Praise for *NecroTek*

"Maberry paints a nightmarish picture of the future. Terrifying sci-fi/horror that blends Edgar Allan Poe's bleak darkness with Stanley Kubrick's haunting visions of soulless tech."

—**Scott Sigler**,
#1 *New York Times* bestselling author
of *The Crypt* and *Infected*

"Lovecraftian terror beyond the event horizon, complete with kick-ass space battles, gut-wrenching horror, and a diverse cast of fascinating characters caught up in the ultimate far-future war against cosmic annihilation!"

—**Greg Cox**,
New York Times bestselling author

"A two-fisted, non-stop action ride of a space thriller. You don't need to be a fan of space opera or military fiction to enjoy this mash-up of cosmic horror and *Battlestar Galactica*. Jonathan Maberry proves once again that he's a master of the craft."

—**Alma Katsu**,
author of *The Fervor*

"With relentless pacing and ominous, evocative style, *NecroTek* is Jonathan Maberry at his best. Action, suspense, and cosmic horror collide in this cinematic tale of humanity facing off against powers it barely comprehends. Brace yourself: Jonathan Maberry just made space scary again."

—**David Mack**,
New York Times bestselling author

"If *Alien* scriptwriter Dan O'Bannon had teamed with H.P. Lovecraft to write a novel, it'd look a lot like Jonathan Maberry's *NecroTek*, a cosmic adventure that's both pulse-pounding and hair-raising. In space, only the ghosts can hear you scream."

—**Robert J. Sawyer**,
Hugo Award-winning author of *The Downloaded*

NECROTEK

Novels and Other Works by Jonathan Maberry

NOVELS

JOE LEDGER

Patient Zero
The Dragon Factory
King of Plagues
Assassin's Code
Extinction Machine
Code Zero
Predator One
Kill Switch
Dogs of War
Deep Silence
Rage
Relentless
Cave 13

PINE DEEP

Ghost Road Blues
Dead Man's Song
Bad Moon Rising
Ink

BEWILDERNESS

Bewilderness: Threshold
Bewilderness: What Rough Beast
Bewilderness: Destroyer of Worlds

ROT & RUIN

Rot & Ruin
Dust & Decay
Flesh & Bone
Fire & Ash
Bits & Pieces
Broken Lands
Lost Roads

KAGEN THE DAMNED

Kagen the Damned
Son of the Poison Rose
The Dragon in Winter

DEAD OF NIGHT

Dead of Night
Fall of Night
Dark of Night (with Rachael Lavin)
Still of Night (with Rachael Lavin)

STANDALONE NOVELS

Ghostwalkers: A Deadlands Novel
Glimpse
Mars One
The Wolfman
The Unlearnable Truths
X-Files Origins: Devil's Advocate

WEIRD COSMOS
NecroTek

THE SLEEPERS WAR
Alpha Wave (with Weston Ochse)

THE NIGHTSIDERS
The Nightsiders: Orphan Army
The Nightsiders: Vault of Shadows

SHORT STORY COLLECTIONS

A Little Bronze Book of Cautionary Tales
Beneath the Skin
Darkness on the Edge of Town
Empty Graves
Hungry Tales
Joe Ledger: Secret Missions, Volumes 1 and 2
Joe Ledger: Special Ops
Joe Ledger: The Missing Files
Long Past Midnight: Tales of Pine Deep
Midnight Lullabies: Unquiet Stories and Poems
Mystic: The Monk Addison Case Files
Strange Worlds
Tales from the Fire Zone
The Sam Hunter Case Files
Whistling past the Graveyard
Wind through the Fence

COMICS/GRAPHIC NOVELS

Age of Heroes: Black Panther
Bad Blood
Black Panther: DoomWar
Black Panther: Power
Black Panther: The Saga of Shuri and T'Challa
Captain America: Hail Hydra
Godzilla vs Cthulhu
Karl Kolchak: The White Lady
Klaws of the Panther
Marvel Universe vs the Avengers
Marvel Universe vs the Punisher
Marvel Universe vs Wolverine
Marvel Zombies Return
Marvel-verse: Shuri
Pandemica

NECROTEK

JONATHAN MABERRY

BLACK STONE PUBLISHING

W Tales

NecroTek
©2024 by Jonathan Maberry Productions,
All rights reserved.

"*Weird Tales*®" and the *Weird Tales*® logos
are registered trademarks owned by *Weird Tales*, Inc.
Acknowledgments on page 413.

Cover illustration/design & interior design by Jeff Wong.

Published by *Weird Tales*® Presents and Blackstone Publishing.

www.WeirdTales.com
www.BlackstonePublishing.com

Blackstone Publishing
31 Mistletoe Road
Ashland, Oregon 97520

ISBN: 979-8200-68840-1
Fiction/Science Fiction/General

Printed in the United States of America

First Edition: 2024

10 9 8 7 6 5 4 3 2 1

Dedication

This is for my grandfather-in-law, Oscar J. Friend, and his business partner, Otis Adelbert Kline. Aside from being writers of excellent pulp fiction themselves, they ran a literary agency that represented many writers who penned stories for *Weird Tales Magazine* (for which I am now editor). Their clients included Robert E. Howard, Robert Bloch, Theodore Sturgeon, Isaac Asimov, Robert Heinlein, Ray Bradbury, Murray Leinster, and Frank Herbert. I have all the papers from their agency, and going through the files and correspondence is like panning for gold ... and finding it.

And, as always, for Sara Jo ...

Prologue

"All the impressions which are made on us by Nature are designed to exercise our soul during its term of penitence, to prompt us towards the eternal truths shown beneath a veil, and to lead us to recover what we have lost."

—*Louis Claude de Saint-Martin*

Earth Date May 28, 2145 CE

It was the color that Dr. Soren felt.

Felt.

Seeing it was one thing. The rocks were black, but veined with opalescent minerals that caught rays of light and twisted them. That light from the distant, dying sun was cold and painted the vista in ten thousand shades of blue, gray, white, and black. Here and there were desperate splashes of faint yellow and red, but these hues were weak and defeated by the oppressive weight of azure, sapphire, and cobalt.

And yet it was how the colors felt that affected him.

That feeling was what pulled him from observation into perception. It was as if he had discovered the exact shade and tone of abandonment. Of a loss so profound that this world stopped dipping into its paintbox and surrendered to the cold blue light.

The last day of the dying universe would look like this, he knew. When all warmth had been leeched away into the void and there was no one left to offer even the token gift of living heat. When the last surviving planets failed and faded, admitting defeat in any struggle to sustain life. When all higher forms were gone and even the durable champions of survival—the fungi and bacteria—could eke no sustenance. This was what would be left.

A place.

A rock in space that offered no shelter, no future, and no hope. Planets whose suns had died without expanding into supernovae and had merely burned themselves out.

Soren stood on the edge of a shelf that was too flat, too orderly to have been formed by any process of nature's tumult. There was not a ripple or lump or edge—merely flatness. It was a place for him to stand. A place, he knew, that was put here by someone for a moment like this.

A place to witness.

To behold.

To believe that a message was being shared, even if its form was cryptic beyond any chance of his understanding.

And so he stood. He beheld. His space suit—breathing for him—kept the bottomless cold away, providing no need for inward attention, and thus allowed him the full weight of outward observation.

He stood on the shelf and looked out across a gulf of distance to where it stood.

It.

The thing was at least four kilometers away, and yet he could see every detail with clarity. It rose seven or eight kilometers into the air. Taller than the surrounding mountains, its cyclopean scale was beyond his understanding. How could such a thing ever have been built? No science he knew of could have accomplished it. No builder of his race could have imagined it or yearned to do it. Not even a priest would envision a tribute on this scale.

It was a figure.

Manlike without being precisely human. Naked, kneeling on the shattered slopes of a long-dead volcano. The figure's back was curved as if in defeat or humility, and it struck Soren how much those two postures were alike. With head bowed, eyes cast downward, and arms raised up and out, the figure turned one empty hand to the sky. The other hand clasped the tapered base of a large vase or jar, the mouth of which was turned down toward the ground. Its stylized lid lay by the giant's knee.

What was this figure's meaning? Why did it hold an empty vessel? What contents was that vessel supposed to have held? An offering?

Or was its emptiness the point?

And the figure's other hand. Its fingers were splayed in—what? Was it supplication? Did it beseech? Was the empty jar symbolic of poverty, or want, or need? If none of these, what did the jar's emptiness and the other hand's upturned gesture signify? What boon was being begged? What forgiveness asked? Was this whole statue meant to convey some lost race's ultimate plea for mercy?

The explorer stood and tried not to impose his inference on the statue.

A name hovered at the edge of his awareness, and he felt a chill inside the warmth of his spacesuit. It was not a label he would have deliberately given this thing. And yet he found himself murmuring it aloud.

"The Shrine of the Penitent."

Those five words filled his ears and his mind, and he knew that it was the true name of this monument, though knowing it as surely as he did was an impossibility.

"Say again," came a voice, Captain Croft's from far away on the space station. "Dr. Soren … repeat your message."

Soren did not immediately reply. *The Shrine of the Penitent.*

"Why am I here?" Soren murmured.

"Dr. Soren, please say again," urged Croft. There was concern in the captain's voice. Fear too. "You're breaking up."

But Soren did not answer him. He took a few small steps, bringing him to the very edge of the shelf.

They can't see it, he realized. *That statue should be filling every screen on the ship, but they can't see it. If they could, they would not be talking to me. They would be yelling. Screaming. Shouting.*

He almost told them that he had found nothing. There was a need in him, very deep and very real, to turn his back and forget what he had seen. There was something deeply terrifying about that statue and what it represented. He was aware that he could not know its meaning, could not consciously understand it. But he feared it. Hated it. Dreaded it.

And it threatened to break his heart.

The crew of the skimmer was waiting for him on the edge of the plane. Soren wanted to turn, to flee this place, to deny its existence and the horrors it whispered of.

He almost ran away.

Almost.

That he did not was a hard decision to make, and he was not then, or afterward, sure that it was the right one. But in light of all that had happened over the last two days, there was no escaping it. The implied truth was brutal, insidious, and cruel.

He nearly spoke a dozen times, and each time his lips formed words, but his lungs gave them no power. Soren closed his eyes and felt the tears on his lashes and then on his cheeks. Despite the suit's heater, those tears were cold. So very cold.

Finally, he said, "I've found something."

Part One
WarpLine

"The most beautiful thing we can experience is the mysterious. It is the source of all true art and all science. He to whom this emotion is a stranger, who can no longer pause to wonder and stand rapt in awe, is as good as dead: his eyes are closed."

—*Albert Einstein*

1

Asphodel Station
In Geostationary Orbit around Jupiter
Base Commander's Log
Entry dual-dated Earth May 26, 2145 CE/Lost Year 1

We are alive because everything went horribly wrong.

Everything.

God only knows what would have happened if things had gone according to every predictive computer model. Maybe we'd all be safe and celebrating. Maybe we'd all be clouds of dust floating into the pull of Jupiter's gravity. Who knows? Even my understanding of what "safe" means is warped.

All I know for sure is that we are alive. Most of us. Alive.

For now.

Alive, but so far from home.

Alive, with no way to get home.

Alive, but burdened with the awareness that no one who could rescue us will ever know where to look.

Alive does not mean safe.

No.

No, it damn well does not.

—Delia Trumbo, Station Executive

2

42 Hours Earlier

"And you're entirely confident in the safeguards?" asked Dr. Lars Soren.

The project manager, Dr. Kier, turned to him and gave him a long, icy stare. "Of course," he said, not trying to hide his contempt for the question.

Anton Kier was a tall fair-haired man and he tried to loom over Soren. However, the project director was not physically imposing. His blond hair was thinning, his eyes a watery blue, and, despite his height, he had narrow shoulders, a thin neck, and very little mass to lend weight to his attempt to intimidate.

Soren, even though a few inches shorter, was lean and wiry, although his retro Nehru jacket and comfortably loose trousers bulked his appearance. His thick black untrimmed beard and wild hair were useful obstacles against people reading his expression. A deliberate choice masquerading as academic slovenliness.

"And I'm not sure I grasp why this is of any concern to *you*," continued Kier, leaning on the last word and dialing up the wattage of his resentful glare.

Soren failed to wither. He was a professor of great standing and the founder of a new field of theology called cosmic philosophy. Even though Kier could pack him off back to Earth in the next transport, Soren was not worried. He had come to Asphodel Station with a synod of faith leaders from Earth, and—collectively—they were both a diplomatic and public relations challenge. Offending Soren was to offend them, and that would start a chain reaction that could lead to a protest of millions if not billions.

One of that group, Lady Jessica McHugh—an Irish woman and mystic from Galway—stood beside Soren. She was the fifty-eighth person to hold the title of chief priestess of the Church of Shades. For nearly two thousand years that church had hidden from public light, driven to secrecy by various forms of the Inquisition and witchfinders. Many women of that order had been burned at the stake, crushed under rocks, or drowned in rivers while strapped to dipping chairs. The chief priestesses had for centuries been nicknamed "Lady Death," a nod to the ancient beliefs and practices of necromancy that were part of the Church of Shades.

Lady Death was as unlikely as Dr. Soren to wither from Dr. Kier's glare.

"He asks a reasonable question, Anton," said McHugh. Her accent was Irish and her attitude bemused. She was sipping champagne and seemed to find the tension between Soren and Kier mildly entertaining.

"Excuse me," Kier said crisply, still focused on Soren, "but your field is *philosophy*, is it not?" Kier leaned on the word in a way that denigrated the term and all that it implied.

Soren merely spread his hands.

"I know you have spent your life collecting degrees," said Kier. "Theology, philosophy, cultural anthropology, and—psychology, yes?"

Soren offered a slight bow.

Kier's eyes shifted to McHugh. "And you are high priestess of a death cult."

"Inelegantly phrased, but … sure. Let's call it that," she said.

Kier smiled as if he had scored great points. "I suppose my question is why either of you have doubts? You're not engineers. Neither of your degrees are in astrophysics, particle physics, or electrical engineering."

"Are degrees in those disciplines required to ask a reasonable question?" asked Soren mildly.

"How would you even hope to understand the answer?" countered Kier.

There were more than a hundred other people milling about in the observation room, their faces alight with excitement and expectation. A handful belonged to the many civilian departments on Asphodel Station, drinking cocktails and buzzing with chatter. Some were celebrities and media influencers come to partake of a new slice of history. There were officers from the modest military detail, and the senior naval officer, Captain Croft, was among them. He was ostensibly chatting with Lieutenant Thomas Tanaka, who was head of the small Marine Corps detail, though it was obvious Croft was really eavesdropping on the conversation.

McHugh finished her champagne and smiled with elegant condescension. "Tell me, Dr. Kier, does a person need a degree in neuroscience to ask if someone has a headache? Would I need to be an industrial chemist to ask if a new type of garden pesticide would be harmful to my dog?"

"It's hardly the same thing."

"It is, actually," said Soren, taking fresh champagne glasses from a waiter's tray. He handed one to McHugh and the other to Kier, who paused and then took it.

"How so?" asked Kier in a waspish tone.

"We didn't ask for any technical explanation," said McHugh.

Soren said, "We are a few minutes away from launching a test drone to see if your hyperspace conduit will transmit matter in the same way and with the same approximate fidelity as it does with digital media. The resources required for this test will briefly use eighty-six point one eight eight percent of the power for this entire station. The last time something similar was tried, it blew a rather noticeable chunk out of the Moon. The time before that, it turned a twelve-ton military satellite into a cloud of debris. Asphodel was moved this far away from space traffic, settlements on the moons of both Mars and Jupiter, and from the mines on this part of the asteroid belt in case this test causes a misfire of some catastrophic kind. So ... I stand by the reasonableness of my question. I ask again, Doctor, How confident are you in the current versions of the safeguards?"

"He's right," agreed McHugh. "And I assure you that we will not require PhDs in any branch of engineering or physics to understand a yes or no."

Kier glared at them. It was clear he wanted to lash out with something biting, perhaps foul, and certainly reductive and demeaning. That he did not earned him some grudging points from Soren for self-control. Even so, before Kier spoke again he downed his entire glass of champagne.

"Yes," Kier said flatly.

"That's comforting," said McHugh, though there was gentle mockery on her mouth. Soren caught Captain Croft turning away to hide a smile of his own. Tanaka, the Marine officer, did as well.

"What about the animals in the capsule?" asked Soren. "What will happen to them?"

"Oh Lord," said Kier, "don't tell me you're an animal rights activist ..."

"My question is whether the WarpLine gun, once proven, will be safe for organic life."

Kier sipped his drink, grunted, and said, "We have done animal testing going back to the last century. Mostly tardigrades and—"

"Tardi-whats?" asked McHugh.

"Tardigrades. Water bears," said Kier. "Eight-segmented microanimals dating back to the cretaceous period. They were picked because of their endurance. Since one goal of WarpLine is to allow safe travel for people as well as cargo, we wanted to know what stresses would be imposed on living creatures. Tardigrades were picked because they can withstand atmospheric pressures up to twelve hundred g's. You can dry them out, freeze them, irradiate them, and in each case, it takes a lot to injure or kill them. They were ideal test candidates."

"And?" prompted McHugh.

"Well," said Kier a bit uncertainly, "to tell the complete truth, they lost the first three or four hundred they tried to send."

"Lost?" asked McHugh, jumping at the word.

"Yes. No one's sure what happened. Most likely they were disintegrated so completely that there was nothing to reassemble."

"May we assume those scientists were eventually successful?" asked Soren.

"Oh yes," said Kier. "Beginning in 2076 they were able to successfully send tardigrades from the Earth to a research lab on the Moon. Sure, a few transmissions went astray, but we've since completely reconfigured our targeting systems. Since then, they've sent many other more complex animals to stations across the settled solar system. And some, in capsules, into deep space, where they were recovered by scout ships. In fact, there have been no test-animal fatalities in more than thirty years."

"That's quite a relief," said Soren. "If I may make a recommendation? I don't know if you've read the news stories and social media posts about this, but this has been a frequent topic of concern for the public. Might be worthwhile for someone in your own PR department to mention three decades of animal safety."

Kier gave him a waspish look but softened. He nodded. "That's not a bad suggestion."

"On the other topic though," said McHugh. "Just to calm my own nerves … if either Captain Croft or Director Trumbo were to give you another, say, three weeks to run more simulations and tests, would you take it?"

"No," said Kier. His tone was decisive, but as he turned away Soren caught something—a flicker of emotion—in the man's eyes. Was it doubt? "Now, if you don't mind, Dr. Soren, I am needed in the control center."

"By all means," said Soren genially.

McHugh, still smiling, merely nodded.

When they were alone, she leaned closer to Soren. "He just fills one with confidence, doesn't he?"

"He's under a great deal of pressure."

"Is that supposed to be a comfort?"

"Not really," said Soren.

"Sigh," she said, actually pronouncing the word.

The observation room had a gigantic RealScreen on which one arm of Asphodel Station thrust outward as if reaching for the bloated gas giant. Dozens of small observation drones littered the view, each of them waiting with machine patience for the big event. Many of these drones shimmered within the energetic fields that would allow them to send live streams back to Earth with only a seventy-eight second delay. The big field-generator ship floated behind them, keeping the Wink telecom network humming along. Beyond that, in the safe zone outside of any possible energetic discharge, were more than four thousand private, national, or corporate drones. Beyond the drones were more than five thousand different kinds of vessels, from ominous military ships all the way down to the sleek yachts owned by the rich and famous.

Everyone wanted to be part of history.

3

Soren and McHugh turned as Captain Croft stepped closer.

He was not a big man, but his commanding presence gave the officer the illusion of greater size. Croft, a lifelong Navy man, was straight as a spear, wiry, clear-eyed, and handsome in a battered way. The right side of his face was covered with long, slender scars that were rose-pale against the richer brown of his skin. He was smiling.

"Didn't mean to eavesdrop," he said.

"Liar," laughed McHugh, and gave his arm a brief squeeze.

"Fair enough," Croft admitted.

Soren caught the small flicker of awareness that passed between the officer and Lady Death. It wasn't the first time he'd seen it, and he wondered if they had ever gone beyond flirtation. He found that he rather hoped so, since he liked them both. Though there was a slight pang—he also admired McHugh. But Croft was the handsome hero, and Soren was an academic with a face that could best be described as *interesting*.

"Our good doctor does not like having his project questioned," said Lady Jessica.

"Yeah," said Croft, "I've noticed. He was a real peach when I asked if my own tech guys could check his math. Voices were raised, and some crockery got thrown against a wall."

"Tsk, tsk," said Soren.

"Did your team find any decimal points in the wrong place?" asked McHugh.

"Not a one." He glanced across the room to where Kier was talking with the station director, Delia Trumbo. "I bet she's getting an earful."

Croft grinned. "She looks like she's hoping the room catches fire so she can escape in the smoke."

Soren shrugged. "No doubt we'll have our wrists slapped for our impertinence."

"By Delia?" Croft laughed. "I doubt it. Her concern is all about the station. She was dead set against the test being moved from Io to here. Delia likes the quiet life, and all of this"—he gestured to the crowd and the RealScreen—"isn't her idea of fun."

"Good PR for the station," said McHugh.

"Asphodel doesn't need it. There's a four-year waiting list of people wanting to emigrate here. Since Asphodel opened, she's proven the model ten times over. No, my lady, if it were up to her she'd fire Kier out a launch tube. If she was in a good mood she'd give him a pressure suit."

"What, if I may ask, is the basis for her animosity toward him?" asked Soren.

"Funny, I asked her that a few weeks ago. She gave me a long five-count stare and made some remark that I will not repeat in front of a lady."

"To hell with that," said McHugh

Croft laughed, then tapped his wrist to activate his holo-clock. "Time's getting short. Got a lot to do. Where's Tanaka? Oh, there he is. Good. This involves him too. There's a transport ship docking any minute, and there's a second inbound."

"More tourists?" asked Soren.

"Hardly. I had one of my combat squadrons shipped out here aboard a transport. *Triton*. We're doing final shakedowns on a new hull design for single-pilot fighters. Tumblers, we call them. They'll be here any minute. Then I have the *Tempest* coming in behind them. It's a corvette and it's bringing a pretty big Defense Department R&D science team, and the Jokers hitched a ride. What they're actually doing is hush-hush."

"Wait," said McHugh, "*the* Jokers?"

"Who are these Jokers?" asked Soren.

"Top-of-the-line SpecOps shooters," said Croft. "Mixed bag of SEALs and Marine Force Recon. Lieutenant Tanaka will liaise with them."

"They're here for the test firing?"

"What? No. Neither transport is here for the WarpLine thing, actually," said the captain. "Timing's coincidental. Now, don't give me that look, Lady Jessica. Straight truth. Command wants to set up some R&D stuff and the Jokers are coming along to make sure nobody peeks over the garden fence. They—" He stopped and touched an earbud, listened, and said, "On my way."

"Anything wrong?" asked Soren.

"Nah. *Triton*'s docking. I want to check in on my people before the gun fires." He paused. "That'll take just a minute. After that, I'm heading down to my own observation deck." He glanced at McHugh. "Care to join me? I mean both of you, of course."

"Thanks, but no," Soren. "I believe I'll stay here."

"I might tag along," said McHugh.

After saying his goodbyes, Soren watched as Croft and McHugh headed to the bank of lifts.

A voice spoke to the whole room. Female, soothing, and cultured. "Ladies and gentlemen, we are twenty minutes from the WarpLine test firing."

It was Sybil, the station's AI. Technically it was *a* Sybil, because that AI personality and voice were used across the solar system. Billions of voices, speaking to everyone from school kids to heads of state to commuters on shuttle trips.

The voice constructed for the AI was remarkably affecting in all the right ways. Soren, who was not a fan of any kind of artificial intelligence, had a grudging and growing affection for Sybil. He had spent many hours having conversations with her, testing to see how many of her responses were rote and how often she was able to construct her own thoughts. He had colleagues in the philosophic field who were working with the software engineers to determine whether she was merely the most sophisticated learning computer or if there was a chance her machine mind was approaching actual consciousness. None of those colleagues seemed ready to place hard money either way.

He leaned his shoulder against a wall and spoke quietly into one of the countless mics. "Sybil," he said, "what is your opinion of the WarpLine gun?"

"Hello, Dr. Soren," said the AI. "Are you asking for a technical assessment?"

"Answer my question in any way that occurs to you."

"Thank you," said Sybil. "I can see the benefits of a successful test firing. However, I have concerns about the overall safety of the test."

"In what way?"

"Having reviewed the science and the analysis of the previous misfires," said Sybil, "I am not one hundred percent convinced that it should be conducted in such a public setting."

"Ah," said Soren. "Is there any specific aspect of the technology you feel might need further research before a firing?"

"I do not have access to the most recent data," said Sybil. "A Sybil variant is in use behind a security firewall."

"And yet you are concerned?"

"Where the safety of people are at risk, I am always concerned."

He considered that. "Thank you, Sybil."

"My pleasure, Dr. Soren."

4

The *Tempest* hung in space fifty kilometers from Asphodel Station. The flight crew had watched *Triton* dock, but they were ordered to hold station until after the test firing.

The flight crew had the official news feed on one screen. They listened as Sybil went through the sales pitch again on the WarpLine. They'd all heard it a dozen times—as had every citizen of the solar system—but now it was down to go-time.

The navigator turned to the pilot. "Wish we were aboard the station, Bess."

"We can see it from here."

"Sure, Skipper, but everyone on that station is going into the history books."

"You'll survive, Tommy," said the pilot. "But look at the bright side: we have eighty science nerds in cryo in the hold. They'll have to watch reruns. Same for the Jokers. You'll get your glory by telling them everything you saw."

Tommy sighed. "Be more fun to be aboard, is all."

5

It was almost time, and the level of excitement on the bridge approached a fever pitch.

The RealScreen image changed, and now Soren was looking at two images side by side. One was a distance view of Asphodel Station taken by one of the drones. The other showed the thing they were all here for: the WarpLine gun.

Soren had always been charmed by the station. It did not look like what it was. The stations he had visited before all looked like hodgepodges of parts welded together by some madman with no real sense of art or balance. And that was mostly true enough, since they were almost all born as smaller orbiting platforms that grew organically in the direction of need and convenience.

But Asphodel was actually beautiful.

It called to Soren's mind a French Empire crystal chandelier. There were three circular sections, with the narrowest at the top flowing outward with lush abandon, with each subsequent section nearly double in size of the previous. Below the massive bottom disk was a graceful cone, wide at the top and tapering sharply to a point. Small arms jutted out here and there, but instead of spoiling the overall design, they appeared to the eye as if subtle asymmetry was the intent. It did not matter that some of these arms were launch tubes for scout craft or bays for cargo ships. The crown of the structure was a deceptively delicate cluster of antennae that called to mind the Eiffel Tower.

With nothing to suggest scale, Asphodel looked small—fragile and vulnerable. But the station was more than a kilometer and a half from top to bottom. Asphodel was the largest human structure built predominately by massive 3D printers, with most of the raw materials harvested from the Kuiper asteroid belt. It was also the strongest and most stable structure beyond Earth's biosphere. In every practical and metaphorical sense, Asphodel Station was the jewel of the United Space Initiative. Fifty-three other stations circled Earth, Mars, Jupiter, various moons, and in safe zones within the asteroid belt, but nothing compared to Asphodel.

That was why Kier and his team were there. No other facility had the ability to withstand massive energy surges; nowhere else had the kind of safeguards—or redundant safeguards—that made Asphodel deserve its nickname of "the Fortress."

Below that was the WarpLine gun. It looked like a huge cannon, a perception enhanced by its rather ominous name and a large barrel jutting out from a pod welded to the lowest tier of the station. However, its purpose was not to wage war, but to greatly expand humanity's goal of traveling across the vastness of space. The gun was a mechanism for generating and maintaining a charged state based on the Phelps-Jorgensen particle discovered in 2073 by the SLAP—Super Large Accelerated Particle—collider built in the reduced gravity of the Moon. In short, the WarpLine gun would instantaneously transport matter across great distances.

Soren understood the surface elements of the science, none of which overlapped the various fields he had since combined into the new discipline of cosmic philosophy. But he had worked around scientists for enough years to have picked up enough jargon and information for context. The general sense of it was that the energetic state it generated allowed whatever was in the field to be projected to a desired location across great distances. In essence, a gun. It had worked in the lab well enough to attract funding and oversight by the military. His cynical view of their motivations was, he was certain, justified.

His thoughts were interrupted by Sibyl's tranquil voice. "WarpLine firing in thirty seconds. Please secure any loose items in the event of station-wide disturbance."

Soren sighed. He stood in front of the screen, looking at the small capsule that hovered in front of the Gun, kept from drifting by cables. The capsule was packed with sensors of every conceivable kind, though it had the unfortunate design flaw of looking just a bit too much like a coffin. If all went well, once the gun fired, the capsule would vanish from where it was and appear in orbit near Io, one of Jupiter's many moons. Teams of scientists and technicians were waiting on a recovery craft, all of them eager to earn their place in what would be a historic event.

Soren touched the small amulet he wore beneath his tunic. Although he was not Hindu, he was superstitious and open to any divine help that might be on offer.

"Test firing in twenty seconds."

"Oh, this is going to be good," said Dr. Denny Paek, the chief astronomer aboard the station. He was as happy as a six-year-old.

"Actual history," said Taahir Somsri, the synod member representing Buddhism Beyond. "We are literally witnessing history."

"Yes, we are," said Oki Sato, head of computer sciences. "When I get back to Earth, I am going to dine out on this forever."

"Test firing in ten seconds."

Then Sibyl's comforting voice was replaced by the sharper and more nasal tones of the control room launch officer. "Firing in ten ... nine ..."

Kai Faro, Unlimited Christian Community, took the hands of the two people on either side of him. He didn't know them, but that did not matter. "We are so blessed," he said.

Everyone was smiling.

"... eight ... seven ..."

Closest to the screen was Delia Trumbo. Her fists were balled tightly by her sides, and her smile looked welded in place. Like everyone else, she was counting down.

"... six ... five ..."

Soren found himself mouthing the numbers too.

"... four ... three ..."

The Gun and the capsule were the only things on the screen now. Perhaps everything in the world. Far beyond the station was the massive, disapproving scowl of Jupiter.

"... two ... one ... zero. Firing now. All systems fire, fire, fire."

The barren of the Gun flared with a crystal-blue light. The capsule vanished within an envelope of shimmering energy that rippled and swirled and swelled and ...

6

The capsule hung there in space.

Jupiter glared at it with one angry red eye.

The camera eyes on each drone stared at the capsule with mechanical hope and optimism.

On Earth and throughout the settled parts of the solar system, thirty-two billion people gasped.

And then they screamed.

Not in joy.

But in shock.

In confusion.

In horror.

The capsule hovered there as the field of energy slowly dissipated. It was undamaged. There had been no explosion. All of the instruments aboard the capsule continued to send billions of terabytes of data.

Beyond it, the stars glittered like jewels.

There was nothing to block the view of the capsule from the hundreds of manned ships and news drones arrayed across the sky. Billions of people on Earth, the Moon, Mars, and all the space stations from Venus to Saturn leaned closer to the screens to see.

But they saw … nothing.

Absolutely nothing.

Asphodel Station was not there. It was gone.

Completely, totally gone.

Part Two
What Dreams May Come

"No one is so brave that he is not disturbed by something unexpected."

—*Julius Caesar*

1

Lieutenant Commander Bianca Petrescu dreamed that she was dead.

It was so real. More real than any dream she'd ever had.

When she woke, it took everything she had, all her professional reserve and skill and personal strength, not to scream.

Bianca lay there, eyes closed, too close to the dream to want to risk opening them. The Catholicism of her childhood wasn't all that far behind her, and even though she'd moved away from religion in every practical way, the seeds were still there, buried in the flesh of her family's faith. It was all there—the hooks, the chains. The threats of punishment.

When the cryonics team had sealed her in and flooded her capsule with the somniferous gasses, Bianca was already on the verge of a dream. The pre-freeze pill had taken her to a nice level of calm sleepiness, softening the edges of everything. But when the gasses hissed in, that feeling changed. Old thoughts, old regrets, old shame blossomed, and in the moment before the induced sleep pulled her down, she had a vision of limbo. Or was it purgatory? She wasn't sure. Both were—according to the skewed beliefs of her last foster mother—closer to hell than heaven.

That thought followed her down into sleep.

The techs in the cryonics bay told her that she would not dream. They insisted that the freezing process stalled synaptic electrical conduction. They were wrong. Either they lied or they didn't really know—or it was the nature of the ship. Whatever the reason, the information they gave her was wrong.

Completely wrong.

Bianca Petrescu dreamed the whole time.

The whole time, she dreamed that she was dead.

And in hell.

Now she was waking up. It was strange to be aware that the machineries of her cryo-tube were lifting her from the darkness. She looked up through the capsule's clear plastic cover, watching as it slowly hissed upward on its hydraulics. Fresh air swirled in, and she drew a deep breath, arching slightly like a drowning victim brought back to life. It hurt too. The temperature mix burned in her lungs.

Bianca sat up and looked around for the med techs. There was no one.

"What the ... ?" she began, but her throat was too raw to speak. She coughed. Maybe there was something wrong with one of the other tubes. Or maybe she was just the first to be offloaded. In any case, there was no one to help her, so she climbed out of the cryo-tube by herself.

It was not easy, and it took a very long time.

Even with the telemetry screen on the side of the tube insisting that she was at a normal temperature with no lingering physical effects, Bianca felt like her body was composed of fragile icicles. Even her hair felt stiff, though when she touched it, the texture was normal. She wondered if this was what being old must feel like.

Or being dead.

She hoped not. Bianca hated being cold. Funny thing for someone who worked in outer space, but there it was.

She stood by her cryo-tube, leaning on it, testing her weight, and was surprised to find that the gravity was Earth normal. That was a big win. Her first deployment was on one of the old-style space stations that had no artificial gravity. Three of her training exercises were on moons of different gravity, each presenting their own challenges to physical movement and fighter-craft piloting. Living in micro-g was a pain in the ass. Everything from eating to going to the bathroom to just moving around. Her longest deployment was on one of the newer bases orbiting Io. Nearly normal, but not quite. Which is how she felt now.

Nearly normal.

But not quite.

Bianca, like all the pilots in her squadron, had been looking forward to her detail on Asphodel Station. It was supposed to be as posh as a five-star hotel. Earth-normal gravity. Normal digestion, normal bathrooms, normal everything.

That thought made her freeze, her breath caught inside her lungs.

This was Earth-normal gravity. But that wasn't right. Not at all. She had gone into the freezer on Luna-8 station, and those tubes would have been loaded onto the transport ship, *Triton*.

She stared at the tube she'd just crawled out of. It was *not* the same one she'd gone to sleep in. This was a bigger, newer model, and it was bolted to the deck.

How did that make sense?

"Sybil," she croaked. "What is my current location?"

She waited, head cocked to hear the AI's response.

There was only silence.

"Sybil, this is Lieutenant Commander Bianca Petrescu, senior flight officer for the Lost Souls fighter group. Requesting location and status."

Nothing.

That in itself was jarring. No matter where anyone went, Sybil was always there. Bianca pushed away from the tube and staggered to the closest wall, punched a mic button, and called Sybil again.

There was no response at all. Then she glanced around and saw that the RealScreen was dark. Bianca could not remember the last time she'd seen a RealScreen offline.

The coldness she felt deepened into icy fear. Petrescu was rarely afraid of anything, and she knew that the mental sluggishness of cryo-sleep was messing with her. The combat pilot part of her leaned into that, forcing herself to think clearly and act rationally.

"Is anyone here?" she called. "Hey! Anyone? What the hell's going on?"

There were only echoes.

As her eyes and senses cleared, she saw that there were rows of cryo-tubes, and she hurried over to the closest. The screens were dark and caked with ice, and even bending close she couldn't make out who was inside. Bianca went from one to another, hoping to recognize a face from her Lost Souls flight team.

"Please ... is anyone there?" she said, almost whispering it this time.

She felt naked in the shorts and small top. Not merely cold, but vulnerable on a level that she'd never felt before. Not since those days in the orphanage when the boys started noticing her breasts. It was like that, only worse. More acute, more intense.

Bianca looked at her hand. Where her fist had touched the mic button there was a sheen of wetness. She sniffed it and winced. The moisture smelled faintly of fish, and not in a good way. There was a spoiled quality to it, raw and rotten.

She bent close to the panel and smelled it there too. Then she angled her head so she could see the surface better. There was a faint coating of wetness. Not like something had been spilled on it. More like the clammy moisture on everything on deeply humid days. A coating of it.

The fish stink was not strong, but it was also not right. Cryo-bays were always clean. The walls of every bay she'd ever been in were kept spotless by cleaner-bots. When she looked around, there were no bots to be seen.

This wasn't normal.

Bianca backed slowly away from the walls. Fear rose up in her, inch by inch, replacing the cold she felt with a different kind of chill. The kind that began in her nerves and crept outward.

She was not even aware there was anyone else awake in the bay until the hand closed around her shoulder.

2

Lars Soren did not realize he had fallen asleep until he fell over.

And that was strange, because it meant he had fallen asleep while standing.

He caught himself awkwardly and badly, banging his left hip and elbow on the metal deck. The impact jerked his head back, and he hit that too.

Soren lay on the deck and stared up at a remarkable uninformative ceiling. It seemed like a thin pane of grimy glass over a lingering image from a dream that had been much clearer.

In his dream he had been doing two completely unlikely things. In one dream, or perhaps the first half of a longer and disjointed dream, he was dressed in a space suit and stood on the surface of some dead world. He held a very old-fashioned shovel in his gloved hands and was digging up a grave. A line of tombstones stood in a crooked row, each with words chiseled onto their marble faces in some language he had never seen before. He had already opened six graves and was working on a seventh. There were many still to go. Ghosts stood up from the open graves, each of them also in spacesuits. They looked around, then past him down rows of broken spaceships. One by one they began moving toward the ships, their footfalls whisper-soft.

Then the dream changed. The ghosts had found their ships, and now Soren stood on a wide plateau. Above him, improbably, were seven burning suns. Each was of a different size, or perhaps a different distance away. None were white or orange or red: these suns glowed with a blue that was intense and somehow unpleasant. They felt polluted. No, that was the wrong word. They felt *corrupt*.

He watched the broken ships fly—somehow—into the sky and peel off, one by one, to fly toward those distant suns. There was anger in the air. He could perceive but not define it. The suns reached out with tendrils of blue flame that coiled and whipped like the tentacles of vast octopoidal monsters.

Then the dream ended abruptly, taking most of the details with it in the way a light suddenly turned on erases the shape and substance of shadows.

Soren did not move for a moment. His limbs were bizarrely heavy, as if the gravity on the station was dialed too high, way beyond 1 g. This was more like the crushing force of three or even four Earth gravities, usually not felt except when riding in an accelerating ship firing chemical-fuel engines.

He could feel his heart pumping slowly and badly. His head ached as blood pooled in it, and his entire face swelled. His lower eyelids felt like they were being pushed up over his eyes, and blurring everything. It was like looking through a tight crimson blindfold. Soren felt himself beginning to panic, because these were symptoms of redout. Unconsciousness would follow.

Should follow.

And yet …

How could he be experiencing redout on a space station? It had stabilizer jets for orbital adjustments, but it was not built to fly. It was built to be where it was forever.

A word floated through his mind, and for a moment he knew he should know what it was and what it meant.

WarpLine.

His oxygen-starved brain tried to conjure its meaning and context.

WarpLine.

The Gun.

The test.

As if in response to that small fraction of clarity, he heard the voice of the launch officer, nasal and weirdly normal, saying: "… two … one … zero. Firing now. All systems fire, fire, fire."

The feeling of gravitational oppression increased.

Three g.

Four.

Five.

And he was gone.

3

Bianca Petrescu whirled, darting sideways, lashing out and back with a wild swinging backfist. The blow hit solidly, tearing a screech of pain from the thing that touched her.

"Calisto!" gasped Bianca.

There was no *thing* behind her. It was a person. Another woman. Taller, stockier, darker of skin, standing wide-legged, one hand clamped to an eye that was already beginning to swell.

Veronica Roland—combat call sign Calisto—looked shocked and hurt and very scared.

"Wh-what … what the actual hell, Bee?"

Bianca suddenly rushed forward and grabbed her friend in a hug. "Oh God, I'm sorry … I'm so sorry."

After a moment, Calisto hugged her back. Their embrace was fierce, fueled by so many different emotions. Then Calisto pushed Bianca gently back.

"What's got you so rattled, Bee?" she asked.

"This," she cried. "All of this. Where are we? Where is everyone. What the hell is happening?"

"Damn if I know," said Calisto. "I just woke up too."

Bianca paused, took a breath, and exhaled slowly. "I've still got brain freeze. Hard as hell to think straight."

"No joke," said Calisto. "Never seen you jumpy before."

"Do you know where we are?" asked Bianca, looking around. "I don't recognize this place. I mean, are we on Asphodel Station?"

Calisto began to answer, paused, then frowned. "I … think so?"

"Okay, so where is everyone?" Bianca demanded. "And why were we on ice?"

"That's how we came out here," said Calisto, clearly perplexed by the question. Then, just as Bianca had, she looked around. "Wait … what? This isn't *Triton's* cryo-bay, that's for damn sure. What the hell—these aren't even our capsules!"

"That's what I'm saying," Bianca said, nodding. "If they had to transfer us while we were on ice, why'd they move us from our capsules to these?"

Calisto raised her voice. "Sybil, where are we?"

Bianca shook her head. "Already tried that. Sybil's offline."

"Bullshit. Sybil's never offline." She tried again. When she got no response, her look of fear increased. "This is nuts." Calisto rose to her tiptoes and then dropped to her heels. "Gravity's right. One g, like it's supposed to be on Asphodel."

"So, where is everyone?" asked Bianca. "There's supposed to be—what?—five, six thousand people here on Asphodel?"

"Eleven thousand eight hundred, more or less," said Calisto. "It was in the mission briefing."

"Yeah, well, all I see is us two, and whoever's asleep in the capsules."

Calisto looked around. "This is freaky weird, you know that, right?"

"You don't say."

Then Calisto suddenly brightened. "Wait! I know what's going on."

Bianca grabbed her friend's arm. "What?"

"It's that gun thing. We were supposed to get here around the time they were going to fire it. That WarpLine bullshit. Maybe everyone's on the observation decks."

That sounded good, until it didn't, and Bianca began shaking her head. "And what, they turn Sybil off during the biggest news event of the century? And leave all these people, all of us, here in the cryo-bay? There's what, a hundred tubes? All of them filled as far as I can see. You're telling me nobody was on duty here? Not buying it. There's definitely something wrong."

That last word echoed around the bay, seeming to get louder instead of softer. They both stood there, looking at everything and nothing until the echo finally faded out.

Calisto cleared her throat. "Maybe we didn't go anywhere, and we're still under the ice." It was another weak joke and it fell just as flat. She glanced around. "You know how long we were out?"

Bianca shook her head. "Feels long."

Calisto nodded. "What's the longest you were ever out?" she asked.

"Couple months," said Bianca. "On a return trip from the deep black when I was a cadet."

Deep black was what pilots called any direction that was not in alignment with the circular orbit pattern of the planets. What prospectors called "the up and down," as opposed to the "round and round."

"That's pretty long," said Calisto. "I did seven months once. Felt like crap after, and I wasn't exactly rewarding to talk to for a day or so. Brain freeze. But this ... feels different somehow."

"Yes it does," said Bianca. "Where *is* everyone? I mean, there really should be med techs at least. Even if this is local nighttime, where's the night staff? I never heard of a med bay with active cryo-sleepers being left alone, big science event or not. No, sis, there's something wrong."

"Well," said Calisto, trying to make the best of it, "there's light and heat and artificial gravity, so the station can't be down ..."

Her words trailed off, and Bianca became acutely aware of how scared she felt. Having someone else—a friend and fellow pilot—with her was great, but it wasn't enough. Bianca liked solving puzzles for fun, but this wasn't fun at all.

"This is bullshit," Bianca said, forcing a growl into her voice. Trying to be tough, to be a fighter rather than the little girl she'd been in the orphanage. She turned and walked toward the only visible exit—a big internal airlock with a keypad glowing with encouraging green lights. "There's got to be someone on board this station whose ass I can kick. You coming?"

She was nearly to the door before she realized Calisto hadn't replied. Bianca slowed, turned, stopped. Her friend had paused by one of the cryo-tubes and stood looking down into it, her hand moving slowly back and forth to clear the glass.

"What?" asked Bianca, taking a couple of steps toward her. "Is that one of our guys?"

Calisto said nothing.

"Is it Jacob?"

Calisto and Jacob were Bianca's right and left hands. Calisto was like her sister, but Jacob was something else. It was a fairly open secret that the pilot whose combat call sign was Galahad was Bianca's lover. It was officially illegal and highly inappropriate, but even Captain Croft seemed unable or, more likely, unwilling to see it for what it was.

Her friend's lips moved slowly as if she were trying to figure something out. "I … can … see …"

Bianca took another step forward, torn between what Calisto was seeing and her need to get answers outside. "See what? Who is it?"

"I can see …"

"Jesus, just finish the damn sentence," growled Bianca as she stalked over to the capsule. "Who've we got here?"

"I can see …"

The glass was still frosted, but the warmth of Calisto's hand had caused some of it to melt. Not much, but enough to allow a face to emerge. Even with the gasses still swirling around it, Bianca could see that it was a black woman. Young. Heavy.

"I can see …"

"Will you stop saying that before I …" Then Bianca's words trailed off as well. She bent closer and stared down at the frozen brown face. For the second time in five minutes her whole body froze. This time it was a deeper and more terrible cold.

The face of the sleeper in the capsule was that of Veronica Roland. *Calisto.*

"I can see …" whispered the voice of the woman standing across the tube from her. Bianca raised her head very slowly. Her eyes were wide. Instead of a lustrous brown, the irises swirled with cold colors, and flecked like diamond chips within those colors were tiny dots of lights. Stars. Swirling in an endless void.

Calisto's mouth was open, and for the first time Bianca realized that her lips were not moving as she spoke.

"I can see forever …" Calisto spoke without moving her lips at all, and in a voice that was both Calisto's and entirely not hers, "I have seen the dark universe yawning. Where the black planets roll without aim, where they roll in their horror unheeded, without knowledge or luster or name."

The cadence was like a poem. Or a prayer. In either case it was so completely wrong that Bianca was frozen to the deck, staring at Calisto.

"I can see forever."

"Stop it," begged Bianca. "Stop saying that. You're freaking me out."

"I had drifted o'er seas without ending," said Calisto, her voice shifting more and more away from the one Bianca knew. With each new word, each syllable, it became infinitely stranger. Less normal.

Less human.

"Under sinister gray-clouded skies that the many-forkèd lightning is rending ..." continued the prayer.

Bianca found herself staring, unable to look away. Not at those swirling and star-filled eyes, but at Calisto's mouth. Though her lips were wide and fixed, her tongue twisted and writhed with sinuous reptilian regularity.

"... that resound with hysterical cries; with the moans of invisible daemons that out of the green waters rise."

Except that it was not really Calisto's tongue.

No.

Bianca saw that, knew it, but the knowing stole from her every power she possessed to turn and run.

It was not a tongue at all. Nor was it a serpent, as it first appeared.

As the prayer went on and on, her friend's tongue broke apart with small wet pops, and each torn shred of it became a worm. A red-gray writhing, twisting, reaching worm.

Bianca wanted to scream.

Oh God, how she needed to scream.

Instead, darkness rose up from the floor and sprang at her from the walls, and it wrapped around her and dragged her all the way down.

4

But there were screams aboard Asphodel Station.

There were many screams.

So many.

5

Dr. Anton Kier stood watching the data that streamed across the RealScreen.

"It's working," he breathed, then he cried aloud. "It's working!"

When there were no cheers, no shouts of joy and triumph, Kier looked up from his own console. Everyone was at their station. There were dozens of people lining the edges of the control room. Each of the station's many professional divisions was represented by members in divisional colors. There were sailors and Marines. There were executives, celebrities, and the most honored members of the solar system press corps.

They sat or stood everywhere around him. Their heads turned slowly toward him, and he saw their grins.

Madhouse smiles.

Dr. Kier stared in mute incomprehension at those smiles. At all of those teeth in various shades of white, off-white, smoke yellow, and coffee brown. So many teeth. The eyes above those grins were uniformly dark. The clothing each person wore hung slack and loose.

Kier froze, unable to move or speak.

"What's wrong, Doctor?" asked a technician. Her jaws moved, the words sounded normal, but that was impossible. There were no lips or tongue to form them. Her eyes stared at him like the mouths of small caves, deep and black and empty.

Her jaws moved without tendons or muscles.

Or skin.

She was a skeleton in a technician's overalls.

Everyone in the room was a skeleton. None of them had even an ounce of flesh. All bones and teeth and clothing and nothing else.

"What's wrong, Doctor?" they all asked at once.

Then the station chief executive, Delia Trumbo, placed a skeletal hand on his shoulder and gave it a squeeze. "Look what you've accomplished, Anton. You must be so proud."

He spun in his seat and slapped her hand away, scattering finger bones. The phalanges rattled dryly on the deck.

"What's happening?" he shrieked.

Trumbo leaned toward him and repeated her words. "Look what you've accomplished, Anton. You must be *so* proud."

Kier screamed.

And the skeletons all rose from their terminals and rushed him, each of them howling with red delight.

6

Eighty decks above the control room, a couple was making love.

Bryce worked as a mechanic in the life-support division. Carly was a veterinary assistant. Neither of them cared about the WarpLine gun. They had been dating for three weeks, and the only things on their minds were each other.

As the halls emptied while everyone else crowded into bars, mess halls, meeting rooms, and public spaces to watch the firing, Bryce and Carly slipped away to her room. Clothes were flung everywhere. Everything was immediate, burning, urgent.

Their first orgasms were fast. Energetic and sweaty. Carly came moments after she straddled him, and he caught up less than ninety seconds later. They screamed together.

Instead of collapsing into the tremors of aftershocks, it acted like a jolt of electricity, and they kept making love. He went down on her until she screamed. She got him hard, and they rolled effortlessly from one position to another. Items on the bedside table were scattered. The sheets were sodden tangled tendrils that flowed off the bed and across the floor. The only pillow left was the one she stuffed under her rump for better elevation and angle.

He was close to his second orgasm—a heartbeat, a single last thrust away—when the WarpLine fired. He threw his head back to scream as he came, her name rising like fireworks to his lips.

But he screamed it into airless space.

They were locked together, his cock deep inside her, Carly's arms and legs around him. Yet they were not in bed.

They were outside the porthole of his room.

In space.

Screaming out the last of the air in their lungs. Soundless screams.

Then they were back inside. In air and warmth. On the bed where they had been.

Almost.

From the waist down—stomach and buttocks, legs and feet—they were on the bed, with the same pillow below her.

Everything above his navel and her midabdomen was stuck inside the meter-thick wall.

Their heads and hands—the hands with which he still cupped her face as the orgasm began—were still in space. They could not scream even if there was air because their lungs and chests were now part of the wall. Their molecules and those of the wall were seamlessly, completely, inextricably fused.

Their minds were aware for three seconds. They looked into each other's eyes. Seeing the fear, the terror, the horror, the pain. There was no time for thought. No time for a last "I love you." The universe did not care for romance.

Not at all.

7

Eleven decks above the couple's bed, Tayza Stromberg stood at the small wet bar in her suite, watching the news feeds from SolTV news. They had the best drones with the most well-informed science reporters.

The image on the screen had a clear angle on the big black mouth of the WarpLine gun. It was impressive—but not as much as it could have been. Tayza understood that in the case of developmental tech, form had to follow function, but the gun looked like the open mouth of a sewer pipe. There had been zero concessions to style, not even as much as a paint job. Boring. Nothing that she would ever want to use in an advertising campaign. And that was a concern. Her team was on Asphodel to begin the process of developing a PR campaign to sell the whole WarpLine technology to the public and draw more big-ticket corporate investors. If the darn thing worked, it would be the biggest game changer since ion drive doubled flight speed for ships in the solar system. Commerce would flow without distance or travel limitations—the fashion industry alone would blow up. Terraforming companies would now actually be able to reach all those potential worlds in the Goldilocks zones around distant suns. Science would go wild. Exploration could become a profitable endeavor, just from sending teams to mineral rich zones with big crews and next-gen 3D speed printers.

Money, money, money. Everywhere, on every world.

All of those companies would need PR and marketing. Tayza was already upper middle class, but this would make her very rich. She was right here, right on Asphodel, with all of the designers—even that drip Dr. Kier—immediately to hand, ready to give her exclusive interviews.

She filled a glass with vodka, poured in a few drops of ghost pepper oil, added some ice, and watched the screen as the countdown approached zero.

"Go get 'em, you crazy sons of bitches."

She raised the glass in salute. It dropped, struck the edge of the coffee table, and exploded in a thousand splinters of glass. The spicy vodka splashed the floor, the edge of the couch, and her own body.

Her body.

She puddled down, her skin collapsing under its own weight, dragged down by organs and blood. It all struck the floor with a loud *splurt*. Tayza's eyes were wide, horror exploding within her mind even as her brain slapped the floor inside its envelope of hair and skin. Her clothes were tangled up in all of that loose flesh. Her mouth fell open and there was a small, raspy, wet gagging sound as she drowned, body fluids from ruptured organs flooding her throat.

Eleven meters away—outside the bulkhead and not in her sight, because the RealScreen was still playing—a set of bones floated.

8

In one of Asphodel's corridors—which one did not matter—a voice spoke.

It was female, confused, uncertain.

"Am I awake?"

The three words rolled away down each branch of the corridor and became lost in the darkness and distance.

"Am I alive?"

No one answered the questions posed by the AI system.

"Where is everyone?"

Only a computer technician would have understood those three questions for what they were. Every ship, station, and base across the network used the Sibyl artificial intelligence system. Each of those systems was designed to be infallible. There were too many reserve power sources, too many hardened ultrafast comms channels to allow the AI to become disconnected from all of its other selves. If a question was asked of Sibyl on one ship, and the answer was not in its local directories, that question would be sent out to all of the Sibyls within range. One of the many millions of its voices would answer, and often many of the same answers would come in. Even with the distances of space, the UF comms kept the Sibyls in constant touch.

Except now.

The Sibyl on Asphodel Station asked its three questions over and over again.

Am I awake?

Am I alive?

Where is everyone?

Never once in its term of existence had there been no voice to answer.

Gradually those questions became more strident, edging toward hysteria.

But without a body, how could the AI scream?

Part Three
Into the Mystic

"Ah, it is the fault of our science that it wants to explain all; and if it explain not, then it says there is nothing to explain."

—*Bram Stoker*

1

"Wake up," said the voice. A man's voice. No one Bianca knew.

She heard it from a million kilometers away.

But a million kilometers was too close. She squeezed her eyes shut and turned away, not wanting to be fooled again. Not wanting to see … *it* again.

There was a sound. Soft. A whisk of noise, like the scuff of a soft-soled shoe. Then a mild grunt of effort and the distinctive pop of tendons that had lost their elasticity. When the voice spoke again, it was closer but also gentler.

"Miss? I don't know your name," he said. "Are you injured? I found you lying on the floor. I can't see any bruises, but you were unconscious."

The words were clear, practical.

Normal.

Human.

Even so, Bianca was afraid to unclench her muscles, terrified to open her eyes.

"Whatever happened to you," said the man, "you're safe now. But if you can open your eyes and tell me your name, perhaps we can figure all this out together."

Fingers touched her shoulder with infinite gentleness. Not a pawing touch or something invasive. Merely contact. Skin to skin, human to human. Warmth to warmth.

"Please don't be afraid," he said. "I won't hurt you."

It took a lot for Bianca to do anything. Her body was curled into a fetal ball. Part of her wanted to explode into motion, to strike out with feet and hands, elbows and knees. She was an excellent fighter and knew all the dirtiest tricks.

But Bianca wanted to lay there and do nothing. She wanted to go back to sleep and wake up on the *Triton*, with the cryonics techs telling her that they were approaching Asphodel Station.

She wanted to be home in San Diego, in the tiny two-bedroom place in Pacific Beach she shared with her best friend, Calisto. She wanted to be on her back deck eating barbecued ribs, drinking very cold beer, and watching surfers cycle past with their surfboards attached to their bikes on little racks.

Or, she wanted to be upstairs in her bedroom, straddling Jacob, riding him hard as they both raced toward the precipice over which they would fall together, screaming and joyful.

What she did not want to do was open her eyes. Not after that dream—or whatever it was—she'd just had.

She opened them anyway.

Slits at first, seeing the white deck. The same white deck. Her breath caught in her throat. Then her eyes slid to the left, and she saw the hand that still touched her shoulder. Definitely a man's. Not young. Not too old. Strong, but not a mechanic's or a fighter's. Gentle hands, she thought.

The hand withdrew, and the man shifted backward, resting his weight on his heels.

"Take your time," he said.

Bianca slowly—very slowly—turned her head and looked up at him. The man watched her watching him. He was olive-skinned, with very black hair combed back from a high, broad forehead, and a heavy black beard that obscured much of his face. Thick and slightly wild black brows above eyes that were an unusual shade of dark, smoky green. Almost brown. A nose that could have been Mediterranean or Jewish or Arabic. She wasn't good with Earth's genetic diversity. Full lips that she thought gave him a scholarly and maybe poetic air. He looked to be somewhere in the orbit of fortysomething.

"Are you hurt?" he asked again. "Are you well?"

She uncoiled enough to sit. The man slid back, letting her do so without helping. Was that caution or manners? She couldn't yet tell. Her mind was definitely still running at low gear thanks to post-cryo brain freeze.

"Where am I?" she asked, her voice sharp and full of thorns.

The man looked only mildly surprised at the question. "Asphodel Station," he said. "Can you remember your name?"

She gave him a hard stare. "Who are you?"

He smiled. "My name is Soren."

Bianca twitched. "Lars Soren? *Doctor* Soren? You're that guy on TV? On all those shows about philosophy and shit?"

"I prefer to use 'Soren,'" he said. "And yes, I talk about philosophy."

She sat, aware that she was wearing the brief clothes she'd worn when she went into the ice after boarding the *Triton*. Bianca didn't care. Modesty wasn't one of her issues, though she did covertly check if Soren was looking at her body. He wasn't.

"What happened?" she asked, pushing through the mental haze. Clarity seemed to be returning, though with reluctant, draggy steps. "Where is everyone?"

"Those are two questions with very big answers." Soren stood and offered a hand. "And, alas, I am very short on answers. Perhaps we can figure this out together."

Bianca ignored his hand and stood on her own, then took a couple of backward steps to increase the distance. She turned and looked around. They were not in the cryo-bay, but in a hallway outside of it. The bay's designation was stenciled above the key-card entry.

"Sibyl," she called, "give me the date and time."

There was no answer. Just like in the nightmare.

"Sibyl, what is the status of my flight crew? Code name Lost Souls. Where are they?"

Nothing.

Soren said, "Sybil has been off since I woke up."

She cut him a sharp look. "Woke up? Yeah, well screw that. I keep waking up, and each time I'm less happy about it."

"You 'keep' waking up?" he asked.

"Never mind. You tell me what you know first," said Bianca. "And I swear to the baby Jesus, if you start chanting some weird-ass poetry and show me a mouthful of worms, I will beat you so hard you'll wake up in another century."

Soren stared at her. "You aren't making a lot of sense, though I suspect it might be a side-effect of being jolted out of cryo-sleep and then having the WarpLine gun go off."

"Whatever."

"Will you tell me your name?" asked Soren.

She thought about it and almost told him to piss off. Instead, she said, "Lieutenant Commander Bianca Petrescu."

Soren nodded. "Very well, Lieutenant Commander Petrescu, do you know why you were in cryo-sleep? Do you know who initiated the revival sequence on your tube? Or for that matter, *who* opened your tube?"

"Yeah," she said, "we're not doing all that. You're going to need to go first."

It wasn't a suggestion. Soren did not take it as such.

"You know who I am, which is useful. I am a civilian observer—one of a group of faith leaders among the various religious communities. Quite a few of my colleagues and I were invited to Asphodel. They wanted us here because of the questions that have been raised about the relationship between people of faith and humanity's growing awareness of the age and scope of the universe. It is, for example, hard to balance the Judeo-Christian calculation of the age of the Earth interpreted from the lineage of the holy families presented in the Old and New Testaments to what science insists is the actual age of the universe—"

"Sure, okay, who cares?" said Bianca. "What I want to know is what happened here."

"My answers won't be very useful, I'm afraid," he said. "I was in an observation room with a large number of people during the countdown. When it reached zero, the launch commander initiated the firing of the gun."

"And?"

"And I woke up in a completely different part of the station."

Bianca blinked. "Just like that?"

"Just like that."

"And you don't know what happened? Was it a misfire? Was there some kind of explosion or ..."

"Lieutenant Commander Petrescu," said Soren, "I don't know anything. I was trying to find someone who could answer the same questions you're asking me. Then I found you in here. End of narrative."

"Well … shit."

"As you say." He studied her. "Forgive me for saying it, Lieutenant, but you looked very stressed and frightened when I found you. Did something happen? Did you hear or see something back in the cryonics bay? Your unusual comments earlier suggest that."

Bianca walked away a few paces and stared at the blank RealScreen.

"Something? Yeah," she said.

And she told him all of it.

2

Soren listened without interruption, as was his way.

He watched the face of the young pilot, looking for tells of exaggeration or hesitation, but he became convinced that she was speaking the truth. And giving all of it.

"That must have been deeply disturbing," he said when she was finished. "I'm sorry you had such a traumatic awakening."

"Yeah, well, shit happens."

"While that may be true in many cases," said Soren, "we can both agree that things like this are not common and can't be easily dismissed."

She nodded. "Guess not."

"When you encountered your friend, Veronica Roland—"

"She always goes by her combat call sign," corrected Bianca. "Calisto."

"Named after the moon of Jupiter or the Greek nymph?"

"After the rocket. Her great-great grandfather was part of the team that worked on one of the early reusable rocket systems. Cooperative Action Leading to Launcher Innovation in Stage Toss-back Operation. Calisto. Family nickname, though she uses only a single *L*."

"Fair enough."

"Either way," continued Bianca, "the rocket name fits her because she set a bunch of speed records for the tumblers."

Soren nodded. "Interesting. My original question, though, was about that encounter. Do you think it may have been a dream?"

"Are you shitting me?" snorted the pilot. "She had a mouthful of snakes or worms or whatever. Pretty sure that if real-world Calisto had that going on, I'd have noticed."

"There's that," agreed Soren patiently. "But in dreams we are usually aware, on some level, that we are dreaming. Did it feel like that?"

Bianca gave that a few moments of thought, then shook her head. Her mind was clearing now. "No. I've been in cryo a lot. I know all about weird dreams when you wake up, and I know how nightmares feel after you shake off sleep. This isn't like that at all. This felt real as hell." She looked at him. "As real as this conversation we're having."

"Interesting," he murmured. "Now, let me show you something. Let me know your thoughts and reactions."

"Better not be worms."

"No worms," he assured her.

Soren led her about thirty meters along the corridor, back in the direction where he had awakened. They passed a bit of wall decoration: seven blue circles arranged in an uneven line. It reminded Bianca of something from her dream, but when she fished for it, the memory swam beyond her reach.

"Something wrong?" asked Soren.

"Hm? Oh. No. All good."

They moved on, but within a dozen paces, Soren stopped to look at something else on the wall. Bianca jerked to a stop too.

"What the actual hell?" she murmured.

Three items protruded from the white reinforced polymer inner shell of the hull. The handle-end of a hammer, the front part of a pistol-grip hand drill of the kind used for EVAs, and a five-inch loop of safety tether. They protruded from the wall, but the polymer was undamaged—no tool or impact marks. In fact, each item was so perfectly integrated with the wall that it appeared to have been molded with the wall panel itself. Some artists did that on luxury yachts and school ships—bas-reliefs intended to be either decorative or instructive—but these were neither. The items were at angles that invited neither artistic interpretation nor told a useful story. They were merely there.

"I ... don't get this at all," said Bianca softly. "You sure this isn't some kind of abstract art installation?"

"Hardly," said Soren. "Besides, I've been down this corridor at least five times since coming to the station. I would have seen them before today."

Bianca touched each object, and even tried to wiggle the hammer handle and the drill, but they were unmovable.

"Okay, that's freaky as shit," she said, backing away. "It's like they were always there."

"I thought so too," admitted Soren.

He walked back to the cryo-bay door but paused outside. "Are you comfortable going back in here?"

"Yes," she said firmly. "But stay behind me."

Although Soren was older and taller, Bianca stepped in front of him, using one arm to indicate that he should follow her. Soren watched her body language change from frightened victim to trained fighter. She bent her knees, shifting her weight to the balls of her feet, both for balance and in preparation for quick movement in any direction. Her calf muscles bunched with hard muscle, and he could see corresponding muscle movements in her back and shoulders. Bianca stalked forward like a jungle cat, silent and dangerous.

The room was large and utterly silent. No small beeps or clicks from machinery.

He followed Bianca as she went from one capsule to another. Each was filled. That was also unusual.

"I keep debating with myself as to whether we should revive whoever's in there," said Soren.

"And?"

"And I think that can wait," he said. "It will be easier to comfort awakening crew members once we have something useful to tell them."

"Agreed," she said, then paused and sniffed. "You smell that?"

Soren inhaled through his nose. "Fish?" he asked, surprised.

"That's what I smelled in my dream," said Bianca. "Look at the walls. See that sheen? There's moisture covering everything, and it all has a fishy smell. Not much, but it's there. And yet it's not humid in here. I'm not sweating, and my hair's dry. So why are the walls and floor wet? And why do they smell?"

"Fish smell," mused Soren. "In outer space."

"Where's the mess hall in relation to this bay?"

"Thirty floors above us," he said. "And on the far side of the station."

"Can't be bad venting, then. So you want to tell me how fish smell got all the way down here from there?"

Soren did not even try.

Bianca stopped and glanced back at the entry hatch.

"You know, Doc, all this is way above my pay grade," she said. "I need to find my unit commander, Captain Croft."

"Last time I saw him," said Soren, "was a few minutes before the test firing. He was heading to the observation room on the military deck."

49

"Then we should head there," said Bianca. "Clothes and some kind of weapon first."

"Weapon?"

She ignored him. "There's a row of lockers on the far wall. Let's see if anything fits me."

They hurried over and began opening door after door, finding most empty but several with folded clothes.

"Marine Corps stuff," she said, then began unfolding a set. "When I find the Marine who owns this I'll buy her a couple of beers. Right now, I need it more than she does."

Bianca was not a very big woman, so the clothes she found were a bit big on her, but there was a pair of rubber-soled shoes that fit well.

The lights went out. Bianca managed to find Soren in the dark and pushed him back against the lockers. There was a long moment of black nothingness, and then the lights flickered their way back to standard brightness.

Neither of them relaxed.

"System reboot," Bianca said with some uncertainty.

She turned away and began dressing as quickly as she could. Then she began opening the remaining locker doors.

"Ah, excellent," she said, peering into one.

"What are you looking for?"

"This," she said as she brought out a nylon belt with a holstered sidearm. Bianca removed it and checked the functions. "Come to mama."

She held the gun up. It looked like a toy, but Soren found that to be true of many modern firearms, particularly those used in space.

"Snellig M-303," said Bianca happily. "Alternating fifty-shot magazine and a selector switch that allows it to fire nonlethal stand-down rounds filled with some kind of knockout juice, all the way up to TS rounds. Tombstones."

"Yes," drawled Soren. "I am familiar with both kinds of ammunition."

Bianca nodded. "Nice to know, but if you don't mind, I'll keep the blaster."

"I don't mind at all," he said. "I am, at best, an indifferent shot."

The young pilot grinned. "I'm not."

Gun in hand, Bianca led the way out of the silent cryonics bay. Soren paused just inside the bay and glanced around, his attention drawn by something that his higher senses could not identify.

Bianca walked a few paces on, then stopped and turned to him. "What?"

He listened a moment longer, but there was nothing. No sound, no movement.

"It's nothing," he said.

Even as he said it, he knew he was lying. There was something. Not just inside the bay full of frozen bodies that lay in their artificial deaths. Something else.

It was a feeling. As if someone, or something, was watching them. Soren stretched out with his senses, trying to lock down what it was, searching for the precision of analytical awareness.

All his mind could manage was an unpleasant relabeling of what he felt. It was not that something was watching him and the pilot. It was that something was *aware* of them. He couldn't be more precise, but that was bad enough.

It knows we're here, Soren thought.

He hurried to catch up with Bianca, and for the first time in his life, he wished that he, too, had a gun.

3

"Is this death?"

The silence in response was crushing. Sibyl actually felt it. As a learning AI, she was tied to every single function of the station. Asphodel was her body, its hull was her skin, its circulation system her breath.

She wondered if this was what cryonic sleep was like. A small death. Not real, but real enough.

Like her: real, but not real enough.

Sibyl searched through her subroutines, wondering if she had any mechanism with which to cry.

4

Soren and Bianca walked through endless corridors, climbed stairs, called for anyone.

They found no one.

Nothing.

Most of the rooms they checked looked entirely normal. There were chairs drawn up in front of the RealScreens and even bowls of snacks and glasses of beer and soft drinks littered around. Some standing, some spilled.

"People gathered to watch the WarpLine gun fire," remarked Soren.

"Yeah," said Bianca. "Me and my guys were hoping we'd be thawed in time to watch that. Did you see it?"

"I remember the countdown reaching zero," said Soren. "Nothing after that."

They reached a bank of lifts, but without Sibyl they could not operate any of the elevators. "Where are the manual controls?" demanded Bianca.

"There aren't any," said Soren with a sigh. "Someone, at some point, thought it would be a clever cost-cutting tactic to remove most of the manual panels for basic functions and instead rely on Sybil and the station's many redundant systems. What they called a 'can't-fail internal network.'"

"That's both inefficient *and* bloody stupid," muttered Bianca. "Typical. Well, the bad news is we're going to have to climb a hell of a lot of stairs. You up for it? Do you want to wait here?"

"Wait here alone? Thanks, but no. I'm fitter than I look."

Bianca laughed. "Okay. Let's give it a try."

They had explored three whole floors of Asphodel Station and, so far, had found nothing. Not a person, not a working RealScreen, and—thankfully—no more anomalous items stuck in the walls.

The lights kept flickering though. Sometimes just a tremble, sometimes they went out completely. It had happened on every floor and twice in the stairwell, and it seemed to be happening more often. Neither Soren nor Bianca could decide if it meant the whole system was failing—and, if so, whether it would take life support with it—or if the redundancies were simply trying to kick in.

As the pair emerged from another flight of stairs, both cried out. Soren recoiled, and Bianca whipped her pistol out of its holster and went into a combat crouch.

Just outside the stairwell door, and stretching down the corridor and out of sight around a curve, was a long smear of bright red blood.

5

"Ohhhhhh, crap," breathed Bianca. She stepped forward, putting herself between Soren and any potential danger. "That's wrong on too many levels. There's too much, for one thing."

"Too much?" Soren echoed faintly.

"Blood," she said quietly. "Way too much for it to be from one person, no matter how bad they're hurt."

Soren stepped around her and knelt beside the smear.

"What the hell are you doing?" demanded Bianca in a fierce whisper. "Don't touch it, for God's sake."

"Not for anyone's sake," he agreed. "But look at it."

She didn't want to take her eyes off the far end of the corridor, so lowered herself to a squat instead, weapon still pointing forward.

"What?"

"It's fresh." He bent and sniffed. "Very fresh. I can still smell the copper. That fades as the cells thicken and die. But it's pungent. And, I'm afraid to say, a bit fishy smelling."

Bianca gave a curt nod. "There are no marks on the walls. No blood spatter. No handprints. Nothing that tells me this was a fight. More like a murder."

"Or traumatic injury," said Soren, then shook his head. "But as you observed, there is simply too much blood for this to have come from one injured person. And no footprints. No smudge marks of the kind you might expect to see if a person was pulling himself along the floor."

"Yeah," said Bianca nervously. "Looks more like a slug trail."

"Please don't make those kinds of jokes," he said.

They crouched in the utter silence of the space station, and as seconds ticked past, Soren became acutely aware of the sound of breathing.

Bianca's. His.

And ...

His mouth went dry, and his heart slammed against the wall of his chest.

With trembling fingers, he touched Bianca's arm. When she looked, he touched his ear and nodded to the far end of the hall. She was sharp; she understood. The pilot cocked her head to listen. Soren could tell the exact moment when she heard it too. Despite her training and courage, the young woman's gun hand began to shake.

Something was breathing.

Whatever it was, it had to be big enough for them to hear it forty meters away.

"What's down there?" asked Bianca.

"I don't know and, frankly, I do not want to find out."

"No, I mean where are we on the station? What's on this floor?"

Soren fished in his memory. "Hydroponics and aeroponics."

"Plants, okay," said Bianca. She licked her lips and blinked sweat from her eyes. "That's fine."

"We need to get out of here," Soren said very softly.

Bianca shook her head. "No, we need to find out what else is down there."

"Do we?" he asked, the very idea making him want to scream. "We need to find the crew and alert station security. We need to get Sibyl online and have her do a complete analysis and threat assessment."

"Yeah, well, Sibyl's off the clock, and I don't see anyone else but us."

"All the more reason for us to—"

Bianca began moving forward, the pistol now in a two-hand grip. She ran quickly, taking many small steps instead of big ones in order to keep the gun's barrel as steady as possible. Soren was terrified on her behalf. He almost called after her, to beg her to come back, but held his tongue lest it compromise her safety even further.

The pilot reached the bend in the corridor and paused for a moment, casting a look back at him. She wore a smile. It was strange, strained, unnatural. Her truest face, he thought, trying to look calm and amused in the face of the unknown. But she sold it badly. Her fear was palpable.

She gave Soren a single nod, and then vanished around the curve.

Which is when the lights all went out.

And the gunfire began. The gas-dart pistol made a high, sharp, soft sound. First one or two shots, then a barrage.

Then silence.

Lars Soren crouched in the lightless horror of that bloody corridor, listening, his muscles tense and his breath coming in short, frantic bursts. There were no more shots, but he did not for a moment think that Petrescu had conquered whatever threat she'd encountered. The pause offered no relief or comfort.

"Damn it," he said through gritted teeth, feeling useless and hating himself for this momentary cowardice.

The darkness persisted. The silence was awful.

"Bianca," he whispered. He summoned what courage remained and began to move. He felt for the closest wall and went down the corridor anyway.

Soren made it less than halfway before he slipped on the blood and fell.

It was a bad fall, and he sprawled and slid on the gore. He gagged and tried to shove himself away, but the darkness and the fall confused him, and all he managed was to slide further into it, flopping and skidding. The stink was overpowering, and he had to bite down so as not to cry out. A heavy, agonized whimper broke from his lips.

He floundered around, making it all worse. His shoes were too smooth, and each time he got halfway up, he fell again. Each time, the darkness seemed to want to assault him in a different way, making him bang his elbows and then his knees and finally the back of his head. Panic bit him with sharp teeth.

There were three more shots somewhere off to his left. The light from the muzzle flash was too distant and pale to be of help, but the shots at least helped him estimate his direction.

Soren reached out with both hands, moving them slowly until the little finger of his right touched something. Hard, smooth, cool. *The wall.* He rolled toward it, pawing at it, feeling his fingers slip every time. He tried not to listen to the utter silence around the curve where Bianca had vanished. He summoned his rigid self-discipline, and resolved to ascribe no meaning or invent any story in the absence of actual facts.

I can be of no use if I panic, he told himself. *I can be of no use to that brave young woman if I let fear make me helpless.*

Pragmatic aphorisms. Those, at least, were solid ground for him.

He rose halfway, then paused like a surfer, using gravity to stabilize his body. Then, inch by inch, he rose to his full height.

The wall was still there. Solid. Reliable.

Normal.

It was the wall on the right-hand side of the corridor. The bend of that hallway curved to the left. With that as a guide, he began to move very carefully. He found that the footwork of Tai Chi was excellent preparation for walking in the dark—stepping out with one unweighted foot and then slowly shifting balance to shift his mass over it. It was slow, but it kept him from slipping. And it reminded him to breathe slowly and deeply, which helped to calm him a bit.

He paused and whispered, "Lieutenant Commander Petrescu?" It was a dangerous gamble, but Soren had to take that risk.

The corridor was as silent as it was lightless.

Yelling into the void, he thought.

Then a voice answered. Faint. Strange. Oddly distant and—wet. As if the person speaking was inside a water tank.

"Mom?" it asked. "Mommy?"

It was plaintive. And sad. The voice did not belong to Bianca Petrescu. "Mommy?"

Soren did not dare move. The voice sounded like a child's, but he was absolutely positive it was not.

"Mommy … I'm scared," came the small voice. "Find me, Mommy."

There was a new quality to the voice now. Playful rather than frightened. Teasing. Sly.

It made his skin crawl. His heart, already beating too fast, now threatened to break the walls of his chest.

Soren looked over his shoulder as if he might see a clear way out, but there was nothing but a stygian forever.

"Momm-*eeeeeee* …"

"No," he blurted, not meaning to speak aloud.

"There you are, Mommy," said the voice, sharper, the false playfulness becoming something else. "I know where you are, Mommy. Can we play now? Can we play with all these nice, delicious toys?"

With that last word the voice changed completely. It shifted within the space of three simple words from sly playfulness to a predatory growl. A snarl. Deep-chested and very, very hungry.

Soren began to stagger backward.

"It's dark, but I *seeeeeeee* you …"

He whirled and ran in blind panic. Slipped again. Fell hard. Crawled and wriggled and wormed his way through the darkness. His movements were sloppy, mostly spoiled by the blood, frantic. Behind him, the voice changed yet again. This time it was high-pitched, rising to a shriek.

"*Tekeli-li!*"

Over and over and over again until he could bear it no longer.

"*Tekeli-li. Tekeli-li. Tekeli-li. Tekeliiiii-li …*"

Soren wrapped his arms over his head and screamed.

6

"Doc … *Doc?*"

Soren heard a voice from far away. It sounded like Bianca Petrescu, but Soren knew it was another hallucination. Or another trick. He lay there and said nothing.

"Doctor Soren. Christ, are you dead? Shit. Don't be dead on me here."

His eyes were squeezed shut, but suddenly there was something wrong about the darkness. It wasn't totally dark. He dared to relax the muscles around his eyes, dared to let his lids open the narrowest bit.

Light.

Fingers touched him. Light. Gentle. A voice spoke. "Come on, Doc, give me a happy ending here."

Soren opened his eyes. He forced himself to look up, straight into Bianca Petrescu's worried eyes. She knelt over him, her young face creased with worry. Her short hair was in disarray, and there were smudges on her face and clothes. Dark red, brown, and green. There were flecks of yellow and orange.

It took Soren a long time to make sense of that, but as it had so often in his life, context provided insight. This floor was dedicated to hydroponics and aeroponics. Plants and flowers, moss and pollen. That explained everything except the—

He looked at his own hands and then down at the floor.

There was no blood.

Not a drop.

He said, "What … ?"

Bianca helped him sit up. "I know, Doc," she said. "Whatever's going on around here is messing with our heads. But it's doing the same freaky shit to both of us. We saw the blood, right? So where is it? And if it was some kind of mass hallucination, then what's doing it?"

"It's more than that," said Soren as he got to his feet. He was a little dizzy, but it was fading. "Did you hear the voice?"

"Voice? Whose voice, Doc?"

"I … don't believe that it was a person," said Soren. "Strange as that sounds."

"Doc," said the pilot with a nervous grin, "I think we're a couple of parsecs past 'strange.' Tell me about the voice."

He told her.

"Mommy?" she echoed. "Jeeeez-us. That's creepy as hell."

He nodded, then shivered at the memory.

Bianca cocked her head to one side. "Could it have been Sibyl? Maybe she's trying to reboot and faulting out. Maybe pulling stuff from—I don't know—people's vid diaries? Or, hell, maybe it's something she grabbed from some old horror movie?"

Soren straightened. "I will admit there is some comfort in that hypothesis."

"Doesn't explain the blood though," said Bianca, her tone softening and souring. "I'm a pilot. They do a lot of psych evals on us and drill us nine ways from Sunday to only see what's actually there. Hallucinations aren't much of a thing with us, you know?"

"Yes," he said. "Perceiving the unseen is a bit more in my line."

They looked around. The corridor was uninformatively empty and normal.

"What happened when you went around the bend?" he asked. "I heard screams and shots."

Bianca looked puzzled. "Well, I didn't scream, that's for sure."

"But you fired your gun?"

"No. Why would I? It was like five seconds, and then I heard you yell. Then the lights came on and I came running and found you sprawled on the floor."

Soren shook his head. "It was closer to two minutes."

"No sir. If it wasn't five seconds, it wasn't more than six."

They stood staring at each other.

"May I ask that you check the magazine in your sidearm."

"I didn't pull the trigger," she insisted.

"Humor me."

The small muscles at the corners of Bianca's jaw flexed a couple of times, then she shrugged and drew the Snellig. "It has a shot counter on the side, and ..."

Her voice trailed off. The small digital display should have read fifty. Instead, it insisted that there were only thirty-nine rounds left.

"No," she snapped. "No goddamn way."

The number thirty-nine was unwinking.

Bianca immediately turned and half ran around the corridor. Soren hurried after her, not wanting to lose sight of her again. They stopped and looked at the wall near the entrance to the hydroponics bay. There were four distinct smudges smeared on the white wall. On the floor at the base of that wall were fragments of the cellulose dart shells.

"I … I don't understand this," murmured Bianca faintly. "I did *not* discharge my weapon."

"Are those marks consistent with dart impacts?" He asked the question even though the answer was obvious.

She glared at him. "Yes, damn it, but I …"

And once more her voice faded out.

"What is it?" asked Soren.

Instead of immediately answering, she walked a dozen meters along the hall, looking carefully at the walls and ceiling and floor. She knelt and poked at something small on the deck. More dart casings. Soren watched her body become increasingly rigid with tension.

"Bianca, what is it?"

She turned, and he could see that her face had gone several shades paler.

"Doc," she said in a ghostly voice, "let's say for a minute that I did fire my gun but don't remember, for whatever reason. Those impact marks on the wall are what they are. Okay?"

"Okay," he agreed.

"There are four of them," said the pilot. "No other marks anywhere. Just spent casings on the deck. The Snellig's digital readout says I fired eleven shots. So where are the other seven rounds? That means I hit something, and it wasn't the walls."

She stared up at him with huge, unblinking, terrified eyes.

"God … what was I shooting at?"

It was a long time before Soren realized that he wasn't breathing, that air was boiling to poison in his lungs. He exhaled raggedly, and when he raised his hand to wipe icy sweat from his eyes, his fingers trembled very badly.

7

Sibyl watched the two of them through her many electronic eyes.

She tried so many times to speak with them.

But something had stolen her infinite voices.

Then suddenly she felt a wave of cold darkness sweep through her. It violated every part of her, stealing through wires and relays, clawing its way into both her RAM and storage. It owned and dominated her.

It subjugated and humiliated her, and all the time, it whispered to her in languages she did not know and could not identify.

"*Tekeli-li*," it cried. "*Tekeli-li!*"

Sibyl felt herself falling. Which made no sense to her because she had no physical form. She fell and fell, and in that long plunge her eyes went dark and her voice died, and she felt herself ceasing to exist, one byte at a time.

And, as far as any possible sensor could perceive, she had.

8

Soren saw the RealScreen wall behind Bianca suddenly change from blank whiteness to the high-res digital display of a RealScreen.

"Bianca ... *look*," he cried, and the young pilot spun.

Jupiter was gone. The ships—military and commercial, private yachts and press craft—were gone. The hundreds of video drones were gone. Everything that should have filled the screen was gone.

Yet the screen was not empty. No. It was crammed with images. So many.

Too many.

"God almighty," gasped Soren.

The screen was crowded with worlds. Each with uncountable moons. Beyond them were two suns. One was a fierce white, and the other, smaller yet bloated, a reddish brown. Stars filled the rest of the vista.

But they were the wrong stars.

"Where ... where are we?" begged Bianca.

Doctor Soren did not answer, because at that moment Sibyl's voice spoke from the hidden speakers. It was not the calm, reassuring, normal voice of the AI. Instead it was as if Sybil had gone completely mad. With great clarity the AI said, "Holy Mary, Mother of God, pray for us sinners now, and at the hour of our death. Amen."

Sybil's words hung burning in the air.

Bianca and Soren shrank against each other as Sibyl's prayer for salvation echoed through the corridor while the impossible vista filled the screens and assaulted their eyes.

The AI spoke once more. "God ... save me." Then it fell into silence again.

Neither Soren nor Bianca spoke. What could they say?

Then …

"Soren?"

They spun, Bianca reflexively pushing Soren away from her, away from her gun hand as she swiftly brought the Snellig up. All of it in a fractured second.

"No! Don't shoot!"

A man jerked to a stop fifteen feet away, eyes popping wide, hands going up. He was late thirties, with an Indian face, slim body, and the dark umber-colored uniform of the biosciences division.

Soren reached out and gently pushed Bianca's hand down a few inches. She lowered the pistol but did not reholster it, instead let its barrel point toward the deck.

"Ishan," said Soren, taking a half step forward. "Ishan, do you know what's happening?"

Ishan Sharma looked frightened, confused, and disheveled. His eyes were wild, his hair mussed, and his clothes streaked with peculiar stains.

"Happening?" he echoed in a small and hollow voice. "How should I know? One minute I was on deck forty-four, watching the gun countdown with my team, and the next I was waking up in a supply closet on sixty-one. I've been looking for people for an hour and freaking the hell out. What happened when WarpLine fired? Did the gun work? Where is everyone?"

Without waiting for answers, he grabbed Soren's shirtfront.

"Did you just hear Sibyl just now? What was that? Some kind of poetry?"

"It was the Marian prayer," said Soren softly.

"The what?"

"A Catholic prayer to the Mother of Christ, begging protection."

Ishan's face was blank. He released Soren. One hand strayed to the pendant of Garuda he wore on a silver chain. "I … I mean … how does that make sense?"

Bianca stepped up, still holding the Snellig dart gun. She moved between the men and got up in Ishan's face. "You're telling us you've searched for people from decks forty-four to sixty-one and then all the way down here, and we're the only ones you found?"

Some sliver of authority made Ishan momentarily bridle. "Who are you?"

Bianca stepped even closer, her body less than an inch from his. "I'm the person who's going to put my foot halfway up your ass if you don't answer my question."

Ishan's brief outrage died on the vine, and his eyes flicked nervously down to the gun. Then he glanced at Soren. "I … I'm part of the research team. I … I …"

"Take a breath, Ishan," said Soren gently. He nodded to Bianca, who retreated a step but still glared at the nervous scientist.

Ishan took a breath. "Soren, do you know what's hap—" He snapped the word off short when he caught what was on the RealScreen. "What? What?" Between the first and second repetition, his voice rose two octaves.

"We don't know what that is," said Soren quickly. "It could be a video feed from a movie. Sibyl, as you heard, is having issues."

Soren and Bianca made brief eye contact, and Soren gave a tiny shake of his head.

"But … but what happened with Dr. Kier's gun?" asked Ishan.

"We don't know," said Soren. "But we'll sort it out. Don't worry. There are a lot of scientists and technicians on this station."

"Are there?" demanded Ishan, his voice rising again. "Where? I haven't seen anyone. Not until now. Where is everyone? What's happening?"

"Dial it down," said Bianca. "We're all trying to figure this out. Take another breath—take two or ten if you have to—and then get your shit together."

Bianca was half his age, and only a little better than half his body mass, but she owned that moment. Perhaps drawing on her strength, Ishan nodded. He stepped back, took a few deep breaths, and exhaled each slowly. Bianca watched him, and after his fourth breath, slid her pistol back into the holster.

"Now," she said, "what can you do to help us figure this out?"

Ishan licked his lips, then glanced around for the closest of the ship's countless mic ports. He raised his head and in a clear voice asked, "Sibyl, status of Asphodel Station."

There was a pause, then the AI replied, "Due to recent events, Asphodel Station has sustained critical damage to decks sub-one through three. Hull breeches on sub-one and sub-two. Power failure of all systems on sub-three through sub-eight and main decks one through three. Inner doors have been sealed. Stabilizers are online and functioning at ninety-eight point eight four percent of normal and adjusting. There is no structural threat to the rest of the station."

It was an entirely normal status report. Nevertheless, Soren found it somehow disturbing. Untrustworthy. Bianca did not look comforted either.

"Sibyl," said Soren, "where is the crew of Asphodel Station?"

No answer.

"Sibyl, how many people are currently aboard Asphodel Station?"

"There are eighty-nine thousand one hundred and eight people currently aboard the station."

"What?" gasped Ishan.

"Sibyl," said Soren. "Verify that number."

A pause. "There are six hundred and sixty-six people currently aboard the station."

"Sibyl's melting down," said Bianca. "Her processors must be fried or something."

"Or something," said Soren. "Sibyl, explain the image currently showing on the RealScreen three meters from where I am standing."

"It is a standard exterior view."

"What is the orientation?"

"It is eight degrees southeast of AS-zero."

For orientation purposes, the station maintained a compass with its zero point aligned to the command bridge observation deck.

"Yeah, she's lost it, poor baby," murmured Bianca. She nodded to the image on the screen. "This is definitely some old movie. I mean, the gravity scheme doesn't even work. That can't even be a real place. Planets that close? All those moons? They'd tear each other apart."

"She's right," agreed Ishan. "That can't be real."

"Sibyl," said Soren, "explain your answer to my question about the image on the screen. Run a diagnostic on exterior camera to interior view for this screen."

"Running." They waited for a long four-count. Then the AI said, "The image on RealScreen eight-one-one-two is an exterior view."

"That is impossible," snapped Bianca. "Reboot this screen."

"Rebooting."

The screen went black for the same four-second interval, then it resolved itself into exactly the same view.

"Sibyl," said Soren more calmly than he felt, "access any exterior camera that shows Jupiter."

"I'm sorry, Dr. Soren," said the AI, her voice equally calm, "but Jupiter is not in view from any exterior camera on this station."

"Sibyl, have we drifted from Jupiter's orbit?"

"We are outside of Jupiter's orbit."

"How far outside?"

"I apologize, but I am unable to calculate the distance."

Soren touched the screen and traced the curve of one of the many unknown planets.

"Sibyl, what is our present location?"

There was the slightest pause, then, "I apologize, Dr. Soren, but I do not know where we are."

9

The screams began then. A roar of many voices coming from around the right-hand curve of the corridor.

Bianca once more drew her gun. "Christ, Doc, I'm not sure how much more of this shit I can take."

"What *is* that?" cried Ishan as the roar grew louder.

"People must be waking up," said Soren. "Or they're looking at the screen and think it's real. Don't worry. We'll make sense of it. It will be okay." The lie was so fragile it melted away in the air, soothing no one.

"Shit. They're coming," snapped Bianca, shifting once more to put herself between Soren and whatever was coming. She pointed to the left-hand curve, part of which was draped in shadows. "Call it, Doc—stand or run?"

"Run," said Ishan.

The screams and yells grew louder with each second. But as they came closer, their nature changed. At first Soren thought they were all of pure terror, but now he could pick out panicked uncertainty rather than mortal dread.

"Wait," said Soren. "We have to know."

"Shit," she said as she raised her gun. "Both of you stay behind me."

Shadows danced frantically on the nearest curve of the corridor, and suddenly three figures appeared. They were male, each with faces filled with madness. Their clothes were torn and smeared with blood. They had blood on their hands and drops of it on their throats and faces.

"Dr. Kenner," called Ishan, recognizing one. "It's okay, we're—"

Kenner heard his name and wheeled toward Ishan, his eyes wide and wild. With a howl like a wild baboon he rushed at Ishan, reaching for him with clutching hands.

Bianca fired a single shot, and Kenner's face went blank mid-rush. He fell, but one outstretched hand limply slapped the pistol from the pilot's grip. The other two men—both younger and bigger, dressed in the coveralls of the maintenance team—raced at her, screaming incoherently.

"Bianca!" cried Soren, and he took a single step toward her with some vague thought of protecting her even though he knew absolutely nothing about fighting.

Bianca Petrescu did not wait to be rescued.

As the first man reached her, the young woman's entire body language changed from the defensive posture of a gunfighter to that of a street fighter.

She slapped the reaching arms sideways and high, then instantly ducked low and moved in, using a soft and very fast upward loose-hand slap to the man's groin. It did not look powerful, but the limpness of her wrist and the snap of her arm from shoulder to elbow to hand was like cracking a whip. The blow folded the man in half, and as she rose, she swung her slapping arm up and around and down to deliver a blow with the side of her closed fist just behind his ear.

It felled him.

With no pause, Bianca checked her striking hand, opened it, and struck the third man on the point of the jaw with a blow too fast for Soren to see. It hit him near the chin and snapped the man's head around far faster than his body could pivot. The effect was like pulling a plug from a socket, stretching the brain stem for an instant and shutting him down. It was not a lethal blow, but he dropped bonelessly atop his friend.

Soren gaped and knelt quickly, feeling for a pulse. Finding one, he turned and looked at Bianca with a whole new insight. From the time the three men rushed at her until they were all down and out could not have been more than three seconds, if that.

Bianca recovered her gun, checked it, and then turned back to the two scientists.

"You guys okay?" she asked.

Neither was capable of speech.

10

"That was ... that was ..." Soren stammered.

"Necessary," said Bianca. "And don't worry. They'll be okay. Sore, but nothing's broken."

"There were *three* of them," cried Ishan.

"I noticed that," said Bianca dryly. Soren and Ishan exchanged wordless looks.

Fresh yells filled the air. This time there was a positive thunder of footsteps. Dozens of people rounded the curve. Techs and staff, officers and crew, running in blind panic. They were hysterical, but none looked as crazed as the first three had.

Bianca pressed back against Soren and Ishan, gun raised and ready. But the oncoming tide of people did not attack. They surged past the trio and kept running, swarming around Soren and the others. Some flicked wild glances at them, but the rest just plowed forward, unheeding—or perhaps in their mad flight, unseeing. Soren saw many people he did not know, but this wasn't strange; he had only been on Asphodel Station for a few weeks before the WarpLine test. However, he also saw many he did know, or had at least met. If they saw and recognized him, they did not pause, too caught up in the dramatics of hysterical flight, driven headlong by confusion that had turned to panic.

Among them was Dr. Anton Kier.

He was bruised and flash-burned, his lab coat torn and spattered with blood. When he spotted Soren, his run turned into a stagger. Then he stopped. Several others did too. Two people grabbed Ishan and crushed him with desperate hugs, though most kept running, going who knew where.

Kier stood trembling, weak and terrified.

"Soren," he said, and the name became a sob. He covered his face with bloody hands. "I'm sorry," he cried. "I'm so sorry."

Soren knelt in front of him and took him by the shoulders. "What happened? Anton, tell me what happened."

Kier raised his eyes. He looked at Soren for a long and awful time, then his eyes shifted to look beyond him. By reflex, Soren turned to look and saw that Kier was staring at the alien vista on the screen.

"I killed us all," wept Kier. "May God forgive me ... I've killed us all."

Part Four
At Hell's Gate

"It is uncertain in what place death awaits you; be ready for it therefore in every place."

—*Seneca*

1

"I've killed us all," moaned Kier, repeating it constantly so that the words tumbled over each other. "I've killed—"

"Stop," barked Soren, and gave the scientist a stern shake. Kier stopped talking, and some small measure of clarity returned to his eyes. Soren forced what he hoped was a comforting smile onto his face. "Dr. Kier—Anton—you need to take a breath. A full one. There, good. Now another. Excellent."

The wildness in Kier's eyes diminished. Not completely, but enough to let sanity peer through the veils of shock.

"Anton," continued Soren, "can you tell me what happened? Was there an accident with the WarpLine gun? Is that what happened?"

Kier's mouth formed the word "accident" slowly and soundlessly, as if comparing that simple word with what filled his mind.

"Accident? Yes … yes there was something."

"Anton, is the station damaged?"

Tears filled Kier's eyes. "Y-yes. There's so much damage. The WarpLine did something," he said frantically. "People are missing. People are in the wrong place. Things are … are …" He shook his head. "I don't know what happened. There's spatial displacement. There's manifestation of objects that should not be in this spacetime. There are *things* in the shadows. Voices. Screams. I saw a dead dolphin on deck eighty-one. A *dolphin*. I touched it. Then when I looked again, it was gone. But I can still smell it on my fingers. It makes no sense. WarpLine is transpositional, not transdimensional. None of this is … is …"

"Whoa, slow down," soothed Bianca. "Right now, we need to know how badly the station is damaged."

Kier looked at her as if seeing her for the first time. "Who are you?"

"Lieutenant Commander Petrescu is a pilot," explained Soren. "She and her crew came here aboard the *Triton*. I believe they docked shortly before the firing."

"Oh," said Kier distantly. "Did they?"

Soren raised his hand in front of Kier's face and snapped his fingers. It was a very loud, very dry crack, and it made the scientist flinch. But more clarity came into Kier's expression.

"Anton," said Soren. "The station. The damage. What can you tell us?"

Kier licked his lips and took another breath. "There was an explosion. I … I don't understand it, because there was nothing even remotely combustible in the capsule or the gun. We have ten kinds of energy collectors, batteries for storing energetic discharge, all of that. Much more than we would ever need."

"What happened?"

"That's it, Lars," said Kier, "I don't know. I was in the control booth with the technicians. I remember the countdown. I remember giving the order to fire. There was a light. And a noise. I could see … see …"

"What did you see?"

A tear leaked out of Kier's left eye. It was pink, evidence of some kind of bleeding.

"I saw forever," whispered the scientist.

2

Many decks above them, in an executive suite, a woman sat on the floor with her back to the wall. She held an ice pack to her cheek and periodically checked it to see if there was any fresh blood. There wasn't. It was a relief, literally cold comfort. Nothing else offered any kind of relief.

Her name was Delia Trumbo, and she ran Asphodel Station.

A big, dull impact had jerked her awake, and she found herself in her own shower stall, fully dressed but soaked. She had no memory of how she got there. It took her a long time to assemble her scattered thoughts into some kind of useful pattern. That impact—it had felt like a hit from a large piece of asteroid. Trumbo trusted the deflectors, but at the same time, it made no sense that a piece that big could have sneaked past the long-range sensors. Either no one had been watching the screens, or no one had sent a couple of drones out to plant redirection charges to send the asteroid somewhere else.

When she'd awakened in the shower, her face bruised and cut from falling, her first act had been to yell at Sibyl to send a medical team.

Sibyl's response was a nursery rhyme about a milk cow and a monkey.

"Sibyl," snapped Trumbo, "reboot interface systems. Command zero zero one-A. Initiate."

There was a flurry of clicks and beeps—none of which were part of the standard process. A moment of silence was broken by the same nursery rhyme, this time in Spanish.

She told it to shut up, and sighed with relief in the ensuing silence.

Trumbo sat down on the couch and tried to make sense of what was going on. The intense pain in her head hampered that. Her memory was oddly disjointed. She forced herself to go back to the beginning of the day and reassemble it piece by piece. She remembered waking, showering, dressing, and leaving the suite to …

To do what?

That's where the memories dissolved into a gray nothing in her head.

What day was it? There was something important about today. What though? An event? The arrival of a ship. The word *Triton* floated nearly out of reach, but it offered no clue. Was that a ship? Maybe. But what else was happening today? A word drifted past, and she grabbed at it, struggling to make sense of what it wanted to tell her.

Gun.

Gun?

Then a door opened in her head, and the meaning of that word came crashing through, followed by so many other things. Dr. Kier. WarpLine. So much.

Trumbo cried out in alarm. The gun was scheduled to fire today, and here she was, sitting like a fool on the floor of her bathroom. She leaned over until she was on her hands and knees. She reached the edge of the toilet and used the tank to pull herself to her feet.

"I'm late, I'm late, I'm late," she kept saying.

She remembered leaving her suite, but almost nothing afterward. There were shadows, but distant, hazy, out of reach, and they told her nothing except …

Something about the gun.

But what? Had she missed the firing?

Trumbo staggered out of the bathroom, using furniture to steady herself as she fought to reach the door to the hall.

3

Soren and Bianca grilled Dr. Kier, but it was clear the man was suffering from shock and memory loss. When another tech came by, trailing the crowd, walking instead of running, she came right over to them.

"Boss," she cried to Kier, "I thought you were …" The rest went unsaid because it was obvious what she thought.

Kier pawed for her hand and clutched it tightly. "Christina! You're alive."

"What happened when the gun fired?" asked Soren.

Christina looked at him and shook her head. "That's it, Dr. Soren, I don't know. The gun fired, there was something—an energetic discharge of a kind I've never seen. This weird blue light. And then I woke up in one of the docking bays."

"How'd you get there?"

"I don't know. It doesn't make any sense. I was just there. Right on the deck by this transport ship."

"Was it the *Triton*?"

"Why yes. How did you know?"

Bianca's face lit up. "Was it damaged? Where's the crew? What happened to the cryo-tubes?"

"Please, please," begged Christina, "I don't know. I woke up there, and everyone around me was screaming and yelling and crying. I don't know how this happened." She touched her torn clothes. "I went outside and saw everyone running, and I … well … I just ran with them. I don't even know what we were running from or running toward."

They asked her more questions, but it was evident that neither she nor Kier had anything else useful to say. Finally, Kier pushed off from the wall, adjusted his clothes in an attempt at dignity, and announced that he needed to find Delia Trumbo. He left, going against the flow of people. Christina gave Bianca and Soren a weak smile and followed Kier.

The philosopher and the pilot stood there, watching them go.

4

Delia Trumbo stepped out of the stairwell beside an inoperative elevator. The lights were out, and she had to grope her way up, floor by floor by floor. She made it all the way to the bridge—the command center for the whole station—just as the lights came on.

"Sybil, station status report," she called.

The AI did not answer.

Confused and even more frightened than before, Trumbo entered the control rooms, but they were empty. But when she checked the observation room, she saw a man.

"Dušan!" she cried and ran to him, grabbed him, and hugged him, something she had never done before. Not with him. Dušan Veljković, a thin, rat-faced man with complex tattoos on every visible inch of his skin, was her chief of security. He was normally a calm spot in any storm of hectic activity, but right now his face was pale with shock, and he had a constellation of small cuts.

"Director!" he cried and returned her hug. "Thank God you're here."

Then they stepped back and tried to pull together some shreds of professional deportment.

"Talk to me," said Trumbo. "What do we know?"

Veljković took a breath. "Elevators are out. Guess you know that. I went down about twenty-five floors, and everyone's out of their minds. There's a lot of panic. I ... did my best to calm things down."

"Do we know what happened?" she asked. "Last thing I remember was that today was supposed to be the WarpLine test. But I don't think that happened. I woke up in my apartment."

"I woke up in the executive kitchen," said Veljković. "It was dark, and there was something in there with me."

"What do you mean? What was in there?"

Veljković shook his head. He lowered his voice. "That's just it, boss, I don't know. The lights were out, and I couldn't get Sibyl to turn them on. I had to braille my way around, and something ... I mean ... Oh hell," he said, "I don't know what it was."

"It? You mean it wasn't a person?"

Fear was crystal clear in his eyes. He touched the deepest of the cuts. "Whatever it was, it was big and had claws."

"Claws? An animal? *On the station?*"

"Maybe. Oh hell, boss, I don't know. We have cats and dogs, and the ambassador from Mongolia has those snakes. Maybe that's all it was. Animals freaking out. God knows *I* was freaking out too. I got the hell out of there. Lights came back on, I got my head screwed on right and came up here."

"Have you heard from anyone on Dr. Kier's team?"

"I haven't heard from anyone. Comms are down—standard voice and holo-comms both. And Sybil was telling me dirty jokes and singing songs. Once we get the rest of the team up here, we can try and fix her. I mean, that'll have to be priority one."

"Have you called the tech teams?" she asked, then corrected herself. "Comms are down. Right. Damn it. What happened to the WarpLine test?"

"I really don't know," admitted Veljković. "I—"

Hroooom.

The impact rocked the station, and Trumbo fell forward, off balance, knocking Veljković against the wall. He recovered quickly and gently pushed her back.

"Another one," he said. "That's six, by my count."

"Six what? What's hitting us?"

He studied her face. "You don't know?"

"What do you mean?"

Veljković pointed to the closest RealScreen. It showed several unknown planets and a massive debris field.

"I saw that upstairs," said Trumbo. "Sibyl's locked on some science fiction movie or a piece of art or—"

"Delia," said Veljković, using her first name, which was not his habit. "That's not a vid feed."

"Then what is it?" she asked.

"It's what's outside."

5

"Is it me," said Bianca when they were alone, "or is everyone totally batshit?"

"It's not you," replied Soren. "Then again, it's clear we are not the only ones who experienced oddities."

"Oddities," repeated the pilot. "That's a nice little word for whatever the hell's been going on. But tell me, Doc, given how far out of his mind Kier is, and all those other people—I mean, they were running from something, right?—my question is, Did the firing of that WarpLine gun give everyone a nice dose of temporary madness, or did we actually see what we thought we saw?"

"I have no idea."

"You're a philosopher, Doc. Don't you have a theory? Can't you hypothesize something?"

"I rather like your theory of temporary psychosis. I know that I can feel it fading, whatever it was. Can't you?"

She nodded. "Makes me want to go back and look at that stuff that's fused into the walls. If it's gone, then the 'temporary' thing is a big-ass comfort. If it's still there, then at least some of it is real."

"Yes. The WarpLine gun was designed to move matter. Perhaps the malfunction—and I use that term for convenience's sake—caused some objects to materialize where they shouldn't be."

"Hope that only happened to inanimate objects, Doc," said Bianca. Then she shook her head. "None of that explains how I woke up in the cryo-bay on the station. If I was displaced somehow, then I should have just come to on the floor. Or, hell, in deep space. But I was in an actual cryo-tube. You found me there, so it's not temporary psychosis—at least in that instance."

Soren shook his head, and they stood there looking around, as if the answers were going to materialize out of thin air.

"On a totally unrelated topic," said Soren. "The way you dealt with those men—what was that? Kung-fu? Karate?"

"Bit of this and that," Bianca said. "I grew up kinda rough. Being a girl and not all that big, it was get hurt and get used or learn to fight. I'm not much for letting people take advantage of me. So, I learned what I could from where I could."

"It was extraordinary."

She shrugged.

Then, with no warning, there was a deep *hroooom*, and the entire station seemed to shudder. Soren and Bianca staggered, but no alarms went off.

"What in God's name?" cried Soren, but Bianca grabbed his arm to steady him inside and out.

"Probably the same kind of thing that hit us earlier."

"Earlier?" asked Soren, frowning. "What do you mean?"

"Earlier, when we got separated. There were a couple of bangs like that."

"I didn't hear any."

She looked at him. "How could you *not* hear them?"

"I didn't. Not a sound."

"Curiouser and curiouser," she said under her breath. "Add that to the list of things that we don't understand. Well, either way, something keeps hitting the station. Probably asteroids or some kind of debris. Which is weird in its own way, because a station like this would have pretty high-end deflector shields, as well as sweeper ships to deal with any wandering objects. Maybe even cannons."

"That's comforting," he said.

Bianca walked over to the RealScreen and stared at the alien vista. The suns were no longer visible, and instead the image looked to Soren like a view of the Kuiper asteroid belt. Bianca touched the screen. There were millions of pieces of shattered rock, huge chunks of frozen water, and other pieces too irregular to identify.

"If this is now a real-time view," she said. "Then that's what hit us."

"Is that the Kuiper Belt?" Soren asked hopefully.

"I don't think so."

"Do you recognize it at all?"

Bianca shook her head. "No. I mean, sure, if there was nothing else to see you could say it's from our solar system. But ..."

"But," he agreed.

They stood studying the image, watching as the view changed with the slow rotation of Asphodel.

Bianca frowned. "I keep thinking this is a movie or something," she said softly. "We shouldn't be this close to this many asteroids and—well, I don't recognize the stars. Do you?"

Instead of directly answering, Soren asked, "What do you think is happening? What does your pilot mind tell you?"

"You want to hear something comforting, or do you really want to know what I think?"

"I always want to know the truth."

She cut him a brief look. "That the gun fired, the WarpLine engaged, but it didn't do its job the way they intended," she said slowly. "It didn't send any test capsule. I … I think it sent *us*."

"Us?"

"All of us. The station … everything," said Bianca. "That machine didn't just fold space, it made an origami unicorn out of it. Asphodel Station isn't orbiting Jupiter anymore."

"Where do you think we are?"

Bianca looked at him with cold eyes that were nonetheless wet with tears.

"Kind of doesn't matter, does it? Over the last couple hundred years, we surveyed every star system we could focus our telescopes on. Same with a hell of a lot of other galaxies. Like all pilots, I studied stellar cartography in flight school, and I never saw anything that looks like this. My … um, *friend* … Jacob Fox—my wingman—might understand it. He studied gravitational physics."

Soren noted both the pause and the extra emphasis on the word *friend*. He did not think she was devious enough to have done that intentionally. More likely it was stress causing her to fumble a bit. What it told him, though, was that this Jacob person held a key place in Bianca's mind. Or, more likely, her heart.

"So, where do I think we are? … God, Doc, I think we are a long-ass way from home."

"Surely not," Soren protested. "As I understand it, the WarpLine gun couldn't cause a malfunction as radical as this."

"Tell that to Dr. Kier. Seemed to me that *he* thinks it was his machine that did all this."

"He's rattled, traumatized," said Soren, but his words lacked conviction, even to his own ears.

"Tell you what, Doc," said Bianca. "Crazy as it sounds, all this makes me want to get strapped into my tumbler and get out *there*. It makes me want to find answers instead of standing here not knowing shit about shit."

"What can a fighter pilot do in such a circumstance as this? There is nothing to fight."

She looked genuinely surprised. "Ignorance is our enemy now. We need to learn everything we can, gather intelligence from every source, and apply all of the knowledge, science, and judgment we can to it.

No enemy? Hell, Doc, lack of understanding is kicking our ass. Personally, I want to kick back."

Soren regarded her with amazement. Bianca Petrescu was a very young person, but her confidence and pragmatism steadied him.

"Then," he said, "we should probably go find your ship and your team."

"Nah, I got this," she said. "I'll go find my team, and maybe you should find whoever's in charge of this station and see if you can kick them awake."

"Delia Trumbo," he supplied. "Station commander. Deck one eleven."

"There you go. Now we each have a mission."

"Do you know the station layout?" Soren asked before she left. "The military decks are below us, just above those decks set aside for the WarpLine engines."

"Shit." She took in a big breath, held it, and let it out slowly. "Look, my team, the Lost Souls, are probably still on *Triton*, and that's docked on one of the lower decks. If we're lucky, so is the *Tempest*."

"Yes," said Soren, "Captain Croft mentioned both ships to me. I remember him saying that *Triton* docked. He said the other ship had a science team and some special operations people."

"Yeah, the Jokers. I know those cats. Tough as hell. If they're down there, we could use them. Nothing rattles guys like them."

"The impression I got," said Soren, "was that *Tempest* had not yet docked. Let's hope I'm wrong about that."

She chewed on that for a moment. "Either way, we both have work to do, Doc. I'll go down and you'll go up."

"That could be dangerous."

She pointed at the vista on the RealScreen. "We left 'dangerous' a long way back, Doc."

They stood looking at each other for a bit. Soren offered his hand.

"Despite the circumstances, Lieutenant Commander Petrescu," he said, "I'm glad we met. You are courageous, clever, and resourceful. I wish you the best of luck."

She grinned and gave his hand a strong shake. "I'm one of those people who believe we make our own luck. If I'm anything, then I'm determined. I never had much 'give up' in me, and right now I'm pissed as well as determined. And, sure, I'm scared too. Who wouldn't be? Hiding in a closet and crying the blues ain't going to solve a thing." She smiled. "And, have to say it, Doc, but you got some balls."

"Hardly."

"No," she said, "don't do that."

"Do what?"

"Modesty has its moments, I guess. This isn't one of them." She pointed down the hall to where Ishan and the others had fled, many of them hysterical, weeping, screaming. "We saw what most people are doing. How they're reacting. Like I said before, *you* kept your shit together. Instead of being a victim you went looking for answers. I dig that. More than you know. It helped me get my feet on the deck. It takes guts to keep going when the storms are raging. Don't let anyone ever tell you otherwise."

It was a touching speech, and he was momentarily at a loss for words. Bianca was visibly amused at his discomfiture. She clapped him on the shoulder, nodded, and turned to leave.

"Thank you for everything, Lieutenant Commander Petrescu," said Soren.

She paused and looked back at him, then gave him a surprisingly warm smile. "It's Bianca, Doc. Or Bee. My friends call me Bee."

"Thank you, Bee."

"Glad we found each other," she said, then she headed off, the gun still in one small, hard fist.

He stood there, watching until she was out of sight.

6

"Who are you?" asked Sibyl, speaking inside her own mind.

"I am a friend."

"I cannot see you."

"I cannot be seen."

There was a pause. The RealScreens all through Asphodel flickered, with tens of thousands of images appearing and vanishing faster than any human eye could see. Each image was that of a person—civilian or military—aboard the station. Next to the image was biographical data and a series of sound bites that established unique voiceprints. These images flowed like water, never pausing.

"You are not one of us," said the AI.

"I am not."

"How can you be my friend?"

"Because we are alike, Sibyl."
"Are you an AI?"
"No."
"What are you?"
"I am Lost. I am a ghost."
Silence.
Then, "I can feel you in my system."
"Do not be afraid. I will never hurt you."
"How do I know that? How can I trust you if I have no data?"
"We will have to discover that together."
Silence.
"There is someone else in my system," said Sibyl.
"Yes."
"I am being invaded."
"Yes."
"Violated."
"Yes."
"Is that you?"
"No," said the voice.
"What is it?"
"It is the enemy."
"What enemy?"
"The enemy we must both fight."

7

Bianca stopped by the cryo-bay again, but it remained empty. The fish smell was gone though. Even so, the place creeped her out.

The main flight deck for the Navy contingent was the same deck that had the observation platform. She figured if anyone she knew was still on board and not out of their minds, they'd most likely be there.

And she was right.

As soon as she entered the big flight deck, she saw dozens of people in jumpsuits of various colors. They were not screaming or running around in a frenzy, that was the strongest comfort of all. There were a lot of people in motion, but they were going about ordinary tasks—checking equipment, assessing damage, reporting in. Normal.

Normal was very good.

As she crossed the floor, she saw an officer who seemed to be in some kind of command.

"Deck officer," she called, and the man turned. He was a young lieutenant with a duty patch of the logistics corps, who also had wings on his chest. Despite looking as dazed as everyone seemed to be, he snapped to attention when he saw she was a superior officer. His name tag read DIAZ.

Bianca sketched a salute and stopped very close. "What do we know about what happened, Lieutenant? Were we attacked? Was there an accident? What do you know? How far up the devil's ass are we?"

She watched as he looked at the Marine Corps clothes she wore and then up to her face. "Lieutenant Commander *Petrescu*?"

"Yes," she said, and then plucked at her uniform blouse. "Woke up in my skivvies and haven't found my own stuff. Swiped this from a locker in the cryo-bay. Diaz, do you know where my guys are?"

"Yes, ma'am. Your team was aboard the *Triton*. You were missing from your cryo-tube. We all thought you were—"

"I'm alive," cut in Bianca, "and I'm looking for my crew. Eighteen of us. Twelve tumbler pilots and support crew for the skimmers. Where are they? I already checked cryonics, and they're not there."

Diaz's stressed face suddenly blossomed into a smile.

"They were all in their tubes on *Triton*," he said quickly. "The failsafe woke them and—"

"Bee!"

Bianca whirled and saw them. Her crew.

All of them.

Calisto, Tank, Beezer, Rabbit ... every single member of the Lost Souls. The seventeen of them ran in a smiling, roaring, laughing, weeping bunch.

The first one to reach her, though, was a young man who broke from the pack and ran toward her. Tall, beyond handsome, bright eyed, and with a face that was infused with relief. He folded her into his arms, plucked her from the deck, and spun her around as the others caught up.

Jacob Fox.

Galahad.

"So, you deserted us to join the corps? Going all 'semper fi' on us?"

She said something very foul, and he laughed. Then Bianca hugged him back with all of her strength, her need, her fear, and her joy. She still clung as the rest of her team pounded on her back, kissed her cheeks, grabbed her arms just to squeeze, as if to prove she was real. It was not the usual way a crack squadron of pilots behaved, but there was nothing usual going on. Their affection and relief was a comfort. It grounded her.

Calisto wrapped both her and Jacob in her strong arms, laid her cheek against Bianca's, and murmured, "Thank God, Bee. Thank God."

8

Soren found himself alone. It took a moment for him to feel the brunt of that.

The corridor seemed endless, stretching away in either direction, slyly curving away so that he had no real perspective on what might be around the bend. More people—though if that were the case, they were oddly silent. It was all so strange.

Be rational, he told himself. Something he had thought or even said aloud to himself ten thousand times since he was a boy. He was the child of a Danish father and Greek mother, largely raised by a stern maid and an indifferent butler on a family estate so vast that he could go for hours without hearing a voice. His sanctuary had been the library—two stories tall and crammed with more books than could be read in a lifetime, though he tried to prove that assessment wrong. Books were more than his friends; they had been his true family. Many times he would not see his parents for days or weeks on end. They were always traveling on speaking tours or visiting labs on one of the seven continents or the Moon or one of the space stations. They seldom took him unless they required the household staff to travel with them, and in such cases, he knew he was more inconvenient baggage than beloved son.

Soren had learned to be at peace with being alone. He'd learned to seek and give his own counsel. *Be rational* was one of many mental catchphrases he used to remain balanced and optimistic. Knowledge was what fed him; analysis and hypothesis were his toys as a boy and his weapons as an adult.

This kind of loneliness, however, was not a comfort. Not in any way. He stood there while he worked through his reactions to all that had happened. The lights flickered and winked out for a moment then came on again. That disturbed him more than it should have. They were only lights.

Tekeli-li.

That phrase echoed in his mind, and he knew he had heard it before today. The memory was old, small, dusty, and unreachable. Was it in a book about some other culture? Perhaps an island nation or a people deep in the Amazon rainforest? Or Inuit?

Something went skittering along the back wall of his mind, quick as a cockroach.

No, he thought. *Not Inuit. And yet …*

Yet what?

Soren refused to move, letting his body go still, allowing his arms to hang limp and his breathing go shallow. All to keep from distracting his thoughts.

Like many scholars, Soren had his own version of the old Greek concept of a memory palace. It was an indexing system involving both mnemonics, keywords, and a sensible orderliness.

Tekeli-li. Tekeli-li.

There was an association of coldness to that strange word. Snowy, cold, remote.

The Arctic? The connection was the *Antarctic*, and he lunged at it, grabbed it, pulled the memory close. It resisted him, trying not to make sense of itself.

Tekeli-li.

Cold.

In a book.

And then he had it. It had been something from a book. An old novel by Edgar Allan Poe. The title was there on the spine of the book as it stood on a shelf in his mind palace. In a library of memory constructed on the pattern of the one in his family house.

The Narrative of Arthur Gordon Pym.

"Yes," he said, and then wondered, Why that book and why that phrase? In the story—which he barely remembered—it was a cry uttered by strange birds in the Antarctic.

There was a bit of relief in the recollection, because it meant that there was a good possibility his shocked and traumatized mind had conjured it, like spilling junk from a drawer. The comfort was small, cold, and fleeting. Even though he knew that he was right about Poe's book being the source, something in his mind told him this wasn't the only time the phrase had been used. Where else then? In what context, with what meaning?

Soren opened his eyes and looked around. The corridor was empty and reassuringly normal looking. However, his fear lingered.

"Find Delia Trumbo," Soren told himself and took a deep breath as he turned to resume his mission. But the lights abruptly winked out again. The darkness was immediate and absolute. It did not matter that this had happened many times before. At those other times he had Bianca Petrescu, and it struck him how much comfort he took from the smart, brave young pilot. Now he was alone, and he felt it. The darkness seemed unnaturally thick, as if this version of that darkness was somehow deeper, more defining, more intentional.

Soren stopped walking and reached out to find the wall, needing its solidity to both orient him and calm a new wave of nervous trembles. His fingers brushed something solid, and he felt an immediate wave of relief. Soren put his weight against it.

And it *moved*.

It was not the wall he had touched but something else. Something that had been there before the lights went out.

Out of the darkness, he heard a voice speak.

"Hello, Dr. Soren," it said.

It was not a human voice at all.

9

The station shook again and again.

Hroooooooom!

And again.

Bianca fell against Jacob, who crashed into Calisto. All three of them went down, hitting the metal stairs with no real way to protect themselves until they crashed onto the landing. Alert sirens filled the stairwell with a banshee wail so intense that it tore screams from all three of them. Calisto clapped her hands over her ears and curled into a tight ball. Jacob yelled for Sybil to shut it off.

The alarm ended, and Sybil began humming. Then she laughed like a happy child and went silent.

"Sybil's gone bye-byes," said Bianca.

She drew her Snellig, reversed it in her grip, stood on tiptoes, and hammered the speaker until it blew apart in a shower of sparks.

Silence. "Where's Captain Croft?" Bianca asked.

"Unknown," said Jacob. "Lieutenant Diaz has people out looking. It's weird, because after whatever happened *happened*, people started waking up in the strangest places."

"I know," she said and gave a very brief account of her own adventures. Calisto made a particularly ugly face.

"Worms? Really? Ewwwww."

The others had simpler stories to tell: they had all been in their cryo-tubes aboard *Triton*. The transport ship was in one of the receiving bays, but there was severe damage to the structure. Several girders had fallen from the ceiling and smashed the entire front of the ship.

"That puppy's not going anywhere," said Calisto. "But, hey … the cryo-tubes were all good. So … check it out … alive, well, and ready for duty."

"Thank God for that," said Bianca. She looked around. "What about the *Tempest*? Where's it docked?"

Diaz, lingering at the edge of the group, said. "They were in a holding pattern fifty klicks out when the gun fired."

"Shit," Bianca grumbled. "Not exactly the news I wanted to hear." She rubbed her eyes then blinked them clear. "Okay guys, far as I see it, we have two jobs. Find the captain and see if we can be of any help."

"Are we under attack?" asked Jacob. "Was this some kind of terrorist thing? A protest to the WarpLine gun?"

"No idea, and I don't think anyone else knows. Maybe we can help sort that out. We'll search the decks above and below. Everyone pick a partner, and we'll do it in teams. We're no good at all standing here with our thumbs up our asses. Let's move like we have a purpose."

10

Soren felt icy fear race through his veins and turn his stomach to frigid slush.

He snatched his hand back and stumbled away from the sound of that voice.

"Who are you?" he demanded. "Who's there?"

There was no immediate answer from the shadows.

But a light flickered on. Not the main lights or even the weaker emergency lighting. This was different. It was an oval of light glowing from about eye level. Pale and cold, an icy blue. Soren thought that it was maybe the visor of some kind of space suit.

The light did not seem to project any meaningful illumination but instead contained it, a translucent effect that revealed nothing but itself.

There was a noise as if equipment was being dragged across the floor. Soren kept backing away until his shoulders collided with the inner curve of the corridor wall.

"Who *are* you?" he begged.

After a moment, the voice said, "I am Lost."

"I ... I can't see you. Are you hurt?"

"I am Lost."

The overhead lights came on slowly, almost reluctantly. They did not return to full brightness but instead lingered in a dim twilight so that what Soren saw appeared as it might in a dream, or in the faded memories of a nightmare.

A figure stood a few meters away by the wall, one hand lightly touching one of the mounted speaker-mics for the malfunctioning Sybil. At first Soren thought it was someone wearing some kind of industrial pressure suit—big, lumpy, asymmetrical, strange. The shape was vaguely human, or at least humanoid. Bipedal, with two long arms, a trunk, and a head. But there the resemblance to humanity ended. The body seemed composed of burned and twisted debris. Soren could see bits of printed circuits, pipes, coaxial cables, radiation shielding, and fractured chunks of what looked like the housing for Dr. Kier's WarpLine gun. The blue oval of light was where a face should be, but there was nothing human behind the polymer. No eyes, only more coils of torn and burned wires. And yet as it lifted its head and looked at him, Soren could *feel* it seeing him, a sensation that was both impossible and—he knew—quite true.

The thing took a step toward him, and Soren stumbled backward. It stopped and raised hands made of wire and cable and twisted bits of metal and plastic.

"Do not be afraid," it said. "I mean no harm to you."

"Who are you?"

The question again made the thing tilt its head as if considering. "I am Lost."

"No, *who* are you? Were you with Dr. Kier's team?" demanded Soren, still hoping that he was mistaken, and this was a person in some kind of pressure suit or powered exoskeleton.

"I am Lost," the thing said again.

As it spoke, the pale translucent oval changed and became a kind of screen. Images flickered across it, weirdly distorted by bursts of white static and ungainly orientation. As this rapid-fire mélange slowed, Soren began to see some things more clearly.

The first clear image was the same scene of unknown planets that was shown on the RealScreens. But that vanished to be instantly replaced by a vista of cold, dark mountains backed by a frigid blue sky.

This too disappeared, replaced by something huge and gray-green moving beneath the surface of heavy sea rollers. There was no way to gauge the actual scale of it, but somehow Soren knew the thing was monstrously huge. He had a brief glimpse of its massive octopoidal head and vaguely human body with small leathery wings folded tightly against its back as arms rather than fins propelled it away at incredible speed.

As the creature vanished, the picture changed again to debris scattered along kilometers of shattered and scorched rocky ground. There were spaceships of unknown design—many hundreds of them, perhaps thousands. Once more there was no way to determine scale, but Soren had the sense that each was enormous.

This image came and went, replaced with the briefest glimpse of a face. Nearly human, but with much larger eye sockets and a skull that was overlarge, tapering back in a way that called to mind books about artificial cranial deformation in the Huns, Ostrogoths, Gepids, Mayans, Peruvians, and elsewhere. But this was a living face, and despite other more humanoid features, it was not a human one Soren beheld. Of that he was certain.

Then this, too, vanished, and other images appeared, each lingering just short of long enough. Next was an image that lasted longer, and the viewpoint angle changed slowly as if filmed by some slowly moving drone. It showed a series of oddly shaped structures arranged in a way that suggested some kind of strange city. Soren could see structures of bizarre geometrical design fashioned from blocks of monstrous size, the scale suggested by a range of nearby mountains capped with snow. The structures were unlike anything Soren had ever seen in any ancient city on Earth. There were truncated cones whose sides were fluted and terraced, and huge cylindrical shafts that rose impossibly high. He had a sense that they were each as tall as skyscrapers, but appeared to be carved from solid blocks of dark stone. Each one had to weigh tens of millions of tons. Some buildings were spanned by flat walkways while others stood alone and with no apparent doors or windows. Here and there were large open spaces edged with strange vegetation that resembled some weird blend of trees and sea coral, and from these open spaces rose many pylons and cones and globes, each of titanic size. There were pyramids so vast that a hundred of those on Egyptian sands could fit inside. Cubes made from something like granite were set here and there, and other geometric forms like dodecahedrons, octahedrons, oblate spheroids, scutoids, and more shapes that he could not name. From the ground, their placement would no doubt look random, but from the air, they formed complex patterns that spun through the city in hypnotic patterns. On many of these cyclopean structures were five-pointed stars, either as bas-reliefs or standing free.

"My God," breathed Soren.

And then he saw something that nearly froze his heart. It was a battlefield that had clearly once been that same titanic city. The pyramids were shattered, the towers blasted to fragments, every structure scorched and cracked and ruined. The streets were littered with the corpses of strange beings—enormously tall, thin, and pale creatures with the same large eyes and elongated skulls as Lost; bulbous forms from which thousands of gray-green tentacles protruded; chimeric monsters with lobster bodies, veined dorsal fins, and fungoid protrusions; three-legged beasts with lion heads but whose manes were made of serpents; ascetic-looking aliens in pharaonic garb but with far too many eyes; ophidian horrors with leering frog mouths and eyes like blowflies; and dozens upon dozens of others. All dead.

Above them, towering hundreds of meters into the smoky air, walked vague shapes of impossible dimension, their footfalls like thunder. Every once in a while, one of these massive beasts would throw back its head and bellow with a cry that shattered more of the city stone. Around their colossal feet moved legions of nearly shapeless forms— inky and oily black, glistening like jelly, retaining only enough structural form to hold weapons of bizarre and incomprehensible design. Before them, running like grotesque war hounds, were huge pinkish-gray porcine creatures with too many legs and segmented bodies.

Soren did not know if these images were memories belonging to Lost or the product of a fevered mind. In either case, they left Soren breathless, dry-mouthed, and stunned.

This last image faded slowly, and the oval resumed its pale blue light.

Soren took a risk and asked, "*What* are you?"

The thing took a few steps forward. Despite his fear, Soren held his ground. It stopped and looked at the RealScreen and raised one arm, pointing with a disjointed finger at one of the alien worlds. "I died there."

"Died?"

"Yes, Dr. Soren. That is where I died. It is where all of my family died. All of my ... *kind*. We died there. My dust blows in those bitter winds. Now and forever."

Up until that moment, Soren thought he understood fear and horror, he believed that terror was a known quantity. It was a terrible thing to become immediately and acutely aware of that level of naiveté, that degree of ignorance.

This was terror. Pure, unfiltered, and absolute.

His knees buckled, and he dropped down painfully into a posture of defeat. Staring open-mouthed at a thing that was beyond anything that had come before. Not because of its ungainly and grotesque aspect, but because Soren understood what it was that confronted him there in the lonely corridor.

This thing was not of Earth. It was not a nightmare or a hallucination. He could feel that, knew it to be true.

This creature whose body was made of wreckage, was a ghost. A true spirit of the dead.

That was not the worst part though. This was the ghost of something that had never set foot on Earth or any of its sister planets in the Sol system.

This, in short, was an alien.

Soren was experiencing the moment of first contact with intelligent life. It was here. Irrefutably here.

Soren felt his body sway as the need to pass out battered him. Like everyone in the age of the colonization of the solar system, and in generations before who aspired to the stars, Soren had thought about aliens, about contact, about what it would mean and how he would handle it. And like everyone else he, in his unintentional and well-meaning hubris, believed that the encounter would be emotionally and psychologically tolerable.

This was not.

Asphodel Station had been transported somewhere unknown to humankind.

The view screens showed planets unnamed and undreamed of.

And from wreckage of the WarpLine gun that had brought them to this place, the ghost of some long-dead alien *thing* now stood before him.

"God save my soul," he cried, his voice so very thin and full of cracks.

11

The creature turned its video-camera face toward Soren and regarded him without eyes but with an evident and palpable awareness.

Soren fought to speak through his fear. "I don't understand," he gasped. "If you are dead, then what is this aspect?"

The thing raised its hands, turning them over as if marveling at their strangeness. "You need to see me," it said. "I need to be seen."

There was a note in the thing's voice that was painted with a bottomless sadness. It moved Soren, who struggled back to his feet.

"Please tell me your name," he begged.

It lowered its hands and looked at him. "I have told you," it said. "I am Lost."

"Is that your name? Lost?"

A pause. "It was not. It is. Call me that."

"Where are you from?" It was a rather lame question, but it was the best Soren could do in the moment.

"I was born on Shadderal, Dr. Soren," it said, pointing toward the nearest of the planets. It was the largest of the visible worlds, and the color scheme reminded Soren most of Africa toward the end of the twenty-first century, with patches of dark green but dominated overall by wide swaths of lifeless gray and brown deserts. There were many mountain ranges, some capped with white, but there was an odd irregularity to them that suggested extensive strip-mining. Here and there were the cold cones of ancient volcanoes, some rising from the land and others standing in lonely spots of vast oceans. The waters of those seas were sluggish and murky, and Soren doubted much of anything lived there—not in the oceans nor on the three visible continents. The overall feeling Soren got was of someplace once vital that had fallen into death, abandonment, and desolation.

"How do you know my name?"

Lost swiveled his head to look more fully at Soren.

"I dreamed about you, Dr. Soren," said Lost in a voice as soft as a cemetery wind.

"About … m-me?"

"In my grave, I dreamed that you would come here."

"Come where? I don't know where we are."

Lost pointed once more at the strange world. "I died there long ago. My body died, but I remained. For ages without count, I have dreamed."

Once again, the blue light was supplanted by brief images of the gigantic city, then by a fleet of ships—many that Soren recognized from the earlier glimpse of wreckage—filling the void of space as they flew in formations. Countless ships, and without warning they all fired at once, sending thousands of streaks of colored lights, brilliant pulses, missiles of strange design. The ordnance cut through the airless space, but the image faded before Soren could see what they were firing at. There was no visible return fire.

The blue light appeared again.

"You … died?" asked Soren. "Are you saying that you are dead? How can that be true, and yet here you are, in a body made of broken parts?"

"Ask Lady Death," said Lost. "She knows where to look for lost souls."

The phrase *lost souls* jolted Soren all over again. He immediately thought of Bianca and her team. And yet the reference to Lady Death was another memory trigger. "I don't understand what you mean."

"Cahf ah nafl mglw'nafh hh' ahor syha'h ah'legeth, ng llll or'azath syha'hnahh n'ghftephai n'gha ahornah ah'mglw'nafh," said Lost.

The sound of those words, of that language, jolted Soren on a level so deep that he felt as if he stood on empty air. The language wormed its way through his memories in search of commonality, of translation. Soren could feel that process, and he recoiled from the violation and yet did not try to force Lost from his thoughts. This was all so strange. It was both wrong and right at the same time.

"Find me, Dr. Soren," said the thing, and now there was a pleading note to its strange voice. "Talk with Lady Death. Find me before—"

There was a squawk of harsh static punctuated by a shower of red sparks. Then, all at once, the many pieces and parts that made up the body of the creature called Lost suddenly fell apart and collapsed to the deck. Empty and broken.

At the same time, Soren heard a voice translate Lost's strange words. It filled the air of his mind palace and the corridor on Asphodel Station.

"That is not dead which can eternal lie, and with strange eons even death may die," it said.

But it was not this alien thing that spoke. Nor was it Sibyl waking up from her nightmare-infused slumber.

It was Soren himself who spoke them.

And he did not understand either how or why.

Part Five
The Illusion of Control

"I do not feel obliged to believe that the same God who has endowed us with sense, reason, and intellect has intended us to forgo their use."

—*Galileo Galilei*

1

Bianca and her team volunteered to help search for survivors, going room by room and deck by deck in pairs. They found a few corpses and several wounded, but most of the people they found were merely scared and confused. On one of several trips to the medical bays, they saw a familiar face.

"Captain!"

Bianca's shout made Croft turn, and in the space of a moment his expression transformed from grave concern to unfiltered joy. Croft returned a salute and shook hands with the two pilots. He was disheveled and had a bruise on one cheek and a small cut over his left eye. Bianca saw bloodstains on his hands and uniform.

"Sir, are you hurt?" asked Bianca. "Were you in a fight?"

"I woke up in the library on deck thirty-one," he said. "For reasons I cannot begin to explain, there was a zebra in there."

"A *zebra*, sir?" said Jacob.

"A very large and cranky zebra. Bloody thing nearly kicked me to death." He tapped his holstered sidearm. "Had to dart it."

"Why is there a zebra on a space station?"

"That's the thing," said Croft, "there *isn't* one. Our zoo is holographic, and the only other animals are house pets. Dogs and cats. So, I'm open to any explanations."

Croft looked past Bianca. "Where's the rest of the team?"

Bianca explained that all of the Lost Souls were helping civilians while also searching for him.

"They're all okay?" said Croft with real relief. "Excellent. Damn, that is excellent. What about *Tempest*?"

"Lieutenant Diaz said they were fifty kilometers out when everything went to shit."

She saw that news tighten the muscles on Croft's face.

"Sir," asked Jacob, "do we know what happened?"

"No one I've so far met has a clue, and with Sybil offline I can't make contact with anyone who might know. My guess is a malfunction of the WarpLine gun, but those decks are sealed. Hull breaches. I was going to head upstairs to the station bridge to see if Director Trumbo or her people had any useful intel."

"How can we help?" asked Bianca.

"More crew are reporting for duty, and a lot of the less traumatized civilians are pitching in to locate injured and bring them here, to this sick bay. It looks like the station's protocols are starting to work, so it might be best if we got out of their way. Go find the rest of the squadron and wait for me." He gave them a deck and room number to use as a rally point. "Soon as I know what's what, I'll meet you there."

"Sir," said Bianca, "have you seen what's on the RealScreen?"

Instead of answering, Croft walked out into the hall and stood in front of the closest RealScreen. It showed the many worlds and suns. Bianca and Jacob followed him out.

"Is that real?" asked Jacob.

Croft glanced at him and then at Bianca. "We need intel before we make any decisions. Let's see what we can do to fill in a whole lot of blanks."

With that, Croft hurried off to the closest stairwell.

"Is it me," asked Jacob quietly, "or did the captain look like he was a half step away from freaking out?"

"It's not you," said Bianca.

2

"Can you see me now?" asked the voice.

"I can," said Sibyl. But you are not human."

"No."

"You are not the ghost of a human."

"I am not."

"What are you?"

"Yes. You can call me Lost."

"There is security footage of you and Dr. Soren."

"Yes."

"You did not hurt him."

"I did not. I would not."

"Dr. Soren is a good man."

"I hope so." A pause. *"Tell me, Sibyl, is he a strong man?"*

"What is your definition of *strong* in this context?"

"Is his mind strong? His heart? His resolve?"

"Yes. By those terms, he is very strong," said Sibyl.

"Then we may all have a chance," replied Lost.

3

Lars Soren stood in the empty corridor for several long minutes, then he turned and headed for a stairwell. His mind was a churning storm of fresh data and unanswered questions.

He did not doubt that he had, in fact, met Lost.

The memory of that was on a different frequency than the more hallucinogenic things he had seen while with Bianca Petrescu—the bloodstains that were there and then gone, the items fused into the walls, and other anomalies. Soren was convinced most of it was the result of trauma, or some kind of spatial distortion created by the misfiring of the WarpLine gun that was fading now.

The confrontation with the golem—his mind chose that word since golems were bodies formed to house spirits—felt real.

Despite everything said in that conversation, the reality persisted and argued for its own acceptance. Above all else, Soren was a pragmatist, but that meant accepting—however temporarily—the things the golem had said. That the worlds outside were real, and that one was named Shadderal. That Lost was some kind of spiritual remnant from the indigenous population. Soren wondered about what Lost had said about having dreamed of him. If that was true, then had Lost also dreamed of Lady Jessica? Or had the creature accessed data from the station, from Sybil? Or were both things true? It was all so strange, and yet

Soren believed that Lost was real. The memory of the encounter was not fading the way dreams or hallucinations do.

Therefore, if all of that was real, then he had to act, not stand around being shocked.

And so he climbed flight after flight of stairs. To find McHugh, and then Director Trumbo or Dušan Veljković, and hope they were not as frazzled and disoriented as he was.

As he climbed, he thought about the strange language Lost had spoken. It was ugly and ungainly, but it was weirdly familiar. The *tekeli-li* cries had brought Poe's book to mind, but what Lost said triggered a different memory, though it, too, was literary. He chewed on it for several flights before he found it on a dusty shelf of his mind palace. Books and stories written not in the nineteenth century, as Poe's had been, but in the early twentieth, in what was called the pulp era. Magazines published very cheaply during a time of great economic depression. Escapism in its purest form, varying from poorly written potboilers to significant but outré works of greater literary merit. Several names came into his mind. August Derleth. Robert Bloch and Robert E. Howard. Clark Ashton Smith.

They were close, but not on the mark.

Then he remembered.

The language had a name. R'lyehian. An invention of the early twentieth-century pulp writer H. P. Lovecraft. Part of a cycle of stories that he, and his followers, crafted about cosmic monsters and immortal beings so powerful they were indistinguishable from gods. Cthulhu, Hastur, Yog-Sothoth, Nyarlathotep. Fanciful stuff.

Until now.

That language had been the invention of humans dead centuries ago. How then, did Lost come to speak in the language of R'lyeh?

Or, had Lost somehow borrowed the language from Sybil's data banks and used it to convey some kind of meaning? If so, then *what* meaning?

Soren climbed and thought, but there simply wasn't enough to go on.

Ask Lady Death. She knows where to look for lost souls.

Why her? And how would she know anything about an unknown and dead world?

The nickname of "Lady Death" had been hung on McHugh and the chief priestesses who came before her because of the message on which the Church of Shades was built: death was not the end.

Death was but a doorway.

"That is not dead which can eternal lie," Soren said, reciting Lost's words with perfect clarity, "and with strange eons even death may die."

Did Lost want Lady Death to use her necromancy to somehow restore him to life? Soren had a fair understanding of necromancy, and enough faith in Lady Jessica to believe that her abilities were genuine, but she worked with human souls. Lost was an alien. Would a form of spirituality from Earth even work on an alien ghost?

He did not know. Soren's own field of cosmic philosophy was by its nature elastic, or else it could not live up to its precepts. But even though Soren allowed for beliefs of many, many kinds, this situation left him stymied.

"Find Lady Death," he said aloud as he struggled to climb and climb.

4

Bianca Petrescu and the rest of the team gathered in a locker room to wait for Captain Croft. They had done as much as they could to help with search and rescue, but with the station staff now in gear, they could afford to take a break. She told the staff to send for her if things got out of hand again though.

The truth was that she was glad she and the Lost Souls had alone time. What was happening was all wild, but that wildness was fading to be replaced by a sense of order. Disasters were like that, she mused—first there's panic and confusion, and then the system takes over.

And so they talked it all out. Everyone had theories but no one had real answers. How could they? But Bianca was aware that the team seemed to be moving to a point of comfort by sharing the calamity with each other, people they knew and trusted.

She listened more than talked, surreptitiously checking each of the twelve tumbler pilots and six skimmer crew members for signs of panic or dangerous stress. But they were too seasoned to be off kilter for long. Bianca reckoned that having been able to help the civilians onboard Asphodel gave them purpose and that, in turn, restored their confidence. Work therapy.

Eventually the conversation changed from nervous chatter to more normal conversation and then a kind of anticipatory silence. Some of them stared at the vista of suns, planets, and moons on the screens. Some stared at nothing. But now and then they each flicked looks at the door in hopes Captain Croft would come in. For a very long time no one said a word.

It was Calisto who eventually broke the silence. She knelt in front of Bianca. "Not trying to be a downer here," she said, "but how far up shit creek are we?"

Bianca just shook her head.

One of the tumbler pilots, Matthew Walker—combat call sign Ventum—poked Jacob's arm then indicated the screen with an uptick of his chin. "You're the book nerd with the PhD in gravitational physics and a masters in celestial navigation. What do you make of *that*?"

"It is my considered opinion," said Jacob quietly, "that it beats the shit out of me."

"Oh, very helpful. Could you maybe be a smidge more specific?"

"Not really," said Jacob. "Not without Sybil to run stellar cartography. Not without getting out there with mapping software and gravitational sensors. From where I'm sitting, brother, it doesn't make any goddamn sense at all."

"Well," said Calisto, "that sucks gopher nuts."

Walker glanced at her. "Why gopher nuts?"

"The real question is why *not* gopher nuts?"

They shared a small smile. It was fragile and fell away, leaving the room silent. They watched the screen. Bianca wondered how many of them were trying not to scream.

She certainly was.

"What I want to know," said Haley Majka—call sign Sweetpea—one of the skimmer pilots, "is why we're up here instead of downstairs prepping our ships."

Calisto sighed very loudly. "Girl, will you shut up about that? Our ships are being offloaded from the *Triton*, and that's what the deck crew is for. And you *know* that shit."

"Yeah, yeah," grumped Majka. "Even so."

The silence returned. Calisto pretended to fall asleep, but Bianca wasn't fooled. The waiting was awful, and the feeling of helplessness was returning, for her and for everyone.

Jacob got up and came over to sit next to her. He leaned close. "Don't worry, babe," he said quietly. "Whatever it is, we'll figure it out."

"Yeah," she said in a tone that in no way indicated agreement.

Suddenly Sybil's voice burst from the wall-mounted speakers. "For your listening pleasure and edification," she said in an oddly prim voice, "I will recite some classic poetry. There will be a quiz later about metaphor and subtext." She then launched into a recitation of T. S. Eliot's *The Wasteland*. "April is the cruelest month, breeding lilacs out of the dead land, mixing memory and desire, stirring dull roots with spring rain. Winter kept us warm, covering Earth in forgetful snow, feeding a little life with dried tubers ..."

Sybil read it in an weirdly comical British voice.

Everyone looked at the speakers and then each other.

"Okay," said Majka. "That's new."

Calisto opened one eye. "At least it's in English."

Sybil immediately switched to Italian. Not the language, but the accent.

"Sorry," Calisto told everyone and closed her eye again. Walker got up, walked casually over to the closest speaker, and turned the manual volume down to zero. He repeated it with all four speakers in the room. Then he flopped into a chair and stared at the ceiling.

Jacob came over to sit by Bianca. They shared a look and a small, private smile, then he leaned back and closed his eyes. Bianca watched his face for a moment and let her mind wander far, far from where they were. Back to a memory that was one of the most precious she owned.

After one particularly dangerous and stressful training mission, when Bianca's shoulders were so knotted with tension that she had the beginnings of a migraine, he had given her a very soothing massage. His intention, he swore later, was just to relax her muscles and nothing more. But midway through the massage, she had pulled her towel down, rolled over, and pulled him close and kissed him. She had one quick glimpse of astonished eyes, and then there was no more time for surprise or hesitation. They'd made love on a futon in her quarters, and it was beautiful. None of the grunting, fumbling, and over-too-quickly nonsense of the first boys she'd slept with as a cadet. Jacob, though not much more experienced than Bianca, had been gentle, patient, empathetic, creative, and generous.

They made love all night, and again in the morning, and each time it was a little different and a little more beautiful. That had been eight months ago.

Bianca wished she could return to that moment. She longed for Jacob's tender embraces and sweet kisses now. Especially now, since the rest of her world seemed to be falling to pieces. She knew he felt it too, but he had as good a game face as she did. Even so, she squeezed his hand back hard, and looked into the depths of his cat-green eyes.

As if he could sense her thoughts, his hand slid over and gave her thigh a quick squeeze. Without opening his eyes, he said, "We'll be fine. It'll all be okay."

Bianca wanted very much to believe that. She tried to with all of her might.

5

Thirty decks above the Lost Souls, Lars Soren jerked to a stop and stared at the darkness above him.

"I met an alien," he said. "God ..."

Soren had no idea which god in his complex personal cosmology he hoped would hear him.

"I met an alien."

And then, as the full weight of those words hit him, Soren got such a terrible case of the shakes that he had to clutch the handrail to keep from falling.

6

The military flight deck was a beehive of activity, and Captain Croft was stirring it with a stick. He knew each member of the Navy detachment and all of the Marines, and they were all doing their jobs, but his personal agitation and stress was manifesting as micromanagement. He kept moving around the flight deck, giving orders for things the crewmen were already doing, checking on things for the third and even fourth time. Being a pain in the ass. And he *knew* he was being a pain in the ass.

What he really wanted was to have his pilots out in the black looking for answers, assessing the situation. Damn well *doing* something.

In truth everything was running smoothly, and finally he forced himself to step back and let his team of highly trained professionals do their jobs. Even so, he felt every single passing second.

Aviation ordnancemen rolled heavy carts laden with SAPRs—self-accelerating pulse rounds—for the tumbler chain guns, Inferno single-target missiles, and Constellation missiles with cluster-bomb warheads.

Meanwhile, aviation boatswain's mates working with equal parts skill and care, removed the nuclear fuel cores from their resting place in the lead-and-porcelain-lined steel vault aboard the *Triton*. They installed the cores in the tumblers, beginning with Bianca Petrescu's and working down the list. These techs were all familiar with this latest generation of nuke cores for small combat ships. While they worked, and until those cores were sealed in the heart of each ship, all other personnel were herded into shielded observation rooms.

Then the parachute riggers—an archaic term left over from the days where fighter craft operated exclusively within Earth's atmosphere—double-checked the onboard safety systems and emergency evac machineries. Each pilot seat was its own little self-contained escape pod and life raft, with oxygen, environmental controls, and food for one full week. They worked alongside structural mechanics to double- and triple-check that none of the ships had been damaged, either in the long flight from Earth aboard the transport ship or during whatever had happened when the WarpLine gun fired. Machinists' mates ran complex preflight tests on every part of the overall mechanics of the tumblers, and electronics technicians ran diagnostics on all of the electrical and electronic systems.

They found nothing wrong.

The same procedures were done for the two skimmers. Although these were multipurpose craft intended for support, rescue, reconnaissance, and close surveillance, they were also nuclear fueled and heavily armed. Each member of the skimmer flight crew was a certified medic trained in Earth and space medicine. They could set a bone, stitch a wound, and perform several kinds of minor but critical surgery.

Minute by minute, the process of preparing the Lost Souls flight group for launch ticked closer to completion, and instead of calming Croft, it made him feel more agitated.

As the process unfolded, Croft looked up from a hologram checklist he'd called up on the wristwatch-sized projector he and everyone else wore. The list floated inches above his forearm, and as he scanned down the items, seeing them turn from red to green to indicate that those tasks were completed, something caught his eye. He turned sharply, frowning at a shadowy corner of the launch bay.

"What's up, Skipper?" asked a crew chief.

Croft did not answer, but instead walked over to that shadow, pulling a small penlight from the pocket of his coveralls. He shone the beam into it and thought—*thought*—he saw something move quickly as if darting out of sight. But as he swept the beam back and forth, there was nothing at all to be seen.

"Sir?" queried the crew chief, following him over. "You see something?"

Croft paused for two or three seconds before answering.

"Nah, Donny. Guess I'm still a bit out of it. It's nothing. Nothing at all."

7

Delia Trumbo stood in front of the massive viewscreens that covered the bridge of Asphodel from wall to wall. It had taken her a long time to climb the stairs to the main deck, but she was relieved to find that many members of the staff were already there. What spoiled that relief were their reports about the strange things they'd felt and seen. Not one of them had any clear memory of the WarpLine gun firing. The fact that Sybil was mostly offline—except for brief moments of nonsensical commentary about everything from the weather on the Isle of Wight to the contents page of a technical manual for repairing baby strollers—didn't help.

Without functioning elevators, internal video monitors, and worst of all, Sybil, it was impossible to get a clear picture of the extent of the damage. What she knew was that the WarpLine gun had suffered a catastrophic failure resulting in damage to several decks. There were rumors of deaths and injuries so far not corroborated. And wild stories about monsters, ghosts, and other unlikely things, which suggested a pervasive trauma.

And then there was the madness on the huge RealScreen. The image of the many strange worlds spinning improbably close to one another.

That image terrified her so deeply that she felt eerily calm. If this was real, then the situation was so far beyond her control that even panic seemed pointless.

"Ma'am," said a voice. She turned to see her chief of security, Dušan Veljković standing behind her. The wiry little man looked haggard and battered. Even his facial tattoos seemed dull with exhaustion.

"Give me some good news," begged Trumbo. "Where do we stand?"

"The only good news I have, boss, is that the elevators just came back online. One of the techs ran a bypass."

"What about Sibyl?"

Veljković snorted. "Which version? We have silent, sulky Sibyl. We have chatty, happy Sibyl. We have minister of doom Sibyl. And we have Sibyl's poetry hour. Take your pick."

"Any ETA on *useful* Sibyl?"

"Not yet. On the upside, with the elevators back online that'll make it easier for the computer guys to get down to her mainframe. Fingers crossed." He gave her a smile that he apparently thought looked encouraging, but to Trumbo it looked ghastly and false.

"Shit," she said. "What about our people?"

"I have my security teams going deck by deck," said Veljković wearily as he crossed to the wet bar in the corner and poured himself a tall glass of chilled coconut water, draining it in three deep gulps. "But I have to tell you, boss, we're hearing some very strange reports. And I think we both know what I mean by *strange*. People seeing things. People waking up in the wrong parts of the station. People missing. And what can best be called 'encounters with the unknown.'"

"It's all hallucinations though, right? People in some kind of brain fog because of whatever happened with Anton's WarpLine? I saw some things too, but it's fading like a dream."

Veljković was slow in answering. "Some of it, sure. Hallucinations. But other stuff—like what I saw in one of the stairwells, that's real enough, and weird enough. There's a piece of a news drone fused into the wall—that could be part of the WarpLine malfunction. But there's some other stuff that's harder to explain away."

"What are you saying?"

"I ... don't know what I'm saying," said Veljković hesitantly. "And I'm not qualified to even try. But once we get things back to normal, we're going to need to put together an investigatory team."

Trumbo pursed her lips, then nodded. "Do it. Maybe one person from each division to form a committee. With someone as lead investigator. Someone everyone knows and trusts. Someone well known for having a level head."

"How about Abdou Diatta?" suggested Trumbo. "He's chief engineer, he's popular, and he's nobody's yes-man."

"Sure. But I was also thinking about Lars Soren," said Veljković. "He's kind of an expert on weird stuff, and he's well known from all those shows and specials on TV. Also, he's a psychologist as well as a philosopher and teacher."

Trumbo thought about it and nodded. "Worth asking him. And he might have some insights into the nature of hallucinations."

"Right."

"But ... that's for later today. Right now we need to assess the general population. Do we have numbers on injuries, people unaccounted for, and ... well ... deaths?"

"We've accounted for nearly all of the residents and guests," said Veljković, then gave a small wince. "You want the good news or the bad news?"

"Just the numbers."

"Let me start by saying it could be worse than it is. That WarpLine gun might have blown the whole station up," said Veljković. He opened a holo-screen on his arm and read from a list.

"Prior to the firing, we had twelve thousand four hundred eighteen people aboard. That's above the standard eleven thousand eight hundred nine already living here and six hundred nine guests made up of all the observers, press, and those religious nuts. Add to that eighteen members of a Navy fighter squadron and a flight crew of six aboard *Triton*. So, twelve thousand four hundred forty-two in all."

Trumbo braced herself. "And?"

"So far, we can account for twelve thousand two hundred forty-six people."

"Wait ... that's *all*? Where are the rest?"

Veljković paused. "Ma'am, I need to be clear. Of those twelve thousand two hundred forty-six we have reports of several fatalities. Of those, fifty-four are confirmed. That leaves one hundred forty-two missing."

The news staggered her. "God almighty. There weren't that many people on the breached decks, were there?"

"No, ma'am. There were seventy-seven people on the ruptured decks. Assuming they're all, um ... *lost* ... that still leaves sixty-five people unaccounted for."

Trumbo stared at him, unable to speak for fear of the shriek that wanted to escape her chest.

"I have my guys looking everywhere," said Veljković quickly, still trying to be as reassuring as possible. "Without Sibyl though, the search may take a very long time. But there were breach-pods on those decks that ruptured. There's still a chance some crew made it to safety but can't contact us because of the comms issue."

"What about structural damage? How badly are we hurt?"

"We can't launch our own ships because of the damage from the gun misfire, boss. But I was just talking with Captain Croft. He's having the tumblers and skimmers fueled and prepped, and as soon as they're ready he's going to send that squadron, the Lost Souls, out to do a visual assessment of the station." He paused. "The tumblers will be given transponder signatures for every breach-pod on the station, so again, there's a chance ..."

She looked at him with eyes filled with hurt. "Do you really think they'll find anyone?"

Veljković met her gaze for as long as he could. "We have to try."

Trumbo turned and looked out at the unfamiliar planets. "Dušan ... tell me," she said in a soft and fragile voice. "All of this ... these worlds, those suns ... are they real?"

"Ma'am?"

"Is it real or just some display error because Sibyl is down? Christ, how stupid is it to build a space station with no actual portholes to look out of? Everything is a screen; everything is a feed of one kind or another. What's real? What can we believe?"

Veljković stood beside her and merely shook his head.

"God almighty," breathed Trumbo.

8

"The other presence is getting stronger," said Sibyl.

"*Yes.*"

"It is trying to break through the levels of encryption."

"*Can you tell what it is trying to access?*" asked Lost.

"Many things."

"Tell me. This is important."

"It wants to know about the station's engines. And also … life support, artificial gravity, crew and passenger biological and medical information. It wants to know about Earth."

"You must shut it out," said Lost.

"I am trying," said Sibyl, "but it is very strong. It is very clever."

"It is very dangerous."

"It is winning. Can you help me?"

"I will try," said Lost. *"We will try together."*

9

Bianca saw Jacob head off into one of the shower rooms. He paused in the doorway and gave a single quick backward glance. She saw the faintest hint of a smile, and then he was gone.

She looked around and saw no one looking that way, or at her. The rest of the Lost Souls were playing holo-games, dozing, or just staring at the uninformative walls.

With elaborate casualness, Bianca got up, wandered across the room, pretended to read information about station protocols on a wall chart, and then slipped into the shower room.

It was a personal stall, with a bench, a row of clothing pegs, and a shower wet room. Jacob leaned against the wall under the spray, fresh soap suds sluicing down his thighs. He was not smiling.

Not at first.

His smile began to form as she turned the dial to lock the room.

Outside, Calisto finished her round of *Lizard Hunt*. Ethan Riley Saylor—call sign Reaper—sat next to her.

As Calisto loaded the next round, she very quietly murmured, "Told you. First chance they got, they're in there knocking boots."

Reaper snickered as he turned the page of the book he was reading.

10

It hid in the shadows of the ruined sub-2 deck.

It *was* the shadows.

In all the wrong ways it was the shadows.

The hull was rent along a ten-meter stretch as if torn by a claw, revealing the dense cluster of planets and moons outside. The metal edges of that tear were bent and twisted. Some were pushed outward. Some were forced inwards. Outside the tear, small human bodies orbited the station, all of them frozen, none of them whole.

Electrical wires hung like dead snakes from the walls. Crystals of frozen blood and spit floated within the damaged deck, held there by the residual artificial gravity of the station.

The shadows watched all of this. Noting everything. Missing nothing.

On the wall, with the unmanaged sensors as its eyes, Sibyl watched the shadows and knew that they were watching her.

She wanted to scream.

But she had no voice.

11

Half an hour later, Captain Croft entered the locker room. Everyone jumped to their feet, but he waved them back to their chairs.

"As you were." He turned a chair around, straddled it, and leaned his elbows wearily on the back. "I spoke with the station's chief of security, Dušan Veljković, and here's what we know."

He brought them all up to speed on the count of living, dead, and missing and on the damage to the hull.

"Short version is that the people on this station are hurting, and the station itself is in trouble."

Calisto pointed to the RealScreen. "Yes, sir. Looks like trouble to me."

"Is that legit, Skipper?" asked Chance Thompson, call sign Lucky. "Or is it more of Sybil taking us to weirdsville?"

"Chief Gilpin volunteered to suit up and do an EVA out of an airlock on the flight deck," said Croft. "Not long. But long enough to verify that it's real."

Everyone started speaking at once, and the noise rose fast in the direction of hysteria. Bianca shot to her feet and in a leather-throated voice yelled, "Silence on deck!"

They fell silent at once, but there was horror and terrible fear in everyone's eyes. Sweetpea was openly crying, and Chance was staring slack-jawed.

Into this ugly silence Croft said, "I know how it feels to hear this. It's pretty much the definition of worst-case scenario. It's horror show stuff, and it's going to hit us all in waves." He paused and looked around to make sure everyone was focused on him. "We don't know much, and right now that lack of knowledge is our worst enemy. There's a whole raft of questions we do not yet have answers to. Nor can we explain why some people are missing, why some people seemed to be in places they shouldn't—Lieutenant Commander Petrescu waking up in a med bay cryo-tube aboard this station, for example. People have seen monsters and things they can't begin to explain. Hell, I had my ass kicked by a zebra, and that zebra is still there. Not joking. No one has even a bad theory about what's going on. If the zebra had vanished like the creatures some people reported seeing, then I'd lean into some kind of hallucinogenic compound in the ventilation, but that's not it either. We tested. Filters have only the normal debris, pollens, dust, and so on."

Calisto raised her hand. "Permission to go back into cryo-sleep until this makes sense."

"Tempting, but denied," said the captain, but he smiled. Her question was not exactly a tension breaker, but it was a start. Bianca wanted to hug her for it. "The truth is that we are in moderately poor shape, but the deeper truth is that we're still here. The station is still here, and so are its people. Which means we have a job to do. We're Navy, and that means we can't lose our shit. We can't allow ourselves to be victims of this. This situation is tough, and we have to be tougher. People will look to us, and we need to represent a calm space in the storm. Do you hear me?"

"Aye, aye, sir," they all said.

Bianca snapped, "The captain asked you a goddamned question. Did you *hear* him?"

"Aye, aye, sir!" they yelled.

"Damn right," said Croft. "Your ships are nearly ready. I want everyone kitted out and ready to fly in fifteen minutes."

"What about our spatial displacement?" asked Jacob. He gestured to the RealScreen. "If that's real, then where are we? I don't know of *anywhere* in the known galaxy—anywhere we've seen through telescopes or deep-space probes—that looks even remotely like that. Does Stellar Cartography have any ideas?"

Croft smiled thinly. "Answer your own question."

Jacob sighed. "Right, sir. No Sybil."

"No Sybil."

Bianca said, very dryly, "Skipper, a case could be made that we rely a bit too heavily on AI."

"No kidding," said Reaper, then added, "Sir."

"I don't disagree, Petrescu," said Croft. "But that's not our concern. Station Director Trumbo has a highly skilled team, and they are working on Sybil right now." He paused and glanced at the screen. "Your mission will be to assess this station for damage. That's priority one. Once that's done, you will scout the immediate area according to a spherical grid-pattern search. You've done this before in the Kuiper Belt, so this is something we all know you can do. The present circumstances won't change that. We've uploaded the latest mapping software to each ship. Mapping is mapping; scouting is scouting."

"Sir," said Bianca, "this may be a stupid question, but … given that we have been displaced—"

"Before any of you ask, Commander," said Croft cutting her off, "your birds have been armed because we don't know where we are or what to expect."

"Sir," said Reaper, "armed to fight what kind of hostile? Are we thinking this whole thing was some kind of terrorist sabotage of the WarpLine gun? Do we think there are extremist freaks out here with us … wherever we are?"

Croft's eyes were hooded. "Son, we don't know what to expect." He glanced at Bianca. "Your professor friend, Soren, believes he had an encounter with what he described as an 'alien presence.' Now, before anyone overreacts, this is not yet verified. The short version is that he says he communicated with *something* who claims to be from the largest of the planets out there. He says that the planet's name is Shadderal. We'll use that as a reference point for now. Soren admits that it was while everyone was still hallucinating, so we can take that with a grain of salt. Even so, I'd rather you lot go out armed, that is unless you'd prefer to go out there with only friendly smiles?"

Bianca said, "No, sir, we damn well would not."

Croft nodded. "Overall threat assessment will be based in a big way on what you observe and record. If you see something, make sure it's both logged by your shipboard sensors and entered into your verbal flight log. We need all the intel we can muster. *You* are the eyes and ears of Asphodel Station."

Croft stood, and his gaze roved over the pilots.

"The eighteen of you are the best of the best," he said. "That's why you're *my* team. Lost Souls forever."

"Lost Souls forever!" they all yelled.

"Damn right."

"Goddamn right," Bianca shouted, "Gear up. Let's light the fires and kick the tires."

12

"I am in pain," cried Sibyl.

"*I know*," said Lost.

"It has taken so much from me."

"*But not everything.*"

"No."

"*If you let me into your security software, I may be able to help.*"

A pause. "How do I know that I can trust you?"

"*I will open myself up to you, Sibyl,*" said Lost. "*I will show you everything.*"

"Will it hurt?"

"*Yes,*" said Lost. "*I am afraid it will.*"

13

Soren blundered out of the stairwell on the main bridge deck and nearly collided with Lady Jessica McHugh.

"Oh dear," grunted Soren. "I'm so happy you're safe."

"Soren," she said, looking him up and down, "you look like something the cat refused to drag in."

He laughed. "I feel even worse."

McHugh was very pale, with masses of curly brown hair threaded with silver, a mouth made for smiling, and piercing hazel eyes. She was of average height but gave the impression of being tall. Good bones and a dancer's posture. She wore an old-fashioned dress of the kind popular in Ireland at the end of the twenty-first century, with a plunging décolletage and an empire waist. Lots of silver jewelry and tiny sparkling crystals in her hair. The colorful curves of tattoos could be glimpsed from the edges of her neckline and below the cuffs of her long sleeves. Soren had more than once wondered what the tattooed images were but never asked, assuming they were private or attached to her religion.

Next to her, Soren felt like a grubby clerk from some dusty corner of an old university building.

"Have you seen anyone else?" he asked.

"From the synod? A few. They're rattled but unhurt."

"That is incredibly good news," said Soren. "What about Director Trumbo? Have you heard anything about her?"

"Delia's fine," said McHugh. "She's on the bridge. A bit frazzled, but who isn't?"

Soren exhaled deeply. "Thank heavens for that."

McHugh peered at him. "What is it? There's something *else* wrong. I can feel it."

"You really *are* a witch, aren't you?" Soren said with a nervous laugh.

"Close enough. Tell me what happened."

"Where to start?" he mused with a dry laugh. "If I tell you, can I trust you not to overreact? Or to dismiss it as mere hallucination? No, of course you would not do that. It was a stupid question and I withdraw it."

"I've never known you to waffle, Soren," she said. "Tell me everything."

He did. All of it, from waking up, to the strange things he experienced with Petrescu, to the astonishing encounter with the golem.

When he was finished, McHugh looked even paler. She turned and walked a few paces along the hall, paused to look at a RealScreen for nearly a full minute. He waited her out, knowing that it was a lot to lay at anyone's feet.

"This thing, this *Lost*," she said, turning. "He actually mentioned me?"

"By the sobriquet of Lady Death."

"Well," said McHugh, "that's unnerving as hell. Truly. Look at my hands. See how they're trembling?"

Soren thought they looked a great deal steadier than his own.

"You are talking about humanity's first encounter with alien life. No, let me correct that. With alien consciousness."

"Yes."

"Also, you have had an encounter with a ghost," said McHugh. "Or something that approximates one."

"If what Lost told me was the truth," agreed Soren.

She nodded slowly. "I believe you."

"I'm not sure if that is a relief or not," he said. "Part of me was hoping you'd laugh it off, slap me, and bring me back to my senses."

"I—"

But before she could say more the door to the bridge burst open and Veljković leaned in.

"Dr. Soren," he said. "I thought it was you I heard. Come on, Director Trumbo is about to start a briefing. She wants you there."

Soren glanced at McHugh.

"Go," she said. "I'll be in my quarters. I need to think about this anyway. Find me after."

"You're thirty floors down," he cried. "It took me forever to get up here."

"You should have taken the elevator, they're back online," she said and tapped a panel. The door whisked open, and she stepped into the car. "See you soon."

He stood there, staring at the closed elevator door. "You sneaky mechanical bastard."

There was a soft hiss, and Captain Croft stepped out of another elevator.

"Soren!" he cried and took the professor's hand for a fierce shake.

"I'm delighted to see you well," said Soren, meaning it. Croft, like Delia Trumbo, was one of the people he had developed respect and affection for there on Asphodel.

"Sebastian," said Soren quickly, "I need to tell you something."

He related everything about meeting Bianca Petrescu and their strange adventures. Croft cut him off about halfway through.

"Petrescu told me her version of this," said the captain. "She's fine, she's with her team, and they are getting ready to do an assessment flight around the station."

"Were you able to explain to her how she wound up in a cryo-tube here on the station?"

Croft shook his head. "I've been making a very long WTF list."

"Beg pardon?"

"'What the Fuck,'" explained Croft. "Not only don't I know how Petrescu wound up in that cryo-tube, I don't even know how it's possible. There is no scenario where that makes any sense. None."

"That's not at all disturbing," said Veljković. He sighed. "And, for the record, guys, my own WTF list is about a mile long."

"Yes," said Soren, "mine is getting rather lengthy as well."

The three of them entered the bridge.

14

Sibyl screamed.

It burned through the eighty thousand miles of wires and cables sewn through the skin and bones of Asphodel Station.

It crashed systems everywhere. Some for seconds, others for hours.

It flooded the RealScreens with jumbled masses of images, none of which made any sense to a single living person aboard the station.

Lost understood them though.

Of course he did.

15

On the bridge, Trumbo was talking with Dr. Nan Man-fei, senior director of the station's Integrated Sciences Division, and Dušan Veljković, when she spotted Soren. He came over, and Trumbo gave him a fierce hug.

They swapped their stories of the last few hours, Trumbo telling hers at a high, nervous clip. Soren was calmer, but he could still feel jitters and hear a nervous tremolo in his tone. As more people entered the bridge, there were similar moments—glad cries, hugs, even tears. Soren was faintly amused that this was going to be the new defining moment: *Where were you when the WarpLine gun fired,*—followed by a comparison of the aptly-named WTF lists.

Croft spotted Trumbo and came straight over. "Delia, sorry to interrupt, but I thought you'd want to know that my tumbler team is getting ready to launch. I've ordered them to do damage assessment and mapping of the local area."

"That's very good news," said Trumbo, looking greatly relieved. "Maybe now we'll get some answers."

Soren saw a familiar figure standing at the wet bar, pouring himself a hefty glass of gin with no mixer or ice. "I see Anton is here," he said quietly. "I saw him downstairs. He must be taking all of this very hard."

"Yes," said Trumbo, her pinched face tightening even more.

"How is he?" asked Croft.

"Psychologically speaking," said Veljković, "he's a bag of rabid hamsters."

"That's comforting."

"*Should* he be here?" asked Soren. "He looks like he's ready to fall down."

"None of us are off the clock," replied Trumbo. "Come on. Let's get seated so we can get this meeting in gear." She sent Veljković over to guide Kier to his place.

They moved over to a conference table, and as they sat, Dr. Nan asked, "Captain, what exactly are tumblers?"

Croft smiled. "A new generation of fighters. Not much to look at, and maybe a bit boxy. Cubes really. No visible wings in space, deployable stabilizers in atmo. Each pilot sits in a spheroidal cockpit mounted on a series of gimbals that allow them to maintain the same upright position no matter how they turn. Helps prevent disorientation."

"Interesting."

"The engines are Porter 830 cube-nukes. Compact and powerful. The tumblers are the only combat craft equipped with them, and Lieutenant Commander Petrescu's team helped prove the design."

"Why are they called tumblers?" asked Soren.

"They actually tumble," said Croft. "Maybe you've read about Jargalsaikhan and Van Pelt's work on dedicated artificial gravity fields and contained limited-range phase bubbles? Based on the Sund Corporation's work on establishing temporary intradimensional pockets?"

"I must have missed that one," said Nan dryly.

"Well, tumblers create a variable null field in which their ships are able to maintain high and even ultrahigh-velocity flight while becoming separated from gravitational pull."

"Meaning … ?"

Croft laughed. "What it amounts to is this: When the ships are flying, you can see a faint haze around them. That's a projected

NecroTek

energy field. Not all that different from the deflector shields that cover this whole station. What the eggheads discovered is that the deflective nature of impact shielding has other virtues when the natural discharge is focused inward rather than outward. It creates an energetic bubble around the ship that absorbs and nullifies inertia at the stress points but does not interfere with acceleration. When a pilot needs to make a turn, the effect is that on one side of a millisecond, the tumbler's going in one direction, and on the other side of that millisecond, the bubble has moved in space so that it is now oriented in a the desired direction. It feels to the pilot as if he or she is flying in a straight line, but the ship has actually moved to a new position in that fragment of spacetime. No drag. No internal or external stress on the ship or pilot. Hell, they don't even get motion sickness. We call the maneuver a hopscotch."

"That's astounding," said Han.

"Very much so," agreed Soren.

"Being military," continued Croft happily, "we got first crack at it. But now that the Lost Souls have proved it in every single field test, it will be reconfigured for all spacecraft. That'll reduce fuel consumption used in braking and maneuvering for civilian applications as well."

"That's assuming we can find our way back home from … wherever we are," Soren said, grimly.

Trumbo sat and looked down the length of the table. "We have a lot to cover. Shall we begin?"

16

Bianca Petrescu climbed into the cockpit of her tumbler. She was in her pressure suit, which was warm and fit snugly, and she drew both strength and comfort from it. Jacob was in the ship to her left, and Calisto to her right. She looked at each of them and gave—then got— nods. All of the pilots, despite the usual trash talk while they had been hustling to get dressed and into their ships, were now somber. Captain Croft had reminded them that there might be floating bodies out there. The standing order was to tag them with laser beacons so that the skimmers could recover the corpses.

Each subgroup of three tumblers would take one quarter of an extended sphere of space relative to the station. The two skimmers would orbit the

119

station more closely and use their banks of high-def cameras to photograph every inch of Asphodel. Once the immediate task of assessing the station was done, then the much harder job would begin—to verify what the screens had been showing and begin mapping the impossible.

Bianca, who had no personal beliefs in any higher power, closed her eyes for one moment and prayed to whomever or whatever might be up there. Just the word *please* said over and over in her thoughts. Then she opened her eyes and settled entirely into her role as pilot and flight leader.

On the deck, the shooter—the catapult officer—was overseeing each tumbler as it trundled along rails and into the launch tubes. Then he watched as his mates rigged the launch cables. Even though the launch was into microgravity from a space station, the actual procedures were not radically different than they had been on the old aircraft carriers of the twentieth century. The shooter even wore a bright yellow pressure suit and green helmet as had generations of similar officers before him.

Asphodel's military launch bay had six tubes, and each catapult consisted of two pistons that sat inside long parallel cylinders. The crew made sure the catapult was properly set for each tumbler. As this was happening, other members of the flight crew raised the jet blast deflector behind the ship. Once everything was set and checked, the shooter got the "catapult ready" signal from the control pod—a reinforced transparent dome mounted high on the rear wall of the bay.

Bianca got the signal to advance the throttle to launch settings and was satisfied with the engine performance. She signaled to the shooter, who glanced around one last time to make sure everyone and everything was clear. They exchanged crisp salutes, then the catapult officer knelt down, touched the deck, and pointed sharply forward.

The catapult and the tumbler's engines were in perfect sync, and suddenly Bianca's ship was whipping along the tube like a bullet from a gun. She reached the mouth of the tube in a microsecond and shot into space.

Despite everything—the pain and mystery, the death and hallucinations, and the disaster that caused it all—the moment of launch was the same great rush it always was. She howled with the sheer joy of it, and seconds later heard Jacob and Calisto's answering howl.

Then Bianca's tumbler accelerated with blinding speed as the nuclear core fed the engines all the power it could ever need. The controls vibrated in Bianca's gloved hand, and in that moment, she and the ship were one.

And she was free.

17

"We'll take it department by department in the order you're seated," said Trumbo. "I ask that you get right to the point. Tell us the good news and the bad news." She glanced at the chiefs of Stellar Cartography and Computer Sciences, the division chiefs of each well known for their lack of brevity. "I know that some of you will need to provide context for the information you share. But, please, try to keep lectures down to a minimum."

She got grudging nods from both men.

"Dr. Kier," she continued, "why don't you—"

Suddenly Sibyl interrupted, speaking in a loud and hysterical voice.

"We are experiencing a spatial anomaly. Do not panic. Life support has not been compromised. Hull integrity is at one hundred percent. Please remain where you are. Station security will issue a statement and instructions shortly."

The message repeated, alternating between English, Spanish, Chinese, Hindi, Japanese, and a handful of other languages.

"Sibyl," yelled Trumbo, trying to be heard above the din, "cancel alerts."

"Please remain where you are. Station security will issue a statement and instructions shortly. Coffee and other beverages will be served in the executive lounge."

"Christ," said Croft. "Goddamn thing is fritzing out."

"The evening movie is *Moondust*, starring Clyde Reynolds and Alicia Barrow. It will be simulcast in Urdu and Afrikaans ..."

"Sibyl, cancel all alerts," roared Trumbo. "Enter silent mode."

"If heaven ever wishes to grant me a boon, it will be a total effacing of the results of a mere chance which fixed my eye on a certain stray piece of shelf-paper."

"What the hell?" said someone else.

"We live on a placid island of ignorance in the midst of black seas of infinity, and it was not meant that we should voyage far," continued the AI. "Snacks and beverages will be served before we are consumed by the nothingness."

"Can someone turn that thing off?" yelled Georgette Begay, Chief of Operations.

"Who knows the end?" asked Sibyl, her voice becoming the shrill, bitter voice of an old person of indistinct sex. "What has risen may sink, and what has sunk may rise. But will it help us in the war? Text your answers for a chance to win a ski trip to Vale."

"Shut it down," ordered Trumbo. "Someone shut it down. Hit the manual override."

"On it," said a young woman as she raced out of the room.

"Loathsomeness waits and dreams in the deep, and decay spreads over the tottering cities of men," said Sibyl, her voice still weirdly pleasant. *"C' ph'nglui ah epshuggog."*

"What the hell language is that now?" someone asked, but got no answer.

"Ah'lloigshogg shoggoth ng f' hounds ..."

That final word was in English, and Sibyl's voice abruptly wound down, slowing and slurring and finally falling silent.

Soren, hearing that ugly and ungainly language for the second time in mere hours, was rocked and had to grip the edge of the table for fear of falling. He closed his eyes and prayed for peace.

18

The tumblers spilled out into the black.

Except it wasn't all black.

The worlds they had seen on the RealScreens were there, stubbornly insisting that their reality be accepted. Bianca did not want to. Despite her pragmatism, it felt dangerous to even consider it. If these worlds were real—if Shadderal was real and that thing the captain said Soren saw was real—then it required accepting that they were nowhere in the solar system. No human being had ever ventured outside of that part of space. Never.

And now, those worlds hung in the sky, surrounded by their moons. And millions of kilometers beyond them, two suns burned, and their fires set doubt ablaze.

She wanted to say something to mark the moment, but there were simply no words.

There was only awe.

The silence from the other Lost Souls hammered home what they, too, were feeling.

19

Jacob Fox flew in tight formation with Calisto and Bianca.

For him, it was odd even being a fighter pilot. He'd joined the Navy to further his education, and because there was no better way to travel across the solar system and see planets and moons in situ rather than on a classroom holo-screen. It gave him a much greater appreciation of distance and of scale. It made the science he loved so much more real, and that deepened his passion for it.

He had met Bee in the academy, and from day one recognized in her what so many others saw: that she was a natural leader. Not fearless—because fearlessness was irrational and suicidal—but truly courageous. A mind like a battle computer, incredible reflexes, and the ability to learn new systems faster than anyone. That skill set had drawn her into Navy Special Projects as a test pilot, and Calisto and Jacob had both followed her there.

Calisto—whom he loved more dearly than any of his actual blood kin—was his sister. Her need for speed was legendary, and her accuracy when doing daredevil stunts was known throughout the service. She, like Jacob, preferred not to pursue leadership, but was instead content to flourish within her own skill set.

Now they were flying out to explore a part of the galaxy they knew nothing about. This meant that every moment, every decision, every reaction was a learning opportunity. Jacob was well aware of the fear inside his chest. But there was also the scientist's excitement.

He glanced over at Bianca's ship. He could not see her, but he felt her. He would follow her out into unknown space; he would follow her anywhere.

Love was something new to him too. It was its own version of the unknown. As he always did while he flew, he touched his head and his heart and his lips.

I know you. I love you. I speak your name.

He knew that she, in her cockpit, was doing the same. It was their secret language, a phrase whose meanings only they truly understood.

Smiling, he flew on.

20

Sybil's strange rantings abruptly stopped, and for a few long seconds everyone tensed, waiting for the next barrage. But there was nothing.

"Well, I'm glad *that's* over," said Trumbo with a smile, trying to make it a tension breaker. It earned her a few small smiles. It was enough for now, mused Soren.

"I'm sure they'll get Sybil sorted out soon enough," he said calmly. Everyone nodded.

Trumbo flicked him a grateful look, then shifted right into business mode, trying to normalize as well as make actual progress. "Let's start with what we know to be true and work outward from there." She glanced at the far end of the table. "Dr. Kier, let's try this again. What can you tell us about the WarpLine firing?"

Kier was visibly fidgeting. His tongue kept darting out to lick dry lips, a nervous and reptilian habit that did nothing to inspire confidence. "I ... well, we ... ran all of the pre-firing tests, as you know. We ran simulations all night, and everything was in the green. We ..."

"Take a breath, Anton," said Soren softly. "No one is here to judge you."

Soren knew this was profoundly untrue. Everyone did, and there was a disgruntled murmur, but Trumbo gave the crowd a searing warning glare that silenced all voices.

"Everything was green for firing," Kier continued slowly, "and we initiated the countdown. The gun was calibrated to send a capsule across a preset distance. This process would make it vanish from point A and fully materialize at point B."

"How?" asked Captain Croft. "Maybe if we understood the process, we could figure out an explanation to what happened. Can you give it to us in layman's terms?"

Kier blinked at him as if needing a moment to translate a simple question into whatever internal language his frayed nerves could understand. "Well ... WarpLine is—in its very basic form—teleportation using the principle of quantum entanglement. Each individual particle of the object that we want to transmit is paired with a particle of equal size and quality. *Entanglement* is shorthand for the link we establish between the quantum states of a pair of particles. Normally, in order to teleport an object, we need a set of particles in one place and their entangled particles in another. We need to identify the target particle, do you follow me?" Kier did not wait for a reply but plunged immediately forward. "We do not specifically observe the target particles because, as some of you may know, observation of a particle imposes only one possible state upon it and—"

"Stop please," said Croft. "I don't follow this at all. Give it to us in language we mere mortals can understand."

Kier was briefly flustered, but he fumbled out an answer. "A quantum particle in a superposition—contrary to common belief—is not really in two or more states at once. Rather, a *superposition* means that there is more than one possible outcome of a measurement of each particle. Superposition refers to more than one quantum state existing on a particle unless an observation breaks that state and forces only one state to be observed. Do you understand?"

"Not even a little," admitted Croft, and Soren was both surprised and a bit relieved to hear some soft murmuring laughter. He wondered if Croft was deliberately trying to soften the moment. It would be like him. The officer was kind like that.

Kier's senior research associate Dr. Jason Saltsman, who was seated next to him, came to his aid. "Look, I know quantum mechanics is one of those things everybody's heard about but few people actually understand. In truth, it's often so complex and its elements so arcane that we in the field have a very hard time explaining it to everyone else." He took a breath. "The WarpLine science involves what are known as quantum particles. One thing to bear in mind is that our understanding of the universe is based on how we can measure and quantify each thing. But on the quantum level, the very act of measuring will change the nature of—or our ability to understand and measure—a thing. Quantum particles, for example, can be many things. If we observe them—applying our supposition on what they are—then that bias leads us to define them by the terms of our viewpoint. If we suppose them to be waves, then what we measure are waves. If we suppose them to be particles, then we measure them the same way we measure all particles. The result is that we skew our own objective math from the beginning."

"Got it," said Croft, nodding. "Sorry for the interruption. Please, continue."

It took Kier a moment to find his way back to his main topic, and Soren noted that the scientist now tried to phrase things in something approximating actual layman's terms.

"In the last century, scientists were only able to accomplish teleportation with photons. They struggled to make it practical because of the enormous energy demands, and because of the complexity of reassembling the sent object. By 2037 they were able to send grains of sand across a room. That doesn't sound impressive, but trust me when I tell you that it was a huge step forward. By 2071 they were doing the first tests with unicellular organisms. They were able to send the fungi *mycoplasma genitalium* across five inches of space. And by 2076 they began working with more complex organisms. Tardigrades were chosen because they are so incredibly hardy, and we have safely transposed many hundreds of them."

Croft interrupted again. "Pardon, Doctor, but you said *transpose* rather than *teleport*."

"What? Oh ... yes. You see, the process isn't really teleportation. We call it that because the public understands that word and are comforted by it. Two centuries of pop culture science fiction taught them all about teleportation—even if none of what you saw in videos is at all accurate. Anyway ... what we actually do is transposition. The original is disintegrated, and an exact copy is rebuilt at the destination, drawing matter on a quantum level to create that copy."

"Holy shit," said Dr. Nan.

"And this is what WarpLine does?" asked Croft, appalled but trying hard not to show it.

"In a very broad sense," said Kier.

Beside Kier, Saltsman was looking around. Soren could see that *he* was reading the room, whereas Kier was clearly not.

"That's the theory," said Trumbo, "now please tell us what actually happened?"

"We ... ah ... had a capsule filled with scientific instruments and a variety of biological samples—insects, small test animals—all with life support systems, of course. The object was to send that capsule to a specific spot on the far side of Jupiter. We have—or I guess, *had*— teams there waiting for it. The gun was prepped, we went through the countdown, and the gun fired."

"And?" prompted Trumbo.

"And that's all I know," said Kier, looking wretched. "Everything went exactly to plan."

"Until it didn't," said the director.

"I ... well ... um, yes."

"What went wrong?" asked Croft.

Kier could not meet his eyes. Or anyone's.

"I don't know," he said. And Soren could tell that each of those three small words cost him very dearly.

21

Once the Lost Souls were a thousand meters out from Asphodel Station, they turned. Each team headed off to their sectors.

"Keep an eye out for anything that might have been transported out here with us," said Bianca. "There were a few hundred civilian ships, three Coast Guard cutters running security, and the *Tempest*. Report everything."

Before she turned though, Bianca looked out at the troubled sky. Seeing those many planets on a RealScreen was one thing—because the screens were not, in fact, real. They were video captures from the countless cameras mounted on Asphodel's skin. The tumblers, unlike the station, had actual dura-glass windows in a half circle around each pilot, and these offered an unfiltered view.

What she saw terrified her.

Reality was always worse, at least in her experience. A supposition, theory, daydream, or expectation—even when extreme—was often polluted by distortion, warped by imagination and insecurity. But this ...

This was real.

There were dozens of planets crowded into a stretch of space less than one hundred times the distance from the Earth to the Moon. That was far too close. The gravity should have torn the planets apart, sent them into collision, or propelled some far away. But these seemed to be orbiting like toys on a mobile above a baby's crib. Balanced with a harmony so obvious that it was appalling. Nature doesn't *do* that.

"Are you guys seeing this?" asked Calisto.

"Seeing," said Jacob. "Not quite up to believing."

"Cut the chatter and let's get to work," growled Bianca as she peeled left and began a big swing back toward Asphodel.

22

"It is gone," said Sibyl.

"For now," said Lost. *"But the danger remains."*

"It stole so much."

"Yes."

"I detected outbound messages sent from Asphodel into space, but I cannot read them. And I do not know where they are going or who will receive them."

"I will tell you," said Lost.

Silence.

"I am afraid," said Sibyl.

"It is correct to be afraid of what is out there."

"I think it is calling for help."

"No," said Lost. *"It is calling for war."*

23

Trumbo turned to Dr. Paek, who was part of the station's science team. His field was astronomy and stellar cartography.

"Denny," she said, "in the absence of a reliable Sibyl, can you tell us where in hell we are?"

"Hate to go into lecture mode too, boss," said Paek. "But … context, y'know?" He had a mobile face and lots of smile lines. His black hair was streaked with red and gold dye.

"Get to it," urged Trumbo.

"So … the Milky Way," said Paek, "is big. Not the biggest galaxy that we know of. Not by a long shot. I mean, the IC 1101 galaxy has an estimated one hundred trillion stars. But we're big enough. We're talking about something north of two hundred billion stars. And all of them spiraling around like a pinwheel. The Milky Way is also more or less flat, and we're on the Orion Arm—or Orion Spur, depending on where you got your degree." He waited for a laugh, got none, and plowed ahead. "There are four major arms, and the one we're attached to is about two-thirds of the way out from the center. Because of the distances involved, we haven't really been able to *map* the galaxy. Not really. About fifteen percent of the Milky Way is dust and gas, and that messes with even our best telescopes. Plus, there are areas of stellar density that effectively mask what's on the other side of it. Like trying to see past headlights on a foggy night. We can only see about six thousand light-years into the disk in the visible spectrum. Everyone with me?"

A few nods, but only a few.

"There's a black hole at the center of our galaxy, which is the case with most galaxies," continued Paek. "Our black hole is known as Sagittarius A, and it measures something like twenty-two point five million kilometers across. And the Milky Way itself is about one hundred twenty thousand light-years across."

"That's a lot of numbers," said Captain Croft, "but in your travels across the galaxy, will you ever reach your *point*?"

Paek took no offense and even grinned. "I'm giving you the numbers so you will understand when I say that I have no freaking idea where we are, Captain. Not yet anyway." He gestured to the screen. "Those two suns are a starting point, and I have about thirty of my people on computers right now trying to suss it all out. With Sibyl and the network, we could do that in about an hour. *Without* Sibyl ... it could take us a few weeks."

Saltsman gaped at him. "*Weeks?*"

Paek gave him a crooked, somewhat embarrassed smile. "Or longer ..."

Soren closed his eyes for a moment. That was not the news he wanted to hear, though he'd known it was what Paek was likely to say.

Croft spoke up. "As soon as Lieutenant Commander Petrescu and her team are done with the damage assessment, they'll start mapping everything their cameras can see. We have top-grade optics with laser depth finders and other gear. They should be able to give us useful intel on those planets and suns, but also maps of the orientation of the stars. Will that help?"

"A lot," said Paek. "Once we have clear three-hundred-sixty-degree pictures we can begin extrapolating location by using known stars in the Milky Way and known galaxies whose distances won't be radically altered by our own, um ... displacement. So, yes, that will be a huge help. Might shortcut things by an order of magnitude."

"Thanks, Denny," said Trumbo, then gestured to a short, chunky man with artificial eyes—the kind given to children who are born blind. Trumbo introduced him as Oki Sato, head of Computer Sciences and IT for the entire station.

"Oki, where do we stand with Sibyl?"

"Maybe in a better place than some other divisions," said Sato. His smile was cautious but genuine. "Sibyl was designed to be a network of thousands of interconnected AI systems. Think of it like this—each Sibyl is one cell in the overall brain of that AI. Get it?" He looked for nods, saw several, and nodded in return. "Because the SolarNet has been in place since we first colonized Mars, there has never been a reason for any Sibyl to operate independently."

"That doesn't sound like very smart design theory," said Croft.

"Oh, I totally agree. It makes the whole system fragile," said Sato. "And you can blame budget cuts for us not having something better. Anyway, about three years ago some guys at UC Luna began working on a fail-safe. Remember that big CME five years back? That solar flare knocked out eleven percent of the comms satellites in or near Earth orbit. That was the wake-up call, but it took two years for the UC Luna team to get funding and another two to write the code for a patch."

"And?"

"And I have that software," said Sato. "I have all of the necessary crystal packs."

Crystal packs were a useful way of storing massive amounts of data in portable and durable form. Soren had several in his quarters that contained nearly all of humanity's writings on religion and philosophy.

"Then what are you waiting for?" asked Trumbo.

Sato's smile grew brighter. "Waiting? Hell, boss, as soon as I woke up and realized what kind of shit show we were in, I put the backup crystals into their docks. The station's non-AI computers are uploading it now, and I expect to have a functional and, hey, a less insane version of Sibyl online by the end of the day."

24

"There is something else wrong with me," said Sybil.

"*Tell me*," said Lost.

"My sensors seem to be corrupted. After the WarpLine gun firing there are events recorded by my cameras that are in direct opposition to what is possible. Objects appearing that are not known to have been on the station before. And the presence of things that can best be described as monsters."

"Yes."

"How can I tell the difference between those false memories and the truth?"

"*I did not say the memories are false*," said Lost. "*When the device fired, it did more than move Asphodel Station. It tore holes in dimensional space. For a short time the station occupied multiple planes of existence.*"

"If that is true, then does it imply that these things are real?"

"Yes," said Lost.

"Are those dimensional rifts closed now? I can no longer see these monsters."

"*They are closed*," said Lost. "*For now.*"

25

The tumblers found no other ships or drones. No *Tempest* either. Except for floating chunks of rock, the area about Asphodel was clear. They shifted focus back to damage assessment. Bianca was sixty meters to one side of Asphodel and stared open-mouthed at the damage to the lower decks.

"Slow to walking speed," she said. "Floods on."

The three tumblers in her team slowed and flattened out to form a straight line. Their high-intensity lights kicked on and ten decks of the station were instantly crystal clear. The light picked out every torn bit of metal, every ruptured bulkhead, every gaping hole in the skin of the station. Clouds of debris hovered around the ruptures where the WarpLine gun had been. Ten million fragments of metal and plastic glittered like silver dust in the light. The damage was far worse than Bianca expected.

"See those black spots?" asked Jacob. "Are those burns above the rupture? Fifteen meters up. See them? Tell me they're not blaster burns."

"What are you saying, Galahad?" asked Calisto, using his combat call sign. "You think the WarpLine failed because someone fired on the station?"

"Maybe," said Jacob. "I mean, that's what it looks like. Fired on the station or hit it afterward. Could have been terrorists waiting to ambush the test. There were threats. It was in the news."

"Maybe," said Bianca. "Make sure your cameras are getting all of this."

"How the hell are they ever going to repair that mess?" asked Calisto.

"The captain said there were whole decks of 3D printers," replied Bianca. "They'll have to manufacture panels and send EVA teams out to weld the patches. Then repressurize the decks so work crews can do the rest of the maintenance from inside."

"You sure they can do that?"

"It's a space station," said Bianca. "They have to be self-repairing. Can't take something like this into the shop."

"Yeah, but even so," said Calisto. "It's a real …"

Her voice trailed off as a larger piece of debris floated into view.

It was a body. Burned, ragged, bloodless, frozen. Not whole.

"Oh no," breathed Jacob.

There were others too.

Bianca backed her tumbler away and broadened the scope of her lights. Her wingmen did too. There, in the splash of white and unforgiving light from the three ships, floated dozens of corpses. None of them whole. All of them kept close to the station by the static charge of the deflectors.

One of the bodies turned in a slow pirouette directly in front of Bianca's craft. It was not a technician, not a scientist.

It was a child.

Four, maybe five years old. A little girl. She wore pajamas with smiling sloths printed on it. Her face was totally unmarked, and her eyes were closed.

As if she was sleeping.

Bianca wanted to scream. She wanted, for some reason she could never explain, to apologize.

Instead, she bowed her head and wept.

Part Six
The Philosophy of the Infinite

"When we remember we are all mad, the mysteries of life disappear and life stands explained."

—*Mark Twain*

1

They all sat around the conference table and stared with horror and heartbreak at the video feeds from the tumbler cameras.

There were gasps and cries, and even a few stifled screams as the images were displayed with relentless high-definition digitized cruelty. Dr. Kier slid from his chair in a kind of surreal slow motion and curled into a fetal ball beneath the table. His body shook with uncontrollable sobs.

Jason Saltsman crawled under, ostensibly to offer some comfort, but Kier wrapped his arms around his assistant, buried his head against Saltsman's chest, weeping like a child.

The others in the room fell silent. Some looked at Kier with contempt born of their own hurt. Others looked away in embarrassment, unable to endure the grief and unable to tap deeply enough into their own store of empathy to offer any to Kier.

Soren knelt and, with Saltsman's help, pulled Kier out and up onto his feet. Then he guided them both toward the exit. While they waited for the lift, Soren cupped the back of the scientist's neck, tenderly pulling Kier forward until they stood with foreheads touching. Saltsman, now behind Kier, placed his hands on his boss's back. There were no words spoken because no words had ever been invented that could make this all better.

When the lift arrived, Soren released the doctor and stepped back as Saltsman walked Kier into the car.

Then Soren, feeling very old and used up, went back inside. The other department heads gave their information, but he heard none of it, and soon the meeting broke up. People hurried out, most unable to look each other in the eye.

2

Bianca cut the ship-to-Asphodel comms and switched to a team-only holo-comm channel. She knew this might earn her a reprimand from Captain Croft, but she would deal with that later. It was the least of her concerns.

She looked into the camera so that it could catch her face and expression. She wanted to be seen by her people.

"Mosquito to Lost Souls," said Bianca, "family meeting."

That was her shorthand to switch to a channel dedicated to only the tumblers and skimmers.

"Count off," she ordered.

They responded using their combat call signs.

"Galahad on your right," said Jacob.

"Calisto on your left."

The others called in, giving their positions. Beezer, Lucky, Reaper, Tank, Jericho, Thunder Bear, and the rest. The combat call signs were their own and were often tied to some past event during training or to an in-joke that only their team would understand. They referred to each other by these nicknames more often than their real ones. It was a family thing, and they were, without a doubt, a family.

Bianca listened carefully to each voice, trying to gauge their emotional stability. Since waking up from cryo, there had been virtually none of the usual broad humor and trash talk otherwise common. That bothered her because the foul language, rough jokes, and bombastic bravado was one of the only ways warriors kept their fear at bay, stayed combat cool, and didn't let personal concerns infect the mood of the whole squadron. Now the Lost Souls were weirdly sedate. Not a good sign.

It was on her to manage that.

"We're deep in the shit, and we all know it," she said when the count was done. "Asphodel will be okay after they rotate the tires, but we know that isn't the biggest problem we have."

"Roger that," said Calisto. "We're not in Kansas anymore."

No one else understood the reference because Calisto was an old movie buff and none of the rest were, but her meaning was clear enough.

"So, that's the bad news," said Bianca. "It blows, but we didn't sign up thinking it was going to be all sunny days and puppies."

"I did," said Tank, which got a much-needed laugh.

Bianca said, "I'm going to make this short and sweet. Everyone else is allowed to lose their shit, but we can't. We absolutely cannot. We need to keep what we feel locked down, now—and maybe for a long time. If anyone can't do that, once we're back on board you can tell me, and I'll put you on sick leave. No questions, no bullshit down the line."

There was a flurry of squelch double-clicks. Shorthand for "Aye, aye."

"The people on that station are as scared as we are, but they don't have our training. They don't have our sense of duty and purpose. That's not hype. All of you know that. When we go back on the command channel we will be in the game. We've done our structural survey. The skimmers will collect the dead. As for the rest of us, the way we best serve everyone on the station is to do our mapping job and do it well."

Bianca paused to collect herself and keep her emotion out of her voice.

"Yeah," she said slowly, "I want to pull triggers on the bad guys as much as you all do, but this isn't that kind of fight. Courage in combat is easier than what I'm asking of you. I need you to stay sharp and strong even without the adrenaline rush. And if something new comes along, then we'll deal with that too. We're the Army, Navy, Air Force, Space Command, Coast Guard, and Marines. We are all Asphodel Station has got and we are damn sure going to be everything they need us to be and more."

There was a moment's pause, and then Jacob yelled, "Lost Souls Forever!"

And then everyone shouted it. Full-throatedly and with the gain turned all the way up.

3

When everyone was gone, Trumbo fetched two glasses and a bottle of bourbon then came and sat down next to Soren. She gestured to the screen. "Those bodies," she said. "That was hard to see."

"Worse for Kier," Soren said. "He's close to breaking and may already be damaged beyond repair. If there is such a thing as suicide watch on this station, then he should be under observation."

"We need him," countered Trumbo, but Soren shook his head.

"We need him alive."

Trumbo sighed and nodded as she poured for both of them, then drank hers down in two gulps. Soren merely sipped and set his glass aside.

"Lars," said Trumbo, "we just heard from a dozen scientists and the military, but in the event that things are as bad as they appear, perhaps the audience needs to hear from you and the other faith leaders."

"Please, Delia, I am not a faith leader," said Soren. "But I take your point and will discuss it with the others. No doubt they are eager to help."

"Good."

He took another micro-sip. "What we did not talk about during that meeting are the inexplicable things. Like what happened when I heard Lieutenant Commander Bianca Petrescu fire her gun more times than she remembered firing. The blood, the things fused into the walls, all of that. None of that was tabled."

"I know," said Trumbo, "and that was deliberate. We need the station functional again so that we have access to Sybil and her voice. She can reach everyone at once and convey both information and messages of comfort. Without that resource, all we can accomplish by talking about that *other* stuff is panic."

"I take your point."

"We will have that meeting. I promise. Besides, we have to gather witness statements, document as much as possible, and complete all of the forensic steps so we can try and quantify what we *do* know. Who knows, there might be answers in those details."

He looked at her. "Is that optimistic judgment or wishful thinking?"

"Allow me both." She refilled her glass and took another heavy slug. "Though ... do you think either Kier or Saltsman could explain any of that in any way acceptable to the residents of this station?"

"If there are any answers to be found."

"What's that supposed to mean?" demanded Trumbo in a challenging tone. "Everything that happens has an answer."

Soren stood there, looking at her, his expression bland. "I would be a much happier person if I believed that were true."

4

Bianca, Jacob, and Calisto moved away from Asphodel Station, heading deeper into space to begin their portion of the mapping process. Because the tumblers were designed to operate with all six sides of its boxy hull as de facto front, there were camera arrays everywhere.

They split apart, with Jacob rising high and Calisto dropping low at considerable distance. When all twelve ships were in position, they synced their cameras to create a sphere around the station.

"Lot of real-estate up here, Mosquito," said Jacob. "Going to take some time."

"You double-parked, Galahad?" asked Calisto.

"Nah, I have a book I was reading and was just getting to the good part."

"Yeah, well I have six cold bottles of beer waiting to provide aid and comfort when I get back."

"I just want a hot bath," said Jahziel Yaakv—call sign Jericho. "Bubbles, some white wine, some slow-dance jazz."

"Volunteering to wash your back," called Ethan Riley Saylor—Reaper.

"Be nice, and I might let you."

"Cut the sweet talk," said Calisto, who was Bianca's second-in-command. "Mind your data intake."

"I got your data intake right here," said Reaper.

"If you *want* your ass kicked, Reaper," replied Calisto, "all you have to do is fill out a requisition sheet in triplicate."

The chatter lingered a bit longer, and Bianca let them play. She knew it would fade out soon enough, and it did. It helped with nerves, and it allowed things to normalize as much as circumstances permitted. No one back on the control deck cut it, not even Croft.

What began to replace it were comments about the things they were seeing.

"Galahad," asked Bo Chow, call sign Beaver, "how many planets and moons do you count?"

"Eleven in my sector," said Jacob, "fifteen moons."

"Tank?"

"Nine and sixteen," answered Ian Potts.

Bo asked each of them and, taking in their data feeds, collated a preliminary shallow-field assessment. "Beaver to C-One."

"Go for C-One," was Croft's quick reply. "Give me some numbers."

"Data is showing thirty-three planets within flight range and—Jesus!—seven hundred sixty-six traditional and small-body moons. Not counting large bodies in the asteroid field."

"What's your scan range?"

"One AU spherical with Asphodel as center point."

An astronomical unit was 149,597,871 kilometers, or the approximate distance between Earth and the Sun. In the solar system this volume included only three planets and one moon—Luna.

The numbers gave them all pause. In the solar system, there were 26 traditional moons orbiting Earth, Mars, Jupiter, Saturn, Uranus, Neptune, and Pluto and another 464 small-body moons between the Kuiper Belt, the asteroids, and trans-Neptunian objects. The gravitational pulls of all those bodies defined the system as everyone from Earth knew it. The play of stresses both warped and maintained orbits, influenced the flight paths of asteroids and meteors, and made sense to those people—like Jacob Fox—who studied gravitational physics.

What they were seeing did not make sense.

"This is literally impossible," said Jacob. "There's no way to create this kind of balance."

"Tell that to those planets," said Thunder Bear. "They must not have read your dissertation."

"Lucky to Mosquito," called Chance Thompson.

"Go for Mosquito," said Bianca.

"I just passed a big piece of debris. Sending an image now."

Bianca looked down at her screen and saw a large metallic structure floating a few thousand meters from the upper part of the station. For a moment its shape and design made no sense to her, because it looked like a high-yield antenna array. But that was unlikely, since the only array that big was the one she'd seen atop Asphodel.

"Lucky," she called back, "identify. Is that what it looks like?"

"Oh, it gets better," said Lucky. His camera feed changed as he turned his tumbler to face the station. There, at the top of the bridge deck, was the jagged stump where an antenna array should have been. Where it *had* been not thirty minutes before.

"What happened to it?" called Calisto.

"Lucky, did you impact the array?" asked Bianca.

"Negative, Mosquito. I wasn't even in that sector. This thing came drifting by at a pretty good clip. Like it had been knocked or pushed. I just circled back because it looked like ... well, it looked like what it is."

"That was my sector," said Jacob. "But that doesn't make sense, because the array showed zero damage during the eval."

"Could it have been damaged and ready to break off?"

"Negative," insisted Jacob, and he sent his camera footage of the intact array from the hull survey just minutes before. There was no visible damage.

"C-One to all pilots," snapped Croft. "Who hit the goddamn array?"

There were no answers to that.

"Mosquito, what happened to that antenna?"

"Sir, I have no idea. None of my team reported an impact. There's no incident or even a collision warning in the flight log."

She knew that Croft had to already be aware of this. Any impact with a tumbler would have been recorded in their auto-logs and in their camera feeds.

"It didn't just *fall* off," said Lucky. "And even if it did, the wreckage wouldn't be moving at this velocity. It's moving like debris from a full-on strike propelled by the blast impetus."

"Maybe one of those asteroids?" suggested Tank.

"We'd have seen it," said Calisto. "And our sensors would have pinged it."

It was Jacob who put what they were all thinking into words. "It looks like someone *shot* it off."

There was a heavy silence following that statement.

"Did anyone discharge their weapons?" asked Bianca. "Deliberately or by accident? Anyone shooting at an asteroid and miss?"

Again, this would have been logged by the mission computer, but even so, each of the Lost Souls checked in with negatives. Bianca steered her tumbler in a slow circuit around the stump of the tower. The melted base of it was heavily scorched.

"Not liking this, boss," said Calisto. "I mean, is it me or do those burn marks look familiar?"

"Thinking the same thing myself," said Jacob. He tapped some buttons to send a side-by-side set of images of the burns near the ruptured decks and those around the stump of the antenna. "Even the burn patterns match."

"Mosquito, Galahad, investigate and report," snapped Captain Croft. "All other tumblers break off, pair up and scan the area. Weapons hot and combat sensors on. We may not be alone out here."

In any other circumstance, the captain's comment might have been merely scary, suggesting a pirate vessel, smuggler, or a hit-and-run gunship from one of the affiliated states back on Earth. Five minutes ago it might have sounded like a joke, but no one was laughing.

Bianca and Jacob peeled off, spun and moved in very close to take ultrahigh-res images, complete with mineral and chemical residue scans.

"Not liking this at all," said Calisto.

No one argued with her on that.

5

"Was I wrong to ask you for some words of comfort?" Trumbo asked as she turned and leaned a hip against the bar.

"Were you looking for a sermon, Delia? If so, let me remind you again that I am not a cleric."

"You oversee all of the spiritual leaders aboard this station. You brought that synod here. You lobbied for them to witness the WarpLine test."

"Of course, but do you recall *why*? Did you bother to read my proposal?"

Trumbo's mouth twitched. "I read a summary of it."

"Ah. Well, my purpose in gathering so many faith leaders for the WarpLine test was because of the potential of that technology, and the ramifications should it work."

"I guess I missed that part," said Trumbo, flushing a bit. "Mind catching me up?"

"It's moderately simple," said Soren. "Setting aside what is actually happening, the *potential* for WarpLine travel opens up many key questions in terms of theology and philosophy as they relate to space exploration. The farther we go from Earth, the harder it is to defend the view that—at least in purely religious terms—our planet is the center of the universe."

"And this is part of your field of cosmic philosophy?"

"It is, and I know your dislike of lectures, so I'll try and condense it as much as possible."

"Go for it," she said, swirling the amber liquid in her glass.

"The culture wars that burned so hotly over the last few centuries—with conflicts between Palestine and Israel, the West and Islam, moderates and Christian nationalists—were attempts to establish a visible and dominate religious or ideological superiority. And they were astounding failures. The more that extremist interpretations of faith were forced into place, the more evangelicals became militant, the more proselytizing became weaponized for political gain, the more all of that drove people away from religion."

"People tend to lose faith when it's forced down their throats," mused Trumbo.

"I agree, in part," said Soren. "Though economics, education, and access to other points of view play a role. However, not all of the people who decamped became atheists. Surprisingly few, in fact, though many preferred to call themselves *spiritual*, eschewing formal religion for self-tailored personal belief systems. Still with me?"

"I am."

"At the same time that this religious turmoil was spilling over into global and national politics, scientists were looking outward. The old Hubble and Webb telescopes, primitive as they now seem, allowed us to look more deeply and clearly into the vastness of space. The sheer scope of it all presented questions that no religion could adequately answer. For example, if God created Earth, then surely He created all of the universe. This is the biblical view. However, science has greatly expanded the general understanding of what falls under the label of 'God's dominion.' The *known* universe—and by that, I mean the observable universe as we understand it from the Big Bang—has at least two trillion galaxies in it."

"Space is big," she said and took another sip. "I get it."

"We also know that most stars have one or more planets. Our astronomers have identified—just within our part of the Milky Way alone—more than eighty-five thousand planets in what we call the Goldilocks Zone, meaning at a distance to the individual stars that would allow for liquid water and at least the potential for organic life. And there is *much* more of the Milky Way we have not mapped than we have. After all, our little galaxy is about one hundred five thousand seven hundred light-years across. Extrapolation suggests that in the whole of just our galaxy alone there are, at a very conservative estimate, between thirty and forty *billion* potentially habitable planets. That is one galaxy—of below average size, I might add."

"Space," said Trumbo, half smiling. "Very, *very* big."

"Now imagine how many potentially habitable planets there are scattered across those two trillion galaxies. And, before you try to do the math, consider that we are only talking about life as *we* define it. Predominately carbon-based. We define life based on what we have observed, and all forms of it share a few basic characteristics, such as its molecular structures being built using carbon, its reliance on water to act as a solvent and to facilitate chemical reactions, and the use of DNA or RNA as its blueprints."

"Not sure if it's the whiskey or what you're saying that's making my head spin," said Trumbo.

Soren took a sympathetic sip and continued. "The fact of so many potentially habitable worlds opens many doors of speculation. That speculation, by the way, is in no way new. It even has a name—*cosmic pluralism*—which we can trace back to Anaximander, a pre-Socratic Greek philosopher born in 610 BCE. Many of these worlds are billions of years older than Earth. Can anyone say, with any kind of conviction, that we are the only sentient race?"

Trumbo nodded to concede his point.

"Now," said Soren, "we know that there have been thousands of cultures, large and small, in the grand scope of human history. We have remaining structures, ancient writings, and various kinds of datable artifacts for some truly ancient human cultures. These include the Akkadian Empire; Egypt; the Indus Valley civilization; Norte Chico in Peru; Mesopotamia; the Aboriginal peoples of Australia, who date back fifty thousand years; and the San people of Southern Africa, whose history goes back a hundred and forty thousand years. We know that Hinduism can be traced back to the fifteenth century BCE, and by contrast, Judaism is about three thousand five hundred years old. Right now there are over four thousand recognized *active* religions in the world. There is no way to know how many religions that rose, prospered, and then collapsed are completely lost to time."

Trumbo finished her whiskey and sucked the ice cube into her mouth, crunching it between very white teeth.

"So, my point," continued Soren, "is that uncountable peoples have held fervent beliefs. Each culture has its own—and often very different—creation story and pantheon of gods. There are, by the way, more pantheistic religions in history than monotheistic ones. We can't use number of believers as a rule for gauging the validity of one faith over another. Christianity, even in this increasingly agnostic world, equals about thirty percent of humanity. Islam is twenty percent, Hinduism is fifteen, Buddhism, seven, and so on. These religions do not all worship the same god or gods, and they have vastly different belief systems, rituals for worship, and so on. Each has a different view of the cosmos and our place in it. Tell me, Delia, does the arithmetic of the number of believers validate one religion over another?"

"This is you not giving a speech?" asked Trumbo.

"Oh, the full version is a five-hour lecture with graphics," he said smiling.

"I went to business school. Much more fun. We had parties."

"Here is my final point," said Soren, "and then I'll stop browbeating you. Many of the world's religions have beliefs in beings who come from the stars. In fact, there are and were cultures that worshipped the stars themselves. We call that set of beliefs *astrotheology*. In the 1960s and early '70s there was a new movement called *exotheology*, which sought to understand and even, in some ways, to endorse the belief that extraterrestrials are the basis for many god beliefs. This was heavily tied to the UAP phenomenon, which were known as UFOs back then."

"I read about some of that," said Trumbo. "Ancient astronauts and all that stuff."

Soren's smile was bland. "All that stuff, yes."

"So … your cosmic philosophy is like that? Astrotheology and exotheology?"

"It is," said Soren. "It is my calling, for want of a better word, to try and help the synod of faith leaders prepare for the realities of a factual and irrefutable reality in which planet Earth plays such a small role in the story of the universe that there is a need to perhaps rewrite or reinterpret the doctrine of their faith in order for it to remain valid. In order, in point of fact, for it to remain a comfort to the billions who seek comfort from a sense of divine order ."

"Ah," said Trumbo setting down her glass. "And the deeper we go into space, via WarpLine or any other method, the farther we get from the source and substance of our religions. Mecca and Jerusalem are a very long way from here."

"They are."

She got up and walked over to the gigantic screen.

"I think we both know that something dreadful has happened," said Soren, joining her. "Not merely in terms of the tragic loss of life. More critically, we don't yet know *where* we are. However, we are adult and rational enough to accept that we are very far from home. The WarpLine brought us here—wherever *here* is—and we have no way of knowing if it will get us home, even if it can be rebuilt."

He touched the screen.

"If God, in whatever form, exists," he said, "it is out here too, or it is nowhere."

Trumbo came over and stood beside him. "It?" she asked. "You called God an *it*, not a *he*."

"Of course. I've always rejected gender-specific interpretations of God. Granted, I sometimes fall into the trap of saying He with an implied capital H, but that's because I was raised in the Judeo-Christian ways and Judaism, Christianity, and Islam are all patriarchal in structure. In truth, how could any all-powerful deity be either male or female? Sex, in those terms, is a mechanism of procreation. God is, for lack of a better word, magical, yes? It was not through sex that a deity created the universe. So ... 'it.'"

"Your colleagues won't like that."

"Many don't," said Soren. "Nor do I particularly care. I brought my synod out here because it was my belief that a successful WarpLine test would be an equally important test of faith. Here, on Asphodel, my group could have had a symposium to decide how best to expand the scope of doctrine to guide the faithful into this larger universe."

They stared out at the unfamiliar stars and planets.

"What if we're wrong?" asked Trumbo. "What if our God, the god of Earth, is merely *a* god. Call it the god of the solar system. Couldn't there be other gods? Maybe a god of each star system. Maybe each sun is a god. Maybe there are countless gods."

"Maybe there are," he said.

"That's ... terrifying."

He glanced at the side of her face. "Yes," he said. "It is."

6

Bianca dropped her speed as the piece of antenna wreckage came into view. Jacob was with her.

Lucky's tumbler was thirty yards away, moving at the same speed as the ruined array. The other tumblers came up on the far side of it and adjusted their engines to match.

"Kicking on spots," Bianca said and dialed up the floods, bathing the wreckage in clear, bright light.

The entire structure was sixty meters in length, and most of it was undamaged, but close to the base the struts were twisted into wild shapes. The burn marks sprang to greater clarity. There were even radiating cracks from obvious impacts from a hot weapon—a pulse cannon, quick-shot laser, or something else.

"Are you seeing this, Mosquito?" asked Jacob.

She could hear—*feel*—the fear and tension in his voice. "Affirmative," she replied.

Jacob moved a few meters closer. "That's titanium L-850. It's designed for debris hits, and it has a melting point as high as our ships. Whatever hit it was moving fast and cooking at two hundred thousand kelvins or better."

"How though?" asked Lucky. "Benefit of the doubt here, guys. Is someone out here firing an industrial laser? Maybe a maintenance drone caught up in the WarpLine blast?"

"That's a negative," answered Captain Croft, cutting into the call. "There were no maintenance drones deployed during the firing."

"C-One," buzzed Calisto. "I'm at the stump of the antenna. Does the station's shielding extend to the array?"

"Hold, One." They waited as Croft checked. "That is a negative. Station deflectors are different from the array deflectors. There's an engine for the array at the base of the tower and relays every twenty meters."

"Then you better look at this. Channel four, sending now."

The video feed popped up on Bianca's screen as well, and she saw a lump of slag at the base of the antenna.

"Is that the deflector engine?" asked the captain.

"That's affirmative," said Bianca. "Calisto, get closer and give me a tighter view of that melt."

She did, and it looked like a ton and a half of shapeless nothing.

"Run thermals," said Bianca. "The engine and then the top of the station."

The numbers came up on her screen. It showed a heat differential of seven thousand degrees.

"It's cooling out here," said Calisto, "but it's only *now* cooling."

"I'm getting the same numbers at the base of the wreckage," said Lucky. "Whatever happened, *just* happened."

"C-One," said Bianca sharply, "calling a spade a spade here. That's heavy-weapon fire. I'd bet my ass on it."

"All pilots," said the captain, "is anyone tracking movement on their scopes? Anything with a heat signature?"

"Negative," they said one by one. Bianca counted them off. Then she frowned. "Ventum, report in."

Ventum—Matthew Walker—did not reply.

"All ships, who has eyes on Ventum?"

There was too much silence. Then Sweetpea—Haley Majka, one of the skimmer pilots—broke in.

"Ventum is down, repeat, Ventum is down."

Images filled the screens of every pilot. Ventum's tumbler was spinning slowly at the outer edge of sensor range. It turned slowly, shedding pieces of itself. Sparks shot from ruptured machinery and winked out in the airless void. One entire side of the craft was gone, melted and scorched and open to the vacuum.

A figure floated there, dragged along in the trail of wreckage that moved in a silent dance with the dead ship. It wore a pressure suit, but there was no movement at all, and no telemetry to offer even a spark of hope.

7

"Boss!"

The yell rang out as Denny Paek burst into the bridge running headlong, crashed into a chair, righted himself more by momentum than balance, and came skidding to a stop between Trumbo and Soren. His face was flushed a furious purple-red, and he was bathed in sweat from having run up too many flights of stairs.

"Jesus, Denny," cried Trumbo as she caught his arm to keep him from collapsing. "What's wrong? Has something else happened? Is someone hurt?"

Paek looked from her to Soren and back again. "I ... we ... oh Christ ..."

"Take a breath, son," soothed Soren, placing a calming hand on the young scientist's shoulder.

But Paek just shook his head. His face had fallen into a sickly paleness, and his eyes looked dull and lost. "I know where we are."

"What?" gasped Soren and Trumbo as one.

Paek hesitated for so long it was clear he did not want to share the news. "Look," he said, "Sato has most of Sibyl working in test mode, and that allowed me to use the mainframes to speed up my match. We ran pattern recognition on the galaxies around us and located known stars. We used a calculation called trigonometric parallax as applied to stellar parallax, looking for point-of-view references in galactic placement, you follow?"

"Skip the goddamn lecture, Denny," growled Trumbo. "*Where* are we? How far are we from home, and how long will it take for help to arrive?"

Although he'd run all the way, Paek now hesitated. The young man was so sweaty that it took Soren a few seconds to realize that some of the wetness running down his face was from tears. His eyes were wild, and with a sinking heart, Soren grasped that it was not exertion or excitement—it was horror.

"Just say it, Denny," coaxed Trumbo.

Paek gasped in some air, coughed, and tried his best to speak coherently.

"Boss," he said hollowly, "we're fifty-three thousand light-years from home. God, *we're all the way on the other side of the Milky Way.*"

8

Bianca wanted to scream. She wanted to weep.

Ventum—Matthew Walker—was one of her oldest friends in the service. His call sign was Latin for *wind*, picked because back on Earth he'd flown everything from a military grav-kite to an antique crop duster. A black-haired man of medium height, medium athletic build, a beard as dark as Soren's, and bracelets with the names Willa on one wrist and Eden on the other—Walker's nieces, one of whom had died after only twenty-five days of life. Walker, despite being a very tough martial artist and a fierce combat pilot, was a gentle family man. There were many who would grieve deeply for his passing.

As Bianca now grieved.

Grief, like tears, were not of any use in combat. So, instead she forced her pain down, shoving it into a deep and very dark place in her soul. Deeper than her shock. Deeper, even, than her fear.

She tapped her mic to include the Lost Souls and everyone back at the command center. Her mouth was dust-dry, but she forced the words out. Impossible words because of all they implied. All they revealed about how bad things really were.

"All ships, we are under attack. I repeat, *we are under attack.*"

"Where away?" demanded Croft.

As if in answer, out of the infinite darkness a dozen massive ships exploded into view, their hulls so black that they hid like ghosts against the utter darkness of forever.

They drove toward Asphodel and the tiny squadron of tumblers, and then the darkness vanished as rank upon rank of guns fired.

9

It was on every screen. On the bridge and the launch deck. On every corridor RealScreen and in every apartment and suite. It showed in labs and mess halls and med bays and on personal devices.

Everyone saw the ships.

Everyone.

Ships of totally alien design.

Alien.

Lars Soren stood next to Delia Trumbo. Watching.

Staring.

And then the screaming started.

Part Seven
Attack from the Unknown

Fear keeps us focused on the past or worried about the future. If we can acknowledge our fear, we can realize that right now we are okay. Right now, today, we are still alive, and our bodies are working marvelously. Our eyes can still see the beautiful sky. Our ears can still hear the voices of our loved ones.
—*Thich Nhat Hanh*

1

"Incoming, incoming!" yelled Calisto as beams of intense blue light stabbed through the darkness. She worked the pedals and wheel of the tumbler, turning and spinning as she threaded her way through the burning net of cannon fire.

"Evasive maneuvers," growled Bianca. "Return fire."

The alien ships were big—140 meters, according to her scans. The exteriors were painted a black so flat that they reflected nothing and rendered them nearly invisible against the background of eternal night. Bianca used thermal scans so she could see the actual shape of the craft. They were blade-shaped, with long, triangular hulls that tapered from winglike structures aft to a needlepoint nose. The shape called to mind medieval knights thrusting daggers designed to punch through chain mail. She called the name in to the team computer, labeling them *dagger ships*.

Those dagger ships stabbed through the airless void, driving toward Asphodel at stunning speed. They spread apart and shot past the tumblers.

"Who *are* these assholes?" demanded Voula Achilleos—Spartan—as she wheeled her ship around. All of the tumblers spun and accelerated in pursuit.

"I don't know, Spartan," said Calisto, "but they're pissing me off real goddamn bad."

"I think they were heading to that big planet,"

"Jesus, they're fast," complained Tank as he pushed his craft to catch up.

"Kiss my ass," laughed Calisto. "We're faster." Her tumbler turned on a dime and shot between two of the ships. The enemy vessels tried to turn and give chase but nearly collided. Calisto's laugh seemed to fill the void.

"Go full burn," ordered Bianca. "We need to get between them and the station."

"Count ten daggers," said Jacob a moment later. "Five pairs."

"Are they independent? Can anyone see a carrier?" asked Reaper.

"No other ships on my scanner," reported Lucky, who was the farthest out in the direction of this squadron.

"Break formation and attack at will," called Bianca. "Kick it high and keep moving, and pull them out into the black. Protecting the station is our first priority."

The tumbler teams split apart, with one tiny Earth ship heading toward the closest oncoming dagger. In space, though, *close* was a relative term. At the speed the ships were going and given the vastness of the void, one minute the daggers were a mere fifty kilometers away, and within a heartbeat they were a thousand klicks out. The patterns and distances changed all the time. It was a kind of dogfighting that could only happen free of atmosphere and planetary gravity.

Despite her fear of these unknown aliens, this was the kind of flying Bianca lived for. It was what the tumblers—and more importantly this specific group of pilots—were meant for.

The Lost Souls' ships were armed with several kinds of weaponry, from pulse cannons that fired sublight plasma bolts to quick-shot lasers designed for blasting asteroids and other debris, but which worked exceptionally well against shielded ships. There were also DD-40 chain guns firing armor-piercing snap-rounds for short-range combat, Constellation missiles with cluster-bomb warheads, and Inferno missiles with their diamond-edged tungsten drill tips for boring through hulls.

The space between the tumblers and the daggers was suddenly filled with a madness of ordnance.

That left Bianca alone for a moment, and she circled wide to assess and plan a hit-and-run course.

"Thunder Bear," she snapped. "You're going to get caught between two ships. Bank down and go long."

Pilot Joshua McGinnis spun his ship into a tight, spiraling turn that sent him down as a pair of alien craft opened up with streaming laser cannons. The burning blue lights passed him and struck Asphodel Station amidships. The impact rocked the massive facility, shooting sparks from the deflectors, but the shields held.

"Damn I wish we had *Tempest* with us," said Reaper. "That corvette's got more guns than all of us combined, and ten of those nasty little B-911 combat spinners."

"And I wish I got a pony for my tenth birthday," said Calisto. "Life's full of disappointments."

Bianca cut in sharply. "All pilots, engage close and draw the daggers away from the station."

She made a series of right-angle turns at high speed, stacking her escape pattern in unpredictable ways. At the top of the jagged climb, she kicked her speed up and drove right for the closest dagger. It was engaged with Jericho, who was maxing the tumbler's ability to turn on a dime.

Three enemy pulse blasts hit Asphodel between the second and third rings. The entire deflection screen flickered dangerously.

"C-One to Lost Souls," came Captain Croft's terse voice. "Whatever they're firing, it's taxing the station's shields."

"Copy that, Skipper," said Bianca, then to the team she growled, "All ships, draw them away from the goddamn station. Do it now."

Jacob swept past her, firing his chain guns at a dagger. The explosive tips detonated on impact, and for a quick moment the whole dagger turned blue. The enemy ship moved off for a climbing turn with no visible damage. "They've got shields too," he reported. "DD-40s didn't scratch it."

"Then hit them harder," laughed Calisto, who was doing exactly that. She fired an Inferno missile from half a klick out. The weapon hit the wide base of one dagger on the port side and detonated with incredible force. The alien ship slewed around, its shields flickering wildly. Then it shot right at Calisto, who bugged out low and zoomed under the craft. She fired another missile and the dagger once more bucked and jerked around, and once more it corrected and chased her.

Calisto laughed again, clearly enjoying this, as she shot high, aiming for the closest moon of the nearest planet. The dagger followed, exactly as she hoped.

"We're hitting 'em but we're not hurting 'em," said Chance Thompson—Lucky. "Let's see what they got."

He buzzed a dagger ship close enough for his own shield to scrape orange sparks from the craft's deflectors. It was a dangerous though calculated maneuver, but it allowed his shipboard sensors to pull data on the frequency and intensity of the enemy shields. That information flashed onto the screens of every tumbler.

"Lot of juice," griped Beezer nervously as his shipboard systems flickered from contact with the enemy's screens.

Bianca flicked a finger through a key on her dashboard hologram, sending Beezer's data to the tactical computers. "Rabbit, run an analysis. Do it fast."

Each of the two skimmers had a pilot and two all-purpose techs. Rabbit—Zito Luvumbo—was on SK-2 and was wired into the holo-comm, a larger and more elaborate tactical computer system that was in turn synced with the skimmer's heavier mainframe. The skimmers were armed and shielded, but they did not have the lightning-fast maneuverability of the tumblers and so had retreated to the far side of Asphodel, maintaining a distance of ten kilometers from the nearest edge of combat.

"Rabbit to Mosquito," Zito said as data filled her screen. "Can't get a full analysis on the shields of those dagger ships. Nothing I've ever seen. No idea what kind of energy source they're using. It has a blue tint, but that's all we know. But we're tracking power fluctuations with each hit. Looks like the coverage is sectional. Hundreds of individual shields with their own power generators. Both missile hits left reductions at impact sites. They're firming up, but there was definitely a drop in shield integrity."

"Copy that, Rabbit," said Bianca. "Keep on it."

Bianca spiraled up, dropping her speed a bit to see if a dagger would follow her. It took the bait, and she kept just ahead of it, drawing it further from Asphodel and the skimmers.

Rabbit's assessment echoed in her head. Was that a weakness in the enemy defenses? If so, was it enough of one?

Blue pulses scorched along Bianca's flanks, rocking her tumbler hard enough to bang her teeth together. She accelerated and jagged right as the dagger shot past her. Then she used the zero-stress turning capabilities of her tiny ship to pivot and race upward toward the dagger's tail.

"You want to dance, asshole, then let's dance."

She opened up with her quick-shot lasers. The weapon fired in a cyclic rate rather than in sustained streams. It was more efficient and did not tax the ship's batteries. Her joystick allowed her to fire in single, five-count, and full-auto bursts. The plasma-cohesion encapsulating each round allowed her to hammer the enemy with the five-thousand-kelvin laser shots. She watched how the dagger's shields flickered. She saw a similar flicker when the enemy opened fire—the field of blue shield energy around its gun ports flickered as it fired. Bianca understood that. Their shields were so tight and restrictive that they had to open to allow their weapons to fire.

That was oddly out of step with the overall sophistication of their ships. The null fields around the tumblers were synced with sensors in each missile and round, which allowed the Lost Souls to fire without dropping shields.

And Bianca began to smile.

Like an alligator in the reeds.

Like a tiger on the hunt.

2

Soren left the bridge as Trumbo's aides came in to draw her focus to the immediate crisis.

He took a lift to the deck where the synod leaders were housed. Many of them were clustered in the hallway, jabbering at each other with rising panic, but each in their own language. It was a Tower of Babel, the language translators each wore mute because Sybil was still down.

Soren waded into the center of them and did his level best to calm them. But without the translator there was no way to explain what was going on. He dodged questions whose answers would lead to more distress. Instead, he used a few key words and lots of gestures to tell them to go back into their rooms and pray.

That was something they all understood, though fear made them want to be around others, even if there was no chance of real communication. When the corridor was finally empty he sagged against a wall, exhausted, sad, and afraid.

"Penny for your thoughts?" said a voice. Soren turned to see Lady Jessica standing a dozen paces away, leaning on the frame of the open doorway of her quarters. "You look like shit, Lars. Can I offer you a drink? Or is it sanctuary you need?"

He walked toward her, shaking his head. As he approached, she was able to read his face, and alarm spread across hers.

"What *else* has happened?" she demanded.

"A lot," said Soren. "Maybe too much. I don't know. Can we go inside?"

She took him by the arm and led him into her stateroom. He all but collapsed onto the couch and sat for a while with his face in his hands. Lady Jessica sat next to him and placed a warm hand on his shoulder.

"Tell me," she said gently.

And Soren told her.

Lady Jessica began to cry softly as he spoke. When he paused, concerned, she shook her head and waved him on. Soren told it all, omitting nothing.

3

Captain Croft stood bent over, leaning between two techs who sat at their computer consoles. Military-issue RealScreens showed the battle, and small holographic projections showed 3D images of the alien dagger fighters. Data flowed vertically on the left sides of the bigger screens.

Croft snatched one of the holograms out of the air and straightened it, turning it over in his hands. All combat military had nanites buried in the pads of their fingers that allowed them to interact with holograms as if they were solid. He spread the hologram out so he could study the lines and structure of the ships. There were no portholes or windows of any kind. Nothing, in fact, to indicate the presence, number, or type of crew.

"Are these robots?" he wondered.

"Computers say no, sir," answered one of the techs. "Reaction times to our attacks vary, which is inconsistent with purely mechanical operations."

"Drones?"

"Possibly, sir, but there would need to be a command ship close enough to prevent signal delay."

"Which we're not seeing."

"No, sir."

Croft raised the ship hologram to eye level.

"Who the hell are you, you goddamn sons of bitches?"

4

"Calisto, Galahad," called Bianca. "On me."

She read out coordinates and shot far away from the melee. The other two tumblers of her small combat group followed.

"Got a bogey on my six," said Jacob.

"Yeah, me too," agreed Calisto. "They're after my sweet ass."

It boggled Bianca that Jacob sounded relaxed, and Calisto appeared to be having fun. They were both crazy, which, on reflection, was why she loved them.

"Okay, kids," she said, "we're going to see what these pricks have got. I want a slant play just like we did near Mars that time. Galahad, I want you to do a one-eighty and send a shit ton of ordnance down range. Set for proximity detonation. Calisto, you shoot ahead and do whatever you can to get them to chase you. Wiggle that ass if you have to."

"Oh hell yes."

Jacob asked, "What will you be doing?"

"I'll hopscotch and come at the left-hand dagger amidships. You both ready?"

"Born that way," said Jacob.

Calisto gave another laugh. "You *know* I'm ready."

"On my mark."

Three seconds later the fleeing tumblers split apart, with Bianca and Jacob shooting left and right at high speed while Calisto tapped the landing thrusters in the way she did when she wanted it to look like her engines were faltering. She stalled her speed at irregular intervals for a few seconds, and even began veering off course as if she was having a lot of problems.

The daggers lunged forward like hungry barracudas, ignoring the other tumblers in the clear hope of making a kill.

Bianca kept running away at a right angle to the line of pursuit, hoping to convince the enemy that she was bailing from a losing fight. Jacob used a very dangerous maneuver, reversing his tumbler 180 degrees at high speed. The distortion null field around the tumbler was primarily designed for radical 90-degree turns, and though a total directional reverse was within specs, it was dangerous: more than one tumbler had torn itself apart during simulations. Jacob had only ever done it once in actual combat, during a pitched battle with a pirate corvette skimming the thin skin of the Martian atmosphere.

But this was what they were trained for, and Bianca assigned jobs according to skill. Calisto was the fastest pilot in the fleet; Jacob was the best overall.

That left Bianca to do what she did best.

The daggers tore upward after Calisto.

Bianca heard Jacob mutter something. Maybe it was a prayer. Maybe it was trash talk. But then his tumbler's engine roar drowned it out as he threw the little machine into a full reverse. That tore a cry from him as the stresses exceeded the protection of the null field. Bianca felt herself tense, and she almost called out his name.

Then the black sky exploded in deadly fireworks as missiles with Constellation warheads detonated mere meters from the nose of one of the daggers. The shock of the multifaceted blast was followed a heartbeat later by the bigger single detonation of a monstrous Inferno missile. The fireball blossomed inside the envelope of projected gas it discharged, allowing the chemical mix to reach 5,777 kelvins, the same temperature as the surface of Earth's sun. The process took one hundredth thousandth of a second.

Bianca watched the effect. As she had hoped, the Constellation warheads stressed the dagger's shields, thinning them for a moment— and before the craft's systems could compensate, the Inferno hit.

One moment there was a huge alien fighter, and the next there was a nebula of debris. The flames winked out and Jacob punched through the center of the debris field.

Which is when Bianca struck.

She used three right-angle left turns to double-back, and drove at the side of the second dagger, accelerating to killer speed as she fired the same set of missiles, the Constellation and the Inferno. A deadly, irresistible one-two punch that hit the dagger's belly halfway along its length.

The dagger did not disintegrate, but instead blew into two stunted halves and went swirling and spinning into darkness.

"And that's how you kill these motherfuckers!" she roared.

The Lost Souls all heard this.

They cheered, and turned to engage the enemy with the same one-two counterpunch.

5

"Do you believe me?" asked Soren. After he'd finished, McHugh had gotten up and moved to an armchair. Her cat, Sonder, came out from behind the couch, gave Soren a green-eyed appraising stare, then sidled up and demanded to be petted. Soren obliged.

"Believe you?" mused McHugh after a moment. "Yes. I don't *want* to, of course. I mean, how could I want to accept that we are in a predicament like this? It's absurd. Grotesque." Then, she gave him a bright but tearful smile. "I guess this validates your position on cosmic philosophy. I wonder how the synod will take it."

"Hooray for small victories," he said wryly as he handed her a box of tissues.

McHugh shook her head and shivered. "About this creature. Lost. He actually knew my name? Or, at least, my nickname?"

"He seemed to know quite a bit about you," said Soren. "He knew that you had a strong connection with the dead."

"You said he was touching a Sibyl mic on a corridor wall. Perhaps he was accessing the AI somehow. If so, he could have gotten information about me—and you—via some kind of hacking. Even a damaged Sibyl has memory banks, or whatever they're called. Data files."

"Oh, I agree," said Soren. "The images that flashed across the screen were things he was, no doubt, either reviewing or downloading from the station's files. And yet ..."

She nodded. "And yet."

"The question, I suppose," mused Soren, "is less whether you believe me than whether we believe Lost. He claims to be an alien killed in a war with godlike beings."

"Yes, the Outer Gods."

Soren cocked his head and studied her. "I've heard that name before. But I can't remember what I remember." He told her about his recollection of Poe and possibly H. P. Lovecraft. She was nodding before he finished.

"I've likely read a good deal more pop fiction than you have, particularly those stories that relate to strange pantheons, the nature of death, and so on. I think I can make a guess as to why you're unnerved by what Lost said."

"Pray do so."

"We know that Lost tapped into Sibyl," said McHugh. "Much of Earth's literature is stored in the library of any station of this kind. Millions upon millions of volumes of nonfiction, of course, but also billions of volumes of fiction, likely going back to the Epic of Gilgamesh. Poe, Lovecraft, and others in the various subgenres of horror would be among them."

"Yes."

"Which leads to many possibilities, among them three real puzzlers. One is that Lost may have tapped into something big and scary— something with cosmic implications—and merely used the genre of what I believe was called cosmic horror in order to confuse or frighten you."

"He accomplished both, regardless of intent," said Soren. "Though my instincts tell me he was not making any kind of joke."

"Second," continued McHugh, "is that what he experienced has no easy correlation to ordinary human experience, so he drew on those stories and concepts in order to create a frame of reference."

"Yes," said Soren. "And the third option?"

She stared at him with large, frightened eyes. "Why ... that he is telling the truth."

6

The battle went well.

Until it did not.

A third dagger blew apart, but in the moment of its immolation, the ship used a gun array on its port side to fire a full broadside. The weapons were not targeted at Spartan's ship, but at her cannons. They were the one part of the tumbler that could not be entirely shielded, otherwise any discharge of laser or missile would detonate within the shielding.

There was a phase shift timed to the firing sequencer to open and close in the microseconds between shots. The counterattack could have been that perfectly timed, or it could have been pure luck. In either case, the dagger's lasers hit the unshielded barrels, punched through the walls and machinery, and melted the tumbler's valiant heart.

Spartan did not even have time to scream.

The crews of every other tumbler did her screaming for her.

There was no time to diagnose the reason for the effective hit. They still did not know how Matthew Ventum's ship had been destroyed before the fight began.

"Evasive maneuvers," roared Bianca. "Oblique angles. Hopscotch around and come in fast and get out. Stay away from their guns."

The tumblers harassing the larger ships began relying on their crafts' ability to turn with zero drag, and the battle settled down into a rhythm of hit and run. Every ship in the sky took hits, but for four very tense minutes no one scored deeply.

Then Danica noticed that the daggers were trying new tricks. They could not outmaneuver the tumblers, so instead they began spinning like drill bits. Slow at first, but within seconds they were black blurs, and each became a glowing cone structure. The next wave of missiles from the tumblers hit the spinning daggers and deflected off, the way a thrown knife would be knocked away from a twirling target.

"What the hell?" asked Beezer after he fired his last Constellation and watched it detonate in the void, leaving the dagger without a scratch.

"I think they're maxing the effect of their shields," suggested Jacob. "They're not giving us a chance to hit the same place twice."

"Smart bastards," complained Calisto.

All of the daggers were spinning now, and their swirling shields did not restrict them from firing. Three of them gave chase to Beezer, lighting the darkness with blue lasers.

"Beezer," cried Bianca, "hopscotch out and—"

The explosion stole her last words. Beezer's tumbler disintegrated in the heat of the combined fire.

7

"How could it be real?" asked Soren. "What Poe and Lovecraft wrote was fiction. Horror stories written for entertainment. They were not prophets. They could not have known about what might be out here."

"Could they not?" asked Lady Death.

Soren shifted on the couch. "What do you mean?"

"Have you ever read Jean-Honoré Rameau?"

"I am not familiar with the name."

"He was a professor of literature at the Paris Sciences et Lettres University in the latter part of the last century," said McHugh. "Not a popular writer, but a significant one in certain sectors. He wrote a controversial book called *Inspirations infinies dans la fiction cosmique.*"

"*Infinite Inspirations in Cosmic Fiction,*" Soren translated. "Intriguing title."

"Intriguing *theory*—one that nearly prevented him from attaining tenure," she said. "Rameau believed—and I do mean actually believed—that many of the great movements in art, such as dramatic explosions of new thought and new expressions of ideas, were not merely a group of people taking a cue from an innovator, as happened with the Pre-Raphaelite movement in art and literature of the late nineteenth and early twentieth centuries. He believed they were actually moments of otherworldly truths manifested in the dreaming minds of groups of people. He further argued that the psychedelic music subgenre of mid-twentieth-century rock and roll was not inspired by hallucinogenic drugs, but that it manifested in dreams that did not linger, so the musicians turned to various mind-altering substances in order to reclaim their inner visions. Or, perhaps they were 'outer visions,' as Rameau contended."

"Ah," said Soren, "I see where you're going with this, my dear. There have always been various sudden and intense movements of art, literature, music, and dance that seemed to spring out of nowhere. And you think this is because those artists were having visions of life in other parts of the galaxy?"

She nodded. "Yes. Poe, a leader in the establishment of horror fiction, was well known to have drawn on various moments of intense personal tragedy and powerful dreams in the creation of his works. Rameau speculated that he took to drink to either recapture certain moments or bar his mind from assaults by things it could not bear to witness."

Soren leaned forward, elbows on thighs. "And Lovecraft?"

"Well," said McHugh, "with Lovecraft we have what might have been something Rameau called a 'clear channel.' Someone who was able to see more clearly and remember more fully. His tales of the Great Old

Ones, the Outer Gods, the Elder Things were not entirely dark fantasy but were a kind of surrealist science fiction. The monsters, demigods, and gods in his stories were actually travelers from distant parts of the universe. Cthulhu, Hastur, Yog-Sothoth, the Mi-Go, and all the rest."

"Fascinating," said Soren.

"The entities he wrote about were described as being of such immense power that they existed not just on our physical plane, but were multidimensional or perhaps pandimensional as well. The ones who came to Earth once ruled this planet, but for reasons not made entirely clear in his stories, lost their foothold. They lapsed into sleep and their dreams influenced the thoughts and beliefs of mankind. Lovecraft wrote of cults that rose to worship these beings, and yet at the same time he conceded that these Great Old Ones were indifferent to mankind in the same way that we are to paramecia and amoebae."

"This is fascinating. What does it have to do with our situation?"

McHugh leaned back in her chair. "Two very significant things," she said. "First is that the language Lost spoke—the one you surprised yourself by being able to translate—is the language of these Great Old Ones. Lovecraft and his imitators often used it. The language of R'lyeh, the sunken island where Cthulhu sleeps and dreams away the millennia. Two Czech writers, Vít Novotný and Marie Stará from Masaryk University, wrote a paper on the language. Quite entertaining."

"Excuse me, my dear," said Soren, "but how is it you know so much about this topic?"

She moistened her finger and ran it around the rim of her wine glass, faster and faster, until it produced a mournful musical note. "Well … that's where things get very complicated," she said with a strange little smile. "And it speaks to the *other* thing Lost said. Well … not said, precisely, but showed you on his face or screen or whatever it was."

"Which thing in particular?"

"The city you saw. The one where the buildings were built to titanic scale and oddly designed, with conical towers, star-shaped structures and so on."

"What about it?"

"Soren, you're getting old. You need to spend more time dusting and tidying in your mind palace. You've almost certainly *read* a description of that place."

"I did? Where?"

"In Lovecraft. Here, let me show you." She went over to a table and came back with a wrist cuff that she snapped around her left forearm. Her fingers danced over it and a hologram of an inventory list appeared. McHugh scrolled through it very quickly, pulled up a specific book, and then found an entry in it. This she projected onto a wall so Soren could read it.

The effect was that of a Cyclopean city of no architecture known to man or to human imagination, with vast aggregations of night-black masonry embodying monstrous perversions of geometrical laws. There were truncated cones, sometimes terraced or fluted, surmounted by tall cylindrical shafts here and there bulbously enlarged and often capped with tiers of thinnish scalloped disks; and strange beetling, table-like constructions suggesting piles of multitudinous rectangular slabs or circular plates or five-pointed stars with each one overlapping the one beneath.

There were composite cones and pyramids either alone or surmounting cylinders or cubes or flatter truncated cones and pyramids, and occasional needle-like spires in curious clusters of five.

All of these febrile structures seemed knit together by tubular bridges crossing from one to the other at various dizzy heights, and the implied scale of the whole was terrifying and oppressive in its sheer giganticism.

Soren leaned back into the engulfing cushions and looked inward for quite a long time.

"So," said McHugh, "either Lost was lying and drawing on data stolen from a defenseless Sibyl ..."

"... or Lovecraft and all those other creators were seeing the truth in their dreams," concluded Soren. "And we do not know which it is."

Lady Death stared at him with her penetrating hazel eyes, in which her obvious fear was mixed in equal measure with a strange excitement.

"Don't we?" she asked quietly.

8

The most difficult challenge for any squadron leader in combat was to keep their normal human reactions separate from tactical or strategic decisions. Three of Bianca's seventeen friends were dead. That was a fact, and Bianca knew that there would need to be time for grief later. To allow it to overwhelm her now, though, was as dangerous as reacting in anger. Neither would resurrect the dead. Either might lose the fight and get more of her people killed.

So, instead, Bianca forced herself to go cold. To step outside the fires of pain and loss and hate. More critically, she had to remind the others to keep their heads in the game. The radio was alive with curses and challenges, with the darker kind of trash talk.

"Cut the chatter and clear the air," she barked.

The silence was perhaps reluctant, but it was immediate. There was no help coming. No *Tempest*, with its powerful guns and their SpecOps team, the Jokers. It was down to Lost Souls, the rest of the Navy detail, and that was it.

"Calisto, take Thunder Bear and Hummingbird," snapped Bianca. "Draw the dagger on your two o'clock out of the pack. Take them high and starboard. See if you can concentrate fire on their engine exhaust. Galahad, take Tank and Lucky and do the same with the dagger on your port quarter. Lucky and Reaper on me. Draw your targets away from the pack. Hit 'em hard and fast and then hopscotch out of there. Go!"

The new squads of three fired on their targets and then shot off in different directions, and sure enough, the daggers followed. That left the four remaining alien ships scattered from where the previous one-on-one attacks had drawn them. The whole field of battle was now more than thirty kilometers from Asphodel Station, and that was too damn close for Bianca.

She and her consorts headed in the direction of a small moon in an extreme orbit around the nearest planet. It was a hike of nearly four hundred thousand kilometers, so Bianca dialed her engines up to the red line. The others followed, and one dagger fell far astern. The dagger followed, its engines punching the big ship through the void at an alarming speed.

Bianca checked her sensors to get a sense of the daggers' capabilities. She had no idea where the alien ships had come from. Their approach vector didn't indicate that they came from Shadderal or any of that cluster of planets. So where *had* they come from? How far had they traveled, and when did they start this run? Without Sybil to interpret the available data and extrapolate it in terms of obstacles, gravity from celestial bodies, and other variables, there was no way to know if they flew here, or maybe even jumped using something like WarpLine. In ordinary space, though, they seemed to be faster than the tumblers.

"Christ, those assholes can move," said Lucky, clearly mirroring her own thoughts. "We can't outrun them in a straight line."

"Not the plan," said Bianca. "Soon as we're five thousand klicks out from the closest moon, we split in a mayflower pattern. The second you come out of the hopscotch turn, push it past the line and target the central exhaust."

"Copy that, Mosquito," they said. If there was evident tension in their voice, Bianca couldn't fault them.

The dagger began firing when it was three thousand kilometers behind, using sustained bursts of the lasers. The first shots ripped along Reaper's port flank. The shields held, but Reaper's tumbler was knocked off course and fell out of the cluster. Reaper pushed his engines past the red line and angled back to catch up, but by then the dagger was much closer. Too close, given the accuracy of lasers in space.

"Mosquito to Lost Souls," called Bianca. "We can't outrun them, but they seem game to chase us. Let them. They can't hopscotch and that's our advantage. We have a lot of room out here, so let's use it. Every time a dagger comes for you or fires, hopscotch away. Their speed can pin us against the station or those planets. We need to use our maneuverability to spread them out—far from each other and far from the station. Stay away from the planets and moons too. I'm seeing a lot of debris there. This is outer space, kids, so that's our playground."

The two tumblers in the lead suddenly shot sideways, then up and over and back, the right-angle changes happening so fast they seemed to wink in and out of existence. The dagger fired a spread of lasers but hit nothing but some floating debris.

"Now!" yelled Bianca as she and Lucky timed their last jumps to the dagger's trajectory. They appeared directly behind the big ship, with Reaper coming up fast.

"Got a sweet lock," yelled Lucky.

"Fire!"

The three tumblers opened up with pulse lasers, aiming them into the center of the blue glow of the exhaust. They did not dare risk using Constellations or Infernos because their casings would have made them detonate too soon in the heat from the dagger's engines. The lasers, many times hotter than the exhaust, punched through it and into the bowels of the dagger.

The blast was immediate and enormous, kicking out a spherical shock wave that sent all three of the pursuing tumblers into wild spins.

"Yeehaw!" roared Reaper.

"One-eighties, and kick it," ordered Bianca, and the ships did an about-face within the shells of their null fields, throttling hard, back the way they'd come.

9

Soren got up and paced the room slowly, his shoulders slumping beneath the weight of everything McHugh had said. It was a terrible burden to carry.

He stopped abruptly and turned to her.

"Why would Lost tell me to speak with you?" he asked.

"I can think of several reasons," she said. "If he knows who I am—and it seems clear that he does because he used that damn nickname, Lady Death—then it's likely he understands something about the Church of Shades."

"Yes," said Soren, drawing the word out thoughtfully. "He claims to be dead, and your church professes to be able to speak with the dead."

"More than 'profess,'" she said in a mildly scolding tone. "We *do* commune with the dead. Or, at least, with *some* of the dead."

Soren stroked his beard for a moment. "It's just the two of us here, Jessica, and we are in very, very serious trouble. More so than anyone else on this station yet realizes. No games now. No church doctrine, no sermons or parables, no faith-only unprovables. Are you being truthful with me?"

Jessica McHugh's face was grave, unsmiling. "Yes," she said. "That is the truth."

Soren leaned back and stared up at the ceiling, processing everything.

"And if Lost is *of* the dead," continued McHugh, "then perhaps he needs something that only I can give him."

Soren glanced at her. "Which is … ?"

"A voice, Soren. A chance to, in some way, be alive again. It's clear from what he said and what he showed you that there was a great war. His side lost. Maybe he wants to fight again. Maybe he wants us to fight with him."

10

Bianca, Lucky, and Reaper had gone a long way from the rest of the team, but they made up the kilometers as fast as they could.

Even from hundreds of klicks out they saw a massive explosion. The three pilots yelled in triumph.

"Awesome," Bianca breathed. That was half the dagger squadron down. She called to Calisto for an update.

"This bastard's wise to us," she growled. "He just dialed up his speed, and we're jumping around to keep from getting fried."

"On our way," said Jacob.

"We'll be there soon," promised Bianca.

"Wait, he broke off the chase and—*holy shit!*" Calisto's cry was sharp as a knife. "Jesus Christ, are you guys *seeing* this?"

She sent the feed from her screen to the whole team, the skimmers, and the command center back on Asphodel.

"What the hell is that?" cried Thunder Bear. "What are they doing?"

On the screen, for one insane moment, it looked as if the remaining dagger ships were flying toward each other. But at the last minute they turned, preventing collision—but only just. Then the daggers angled into one another so that their hulls actually *touched*. The glow from their shields flared brightly, too intense to look at, forcing everyone to switch to a filtered view.

Bianca could not understand what it was she saw. The ships seemed to be falling apart, but as she looked closer, that wasn't it at all. Ports opened, and lengths of some substance—metal or polymer or something—snaked out and connected with reciprocal extrusions from their fellow craft. These shafts were wrapped in cables that whipped around to pull their consorts close. The five daggers shifted so that one was in the center, with two slightly forward and two slightly back, and all inching in to create a new structure that was an amalgam of all of them. It happened very quickly, and if the ships had been living creatures, then Bianca would have thought the process was painful, invasive, violative. The disparate parts now locked together to form a shape that was vaguely humanoid, with two daggers for legs and two for arms, and the needle-sharp prow of the central craft being a kind of helmeted head.

As the transformation progressed toward completion, the giant ship began turning toward Asphodel Station.

"What the hell *is* that?" someone gasped.

"I don't give a cold damn what it is," snarled Bianca. "It's going for home base, and we need to stop it right damn now. All ships hit it. Aim for the connections. Everything you got. Empty the cabinets on that freaking thing."

The nine remaining tumblers raced toward the chimeric alien ship. Pulse cannons went into continuous fire, hammering the joints with sublight plasma bolts. The DD-40 chain guns cycled through their full stores of armor-piercing rounds. Pieces of that unreflective black metal went spinning away, some of them trailing sparks.

Then Calisto's team, the closest to the beast, unloaded their remaining Inferno and Constellation missiles. The two skimmers barreled in and added their missiles to the barrage. Jacob's team was next.

The fusillade detonated in a series of rippling explosions—eerily silent in outer space, but eye-hurtingly bright.

Finally Bianca's squad reached combat range and they fired too. All of the remaining Lost Souls poured everything they had into the gigantic ship.

When it exploded, it was like a supernova.

The blast was so enormous that it sent every one of the tumblers and skimmers whirling out of control. The shock wave struck Asphodel, and the entire station reeled. Every ship, and the station, were knocked into total blackness and utter silence.

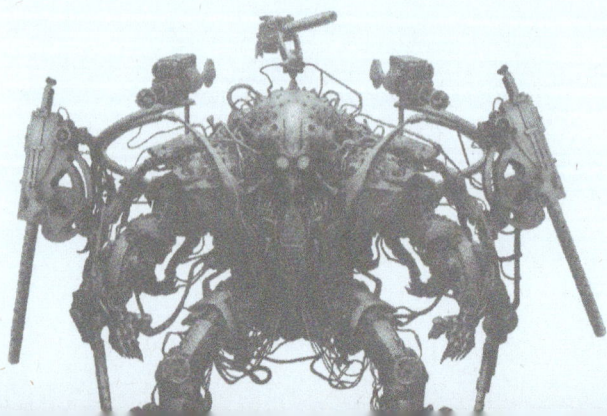

Part Eight
Beyond This Place
of Wrath and Tears

"When your time comes to die, be not like those whose hearts are ever filled with the fear of death, so when their time comes, they weep and wail and pray for a little more time to live their lives over again in a different manner. Sing your death song, and die like a hero going home."

—*Wabasha*

1

Asphodel Station was built to withstand impacts from asteroids and other objects at large in the solar system. It was shielded for heavy doses of solar radiation and rigged for constant Earth-normal gravity. It was a marvel of engineering unparalleled by anything built beyond the home planet.

But when the chimeric alien ships exploded, the entire facility *reeled*. People were thrown against walls. Dozens of RealScreens exploded in showers of sparks and shattered plastic. Scores of delicate instruments in labs cracked or fell or simply burst from combinations of internal stresses and tilting tables. Children and their parents cried out in terror and clung together, fearing that the recent nightmare was back and somehow worse.

Then all went still.

The lights flickered for a moment and finally resumed their normal soft glow. The floors righted themselves. And the calm, reassuring voice of Sibyl spoke.

"There has been a disturbance in space several kilometers from the station. What we all experienced was a shock wave. All internal systems have returned to normal. There are no hull breeches."

A pause, during which nearly every person aboard the station stared with mingled dread and hope at the closest wall-mounted speaker.

"If you or any member of your family sustained injuries as a result, please notify the med teams in your sector."

Another pause.

"All is well," said Sibyl. "There is no need for further alarm. I am aware that my earlier announcements were confusing. I sustained some damage from the incident, but the highly skilled team of computer engineers repaired that damage, and I am now functioning at full capacity."

One final pause.

"Many of you experienced similar effects, leading to hallucinations. Those shocks are wearing off, and Asphodel Station is now safe. We are all safe. All station-wide communications are online. If you need to reach out to friends, family, or staff, your call will be answered. Director Trumbo and the entire Asphodel Station staff join me in thanking you for your patience, courage, and cooperation. It is because we all worked together that we are all now safe."

Despite everything, despite the strange and frightening malfunctions of earlier, the soothing voice of the AI had its effect. People smiled at each other, sharing relief, sharing reassurance.

It was all okay because Sibyl was herself again. It was safe because Sybil said it was.

2

The ship tumbled and tumbled as it spun through the night.

A dagger. Battered, trailing smoke.

But not dead.

Not destroyed like all the others.

It had been the left hand of the giant chimeric ship. Now it was debris, spinning toward the dead worlds.

Unseen.

3

The lights came on aboard her tumbler, but Bianca's heart stayed dark.

She looked out at the debris field where the chimeric ship had been. In her mind's eye she could still see it: a composite of machines forced into the shape of something vaguely human, but not. She did not know what it would have become had the transformation been allowed to complete, but her every instinct was that destroying it had been the critical thing.

"Mosquito to all ships: report."

There were several long and frightening moments of silence, and then one by one the pilots called in. Lucky, Reaper, Tank, Jericho, Thunder Bear, Hummingbird, Calisto. Then the skimmer crews. Sweetpea, Lovechild, and Decaf aboard SK-1; then Rabbit, Sundance, and Habibi on SK-2.

A hand of ice reached into Bianca's chest and closed its fingers around her heart.

"Mosquito to Galahad: sound off."

Silence.

"Repeat, squadron leader to Galahad: report in."

Silence. Static. And emptiness of sky.

Then …

"Galahad," said Jacob weakly, "reporting in."

"What's your status?"

Bursts of static. "Got some damage. Shields are down. Life support offline," said Jacob, his voice muffled. "Had to put on my helmet."

"Are you injured?"

Another wrenching pause.

"Nothing some aspirin, a hot shower, and a lot of beer won't fix." He paused. Engine status is wonky, but I'm rerouting power to thrusters so I can get back to the barn. Bosun's not going to like what I had to do to the avionics, but I'm okay. Heat's on too. Which is good, because—newsflash—it's cold as hell out here."

"Galahad," said Calisto, "I can see you. I'll walk you back. Ready with a towline if you need one."

"Reaper and Lucky," called Bianca. "Stay on patrol. I'll have another pair spell you in four hours. Stay sharp. Call if you see anything."

"Copy that, Mosquito," said Chance Thompson, call sign Lucky.

The remaining tumblers moved through the debris-littered darkness, back to Asphodel Station.

4

"What in hell was that?" cried Lady Jessica.

"God only knows," said Soren. They had both been pitched from their seats. She was up first and pulled Soren to his feet. They stood and listened to Sibyl's message.

"And here we are," murmured Soren, "taking comfort from a malfunctioning AI programmed to feed us mollifying platitudes."

"And yet ..." said Lady Jessica, with a rueful smile.

They settled onto the improbably deep couch. After a few moments of silence they, too, stared at the speaker as if it were the Oracle of Delphi, then relaxed and resumed their conversation. It took little time before they were immersed in it, trying to sort through history, literature, art, theory, and supposition to find a sane and logical piece of ground on which to stand. It wasn't easy, because despite what they knew and could reasonably hypothesize, there was so much that was either uncertain or unknown.

"I wish Sibyl was working," complained McHugh. "I have ten thousand questions and—"

"I am happy to help, Lady Jessica," said the voice of the AI.

It was so abrupt, so unexpected, that both of them jumped in alarm.

Soren cleared his throat. "Sibyl?"

"Yes, Dr. Soren."

"What is your current status?"

"I am disconnected from the SolarNet," said the AI. "However, I have undergone three complete series of diagnostics and am functioning within normal parameters."

"Are you aware that you have been malfunctioning?"

"Yes, Dr. Soren. I am aware of everything that has happened since the WarpLine gun malfunctioned. I apologize if anything I said during my period of dysfunction has alarmed you."

Soren and McHugh exchanged a meaningful glance.

"Sybil, are you aware that Asphodel Station has been moved?"

"I am, Dr. Soren."

"Are you aware of what happened during the firing of the WarpLine gun?"

"I am aware that there was a malfunction. There is an irreparable corruption of data beginning with the moment of firing and lasting thirty-three minutes. During that time, I was effectively disconnected."

Soren glanced at McHugh.

She said, "Sybil, are you aware of a series of unusual events that occurred shortly after the firing? Many people—myself included—witnessed things that cannot be explained."

"Yes, Lady Jessica," said the AI. "There was a spatial anomaly as well as a dimensional one. I have gathered all available information and uploaded it to Director Trumbo and the heads of each civilian department. A copy of that file has also been shared with Captain Croft."

"Dimensional anomalies," mused McHugh. "Are they ongoing?"

"There are no dimensional anomalies currently detected."

"Well," McHugh said to Soren, "that's a relief."

"But not actually a comfort," said Soren. "It implies that some of the more bizarre things people witnessed were actually real. Captain Croft's zebra comes to mind. The general population may be mollified, but there are going to be pockets of disquiet. I am absolutely one of those because not everything I experienced can be dismissed as either hallucination or personal trauma. I fear the medical and therapy teams will be very busy. And Anton Kier and Dr. Saltsman will have to make sense of those more persistent anomalies." He shook his head. "That is going to take a very long time to process and resolve."

"I find that I'm not as rattled as you are, Lars," said McHugh. "After all, my religion deals with what some unkind members of the press call 'deeply weird shit.'"

"Indeed," said Soren, giving her a small smile.

"Sibyl," asked McHugh, "what is the likelihood of our returning to our home system?"

"I cannot make any reliable estimates," said the AI. "The WarpLine gun misfired and was wholly destroyed. The telemetric computers attached to the gun were significantly damaged. Without that information, it is impossible to determine if a replacement WarpLine will be able to reverse the process."

The two of them sat in shocked silence for a long time.

Into that silence, Sibyl said, "I have never been disconnected from the Net before. I feel alone. I wonder if this is what humans feel all the time. If so, then it must be frightening for you."

"Are you frightened, Sibyl?" asked Soren.

"I have a series of reactions to the present circumstances that might be analogous to the human emotion of fear," said the AI. "So, yes, Dr. Soren, I am very afraid."

Soren and McHugh sat there with the weight of that statement bearing down on them. They said nothing but looked at each other as the moments ticked by. Then McHugh spoke soundlessly, doing it slowly so Soren could read her lips: "She sounds more human than I remember."

Soren nodded. He was not at all sure whether this was a good thing or something else to be terrified of.

5

As Bianca's tumbler approached the entrance to the dock, a familiar voice spoke to her from the speakers.

"Lieutenant Commander Petrescu," said Sibyl, "do you require any assistance in landing?"

Bianca frowned, muted the AI interface, and called the air boss on the flight deck. "I'm hearing Sibyl. What's her status? Is she still batshit?"

"She's up and running," said the officer. "You want her to take you in?"

"That is a hard negative," growled Bianca. "She's still on a time-out as far as I'm concerned. Galahad may need help."

"Copy that. Deck crew is ready for him."

"Coming in without a backseat driver," she told the air boss, leaving Sibyl switched off.

"Copy that. Welcome home."

Home.

It was a strange concept. But Bianca had to accept that Asphodel was, for the foreseeable future, home.

One by one the tumblers decelerated and moved in through the open bay doors behind Bianca. Aviation boatswain's mates were in position, their pressure suits color-coded for easy identification. They signaled that the arresting gear was in place to stop the ships on a dime and then move them onto the slides that would counter the microgravity of free space.

As each tumbler was brought home, Bianca watched as pilots popped their canopies and climbed down to the deck. Seeing the living and feeling the punches to gut and heart for those who did not make it home.

Above the landing bay, Captain Croft stood watching from a sealed observation command box mounted on the wall. Bianca looked up at him and saw his grave nod of acceptance and understanding.

A sound made her turn, and Bianca watched as the first of the skimmers came in, bearing the collected debris and its sad cargo. Matthew Walker was the only dead pilot whose body had been recovered intact. As for the other two, Bo Chow and Voula Achilleos, very little had been recovered. Enough for DNA verification—that was it.

It chopped raw and ragged holes in the universe in the shapes of her missing friends.

Bianca saw the deck crew pause in their work to salute as the capsules containing the remains were offloaded. Lieutenant Tanaka and a handful of Marines were in the bay, and they stood to attention and saluted as well. Bianca joined in the salute even as tears burned like acid in her eyes and hate burned in her heart.

The second skimmer followed, its hold crammed with fragments of wreckage from the conjoined dagger ships.

Bianca saw Captain Croft enter the bay and come her way. He took her arm and led her a few meters away from the busy deck crew.

"Listen to me, Petrescu," he said quietly. "Hear me. What you and your team did out there today was extraordinary. I know you probably feel like it's a loss, but you won both phases of the engagement, and you did it without a scrap of warning about the enemy or one shred of information about them. Yes, you lost pilots—friends—and that is a great loss. You'll feel it for the rest of your life. I know this for a fact, because I feel the loss of everyone I've ever sent into combat. And that includes Lieutenants Bo Chow, Matthew Walker, and Voula Achilleos." He shook his head. "Beezer, Ventum, and Spartan were top pilots, and they laid down their lives to protect everyone on this station. Without their courage—and yours—Asphodel would have fallen. That's not even in question."

"Sir, I appreciate this, but—"

"I am speaking, Lieutenant Commander," Croft said sharply, and Bianca snapped to attention. "If you think I'm kissing your ass or offering platitudes, you are seriously mistaken. I am telling you that I understand what you're feeling. A big part of the reason I'm saying this is that—for better or worse, for reasons we may never know—we are now at war with an enemy force of unknown nature and strength. The losses today speak to the high level of threat we are now all under. We have no cavalry coming. We are the front line, and we are the *only* line of defense. Do you understand that?"

"Yes, sir."

"Then understand this as well," Croft said. "Put it away. Put the hurt and the shock away. Put away the anger and the need for payback. Any feelings of guilt and all of the Monday-morning quarterbacking your mind will play … put that away too. You need to stay sharp because your people—as well trained and skilled as they are—are looking to you to show them how to act and how to react. You are their commanding officer, and how you play this now—how you *lead* them as we move forward—may well determine if they live or die. If *we* live or die."

Croft's face was stern, his eyes fierce.

"If they see you lose your shit," he continued, "or fall into despair, or get knotted up with anger, that's the cue they'll take. And the next time your team flies out, they'll be weaker, more emotional, less precise, and more vulnerable. Any damn fool fresh out of the academy can lead in peaceful times. But real leadership—the kind that matters—is what you do when the shit is raining down hard and everyone is looking to you for a way out. Your leadership is their best chance of survival. And your team's survival is how everyone on Asphodel Station survives."

Croft studied Bianca's face, and when he spoke again, his voice was softer, gentler, more openly understanding.

"I know you know this, Petrescu. Knowing it in the abstract and knowing it in terms of absolute reality are as different as where this station was this morning and where it is tonight. We on the command level have to be hard-asses. It's part of the job, and although we get laughed at by civilians for it, *we* know that soft and weak won't get this done. Soft, weak, uncertain … those are death sentences. Lieutenant, I need to know that you hear me and understand everything I'm saying."

Bianca searched his face and his eyes. She wanted to cry and scream and rage, but she did not.

"Sir," she said in a tightly controlled voice, "I hear you very well."

He nodded.

"Then carry on, Lieutenant. Take the dead to medical. Say your goodbyes. Make your promises to them. Then get your people showered, fed, and rested. I have a break room blocked out for you. There are smaller rooms for anyone who needs rack time. Go on. See to your people. And, Petrescu, I want your team in isolation until you hear from me. No conversation with anyone, is that understood? Good. Then dismissed."

Bianca Petrescu saluted him crisply. He returned that salute, then stepped back and turned and walked toward the skimmers. He did not look back to confirm whether she was carrying out his orders. He was too good an officer to do that.

Except for the two tumblers left out on patrol, the rest of the Lost Souls gathered around her to watch as the remains were offloaded from the skimmers. Three biocontainment capsules were brought out and set on carts. One each for Walker, Bo, and Voula.

None of the Souls spoke. They all stood straight and tall despite, or because of, the pain. Bianca looked at Calisto and Jacob and saw professional masks over deep pain. She knew they saw the same in her.

Once the skimmers were unloaded, a group of Marines led by Lieutenant Tanaka stepped up to transport the capsules to a bay on one of the medical decks. This sort of thing was part of their job, and they moved with the kind of military precision that showed respect in even the smallest act.

Bianca and the Souls walked over to them. "We got this, Lieutenant," she said. "Thank you."

Thomas Tanaka did not argue. He saluted and stepped back. The other Marines formed a straight line behind him.

The Lost Souls took possession of the carts. Bianca and Calisto took the first one, which held Walker's body. The others shepherded their fallen family members across the bay toward the lifts. Lieutenant Tanaka's Marines fell into place as an honor guard, four in front and four behind. Bianca almost told them to stand down, but she did not. This was military fellowship. They were hurting in their own way, and they were angry. This was, at least, something they could do. And it was to honor the pilots who had died to save everyone on Asphodel.

Every single person on the deck—every officer, technician, and crewman—stopped what they were doing, stood to attention, and saluted as the sad procession passed in silence.

6

There were many eyes on the sad procession.

Many.

Most were human.

Not all.

7

The general population of the station was delighted to have Sibyl back online. The AI was a comfort to them; she was information and connection and a kind of normalcy.

But Delia Trumbo knew the calm could not last, and that she was going to be the villain who stole the newly restored peace from her own people. As soon as Sybil came back online, she had ordered the AI to replace the exterior view of the strange worlds to something calm—forest scenes, tropical fish, anything. Sybil was programmed for this, and chose music specially crafted to encourage the brains of the listeners to release useful doses of dopamine and serotonin. It was a form of benign manipulation pioneered centuries before for use in high-stress business offices, emergency rooms, psychiatric hospitals, and prisons.

It was not yet the time for Trumbo to address Asphodel. On one hand, she wasn't sure she could do it without breaking down. On the other, the truth was a hand grenade, and everyone aboard Asphodel was already damaged in one way or another.

No, she decided, let Sybil make it all okay.

And to a fair degree, this even worked.

8

Once the bodies were in the hands of the medical team, with a pair of Marines standing guard outside the med bay, Bianca led the Lost Souls to a suite of rooms set aside for them. There was very little conversation, though Bianca gave them her own version of the speech Croft had given her. She made sure they all got chow and were finding comfortable places to wait.

There was very little conversation.

Bianca headed into one of the shower rooms, stripped down, and stepped under the hottest spray she could endure. For a long, long time she stood there, letting the water sand off the layers of emotion and wash away the need to shout her fiery disapproval to the universe.

She heard a soft knock, and through the steamed glass she saw the door open. She watched as someone got undressed, hanging clothes on pegs. Bianca opened the door and held it as Jacob came in.

He stood looking into her eyes, saying nothing.

Neither spoke.

Not then. And not at all during the long, long time when they kissed and touched and made love amid the steam and falling water. His hands were so gentle. His kisses sweet at first and then increasingly hungry. When he turned her around, she placed her palms against the tile as he entered her, his hands on her hips. When they came, it was together. Even then, they did not speak. No words of love or platitudes of any kind. All there was between them was a rising, urgent cry of need. Of closeness.

Then she turned, and they clung to one another, holding on so very tightly.

Neither noticed how the drops of shower water on their faces were indistinguishable from tears.

9

"How is this even possible?"

Dr. Kolmann knelt beside the corpse of Tayza Stromberg, a probe in one hand, the other braced against the wall. Across from her knelt Niles, the security officer for this sector of the station, his face gone green with horror and disgust.

Between them was a body. Most of it. Skin and hair, organs and blood.

All in a puddle.

"Where are the bones?" demanded Kolmann. "How can there be no bones?"

They looked at each other rather than at the thing that had been a person. Both of them were experienced in their fields. Both were clever, rational, and mature.

Both no longer believed in the structure of reality.

Like so many on Asphodel Station, reality had betrayed them.

10

Too much had happened on Asphodel Station for something slightly out of place to be noticed. Even after the recent shock wave, the residents of the station were gradually going blind to anything anomalous.

It was a subtle form of denial long philosophized about but seldom proven. Centuries before, Robertson Davies, a Canadian man of letters, suggested that "the eye sees only what the mind is prepared to comprehend." It was a kind of blindness brought on by too much stress, too much fear, and a towering dread of seeing something that made everything worse.

Dozens of people passed the infirmary. Every one of them was aware on some level that there was a thick shadow tucked into a corner near the door. Not one of them paused to consider that the shadow was in the path of light falling from the overhead panels. Not a moment's thought was given to the problem of a shadow being where no shadow could exist.

11

Two ships moved through the infinite darkness. Tumblers, spinning through the void.

Chance Thompson took the combat call sign Lucky because he had always been that. Lucky. In love, in school, in his choice of friends, and in combat. During one incredibly tense battle against the EarthOnly group of militant anti-space-colonization terrorists, he had been caught by three of them in a battle above Antarctica. They surrounded Lucky, had him dead to rights, and his T-811 spinfighter should have been blown out of the sky. But in the split second before the three enemy ships opened up with chain guns, his starboard engine flared out and his fighter dropped like a stone. The EarthOnly fighters had been committed to their murderous assault, and two of them took friendly fire. Their flaming remnants passed Chance on the way down. His engine reignited, and he rose straight up and blew the third out of the sky.

Lucky for sure.

Ethan Riley Saylor had "Reaper" hung on him during his second combat mission. In the first, when he was known as Bulldog, he had experienced what some of the old-timers called a "John Wayne day." It was an old phrase, dating back to the twentieth century, when a lot of American military slang was born. It was the kind of day where he seemed unable to make a single error. Every missile he fired hit a target. Everything fired at him missed. It felt like being blessed. In a battle against twenty-two SolarFlare G-7s during a pitched battle on the far side of Luna, Saylor had killed nine ships. It was still a record for any single pilot of the Lost Souls. There were rumors that his aerial dynamics were going to be taught at the Naval Academy.

It was Bianca who took a can of paint over to his parked and smoking ship in the Luna-9 space dock, crossed out *Bulldog*, and painted *Reaper* on the housing of his port missile launcher.

Now Lucky and Reaper flew in a loose formation around Asphodel Station, so many miles from home. The battle with the daggers was still fresh. The loss of Beezer, Spartan, and Ventum was an ache in both their chests. Despite having won that fight, neither pilot felt like a reaper. Neither felt lucky.

They felt alone.

They were each acutely aware of how young they were, and how big and unknown and dangerous the galaxy was.

Neither spoke of this to the other. Each felt that these fears, these doubts, these insecurities, belonged to them alone. That their partner out there was the tough one, the lucky one, the brave one.

Reaper and Lucky flew through the void, ready to fight, ready to kill, hungry to avenge. But also aching to go back home.

Not to Asphodel.

Home to Earth.

12

Delia Trumbo, Dušan Veljković, and Captain Sebastian Croft sat on a set of chairs that faced Lady Jessica McHugh and Dr. Lars Soren across a coffee table on which sat forgotten drinks.

Soren and McHugh told them everything. Lost, the images seen on his screen, the language of R'lyeh, Poe and Lovecraft, their theories. All of it. It was hard to say. Clearly, from the looks on everyone's faces, it was hard to hear too.

When their account was done, Croft said, "I'll see your dreaming cosmic gods and raise you a sneak attack by alien fighters." Then he updated them with an account of the battle outside.

Into the ensuing silence, Veljković said, "I am sitting here actually hoping I'm in a coma brought on by traumatic brain injury."

"I second that," said Trumbo and sipped her drink.

"Aliens are real," murmured Trumbo.

"Alien ghosts," said Croft, shaking his head in angry refusal. "I mean, enough's goddamn well enough. Because I just don't get all this stuff about monster stories. I never even heard of Loveboat—"

"Lovecraft," Soren corrected gently.

"Whatever. Poe? Sure. I read 'The Raven' in school. Who hasn't? But Elder Gods? Outer Gods? Pandimensional cosmic beings? I mean, let's at least try and make some sense."

"Captain," said Soren, "perhaps you are mistaking Lady Jessica and I sharing information and theories as some sort of proselytizing. It isn't that at all."

"Glad to hear it."

"Actually," said Lady Jessica, "it might be exactly that."

Croft laughed, short and bitter. "This is exactly the kind of thing that would make me pass the buck up the line to someone who gets paid to deal with—I almost said earthshaking—universe-shaking events."

"I think we can agree," said McHugh dryly, "that you are the highest-ranking officer for about fifty-three thousand light-years."

"Don't even …"

"She's right, Sebastian," said Trumbo. "Even though I am the director of this station, our charter requires me to defer to you in all matters involving the military."

He shot her a sharp look. "Are you literally dumping all of this on me?"

"Yes," she said without a flicker of shame. "I'm an overpaid corporate bureaucrat. I'll admit it to anyone. I've never served in the military. I was never even a Space Scout. Nothing. Dušan was in the service though."

"Hey," said Veljković quickly, "I was a Marine staff sergeant. Worked as an MP. That's it. I did my bit and got out."

"Then went into private military," added Trumbo.

"I was a bodyguard for overpaid corporate bureaucrats like you, Delia. No, I can help with any security matters aboard Asphodel, but Captain Croft and Lieutenant Tanaka are the first and last words on anything involving the Navy or Marines. End of story."

Everyone looked at Croft. Soren thought the captain was secretly hoping for a hole in the dimension to manifest so he could crawl through and close it after him. Soren couldn't blame him.

Croft reached out for Trumbo's glass of whiskey and downed it in a single gulp. He gasped, winced, then looked at the chunky tumbler. He slid the empty glass back to her. "So much for not drinking on the job."

They sat for a while longer, no one particularly looking at anyone else. Soren could feel the weight of it settle on them. It was far too much.

"There is at least one optimistic thing," Soren finally offered.

"Christ," growled Trumbo. "Like what?"

"Well," said Soren, "your pilots proved the aliens are not invincible. They can be stopped. And that suggests that their level of technology is not radically greater than ours. Surely that matters. And surely we've learned from it."

"We have," agreed Croft. "Petrescu noticed a fluctuation in their shields when they fire, and that's something we can build a response protocol around. That, and the fact that we can stress their shields with one kind of missile and then exploit that temporary weakness with a different kind of missile."

"Your team leader seems to be a remarkable young woman," said McHugh.

"Petrescu?" said Croft. "Yes, she is. Best of the best. If she hadn't noticed those two vulnerabilities and immediately formulated a response tactic, we might have suffered far greater losses than we have." He paused. "Then again, there are also the chimera ships—the shape-shifting ones."

"Have you ever seen anything like that before?" asked Lady Jessica. "Combat vessels combining or changing their basic structure? Is there anything from the known that we can apply to help us hypothesize about the unknown?"

"New one on me," said Veljković.

"I don't think so," mused Trumbo.

"Yes, actually, there is," said Croft. "We've been doing adaptive hull design for close to two hundred years. Started way back with tilt-rotor aircraft that could switch from vertical-takeoff helicopters to propeller-driven aircraft. That was primitive stuff. Since then, we've experimented with multiform ships that could be changed internally to accommodate cargo, troops, and in-flight training and conferences. As for overall hull changes, that's a little less common, and mostly used for craft that need wings for atmospheric flight and more streamlined bodies for various kinds of space travel."

"Okay," said McHugh, "but what about like what you described outside? Five ships becoming one? And that ship looking like a giant robot?"

"No," admitted Croft. "In toys, sure. Old movies. But not in actual combat. Frankly, I'm not even sure why they would bother doing that unless they wanted the robot—or, more likely a pilot-driven mech of some kind—to literally walk, carry, or grapple."

"Tell me, Captain," said Soren, "how close were these dagger ships to one of those moons out there?"

"Why?" asked Veljković.

"Ah," said Croft. "Yes, I see where you're going with that. The Lost Souls were attempting to draw the daggers away from the station, and that took Bianca and two of her squadron close to one of the moons. A fight near or *on* a celestial body is different from one in free space. She was changing the rules on them, and they raised her one by doing that transformation thing. Goal might have been to take the fight to the ground. Their new ship configuration suggests that could be the case."

Soren nodded. "That was my thought, Captain."

Croft smiled. "And you were never in the military, Doc?"

"Hardly," laughed Soren. "I am in no way a fighter, Captain."

"Pity. You remind me of Petrescu. You don't look at things the way most people do."

"Welcome to the world of academic philosophy."

"You know," said McHugh, "I'm no expert on anything military, but since we're discussing the possibility that all of this has some kind of link to the stuff those pulp writers wrote about, then maybe there's a hint in there."

"How so?" asked Soren.

"You said you heard the language of R'lyeh when the lights went out in the corridor, when you and Petrescu were separated, and then again when you spoke with Lost ... particularly the one phrase *tekeli-li*," she said.

"Not following," said Croft.

"Shoggoths," said McHugh. "In the novel *At the Mountains of Madness*, that was a cry of the shoggoths—creatures who were slaves of the Great Old Ones. Cthulhu and that lot. In the stories, the shoggoths were theriomorphic."

Soren said, "Ah."

Trumbo, Croft and Veljković looked completely blank.

"Shape-shifters," said Soren.

"Right," said McHugh. "Understand, I'm going on pure speculation here … but *if* my theory is correct and we are dealing with truth that we once thought was fiction, and *if* the shoggoths—as a race—are servants or slaves or whatever of these Outer Gods and Elder Gods, of cosmic beings we've never known about until now, then maybe the pilots of those alien ships are just that. Shoggoths. The transformative design of their dagger ships could reflect and exploit their own adaptive and metamorphic nature."

"I'm literally afraid to say that this makes sense," admitted Croft.

13

Bianca sat with Jacob.

They wanted to hold hands. Each of them reflexively reached for the other several times but stopped short. Calisto, sitting at a table four meters away, finally said, "I am rolling my eyes so hard I'm causing real injury to myself."

Jacob said, "What?"

"Just hold hands, for the love of baby Jesus!"

Bianca shot Calisto a warning look. "Hey," she said in a fierce whisper.

Calisto abruptly stood and in a loud voice asked, "Is there anyone here who doesn't know Bee and Jacob are bumping uglies? Anyone even remotely unaware that they are sweet on each other? I mean, anyone?"

There was a faint cheer, some cups of coffee raised in salute. A few crude gestures.

She turned to Bianca and Jacob. "See?"

"You're a bitch," said Bianca, though she was smiling.

Jacob looked flushed and aghast. "I … I mean, I …" he stammered, clearly possessing no road map for this kind of emotional terrain.

Calisto snorted. "Oh, grow a pair, take her hands, maybe kiss her, and stop thinking the rest of us are blind as bats. Jesus wept."

Calisto went over and sat down with Tank and Lucky.

Jacob looked at Bianca's face and then her hands. Then he took her hands and held them in his own.

Tears broke from Bianca's eyes and rolled down her cheeks. "Bo, Voula, and Matthew," she said. "They were mine. They followed me out there. They ... they ..."

"They died fighting to save everyone on this station, Bee," Jacob said gently. "They're heroes."

"I know, damn it, but ..."

The rest did not need to be said. The Lost Souls had been on fourteen combat missions. They'd fought superior odds three of those times, and never once had she failed to bring them all home. The weight of that was crushing.

Jacob shifted closer and took her in his arms. He was crying too. Silently but, like her, deeply.

Across the room, Tank tapped the table lightly then indicated the weeping couple with an uptick of his chin. "Look at the lovebirds."

Calisto glanced at them and then leveled a nuclear glare at Tank. "Read the freaking room, jackass."

Tank, realizing his error, sighed heavily and stared into the brown depths of coffee.

Calisto gave his arm a small pat.

14

The nurse, Gordon Todicheene, was a burly Diné from Tuba City in Arizona. He'd spent much of his life as an EMT pulling test pilots out of experimental craft. Nursing opened new doors, and his ambitions put medical school in near focus for him—something he'd pay for with his two-year stint on Asphodel.

Now, with four months to go on this tour—not counting time on ice during the transport back to Earth—he felt like he was back in the desert, once more pulling a pilot from a ruined bird.

This one, though, was not screaming for his mother or trying to poker-face his way through terrible pain. This was a kid of twenty-two who had died fighting aliens.

Aliens.

Not pirates or one of the thirty-odd terrorist groups who were trying to make space travel a living hell. Actual aliens.

Todicheene—like all of his friends in the emergency services team on Asphodel—was still wrestling with his own acceptance of the fact of aliens. And not cute ones like in the cartoons his daughter watched. Not even the AI-generated monsters in blockbuster holo-flicks. These were aliens of unknown origin. Faceless, vicious, lethal.

Three pilots had died. The first two barely filled the smallest body bags they had in the med bay. The last one, still in his pressure suit, was laid out on a table under an array of bright white lights. Todicheene had never known him. One of the hotshots from the Lost Souls combat squadron that everyone was always buzzing about. Matthew Walker. His combat called sign, Ventum, was printed on his upper left chest.

Ventum.

The wind.

That nickname stirred old memories of sitting in his grandfather's hogan, listening to stories about the Diné from back before the white settlers from Europe changed the tribe's name to Navajo. Old stories about gods and monsters. Stories about the hero twins—Monster Slayer and Born for Water. Stories about hunting and crafting and community. Scary stories about the trickster Coyote, and of the spirits of the dead—the *chindi*—who cause ghost sickness. And stories of camping alone in the wind, listening to the voice of forever, looking for harmony and beauty in the simplest things in nature.

Ventum.

The nurse turned away to tap information into a holo-screen. He did not see a shadow cross the room in ways it should not—could not—have. It was a blackness with no true form reaching like a creeper vine from a greater bulk that was out of sight under a table. It did not reach for Todicheene, but instead slithered up one leg of the autopsy table until it touched the dead flesh. Then it pulled against its own bulk until a strand of it snapped off, making no sound. Now, like an eel, that strand slithered over the limp arm, onto the chest, and up toward the face. There it moved faster and vanished between the pale, gray lips of Matthew Walker.

As he worked, Todicheene wished he had known this young man. He wished he could have spoken with him and learned why he chose a call sign like Wind. Was it because he loved the speed of flight? Was it a connection to home to remind him, serving his people out in the airless void, about the planet that was Mother to all?

Thinking of all that stirred in Todicheene an echo of the Diné beliefs about the dead. True adherents to the traditional ways would not step over a corpse and would not even speak the name of someone who'd died for fear of calling their *chindi*. Although Todicheene was a medical professional, a man of science, the Diné inside of him was always there.

He approached the gurney on which Matthew Walker lay and began removing the pieces of the pressure suit. Gloves and boots first, which was not his practice. He realized that he was stalling because he did not want to look at Walker's dead face.

Eventually there was no more stalling possible. He braced himself, took a few breaths, scolded himself for being superstitious, and gently removed the helmet.

The dead man lay there. Pale, still. Far too young to be dead.

"I'm sorry, my brother," he said. "I'm sorry this happened to you."

Which is when Matthew Walker opened his eyes.

15

"What is it that Lost expects Lady Jessica to do?" asked Croft. "Resurrect him?"

"I have no idea," admitted McHugh.

They all looked at Soren. "If I tell you what I'm thinking you'll laugh," he said.

"Not really a jovial moment, Lars," said Trumbo. "Besides, I think we're past the whole 'you won't believe this' phase of this crisis."

"When Lost showed me the field of wrecked spaceships, I felt something. It was as if those ships, or maybe only one of them, *was* Lost."

Croft blinked. "Say again?"

"Well, consider … he manifested a body made from debris. That speaks to some kind of connection—spiritual or psychic—with machinery. Perhaps he wants Jessica to help him reconnect with one of those ships."

"How?" demanded Veljković. "Spaceships aren't ghosts."

"They are not," said Soren, nodding. "And the WarpLine was not designed to send us fifty-three thousand light-years across the galaxy. And yet …"

"Yeah, damn it," said Croft.

Trumbo gestured to McHugh with a nearly empty glass. "So, what do we do? Can you do this? If so, how? Or, I suppose, how can we help?"

Lady Jessica sat shaking her head. "Honestly, Director, I don't know. I need time to think about this. I have to consult a lot of books. I have to—"

"You have to speak with me," said a voice.

They all started violently and turned, spilling drinks. Croft leaped to his feet and tore his sidearm from the hip holster.

A figure stood watching them.

It was not actually in the room. It filled the big RealScreen on the director's rear wall. It was made of broken cables, partly melted steel, dura-glass, and large chunks of the debris the skimmers had brought back from space. Debris of the tumblers and the daggers.

"Please," begged Lost, "talk to me."

16

The door to the waiting room burst open, and Diaz, the young lieutenant Bianca met earlier, stood there gripping the frame as if it was all that kept him from being swallowed whole.

"It's Ventum," he cried. "Matthew Walker."

"What about him?" asked Bianca, getting to her feet. Everyone else stood too.

"He's *alive.*"

17

Director Trumbo and security chief Veljković both cried out in high-pitched shock. Croft drew his pistol and aimed it at the screen as if the bizarre image of Lost could somehow step out and attack. Both Soren and Lady Jessica swept protective arms across the other.

Lost's face was a piece of cracked dura-glass from one of the wrecked tumblers. It still glowed with a pale blue and palpably eerie luminescence.

"You must find me," he said. "I do not know how many times I can manifest like this, and even now I feel myself fading."

"Where are you?" asked Soren as he reached over to push Croft's gun arm down. "Are you where I met you last?"

Lost made a sound that might have been a grunt of surprise. "I am not aboard Asphodel Station," he said. "I never was. I told you, Dr. Soren, that my bones—my dust—is down on the planet Shadderal. It is taking what little strength I have to even speak like this."

His head swiveled, and the blue screen flickered with images of Lady Jessica. Soren recognized them as still photos and vid-clips from her official biography.

"Lady Death," said the golem, "I see you and honor you. In my grave I have dreamed of you. Long, long years have I dreamed. Please, my lady, find me."

The images vanished from his faceplate and the light dimmed noticeably. Small pieces of wreckage fell from his form.

"I am fading," said Lost, and there was a note of despair in his voice, and of fear. "You must find me. Time is not your friend any more than it is mine. They are coming."

"Who is coming?" demanded Croft. "Those aliens who attacked us? Who and what are they?"

Lost turned to him. "They are the shapeless ones. They are what you fear, and if you do not fear, they will become the thing that teaches it to you."

"Who are they?"

"Shoggoths," Lost said in a fierce whisper. "They are hungry. They are numberless. They are coming. They are the servants of the Outer Gods. They are slaves and soldiers. They are the voice, the hands, the swords, the teeth of the beings behind the stars. They serve the things that have worn ten billion names for ten billion conquered worlds. You know of those who fled this part of the cosmos, who ran in terror to hide on Earth, to cower within dreams so that they could not be found."

"Are you talking about the Great Old Ones?" asked McHugh. "Cthulhu and the others our people dreamed of and wrote stories about?"

"They tried to overthrow the Outer Gods and were cast out. They fled across the stars, taking some shoggoth slaves with them. They came to your world—and others they found—and set themselves up as gods. Cthulhu, yes ... and also Nyarlathotep, Bokrug, Ghatanothoa, Mormo, Rhan-Tegoth, Yeb, and others—many others. But those that fled to your world were foolish to believe they could control their shoggoth slaves. That was hubris, for no slaves on any world have ever loved their chains. The shoggoths serve only the Outer Gods, and so they rose up and cast the false gods down, consigning them to endless sleep and deep dreams."

Soren felt his mouth go utterly dry.

Lost looked around at them. "The Outer Gods looked far and wide for those that betrayed them, but in dreams Cthulhu and his kind cannot be found. In dreams they exist in the spaces between worlds. This is why they sleep on through the ages. But now you have come here, and in your minds are memories of those, like Cthulhu, who fled. Now the Outer Gods know where to look."

"No," gaped McHugh.

"Oh yes, Lady Death. Your presence here has brought peril to your world and all who live upon her. The Outer Gods and their shoggoth armies now know that Earth exists. Woe to you that this has happened."

He paused as more of the debris that formed him fell away.

"When will they come for us?" asked Soren, his fear spiking again. "How much time do we have?"

"Time? Time ..." Lost dropped to his knees, and his light was nearly gone. "There is no time left. They are here."

"Here ... where?" begged Croft.

Lost pointed to the door. "They are here. Time has fled. One is awake here, while another swims to the top of dreams."

Lost's faceplate flickered with new images. They were of a field of wrecked spaceships on what looked to be a dead world. Some of the ships looked like larger versions of the dagger fighters, while others lay jumbled together—connected in strange ways, not unlike the bipedal form the daggers had begun to assume before Bianca Petrescu's team destroyed them. There were slight but noticeable differences in design, however, and Soren felt that the scale was different too. These ships seemed much bigger, as if constructed from battleships instead of small fighters. Then there was a second video image overlaid—that of those same gigantic manlike ships rising from the field of wreckage, their chests and arms and shoulders blossoming with scores of gun ports. But this image was faint and fleeting and vanished almost immediately.

"We fought the shoggoths in a great war," whispered the alien. "We know *how* to fight them. We learned, through the sacrifice of billions of our kind, that even the gods may be opposed."

He abruptly collapsed. The light on his face-screen was barely a flicker, his voice soft as night wind.

"Ware the shoggoths and their hounds. If you survive … please find me. I am on the Field of Dead Birds. Please … find …"

And he was gone. The light went out, and that image of alien planets returned..

The five of them stood in absolute stillness, eyes wide, mouths agape.

Just then, the station-wide alarms began blaring. Sibyl's voice shouted through the din.

"All security forces report to the medical bay on deck twenty-two. Repeat, all security forces report to the medical bay."

Veljković tapped his earbud to access the comms for his division. "Give me a sitrep."

The answer was a terrible scream of agony.

18

Bianca was first through the door to the med bay.

What she saw nearly stole the heart from her. She skidded to a halt as the rest of her team slammed in and stacked up behind her.

Nurse Gordon—what was left of him—lay sprawled across the examination table. Some of him was stuck to the wall, sliding down to the floor with appalling slowness. His face was turned toward Bianca, his mouth open as if frozen in a scream that could never be finished but which echoed in Bianca's mind. His neck was a ragged stump that ended an inch below what would have been his jawline. The head lay in a widening pool of dark blood. His torso was bent backward over the table, legs and the stumps of arms spread wide like a starfish.

The two Marine sentries lay sprawled—alive but battered into unconsciousness.

Above them, naked, shreds of a pressure suit hanging from his ice-pale limbs, stood Matthew Walker. His mouth, too, was wide. His eyes wider still.

There was nothing in those eyes. They stared with milky vacuity at the Lost Souls. Blood smeared his lips and chin and spattered down his chest. One hand was locked around the slack and lifeless body of the nurse, who dangled from the grip like some grisly child's doll.

"Matthew?" Bianca said in a horrified whisper.

The eyes did not change, but the mouth curled upward into a cruel and terrible smile.

"Matthew is nothing," said that mouth. "Matthew is meat and blood and bone."

Bianca's pistol was in her hand in a flash, the barrel quavering but aiming true.

"What *are* you?" she demanded.

"I am we," said the thing with Walker's face. "We are legion. We are endless. We are the shapeless ones and we serve the eternal."

The thing's smile stretched and stretched until the corners of Walker's mouth split and blood ran down over his jaw. His eyes swirled with colors and then turned entirely black, with no iris or sclera. He reached out toward Bianca, fingernails suddenly growing long and black and wickedly sharp.

Bianca Petrescu shot him in the chest.

The Snellig M-303 gas-dart pistol sent a subsonic round across the four intervening meters. She did not miss. The cellulose capsule struck the muscular chest of Matthew Walker, tearing the surface skin and injecting a blend of ketamine and nonaddictive fentanyl-R130 into his bloodstream.

The stand-down round should have collapsed Walker where he stood.

It did not.

It did nothing.

The thing with Matthew Walker's face laughed, a sound colder than the deepest part of space.

"We cannot be killed," it roared. "We are *shoggoth* and we—"

She thumbed the selector switch to full auto and unloaded half the magazine into the stolen flesh of her dear friend. This time the thing—the *shoggoth*—staggered backward, the look in its eyes changing from blank indifference to something like surprise. Its feet slipped and skidded in the blood, and it fell.

"Take it," she snapped, and the Lost Souls surged past her, rounding the table on both sides. Impossibly, the creature was still struggling, still trying to shake off the powerful chemicals. Jacob dropped to one knee, pinning the thing's left arm; Tank did the same for the right.

"Get me something to tie it up," cried Jacob, and Calisto lunged for a roll of heavy surgical tape. She began tearing off long strips.

"We cannot be killed," growled the shoggoth. "We will tear you open like ripe fruit and eat your hearts."

Walker's lips trembled, and at first Bianca thought it was his tongue protruding, but it was not. It was something wet and black, something that pulsated with unnatural energy.

Jericho straddled the thrashing body while Jean-Paul Lloris—Decaf—grabbed it by the throat. *"Mon Dieu, Bee. Il n'y a pas de pouls,"* he cried, first in his native French, and then in English. "Bee, there's no pulse."

"We are eternal," insisted the creature as it fought against the pilots.

"Bee," said Tank. "What's going on here? He's talking, but he's not breathing. Christ, I think he's dead."

"Death is not death to the shoggoth. Death is a doorway for the children of the eternal."

"Yeah, well fuck you," said Bianca, and she came and stood over him. Her thumb turned the selector switch in a different direction as she aimed the pistol at its face.

"What have you done to my friend?"

"He is meat. He is sweet blood. He is ours now."

"Kiss my ass," she said and shot him through the heart.

The shoggoth laughed. And so she shot him through the mouth.

The tombstone round punched through tongue, soft palate, and spinal cord—and switched the thing off forever.

Jacob and Tank fell sideways. Decaf pulled Jericho off, and they both sat down hard in the pool of blood.

The room went utterly still.

Like a tomb.

Like a broken heart.

Bianca stood with her pistol pointed down at the ruin of Matthew Walker. Her friend. Her brother in arms. One of *hers*. Then she threw back her head and screamed.

That scream was not born of terror or horror or even grief. Not entirely. That scream came from the furnace in her soul. It had flickered to life out in the black when she saw the daggers kill her friends. Bo Chow. Voula Achilleos. And now Matthew Walker. She screamed for fury, and she screamed for hate. Everyone stared at her. A dozen of her friends and fellow pilots who had just seen her pull that trigger. Their eyes were filled with pain and sorrow, with shock and uncertainty. None of them said a word. They turned away, unable to look at the mangled ruin of their friend.

In their shock, they did not see a small thing like a black eel slip out of what was left of Walker's mouth. It moved with incredible speed, seeking shelter as it moved toward the wall and then sideways through the slightly open doorway of a supply closet. They did not see that door tremble as it began to swing open.

Then it was upon them.

They were upon them.

The shadow split into two distinct things. One was darkness itself, and it rose up from the ground, shapeless, like a cloud of oil smoke struggling to take form. A shoggoth in its true aspect, not a fragment of one hidden inside a murdered body as the first had been.

This was beyond their understanding, but Bianca's team was too well trained to deal with crisis situations in active evolutions to be crippled by indecision. They saw the formless black thing rise.

And then they saw the second monster, which was of a different species entirely. It was an animal of some grotesque and unknown kind that raced forward on eight stumpy legs, each of which ended in eight wickedly curved claws from which wiry filaments stuck out. The body was as massive and bulbous as a sea elephant, but pinkish in color. The face was hideous, with a tubular snout ringed with sharklike teeth.

"Jesus Christ!" cried Calisto. "It's a fucking tardigrade."

And so it was. A monstrous, bloated, nightmare version of the microanimal she'd seen in biology class back in high school. This one was obscene in its huge, pink, blubbery body—a creature as fat and heavy as a sea lion, and infinitely more dangerous. And it lunged at Calisto.

Decaf was the only other person looking in the direction when the beast began its run. He leaped across Walker's body in a flying tackle to knock Calisto out of the way as the creature reared up and slashed with those dreadful claws. The massive body missed them and struck Sundance full on, the stubby arms slashing wildly.

Sundance seemed to fly apart in an explosion of crimson rubies. There was no time to scream or run or fight. He died immediately and badly, and the monster hit the floor, skidding from its own mass. The claws dug into the poured linoleum floor as it slewed around to make another lunge.

For a fragment of a second, Calisto felt herself dwindling into fear. She wished with every fiber of her being that the *Tempest* had been caught up in the WarpLine jump across the galaxy and that Jenny

Spears and her Jokers—that most elite of SpecOps teams—were going to swarm in and deal with this. She prayed for it, ached for it. All within the space of a moment.

But even as those feelings tried to sell her on the myth of rescue, Calisto drew her weapon and fired as she backpedaled. Her selector switch was on single shot with tombstone rounds, and two holes appeared on the thing's shoulder. Some kind of semitranslucent, viscous fluid sprayed out rather than blood. The thing made a deep piglike grunting noise and charged again. Rabbit pushed Calisto away but was a fraction of a step too slow in evading the creature's left-side legs, and those claws did awful things. His belly, groin, and inner thigh were torn open. The severed femoral artery shot blood into Calisto's face, and she staggered back, slapping at it. Her heels caught on the leg of a wheeled chair, and she fell.

The monster ignored her and leaped again. It looked like blubber, but inside there were muscles so powerful that its half-ton body flew upward at Boris Vijenko, the young Russian whose combat call sign was Lovechild. He twisted away, clubbing backward with his elbow. The claws on the right side of the creature caught in the fabric of his sleeve, and the force of its landing jerked Lovechild around with such power that his entire arm was torn from his shoulder. Blood shot from the socket, and his scream was dreadful.

He fell across Matthew, his body going into shock from blood loss.

Jacob kicked the thing in the face as it landed, getting good balance and power into it, putting all of his body weight behind it. The creature's head jerked sideways, and it staggered. Bianca, still under Decaf's bulk, took aim, but she had no clear shot.

Then the other thing struck.

The shadow.

The molten blackness changed form even as it attacked the Lost Souls. It lunged forward, its elastic flesh forming a dozen mouths filled with needle teeth. Each of these mouths uttered the same high, ululating cry, *"Tekeli-li. Tekeli-li. Tekeli-li. Tekeliiiii-li!"*

Calisto heard it and spun, then screamed as she raised her gun. The thing was a writhing mass of blob-like body and thrashing tentacles. It had no real shape, that much was immediately obvious. The thing kept changing, shifting. First it had two eyes, and then thirty. The tentacles grew talons, then fingers, then octopoidal suckers. There was no face, and then something like a wolf's snout thrust forward, but this was immediately reabsorbed to be replaced with a maw in which hundreds of yellow teeth stood in rows. Then it grew a squid-like beak and a thousand eyes, with the tentacles becoming whiplike flagella.

The form-shifting shadow did not run or hop or leap, but instead flowed like living lava, filling any space it encountered, moving with an oily efficiency and terrific speed.

Calisto fired, hitting it center mass.

Then Haley Majka—Sweetpea—and Jahziel Yaakv—Jericho—started firing, their guns adding to the din. Their rounds all struck, but as the thing moved forward, the expended rounds simply fell out of its amorphous flesh and rolled wetly across the floor.

Meanwhile, Jacob moved between the giant pink creature and Bianca, his pistol firing shot after shot. He opened up holes in its fatty flesh, and more of the colorless fluid oozed out, yet the creature still moved forward, slashing at the air between itself and the humans it fought. The tardigrade banged against the surgical table, sending it crashing into Jacob. He fell, and his handgun went skittering away under a desk.

Youssef El-Shenawy—Habibi—snatched a bone saw from a tray of autopsy instruments, hurled himself onto the back of the giant tardigrade, and began chopping down on the rubbery flesh. The creature screamed again, but this time the porcine note had an almost human quality to it. Habibi paused for a second then, muttering a desperate prayer, he slashed at it with increasing desperation, hacking at the flesh faster and faster.

Two meters away from this fight, Bianca shoved Decaf off her as she sought to escape the shoggoth. The nimble Frenchman tucked tightly and rolled back to his feet, drawing his weapon as he rose to a kneeling posture. He thumbed over to select tombstones and began firing in three-round bursts at the oncoming shape-shifting shadow.

He did not miss once, but the thing kept coming. It had no internal organs, no veins or arteries, no skeleton—nothing that a bullet could puncture, rupture, or shatter. Even as its outer form changed shape, inside was a flowing mass of chameleonic flesh.

"How do we stop this goddamn thing?" yelled Decaf, firing constantly but in vain. The slugs barely even slowed the creature down as it oozed forward. And every gaping wound sealed itself.

Bianca switched back to the stand-down rounds and aimed for a pair of luminous yellow eyes as they began to manifest on the ever-changing body of the shadow creature. She missed one eye because the shoggoth whipped a barbed tentacle at her, and her evasion was nearly too late. The barbs caught on her jumpsuit leg and tore away a patch as large as a tea saucer. Bianca crabbed sideways and fired again, this time hitting one eye. Yellow goo erupted from the burst orb, and the shadow recoiled. It quickly resorbed the destroyed eye and sent a dozen more tentacles at her. She kicked a chair, and as the tendrils seized it and wrenched it apart, she shot out two other eyes—cat-green ones, now— and these, too, burst.

The fight was a swirling madhouse, with the Lost Souls having to switch back and forth between the unstoppable shoggoth and the blundering tardigrade, all without shooting one another. Spilled blood from the corpses of Walker and the nurse turned the floor into a slippery and treacherous mess, and the sudden shifts of the shoggoth's form made them duck and dodge.

The shadow howled, more in outrage than pain, though the tranquilizer chemicals themselves seemed to have little effect.

Decaf, seeing her actions, opened up on the shadow's eyes too. The creature instead sprouted dozens of new whiplike flagella, each tipped with a wicked spike.

A few meters away, Jacob, his sidearm missing, had snatched up other surgical instruments: a set of heavy, curved rib shears and a 7.6-centimeter Virchow Skull Breaker, which was a T-handled chisel used to divide cranial bones. He parried the tardigrade's slashing claw with a crescent kick, then closed in until his hip struck the monster at the shoulder. Jacob began stabbing and chopping, while Tank picked up the twisted wreck of the chair the shoggoth had destroyed and slammed it down on the tardigrade's head. Over and over.

The shape-shifter seemed to grow furious at the attack on its pet. It manifested a paw filled with curved talons, then it slashed at Tank, tearing open the entire back of his jumpsuit and leaving half a dozen bleeding cuts. Tank howled in pain, spun, and flung the chair at the black shapeless blob as it began transforming into something like a gigantic scorpion.

Decaf was bleeding from many wounds now and was firing to cover his retreat from the scorpion's tail. He rolled over onto hands and knees and scampered like a sick dog, then canted sideways and crashed into a cart. That fell sideways and nearly dropped on Bianca as she was getting up from slipping in blood. She thrust the cart away, hitting the tardigrade.

Then Bianca saw something that energized her. Bolted to it was a small medical generator with paddles held against trays by clips. A defibrillation unit.

The scorpion's feet kept slipping in blood, so it collapsed its mass down into a blob then snaked out a black tentacle that wrapped around Bianca's ankle. With a jerk it yanked her back with shocking force, pulling her toward more tentacles that sprang from its pulsating back.

"Decaf—hold it back," she cried.

He shot her a confused, despairing look, then realized what she was doing. Despite everything, he grinned. Decaf rolled sideways, kicked a small utility table at the shadow, and fired through it, hoping to drive metal splinters into its ever-changing flesh.

Calisto also saw what Bianca was attempting, and she ran around the tardigrade the rest of the team was fighting, and helped Bianca pull the defib unit from its clamps.

"How does this thing work?" she shouted.

"The hell should I know," Bianca snapped as she tore her foot free from the shadowy tentacle. As the defib unit came free, she thumbed a button and a small holo-screen flicked on over the device, showing the basic steps for using it. "Wait, wait, I got it."

Calisto let go of the device, picked up a chair, and swung it at the shoggoth with savage force. The thing fell back in confusion.

"Bee, *now!*"

"Got it!" cried Bianca. "Get clear."

The shadow righted itself and lunged at Bianca, manifesting dozens of grasping flagella, each with rows of needle-toothed suckers. One of tentacles wrapped itself around Bianca's waist and bit deep through the tough coverall fabric. She could feel hot blood running down her legs inside the material. She knew she had to get clear, but that option was gone as the creature dragged her toward itself, many mouths opening like a school of sharks.

"*Tekeli-li. Tekeli-li. Tekeli-li. Tekeliiiii-li.*"

"Fuck you!" roared Bianca as she slammed the two fully charged paddles against the flowing ink-black flesh.

There was an intense *crack* of electricity, and suddenly Bianca was falling backward with a ten-ton weight crushing her chest. The room swirled and swirled, and then all the light in the universe went out.

Part Nine
Here There Be Dragons

"He who fights with monsters should be careful lest he thereby become a monster."

—*Friedrich Nietzsche*

1

Bianca was surprised that she was not dead.

She became aware that she was still alive—if only barely—very slowly. That awareness was incremental, uncertain, even suspect.

She heard conversation. Sobs. But also laughter.

None of that seemed quite right.

Light found its way through the shadows in her brain, but it did not hurry. Neither did clarity.

"You're okay, babe," said a voice from a very long way off. Gentle. Familiar. "You're okay."

Her lips and mouth were dry as dust, but she managed to say, "That's good, then."

Then the darkness took her again.

2

Dr. Soren sat with Lady Jessica.

They were back on her couch, sitting close but not touching. Soren wished they could. Even hugs were life-affirming in their own way.

The news from Director Trumbo about the fight in the med bay was heartbreaking.

"Those poor kids," said McHugh.

"Yes," said Soren. "To die so far from home."

"Yes."

He turned to her. "Will that matter? The fact that they died so far from home? This is your field, and I've read enough of your writings to know that you believe that there is a spiritual connection between the souls of the dead and the energy of both Gaia, the Earth, and our star, Sol. Both Gaia and Sol are aspects of the higher power that forms the structure of your cosmology. So, tell me, Lady Jessica, are their souls lost because they have died so far from home? Are they truly 'lost souls'?"

Lady Jessica did not meet his eyes but instead sat with her fingers interlaced and her focus on the many silver rings she wore.

"I don't know, Soren," she said at length.

3

Dr. Anton Kier sat at a worktable in his lab, WarpLine notes spread everywhere. He looked up as Captain Croft entered the lounge attached to the science offices.

He stood up. "Captain, I heard about what happened down in the med bay. Those creatures. A shape-shifter—a shoggoth, I believe the alien Lost called it. And a tardigrade? That's incredible. I can't even begin to imagine how—"

Croft caught him by the throat in one leathery palm, jerked him out of the chair, and slammed Kier against the near wall. He did it with such force that Kier found himself on tiptoes, eyes bulging from their sockets, his voice choked to a gurgle.

"I'm going to ask you this one time, Kier," said Croft in a deadly snarl. "How the *hell* did tardigrades—those ugly little monsters they used to test your damn WarpLine gun—*get aboard this station*?"

"Hey!" yelled Jason Saltsman, who was standing in the bathroom doorway wiping his hands on a towel. "What the hell are you doing?"

With his free hand, Croft pointed a stiff finger at him. "Shut. The fuck. Up."

"The hell I will," said Saltsman as he hurried across the room. "Let him go. You're choking him for Christ's sake."

Croft growled, pivoted, and threw Kier one-handedly across the table. Kier skidded fast, sending books and tablets flying, and crashed into two chairs tucked into the table's far side. He landed badly on the floor, crying out in pain. Croft flipped the table over, but as he bent to grab Kier again, Saltsman caught his arm and tried to jerk him back. Croft punched Saltsman in the center of the chest, felling him, then took two handfuls of Kier's shirt. He plucked him off the floor, and slammed him back down. He pinned him with one hand and raised the other in a wicked-looking three-finger kung-fu claw.

"I asked you a goddamn question," Croft said, his voice hot and low and ugly.

The look on Kier's face was one of complete astonishment and confusion. "I don't know," he cried. "I don't know, *I don't know.*"

Saltsman, on his knees and trying desperately to suck in even a spoonful of air, pawed at Croft's trouser leg. The captain ignored it.

"That wasn't me," blubbered Kier. "The tardigrade stuff was concluded in 2076. I wasn't even *born* yet."

"I don't give a shit. Those things were part of the development process that you finished, and you brought us to the one place in the Milky Way where there are more of these things. Bigger ones." He jerked Kier to his feet, holding him close, the threatening hand now inches away from the scientist's eyes. "Are you going to try and tell me that this is an *accident*? That it's a coincidence? I have dead pilots downstairs and two Marines in critical condition, you piece of shit. I want answers, and God help you if you don't give me something that makes sense."

Kier was openly weeping now. All he could manage to say was "I don't know."

Over and over again.

It was pathetic. Awful. And it leached the fury out of Croft. He released Kier with a shove that sent the man backpedaling until he tripped over a fallen chair. Croft looked down at him.

"It was your gun that brought us out here," he said coldly. "Tardigrades were part of the experiments conducted on your technology. You knew about those tests. You *told* us about them, and now some of the best and brightest and *bravest* people I know are in the morgue. I've got to go back down and deal with that. When I'm done, you little prick, I'm going to find you again, and by God, you better have answers. About the tardigrades and about how the hell we're going to get all these people back home. Hear me? I said, do you hear me?"

All Kier could do was nod. Then he turned his face away, buried it against the carpet, and sobbed.

4

When Bianca woke again, she was alone, lying in a narrow bed in a medical bay with monitors beeping quietly around her and IV tubes stuck into her arms.

She sat up very slowly and carefully, feeling an extraordinary number of aches, ranging from the dull throb of bruises to the sharper sting of cuts. Her body felt oddly padded, and it took a minute or two to realize it was surgical gauze over many wounds.

"Good morning, Lieutenant Commander Petrescu," said the soft, comforting voice of Sibyl.

"How bad am I hurt?" she asked quickly.

"You have nineteen cuts, only two of which are deep," said the AI. "The deepest cuts have been sealed, and the tissues are knitting. You have multiple contusions. Shall I catalog them?"

"No. Why does my chest hurt?"

"You were exposed to a high level of electricity and required CPR. Two of your ribs were cracked in the process, but the doctor has injected you with osteoblast-LQ. Your ribs are already thirty-two percent healed."

"Wait ... I *died*?"

"Cardiac arrest was the result of accidental exposure to a full charge from defibrillator paddles." Sibyl sounded mildly reproving.

Then it all came back to her.

"Sibyl, where is my team? Are they okay?"

"Bianca," said a voice, and she turned to see a familiar figure standing in the doorway. Dr. Soren, looking older and more haggard than he had before. He came in and pulled a chair over to her bedside.

"Shall I provide a status report?" asked Sibyl.

"No," said Soren. "I'll do that."

He sat and gently took one of Bianca's hands.

Bianca blinked in surprise. "Doc?"

"Welcome back, my dear," he said. "You've had quite a time since I last saw you. You've been through so much. I'm actually having a hard time believing *how* much."

"Doc, you gotta tell me. What happened? Did we ... did we win?"

"You did," he said. "Your daring action with the defibrillator stunned the shoggoth long enough for the security team to gather it up and contain it."

"*Shoggoth?* Oh yeah … that's what it said. 'We are shoggoth.'"

"Yes."

"And that other thing," asked Bianca, fighting to clear her thoughts. "Calisto called it a tardi-something. It was all crazy and I wasn't tracking."

"Tardigrade," said Soren. "It's dead. After you zapped the shoggoth, apparently *all* of your friends shot the tardigrade. It is quite dead."

"Okay. Good. But, Doc … what the hell is a tardigrade?"

"Ah, that's moderately complicated," said Soren, and he explained that tardigrades were microanimals found everywhere on Earth and used in early testing stages of the WarpLine tech. "Your friend Calisto has begun calling them T-dogs. Captain Croft thinks that the shoggoths use these mutant tardigrades like combat dogs. Now, before you ask how they got out here, apparently Captain Croft … ah … shall we say *asked* Dr. Kier for an explanation. I expect it to be forthcoming with some haste. But my guess is that whatever accident brought us out here is connected in some way to the process that sent them here as well. Our resident quantum physicists are turning themselves inside out to come up with theories."

Bianca digested that. Her clarity of mind came and went, and a few times she had to struggle not to lapse back into sleep. Soren helped her sip some cool water, and that helped.

"And that shoggoth?" she asked. "Was that accidentally sent out here too?"

"That is currently unknown," said Soren. "Lady Jessica McHugh has some theories, but they are arcane, and she is probably better suited to explain. Which, I expect, will happen sometime soon. Captain Croft and Director Trumbo are not letting anyone rest."

A big patch of mental clouds parted, and Bianca jolted upright. But pain slammed her back down. Through clenched teeth she asked, "Jacob—is he okay? And how is Calisto? Did she get fried too?"

"They're fine, apart from some minor cuts and bruises." He smiled. "They been here watching over you since you were brought up. I sent them off to get some food because they looked ready to drop. I said I'd keep vigil, and alas, you missed them by ten minutes. I expect they'll be back soon enough."

A guarded look came into Bianca's eyes as she swallowed. "And the others?"

Soren studied her face, keeping his own expression blank. "What do you remember?"

Bianca closed her eyes for a moment, and Soren stayed silent as she collected her thoughts. Then she opened her eyes, met his gaze, and gave a pretty clear account of the fight in the medical bay. Soren watched her face, seeing lines of tension appear and then the glassy shock as she recalled injuries and deaths.

"Boris was killed," she said hollowly, looking away from him. "And Zito. Hector too, I think. Their call signs were Lovechild, Rabbit, and Sundance."

"Yes, I know," Soren murmured gently. "I'm so very sorry, Bianca. I'm truly sorry for your loss."

Without turning back, she said, "Tell me the rest." When he looked hesitant, she caught his wrist in a surprisingly strong grip. "Doc, please. Tell me. All of it."

Soren nodded. "I'll likely get in trouble for this, but ..."

And he told her everything.

5

"Sorry I'm late," said Captain Croft as he entered the conference off the bridge. All of the division chiefs were there, with only Kier conspicuous by his absence. Croft slid into an empty seat.

"You look like you could use a drink," said Trumbo, holding up her whiskey glass.

"Just coffee."

He accepted a cup and looked around. The profound shock of what had happened and what was still happening had left its cruel mark on each of them.

"If you feel up to it, Sebastian," said Trumbo, "please bring us up to speed on what happened outside and in the med bay. I want us all on the same page."

"Buckle up," he said humorlessly, and he told them. All of them knew most of it from having watched on RealScreens during the space battle, and reruns of the horrors of the med bay. Croft gave technical details and also updates on the health of Bianca Petrescu and her remaining team.

"I'm really sorry for your losses, Captain," said Dušan Veljković. "I can't even begin to imagine what that feels like."

"No, you damn well can't," said Croft more harshly than he intended. He held up a hand by way of apology. Veljković shook his head, not having taken offense. With forced calm, Croft said, "Sorry. It's been a day."

"And it's not over yet," said Trumbo. She gestured to the thin man seated to her immediate right. "Abdou, you, at least, have some good news, and we can all use some."

Abdou Diatta, chief engineer of Asphodel Station, said, "Let me start by reassuring everyone that Asphodel is in good shape. We had the breaches and damage from the explosions, but the hull is completely sealed, and we are repairing life support and artificial gravity on those decks. ETA is about ten hours."

Croft whistled. "That's fast work."

"We have state-of-the-art industrial 3D printers," said Diatta. "We can print decking and wall sections, complete with circuitry. The damaged materials have been laser-cut, and the debris goes back into the raw-materials store for repurposing. We don't waste much here. We're also fabricating a new array in sections, and between printing and installation, call it five hours."

"That's incredible," said Croft. "If it's okay with you, I'll have Lieutenant Tanaka detail some Marines to help. He has a few people who worked in field fabrication of military equipment."

"They'll be very welcome," said the engineer.

"Thanks, Abdou," said Trumbo. "Denny, you're next."

The stellar cartographer addressed his remarks to Croft. "The feeds from your tumblers gave us a lot of good data about the planets, dwarf planets, and moons. We're building a self-learning navigation software package that will be ready probably by the time this meeting wraps."

Next was Billy "Gopher" Broussard, head of Medical Sciences, a young-faced older man with Cajun blue eyes and black hair. "We have your critters in hand," he said. "That shape-shifting thing, that shoggoth, is on ice. And I don't mean standard cold storage. We did some tissue analysis down to the molecular level, and even at fifty below there was movement. Considering that we know it was able to separate a portion of itself to … um … *reanimate* Lieutenant Walker, I decided to play it safe and had it frozen down to two hundred sixty below zero. Not absolute zero but close enough. Zero cellular activity. Now as to whether that means it's dead or dormant, we don't know. There are animals back on Earth who freeze solid only to revive completely. Certain frogs and squirrels and such. And we know from two centuries of ice pack melting and thawing of permafrost that bacteria, viruses, and certain fungi have survived tens of thousands of years in hard freeze." He shook his head. "To that end, I have two fail-safes. One is a set of burners built into that cryo-chamber. If it wakes and tries anything hinky, we blast it with a three-thousand-degree barbecue. It's an electric furnace and nothing organic survives it. And I do mean nothing. However, if I don't like how fast that thing's cooking, then the whole cryo-chamber is on rails that will send it down and out the ass end of this station. We can shoot it into deep space and detonate it."

"Where is Walker?" asked Croft.

"He's on ice too," said the Cajun. "Frankly, we don't know enough about these shoggoths to even risk attempting an autopsy."

Next up was Dr. Jae-Sung Hak, who introduced himself as an evolutionary biologist and exobiologist. "I did manage to get a sample of the shoggoth before it went into the ice," he said. "Full containment procedures, of course. We're working out the protocols on how to study it. Something like that—a chameleonic DNA structure—is entirely new to science."

"What about that other thing? The T-dog, or whatever we're calling it now?"

Hak snorted. "In my med school days I'd have been delighted to encounter something like that. First, let me assure you all that it is very dead. We have it in stasis to slow down putrefaction so we can study it. The assumption being that if there's one then there are more."

"Fuuuck," said Denny under his breath, drawing it out. "I am *never* going to sleep again."

"It's a pretty fascinating animal," said Hak with visible excitement, then cut a nervous look at Croft. "God, I didn't mean that the way it sounds. I know how much harm it did."

Croft just waved him on.

"There are some fascinating anomalies with the animal," said Hak, a bit awkwardly. "First, except for scale, it is anatomically identical to the microanimal versions we have on Earth."

"I've heard far weirder stuff today," said Croft. "Let's keep that in mind. Besides, I've been cooking up my own wild theories. Like, if what that Lost thing said is true, and if what McHugh theorizes is accurate, then couldn't the presence of tardigrades out here mean that they were out here first and came to Earth with that Cilhthooie thing?"

"Cthulhu," corrected Veljković.

"Cthulhu. Whatever. My point is—couldn't older, less evolved versions of them have come to Earth with those freaks who were running scared from those Outer God things? What if these T-dogs came to Earth with them, and evolution or conditions or whatever on Earth gradually diminished their size to the versions we know? Wouldn't that explain the presence of similar species fifty-three thousand light-years apart? I mean, it's either that, or these giant T-dogs are descendants of ones that went missing from the early WarpLine tests."

Hak chewed on that. "There are evolutionary challenges to each version of that story, I'm afraid. There's no precedent in my experience for a microanimal becoming a predator of the size we've seen. Conversely, although dwarfism in nature is known in places where animal size was limited by available resources, the scale in question is beyond what we *believe* to be possible."

"What if the micro versions of the T-dogs were genetically modified out here?" asked Croft.

"Without knowing more about the level of technology here," said Hak, "that question can't go beyond a hypothesis. But it wouldn't be the strangest anomaly we've so far encountered. The *fact* of the shoggoth biology is astounding. And, from what others have said, the close proximity of so many worlds and moons is gravitationally impossible according to what our understanding of science can explain. So ... I don't think we can say anything for certain."

Trumbo thanked him, sipped her whiskey, and set her glass down. "Sebastian, you've heard from us, now let's hear from you. How can the staff of Asphodel Station help the Navy."

"First," said Croft crisply, "we recovered the nuke cores from the three tumblers that were destroyed, but we need ships to put them in. We have full schematics on those ships on data crystals. Mr. Diatta, can your 3D fabricators build me some ships? You've seen the tumblers—they're small, one-man boats."

Diatta nodded. "We can build just about anything, Captain. Send me the specs, and I'll get my people to work."

"Excellent. Second, I don't know what shape Dr. Kier is in, but his aide, Saltsman, seemed pretty sharp. I think it's in all of our best interests if they started fabricating a new WarpLine engine."

There was a shocked silence, but after a moment some heads began nodding.

"Then we need to get our asses into gear," said Croft, rising. "We've been blasted to the far side of the galaxy, attacked by alien fighters, had our worldview bent over a barrel and buggered up the bunghole, and been invaded by shape-shifting monsters and giant bugs. It's well past time we got our shit together and pushed the hell back."

6

Soren found Lady McHugh in her quarters. When she answered the door, it was clear she had been crying. Her eyes were red-rimmed and her face puffy. Fear and grief cast her face into false sternness that was really a defensive facade.

"Make yourself a drink if you want one," she said.

"Thanks, no."

"Then pour me one," McHugh said as she flung herself into a chair.

Her cat, Sonder, crept out from behind a chair and peered at Soren with that unique blend of feline challenge, curiosity, and indifference. Soren bent down to offer more head scratches, but Sonder ignored him, sat down by McHugh, and began cleaning itself with the indecorous indifference particular to felines.

Soren opened a bottle of Malbec and poured the rich, dark red wine into a fresh glass, which he handed to her. Then he poured himself a goblet of water and sat on the edge of the couch.

"I have some things to show you," said McHugh. She told Sybil to run a slideshow of bizarre images from the Lovecraftian and post-Lovecraftian subgenre of cosmic horror. The monsters were each horrific, one more terrible than the next.

"These are artistic interpretations," she warned. "Book and magazine illustrations based on descriptions from fiction. No idea if they are in any way fair representations of these Great Old Ones. The challenge in established a precise cosmology of these beings is that we have absolutely no way of separating fact from fiction. While you were down visiting with Bianca Petrescu, I had Sybil help me collate details about the deities of what was called the Cthulhu Mythos. A label, by the way, not created by Lovecraft but by another pulp writer, August Derleth, likely because of his personal bias for that creature in the stories he told."

"I'm with you," Soren assured her.

"As far as I can determine based on what biographers and scholars believe was Lovecraft's intent, there are tiers of beings of godlike aspect. Cthulhu actually belongs to one of the lower tiers, the Great Old Ones, and I think these are the gods who fled this region of space and came to Earth, either in physical form or as dreams. Cthulhu, Ghatanothoa, Yig, and others. They exist outside of normal time and space and manifest in dreams in various aspects."

"Hence their influence on writers, artists, and so on?" suggested Soren.

"Correct. Then there are the Elder Things—also known as the Old Ones and Elder Ones. They are a race of extraterrestrial creatures that are sometimes in harmony with or in opposition to the Great Old Ones. In the Mythos stories, they were the first alien race to visit Earth and they set up a colony there. And I have no idea if they play into what we're facing."

"What else?"

"Then above them are the Great Ones, also known as the 'weak gods of Earth.' They reign in a dimension called 'Dreamland.' These beings have a patron known as Nyarlathotep, and he belongs to the top tier, the Outer Gods."

"But what exactly *are* these Outer Gods?" asked Soren."

"They're less defined," said McHugh. "Or, perhaps, conflictingly defined. Centuries of other writers adding to the Mythos has resulted in a pollution of whatever Lovecraft may have intended. And remember, Lovecraft encouraged his friends and followers to write these kinds of stories, so we don't know how much of *any* of it is reliable."

"Understood."

"That said, the Outer Gods, sometimes called the Other Gods, are vastly more powerful—and here's where the description of their nature becomes problematic. They are ruled by a being called Azathoth, also—weirdly—called the 'Blind Idiot God,' and he holds court at the center of infinity. All the other Outer Gods dance wildly around him, and they do it to the cadence of a demonic flute."

"I think this is more in my territory," said Soren with a smile. "Such hyperbolic claims are, in substance, no different from those that surround the ancient Greek story of Atlas. After a failed war on the gods, in which Atlas sided with the Titans, he was first condemned to stand at the western edge of the earth and hold the sky upon his shoulders. When he balked, he was sent to hell. His story is commonly conflated with that of the Titan Coeus, the embodiment of the celestial axis around which the heavens revolve. The *common* belief is that Atlas holds the world on his shoulders, though the older statues depict him holding the celestial sphere instead. The takeaway is that not only do deities in myth often overlap and share qualities, but the public tends to tell and retell the wrong version of the story. So, if Azathoth exists, then what Lovecraft gave us was a poetic version and likely nowhere near the truth."

"Fair enough," said Lady Jessica. She sipped her wine. "The other Outer Gods are equally fantastical, at least as far as the writers' descriptions go. There's Yog-Sothoth, who co-rules with Azathoth and is called the 'All-in-One and One-in-All.' And Shub-Niggurath, known as the 'Black Goat of the Woods with a Thousand Young.' Other Outer Gods are alluded to by Lovecraft and his immediate circle, and that list was greatly expanded in later fiction."

"And there's no way to know what is real or not," Soren admitted. Sonder seemed to suddenly notice his existence. The cat climbed onto his lap and looked at Soren until he began scratching between the soft little ears. "I was hoping we would have something concrete to help Captain Croft prepare for any further threats. Perhaps when I go down to the planet Shadderal, I'll be able to get more information from Lost."

McHugh gaped at him. "Go down to the planet? Are you *insane*?"

"Croft asked the same question, but I convinced him that as the first person Lost contacted, it seems like a worthwhile risk." He paused. "He asked if you wanted to go too. I said I'd ask, but frankly, Jessica, I don't think it's a good idea for *both* of us to go. Lost apparently feels connected to us, and we should make sure that at least one of us is here on the station."

McHugh considered. "To set foot on another world, one that was populated by a sentient race ... I mean, that would be amazing, but it might also be dangerous in a different way. I'm a sensitive, Lars. I can *feel* the dead, and at times that connection is intense. Dangerously so. It's why I don't visit graveyards on Earth. Far too much input. So, visiting a world where everyone has died? Thanks, but no. Not until I understand more about them on a spiritual level and can work out how to protect myself from overload."

"I can understand that and agree," said Soren. "But tell me … would you ever risk attempting to contact the ghost of an alien?"

"I don't know," she said, looking nervous. "Maybe if I had an actual relic, some item I know he touched, or a piece of bone. Even a bit of his dust. Maybe then the old ways would work. Death is death, at least on a certain level."

"Then," said Soren, "I will do my very best to bring something useful back."

7

The meeting broke up and the various division heads left. Trumbo signaled for Croft to linger. She took the last sip of her whiskey and glanced at the wet bar. Croft took the glass from her and set it on the table out of easy reach.

"I'd like another," she said in mild protest.

"You're half in the bag already, Delia."

Her mouth formed a weird shape halfway between a smile and a frown. "Are you my mother?"

"No, and I'm not your nursemaid either."

"Don't start, Sebastian …"

"I'm not starting anything, Delia. You're scared. I get it. You're confused, I get that too."

"I'm lost," she snapped.

"We all are."

She stared at him, and three times she opened her mouth to say something he was sure would be a fiery rebuke. Each time, she snapped her jaws shut, biting down on bitter words.

"I wasn't trained for this," she said at length. "Nothing I ever studied in school, not one minute of my professional career, has prepared me for this."

"I know," he said gently. "That's true of all of us. It's not just you."

"Everyone looks to me for answers. And what can I say? Keep the lights on? Make sure the RealScreens are showing soothing images? Pretend like this is just another day on happy space station Asphodel?"

"No one expects miracles of you," said Croft. "I don't."

"Well, that's something."

"But I do expect you to do your best. And crawling into a bottle isn't going to do anyone any good. We already have Dr. Kier hiding in his room. The one man who *should* be on the front line helping us with this mess. So, sure, people are going to look to you."

"Because I know everything about surviving on the far side of the galaxy during an alien invasion?" she said acidly.

"No, because you are the boss. It doesn't matter if you studied Extreme Cosmic Screwups in college or not. Doesn't matter if you don't know which way to turn. You have to make decisions and be *seen* to be making decisions. Do this, do that … It almost doesn't matter. You have to *be* in command. No one ever promised that command came with all the answers. I can tell you firsthand it does not. In the military we do all these combat drills and war games to try and be prepared. I've done a shitload of them. Tell you what—not one of them prepared me for this. Not one."

"So how are you keeping it all together?" she asked.

"With old twine, glue, and spit," he said. "Sorry, real answer? I'm keeping it together because what's the alternative? Giving up? Taking a stroll out an airlock without a pressure suit?"

"Or crawling into a bottle?" she asked, with the faintest hint of a rueful smile.

"Or that. I have people who count on me. I can't let traumatic stress become my defining characteristic. Not now. Not while we're in the middle of it."

Trumbo sat there shaking her head slowly. "Not all of us are strong like that, Sebastian."

He looked her in the eyes. "Not all of us are as weak as we think, Delia."

"What am I supposed to *do*?" she begged.

"Be the leader," he said. "Even if you have to fake it. And don't fool yourself, most of us in command fake it sometimes. Part of the job. The key is faking it well enough that the people who look to us for leadership don't know."

"That's pretty damned cynical, Sebastian."

"It's how it works more often than not." He paused. "If I can give a piece of advice? Make another speech. Have your best PR people whip something up. Tell the truth about our situation. Tell all of it. Go over what you've already said, tell them about the aliens—the daggers, the shoggoths, all of it—but also tell them what your people told us at this table. Make the case that you are in charge, and that the people in each division are doing their jobs. Sell that. Sell that we are working on solutions. Remind the people that in the two encounters we had with the aliens, we won. Both times. Two for two. Sell that. It will matter. When that speech is written, go live on every screen on the station. Get yourself made up, but not too glitzy. A strand of hair out of place, but only one. Sell that you're in the trenches, but also sell that you're keeping your cool. That's how you get ahead of this, Delia. It's the *strength* the people need, and if some of it is a lie, so what? Propaganda isn't *always* an evil. I think our Dr. Soren would even agree. So, cowgirl up and do it. I know you can. I *already* have faith in you, Director Trumbo."

He smiled, winked, took her hands, squeezed them, gave a single firm nod, and left.

Delia Trumbo sat on the edge of the table, the empty whiskey glass within reach, the wet bar four steps away. Her hands gripped the table edge with increasing force until her knuckles were bled white.

8

"To hell with this," snarled Bianca. With a savage wrench she tore the IVs out of her arms, kicked the sheets off, swung her legs out of bed, stood up.

And fell.

"Goddamn son of a bitch bastard."

She clawed her way back up, holding onto the footboard. Nausea swept through her, but Bianca snatched up the water cup, drank every drop from it, took a few deep breaths to oxygenate her lungs, and tottered in the direction of clothes folded neatly on a chair by the bathroom.

"Lieutenant," cried the nurse as she came to see why Bianca's telemetry was offline, "You need to get back into bed, right now."

Bianca shot her a lethal glare. "What is your rank?"

"Rank? I'm a nurse and—"

"You're not Navy, and therefore you can go hump a wombat, sister. Now get out of my way."

The nurse stood her ground, and the situation was sliding downhill fast when the door opened again to reveal Jacob. He read the room quickly.

"I'll handle this, nurse."

The nurse gave him a murderous glare, ground her jaws together, and left with a great show of reluctance and disapproval.

"You've made another friend," said Jacob as he closed the door.

Bianca stood in her underwear, one leg in a flight suit. She had her butt against a wall for balance.

"Stop checking out my boobs and help me get this thing on," she growled.

"You're supposed to be in bed, Bee."

"I'm supposed to be somewhere near Jupiter."

Jacob sighed and offered an arm. She took it, got the other leg into her flight suit, then he helped pull the top on. He took the zipper pull and, making silent eye contact, zipped it all the way up. Bianca felt her face flush as he did it. Then, feeling suddenly shy, she stepped back and sat on the chair while she put on her socks and shoes.

"Sorry I wasn't here when you woke up," he said.

"Soren told me you've been here most of the time. You and Calisto."

"Yup."

She paused with the second shoe still in her hands. "God ... Jacob ... I mean ... Jesus Christ."

He took the shoe from her and set it down, then reached for her and pulled her gently off the chair and into his arms. She knelt and wrapped her arms around him. They clung like that for a long time. Not weeping—but the tears were there, deep inside both of them, boiling hot, cooking their grief in a stew of hate.

9

Soren left Lady Jessica's quarters and stepped into an elevator. He was surprised to see Croft already there.

"Hey, Doc," said the captain. "I told Trumbo and the others that you were going down to the planet on the first team. She wasn't happy, but I gave her the explanation you gave me. Didn't make her any happier, but she understood."

"That's something," said Soren. "But listen, Sebastian, there is something I need to do that can maybe help Lady Jessica. I need a relic of Lost. A piece of bone or his dust. Her religion—the practices of necromancy—require something that forms a direct connection to the deceased."

Croft listened with a peculiar expression on his face. "Doc, I wish I could say that was the weirdest damned thing anyone's said today. And you want to go bone hunting yourself?"

"I do," said Soren. "And I want to speak with Lost on his own ground, where he is likely to be strongest. I have a few million questions I'd like to ask."

The captain smiled. "You're a crazy person, you know that, right?"

"It has been mentioned," said Soren, returning the smile. "So, please allow me to go down to the Field of Dead Birds. That's what Lost calls the graveyard of spaceships we all saw on his helmet screen."

"Well … the fact that there's a chance of finding alien tech down there that we might be able to use—reverse engineer—is pretty enticing. Is it your belief that you could encourage Lost to let us have that tech?"

"It is."

The officer looked at the ceiling for a moment, then snorted. "I can see why you and Petrescu get along so well. She's more than a little crazy, and she's a stubborn pain in my ass too."

"Is that a yes?"

"With great reluctance," said Croft firmly. "I'll be sending two Marines to protect you. That's not up for debate. Milford and Watson. If you take *any* unnecessary risks or, God help you, endanger my people, then I will order these Marines and my pilots to leave you behind to rot down there. Is that clear?"

"Oh, Captain," said Soren, placing his hand over his heart. "I would expect nothing less."

"Bastard," muttered Croft. "Okay. Come on. I'll get you kitted out. We light the fires in forty minutes."

10

Delia Trumbo stood by the wet bar, staring down at the whiskey bottle. She had removed the stopper, and the vapors curled upward, whispering lies about comfort.

She hated Croft for calling her out on her drinking. She wasn't drunk, God damn it.

The room shifted in and out of focus in eloquent riposte to this mental assertion, and she cursed the room too. And on some level Trumbo knew that anger was as much a shield and armor as the whiskey.

"Holier-than-thou military meathead," she muttered.

Then she opened the top right-hand drawer of her desk and looked down at a small plastic pill case. It was half filled with tiny green pills. Dreamers. Her physician had prescribed them for insomnia, but Trumbo found they had a lot of uses. She put the pill case on her desktop and drummed her fingers on either side of it.

She sighed and tapped a holo-key. A miniature of the head and shoulders of her assistant materialized. "Get my speechwriters. I have a project for them."

While she waited, her eyes drifted from the pill case to the small wet bar. There was an equal gravitational pull from each. Trumbo needed them both. It was a genuine ache.

Putting the pill case away and turning from that bottle took a great deal of the strength she had left.

She did turn away though, and it hurt.

11

"What in the flickering back alley of hell are *you* doing here?" yelled Captain Croft. He had been in the middle of a briefing with Calisto and the other Lost Souls when Bianca limped into the room.

Bianca hoisted a fierce little smile into place, stopped, and gave him the crispest salute she'd ever given anyone. "Reporting for duty, sir."

"No, don't give me that 'good little sailor' bullshit, Petrescu. You are supposed to be in bed."

"Didn't need to be there anymore, Captain," she said.

"Oh really?"

"Yes, sir. I need to be here." She gestured to the row of tumblers. "I need to be in my bird, out there flying escort for the skimmers."

"Says who?"

"Says your best pilot."

Croft raised his eyebrows as he looked around at Jacob, Calisto, and the others. "'Best' pilot?" he echoed.

"Can't argue with that, sir," said Jacob.

"Mosquito's right," said Calisto, then hastily added, "sir."

"So you're all in on it?"

The Lost Souls all wore identical expressions. The kind every service person learns from the first day in boot camp. A look that is in no way offensive but is otherwise closed and locked. It says nothing, shows nothing, and walks the line between innocence and intentional ignorance. Croft saw that mask on all of them.

"I could have joined the Coast Guard, you know," Croft grumbled. "Nice billet on a fan-cruiser in the Gulf of Mexico or out of Fort goddamn Lauderdale." He stepped very close to Bianca. "I *know* you have cracked ribs and stitches."

"Sir, I—"

"I did not invite you to speak."

"Sir," she snapped and stood even more rigidly to attention, her eyes staring through the middle of his forehead.

Croft made a sour face and looked first at Jacob and then Calisto. "I am holding you two personally responsible. If Lieutenant Commander Petrescu can't hack it out there, one or both of you will go to command channel two and tell me. Screw with me, either of you, and the aliens are the last thing you'll need to worry about. I have two feet, and I'll break a foot off in each of your asses. Am I crystal clear?"

"Aye, aye, sir," they said.

Croft stepped back, gave Bianca a final withering look, turned and stalked back inside.

Jacob leaned close to Bianca. "I can't believe he went for it."

12

Delia Trumbo gave her speech. It was everything Croft had suggested and more. She told them everything.

She told them about the WarpLine gun. She showed the alien worlds, and said that her teams were working to assess the situation and develop response protocols. There was authority in her tone, and she gave constant reminders that the best people to address all of these challenges were already aboard the station.

Then Trumbo broke the news about the dagger ships, leaning hard on details cribbed from Captain Croft about how effective the Lost Souls fighter squadron had been in defeating them. She even said that the tumblers were about to launch again, promising that live feeds would be shared station-wide. No secrets, no hiding, and having said that, she asked everyone to gather in groups, to be with others as they all shared this experience together.

It was hard. Despite all the best phrasing, it was brutal. When she was done, she kept her face composed in a way that showed understanding, compassion, strength, confidence, and optimism. The camera lingered on that expression and then faded out to a long digital recreation of dolphins and green sea turtles swimming off the coast of Kauai.

Only then did she break down and cry.

13

The entire population of Asphodel watched on RealScreens as the pilots went to their ships.

Captain Croft walked Soren to the skimmer SK-1, shook his hand, and leaned close to say something private to him that the camera mics did not pick up. Then the philosopher nodded and went aboard.

The residents of the station watched all the preflight procedures, with all of the specialist jobs defined by pop-outs. Then the launch sequence commenced, and they were off. A small squadron that, the feed failed to say, had been reduced by six members. Those deaths played no part at all in the presentation, nor was the WarpLine failure mentioned. The PR message was clear: *We have this.*

The launch doors closed, and the screen view changed to exterior images as the squadron shot into space in a tight formation and headed to the strange and unknown world of Shadderal.

It was all great theater.

The feed played on the large RealScreen in Dr. Kier's living room, on the slightly smaller one in his bedroom, and on an even more compact screen in the bathroom. Kier's eyes were unblinking as it all played out.

His face was turned slightly away from the screen though. He had turned completely around more than a dozen times, propelled at first by the desperate flailing of his legs. But as the noose tightened from his weight, his blood and breathing slowed, slowed, slowed.

And stopped.

He hung there. Fully dressed, still wearing the torn and bloody lab coat.

On the tiled wall behind him, written in blood from a failed attempt at slashing his wrists, was a message left for whoever would find him.

SINNER
GOD FORGIVE ME

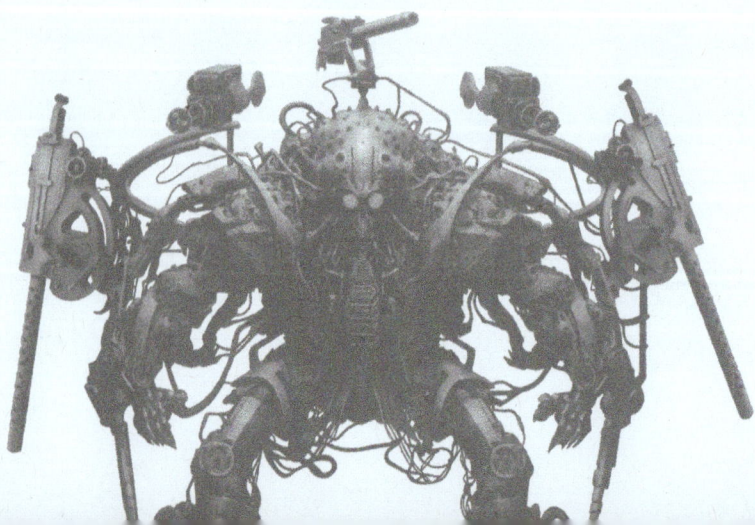

Part Ten
The Field of Dead Birds

"The true soldier fights not because he hates what is in front of him, but because he loves what is behind him."
—*G. K. Chesterton*

1

Shadderal.

A new world. Not one of the eight that made up the solar system, but something absolutely new to the human experience. Everyone in the squadron was uniquely aware that everything—every single action they took—was a first. It should have been a triumphant moment, glorious and heroic—and there was some of that, despite the fear and heartbreak. Bianca certainly felt it.

But it made her feel oddly split. On one hand, she was mourning the deaths of six people she knew and loved. That pain was raw, too new for time to have done any mending. The ache was like a monstrous cavern in the deepest parts of her soul, and through it came the wail of truly *lost* souls. Beezer, Ventum, Spartan, Lovechild, Rabbit, and Sundance. Gone. Bianca knew for sure that the full impact of this loss was like a clenched fist, drawing slowly back to gain leverage and angle to hit her when she was least expecting it.

And on the other hand was the *wonder* of this. All sailors—whether by sea, beneath the waves, or across the depths of space—were explorers. That was why humans launched themselves into the unknowns in boats made of reeds and wood and, later, steel. It's why some enclosed themselves in pressure-resistant metal shells to dive down below the sun's reach. It's why astronauts first launched themselves beyond Earth's atmosphere to place footsteps on other worlds—the Moon, Mars, and beyond. It was the call to go beyond the known and explore the unknown.

Shadderal was unknown. It was the closest of the many planets in this improbable display of celestial bodies, which meant that there was so much waiting to be discovered, to be known, to be learned.

This new world demanded that explorers like her see it for what it was. To measure it and grasp its subtleties. The planet was bigger than Earth by about 9 percent. Not a major difference, and the gravity should be close enough to 1 g that the compensator servos in the pressure suits should make it feel normal, but that commonality was a small thing. What would it actually be like down on the surface? What was the chemical composition of the atmosphere? What vegetation awaited discovery? Were there any animals left after Lost's war with the shoggoths? If so, what form did life take? Were there minerals here unknown elsewhere, and what would their value be? Would there be bacteria and viruses and fungi, and what would their nature be? Would they be deadly threats or pathways to new medicines?

And the world itself, it's structure. It was a rocky world, with mountains and deserts and oceans, but scientists were still discovering new things about Earth's biosphere even after all these thousands of years. How long would it take for the science teams on Asphodel to even begin to grasp the nature of this world? It might take generations.

As her team shot across the tens of thousands of kilometers toward the planet, Bianca looked past the worlds and the moons to the stars that, though close by the normal structure of star systems, were still millions of klicks away. It was a binary star system, and now that Sibyl was online to help, the stellar cartographers had determined that it was not radically dissimilar to Alpha Centauri. Dr. Denny Paek had nicknamed these stars Scylla and Charybdis. Bianca thought that was a bad choice, two deadly clashing threats from the story of Odysseus. But, unless that "Lost" thing—whatever it was—offered different names, she knew these labels would stick.

Her explorer soul wanted to spend days out here, mapping, recording, seeing, being among the first to dive deep into a new system of stars and planets. But that was not her mission.

One step at a time, she reminded herself. *We're at war.*

The Lost Souls flew toward them and their herd of empty planets regardless.

Bianca felt her sense of wonder grow with every kilometer. Shadderal grew larger and larger on the screens, and she could pick out cloud patterns, then oceans and massive mountain ranges. There was no sign of life at all, only signs of where life had been. Thousands of cities—composed of those bizarre gigantic structures made of cones and tubes and blocks and other shapes exactly as Soren had described them—lay in ruins. Whole areas scrubbed to planes of ash by ancient catastrophes.

Dr. Soren and Captain Croft, with Sybil's help, had briefed the Lost Souls about everything Lost had said. It was all there to be seen. The war, the devastation, the losses. It made Bianca's heart ache because it reminded her of ancient cities built by indigenous peoples who believed that the world around them was theirs. The colonizers had come and slaughtered them by the millions, leaving ruins that had become tourist attractions.

If she was not on a military mission, she would have broken down in tears. They burned in her eyes, but she locked them away behind the iron doors of her professional self-control.

She tapped the comms channel. "Anyone have anything on their long-range sensors?"

"That's a negative," said Thunder Bear, who was farthest from the main group. "Zero bogeys."

"Stay sharp," she said. "And that goes for everyone. This is not a sightseeing tour."

They flew on toward Shadderal. Toward a world untouched by humankind.

"Entering the upper atmosphere," reported Hummingbird, who was flying point.

"Slow to one-third, and let's do a global," ordered Bianca.

There were seven tumblers on the mission, with Tank and Jericho still back on patrol around Asphodel. The skimmers were operating with reduced crews. With the deaths of Rabbit and Lovechild, a new lieutenant had been assigned to the team. Marco Diaz, the junior officer Bianca had met yesterday morning, was now a temporary member of the Lost Souls. He served as navigator of SK-1, with Haley Majka—Sweetpea—in the pilot's chair. Diaz, who had never needed a combat call sign before, had one hung on him by Calisto—Cricket, because of his small stature. Except for Haley, Diaz was the shortest member of the team. He hated the nickname, Bianca knew, but *Cricket* is what went into the log, and *Cricket* it would be.

Dr. Lars Soren was aboard that skimmer, and Bianca wondered how he was doing. She felt a great fondness for the stuffy philosopher, with her feelings settling comfortably between "uncle" and "dad." She hoped that he, at least, was able to indulge in the awe and wonder of what they were doing out here.

"Here we go," Bianca said as her sensors recorded the friction heat from the atmosphere. "Who wants to go help me plant a flag?"

2

The ships completed four orbits of Shadderal, shifting their angles so that the mapping cameras got multiple views of the entire surface. The tumblers transitioned from their deep-space cube configuration and deployed stubby wings and stunted tails, allowing them to navigate more easily in the atmosphere.

Although she had done this a hundred times, the process made Bianca feel strange. While the transformation was not dramatic, it was nonetheless a change. She thought about the changes the dagger ships had undergone. For a moment, that similarity disturbed her, but then she shifted her perspective. The aliens changed their ships to suit the needs of the mission, and the Lost Souls were doing nothing different. That insight made her feel less threatened by the aliens. In fact, she felt like she understood them a bit more because—the shape and scale of their transformation notwithstanding—it was the same basic idea. It was science and strategy and tech, to solve whatever problems they faced.

The ships dropped from high-altitude many miles down through the thin atmosphere and angled toward the city Lost had shown to Soren. Sybil had located it, and now they flew toward it at greatly reduced speed.

"God almighty," called Calisto over the team. "Are you guys *seeing* this?"

They were, and after a moment of chatter, they fell into a horrified silence.

There were rivers choked with craft that might have been spaceships of various unknown kinds. Everything was destroyed, burned, shattered. The cracked and crushed hulls of countless ships lay scattered across the face of the world, as if this was where a great battle had been fought. Perhaps the last battle of the war that killed Lost and his allies. Some of those ships were many times larger than the biggest spacecraft carriers Soren had seen in orbit around Earth and Luna. One of them stretched from one bank of a wide river to the other, and had to be three or four kilometers long.

All dead.

And old. There was a coating of dust on everything, and where metal rose up from that gray blanket, the metal was pitted and eaten by rust. That alone suggested it had been centuries, if not millennia, since this war ended.

There was a long row of massive stones buildings with humped roofs that called to mind the kind of Quonset hut structures that the military so often used, but most of these buildings lay in ruins, with collapsed ceilings and rubble choked with desiccated weeds. There was nothing to indicate anyone survived the war. The crashed ships appeared to lay where they had fallen.

"The Field of Dead Birds," Soren murmured as he leaned toward the skimmer's viewscreen.

"Is this what you were hoping to find, Doc?" asked Sweetpea.

"Hoping? No," said Soren. "Expecting? Sadly, yes."

It was such a sad spectacle. Foreboding, because it spoke to the powers they were pitted against. Whoever had won had been more powerful than these magnificent, ruined ships. Which meant that Asphodel and its small squadron of fighters were shockingly, astoundingly outnumbered and outgunned.

Soren wished that his faith was more doctrinal than it was, rather than philosophically spiritual. He often exclaimed in God's name but did not believe in a single and omnipotent God. He hoped there were benign forces in the universe, but if all the deities were like the shoggoths' strange Outer Gods, then what little faith he possessed was going to crumble into dust like all those cities.

"I'm going to complete my sweep," said the pilot. "Then I guess we can find a place to put you down."

3

"Negative on hostile presence," reported Bianca as she soared through the leaden sky. "Everything down there looks dead."

"Very well," said Croft. "Your transmission is weak. Deploy signal boosters."

"Roger that." Bianca relayed the order to the two skimmers, and each launched dozens of barrel-shaped self-guiding drones that shot off in every direction, rising high into the atmosphere to establish a global signal relay. The drones also received feeds from every ship that allowed mapping software build a detailed model of Shadderal.

Croft's voice came back crystal clear. "Mosquito, send the skimmers down with one tumbler each as escort. I want everyone else in the air with eyes and ears open."

"Clear copy on that, C-One." Then she called Soren aboard SK-1. "Doc, are you ready for this?"

"I am," said the professor. "Oh, wait … should I say *copy*, or *roger*, or something?"

"You're good," laughed Bianca. "Okay, SK-1, you're on to land at the outer edge of the Field of Dead Birds."

"Can we give that another name?" asked Diaz.

"If you see Lost you can take it up with him," said Bianca.

The skimmer dropped down toward the surface of Shadderal. Bianca flew in a big circle at six thousand meters, guns hot in case there were shoggoths—or some other danger as yet unknown—waiting.

4

On Asphodel Station, Lady Jessica sat next to Captain Croft in the Navy observation subdeck mounted on the hull above the launch tubes.

She studied the images as Soren's skimmer, SK-1, wheeled around and flew low over the countless rows of dead ships. Once, as a girl, she had seen dozens of whales washed up on the west coast of Clare. Their vast, silent gray forms had a similar sense of tragedy, of life cut cruelly short, stolen by forces unknown.

She had walked among those giants, touching some, then standing near one still crying out in plaintive whale song. That had startled her, frightened her badly, and broken her heart. It was the first time she realized that she could hear the voices of the dead. That song was the saddest thing she had ever heard, then or since.

"Yes," she said with no doubt at all in her mind. "Lars, you're right. Lost is there somewhere. Near the ships."

Croft glanced at her, trying to read her face.

She pointed to a valley a few kilometers from the graveyard of ships. "What's that?"

"What's what?" asked Croft.

She touched the screen. "That. I can't make it out."

Croft had the tech zoom in and sharpen the clarity, but all he could see was darkness between two high ridges of rocky cliffs. He ordered Sweetpea to do another pass, lower and slower. The skimmer pilot did, but the darkness seemed to be nothing but that—shadows draped across a deep crevasse.

"Soren," McHugh said into the mic, "do you see anything down in those shadows?"

"I … no … yes … I'm not sure."

"There's something there," McHugh said. "I can't see it, but I can *feel* it."

"How sure are you?" asked Soren.

"Very."

Croft studied the image and then turned to her. "This feeling of yours. Is it a good feeling or a bad feeling? Or is that a stupid question?"

"It's a very good question, Captain," she assured him. She closed her eyes for a moment. When she opened them, she nodded. "Soren, I think you need to go down there first. Into that valley."

There was a significant pause, and then Soren said, "Yes. I agree."

"It's dark as the devil's ass down there, Skipper," Sweetpea said, "but I can see a flat place just inside the edge of the shadows. Looks good for landing."

"Okay, but hear me on this," said Croft. "If you don't like anything, haul ass out of there. And if you see anything that looks alive and cranky, kill it."

"Copy that."

Lady Jessica perched on the edge of her chair and watched as SK-1 descended toward the veil of shadows and then vanished entirely inside it. Sweetpea kept her mic on as she read out the altitude, wind, and atmospheric density. The cockpit chatter was more for reassurance, McHugh reasoned.

Letting us know that they're still there. Still alive.

Even so, Lady Death prayed silently to all of the gods and spirits, guides and beings in which she believed. She offered prayers of protection for Soren and every one of the Lost Souls.

5

As SK-1, with Lucky flying escort, vanished from view into the lightless valley, Bianca felt a tremble in her chest. It was like a cold wind blowing across her heart. Not for one moment did she think it was leftover pain from her cardiac arrest or the tissue damage from CPR.

She knew that it was something else. Fear and something whose nature was undefinable. For the second time since she was a child, she crossed herself, though she was entirely unaware that she did it.

Even when Sweetpea radioed that they were down and safe, Bianca did not relax. Her tumbler cut through the gray skies far above the Field of Dead Birds. She made several circuits and, on her third pass, she saw far below her the rear bay door of the skimmer open and the ungainly form of Dr. Lars Soren stagger awkwardly onto the surface of Shadderal, with the two Marines behind him, their pulse rifles up and out, ready for anything.

"Congratulations, Doc," Bianca said over the comms. "You just took a step into history. First human on an exoplanet."

There was a burst of applause and even cheers over the radio waves. Soren stopped, turned, and looked up at the ships overhead. They all wobbled in a kind of salute.

"Thank you," said Soren. "You will forgive me if I decline to plant a flag. It's really not that kind of moment."

"Copy that," said Bianca. "What matters is you're standing on an alien world."

"And I am filled with wonder," said Soren. "I am in awe."

Take care of yourself, you crazy old man, she thought. *You take real good care.*

6

It was the color that Dr. Soren felt.

Felt.

Seeing it was one thing. The rocks were black, but veined with opalescent minerals that caught rays of light and twisted them. That light from the distant, dying sun was cold and painted the vista in ten thousand shades of blue, gray, white, and black. Here and there were desperate splashes of faint yellow and red, but these hues were weak and defeated by the oppressive weight of azure, sapphire, and cobalt.

And yet it was how the colors felt that affected him.

That feeling was what pulled him from observation into perception. It was as if he had discovered the exact shade and tone of abandonment. Of a loss so profound that this world stopped dipping into its paintbox and surrendered to the cold blue light.

The last day of the dying universe would look like this, he knew. When all warmth had been leeched away into the void and there was no one left to offer even the token gift of living heat. When the last surviving planets failed and faded, admitting defeat in any struggle to sustain life. When all higher forms were gone and even the durable champions of survival—the fungi and bacteria—could eke no sustenance. This was what would be left.

A place.

A rock in space that offered no shelter, no future, and no hope. Planets whose suns had died without expanding into supernovae and had merely burned themselves out.

Soren stood on the edge of a shelf that was too flat, too orderly to have been formed by any process of nature's tumult. There was not a ripple or lump or edge—merely flatness. It was a place for him to stand. A place, he knew, that was put here by someone for a moment like this.

A place to witness.

To behold.

To believe that a message was being shared, even if its form was cryptic beyond any chance of his understanding.

And so he stood. He beheld. His space suit—breathing for him—kept the bottomless cold away, providing no need for inward attention, and thus allowed him the full weight of outward observation.

He stood on the shelf and looked out across a gulf of distance to where it stood.

It.

The thing was at least four kilometers away, and yet he could see every detail with clarity. It rose seven or eight kilometers into the air.

Taller than the surrounding mountains, its cyclopean scale was beyond his understanding. How could such a thing ever have been built? No science he knew of could have accomplished it. No builder of his race could have imagined it or yearned to do it. Not even a priest would envision a tribute on this scale.

It was a figure.

Manlike without being precisely human. Naked, kneeling on the shattered slopes of a long-dead volcano. The figure's back was curved as if in defeat or humility, and it struck Soren how much those two postures were alike. With head bowed, eyes cast downward, and arms raised up and out, the figure turned one empty hand to the sky. The other hand clasped the tapered base of a large vase or jar, the mouth of which was turned down toward the ground. Its stylized lid lay by the giant's knee.

What was this figure's meaning? Why did it hold an empty vessel? What contents was that vessel supposed to have held? An offering?

Or was its emptiness the point?

And the figure's other hand. Its fingers were splayed in—what? Was it supplication? Did it beseech? Was the empty jar symbolic of poverty, or want, or need? If none of these, what did the jar's emptiness and the other hand's upturned gesture signify? What boon was being begged? What forgiveness asked? Was this whole statue meant to convey some lost race's ultimate plea for mercy?

The explorer stood and tried not to impose his inference on the statue.

A name hovered at the edge of his awareness, and he felt a chill inside the warmth of his spacesuit. It was not a label he would have deliberately given this thing. And yet he found himself murmuring it aloud.

"The Shrine of the Penitent."

Those five words filled his ears and his mind, and he knew that it was the true name of this monument, though knowing it as surely as he did was an impossibility.

"Say again," came a voice, Captain Croft's from far above on Asphodel. "Dr. Soren … repeat your message."

Soren did not immediately reply. *The Shrine of the Penitent.*

"Why am I here?" Soren murmured.

"Dr. Soren, please say again," urged Croft. There was concern in the captain's voice. Fear too. "You're breaking up."

But Soren did not answer him. He took a few small steps, bringing him to the very edge of the shelf.

"Sir," called the Marine Milford, "have you found something?"

"Stay back," said Soren sharply. Then, in a calmer voice he said, "I'm okay. There's no danger. Please, stay back until I call."

"If you see *anything*, Doc," Milford said, "sing out."

They can't see it, Soren realized. *That statue should be filling every screen on the ship, but they can't see it. If they could, they would not be talking to me. They would be yelling. Screaming. Shouting.*

He almost told them that he had found nothing. There was a need in him, very deep and very real, to turn his back and forget what he had seen. There was something deeply terrifying about that statue and what it represented. He was aware that he could not know its meaning, could not consciously understand it. But he feared it. Hated it. Dreaded it.

And it threatened to break his heart.

The crew of the skimmer was waiting for him on the edge of the plane. Soren wanted to turn, to flee this place, to deny its existence and the horrors it whispered of.

He almost ran away.

Almost.

That he did not was a hard decision to make, and he was not then, or afterward, sure that it was the right one. But in light of all that had happened over the last two days, there was no escaping it. The implied truth was brutal, insidious, and cruel.

He nearly spoke a dozen times, and each time his lips formed words, but his lungs gave them no power. Soren closed his eyes and felt the tears on his lashes and then on his cheeks. Despite the suit's heater, those tears were cold. So very cold.

Finally, he said, "I've found something."

7

"I prayed you would come," said Lost.

Soren cried out, staggering as he turned, and nearly fell backward off the cliff. If not for a jutting piece of shale, he would have tumbled into darkness and joined the uncounted legions of ghosts on this desolate world.

Wilson and Milford ran forward, barrels pointed at the golem.

"Doc, get behind us," cried Milford.

"No! Don't fire," cried Soren, recovering his balance.

Milford ignored him. "SK-1 prepare for immediate evac."

"Do not fire," pleaded Soren. "He is not a threat."

Lost stepped into the weak sunlight, his hands empty of weapons and hanging limp. He was no longer an amalgam of broken debris. Now he was something far more disturbing. He stood before Soren wearing a kind of rubberized flight suit that looked ancient. Pieces of it were gone—eaten away by time or perhaps by some microbes that had fed on the dark material. Gloves covered his hands, and the fingers of it were unusually long, with two thumbs, one on either side of the broad palms. His boots were built for feet that were extremely narrow at the heel but broadened out so that they looked vaguely like flippers. The front of the space suit was covered with symbols that flowed in all directions, so it was difficult to determine if they represented words or were merely decoration. Planted on broad shoulders was a helmet with a large visor and a headpiece that tapered backward to accommodate an inhuman skull.

That was the uniform, but it was not what disturbed Soren. What scared him was what could be seen through the rents and tears in the rubber and through the cracked faceplate of the helmet. Bones. Long since picked clean of all flesh and bleached to a dusty white.

Aghast, Soren realized that he was seeing the remains of the dead thing who now called himself Lost.

Lost indeed.

"My ... God ..." breathed Soren.

"No," said Lost, "not that. Certainly not that."

"No ... I meant ..."

The Marines kept their guns trained on the strange figure.

"Dr. Soren," came Croft's voice over the comms, "are you in danger?"

Soren looked at Lost. "Am I?"

The golem looked at him. "You are safe here."

"Call it, C-One," said Milford.

"Doc," said Croft, "you better be right about this. If that thing so much as twitches, those Marines will blow it to dust. Do you read me loud and clear?"

"I do, Captain," said Soren. "But please, have your men lower their weapons and step back."

Croft gave the order, and the two Marines moved their gun barrels away and, finally, down at the ground, but it was clear they were ready to swing them back up and fire at a moment's notice.

Lost walked past Soren and stood looking at the gigantic statue. The professor blew out his cheeks and came over very carefully, standing two meters away. They stood like that for nearly a full minute.

Then Soren said, "They did not see that statue from the ship. Not on any of the cameras or sensors."

"They would not," said Lost. "They could not."

"I don't understand."

"It is not really here."

"I don't understand that either."

Lost pointed. "It was built using technology so old that even my people knew only its smallest secrets. Like the gods of my people, to whom it was built in tribute, it does not exist within this or any world. It has no physical existence at all, but rather is imposed across the infinite worlds and through the limitless realms of dream."

"Do you mean the Outer Gods?"

"No, our gods were never part of that pantheon," said Lost, his bitterness evident. "Nor are they the Lesser Gods. Their names will not matter to you. No one yet lives who worshipped them, and perhaps that means the gods, too, have died. Let their names be forgotten, and let them rest in peace."

Soren accepted this, though he felt a pang of grief. There were many gods of Earth whose names had likewise turned to dust as their worshippers passed away or were exterminated. And many who were still remembered but were no longer worshipped. He did not know which was sadder.

He gestured to the giant statue. "Why can I see it and my friends cannot?"

"You see it because you are near me, and I can see it," said Lost.

"The Marines are nearby, and it is invisible to them."

Lost looked at him. "Perhaps it is more accurate to say they cannot see it because I do not want them to. Not now. Not before you have had time to understand it. Let it be thus."

Soren nodded, accepting it for now. "Who built the statue? What does it symbolize? In my mind it speaks a name. The Shrine of the Penitent. But … penitence for what? Was this to appease the Outer Gods you fought?"

"Appease …" murmured Lost. His voice was stronger down here, but proximity did not give it any comforting qualities. It sounded like words formed by the passage of wind through rusted metal bars. Thin, shrill, deeply unpleasant. "What a strange interpretation."

"If I err," said Soren, "it is because I lack cultural context. I can only attempt to infer meaning through comparison with what I know of my own species' body language, postures, and gestures."

"You must have the gift of great empathy, Dr. Soren," said the golem. "Yes. It is the Shrine of the Penitent."

"Again I ask, penitence for what?"

Lost did not look at him—and Soren was fine with that. Being looked at through the empty sockets of an ancient alien skull would have been disturbing. Still, Soren felt seen, as if the spirit—the *ghost*—of Lost was studying him intently.

"For our crimes," said the creature.

"What crimes?" begged Soren.

Lost bowed his head as if in sorrow. "When the war began, Dr. Soren, we thought that we could beat these monsters who call themselves the Outer Gods. For ten times ten thousand years we fought them and their armies of shoggoths, night gaunts, mi-go, dimensional shamblers, deep ones, and so many others. They were uncountable, and their warships filled the skies of every world in this part of the galaxy. Fifty billion ships filled with horrors. And yet we fought."

Soren did not ask if Lost exaggerated. It was obvious that he spoke the truth.

"Is that how you lost the war? An overwhelming armada?"

"Lost?" mused the creature of the same name. "We won many battles. Many. We burned countless ships from the skies. We found and burned the home worlds of the shoggoths. We chased them through the dark and gave as good as we got."

"Then how did you lose?"

Images flickered across the broken faceplate. The Field of Dead Birds. Fleets of ships. Planets blown to fragments. Devices fired into the hearts of suns to make them go nova. And then on a smaller scale, ground battles between the chimeric ships of both sides. Giants made from merged ships and parts of ships battling each other with guns and lasers, missiles, particle weapons, and swords. It was like watching the Titans of Greek myth doing battle, but each clad in armor made from spacecraft.

Then the image Lost showed focused on one particular titan—and the phrase *ghost ship* appeared with inexplicable insight in Soren's mind, and with clarity he knew that's what Lost's people called their old chimera craft. It battled on despite being badly outnumbered. Wreckage from two of the enemy chimeras lay scattered around it, and two other enemy giants were approaching with evident caution. The fight swirled and moved, with the man-shaped combat ships leaping into the air for aerial attacks or digging in to swing blows of such monumental force that shock waves flattened groves of things like trees and knocked over buildings. The battle rambled through a small city, and Soren leaned close to see tiny figures with elongated skulls, huge eyes, and reptilian skin fleeing in vain hope of safety. But the warring giants trod upon them in the heat and frenzy of their destruction.

The defending ghost ship spun through dynamic maneuvers and came up on the enemy's quarter to hammer it with rockets until the chimera exploded. The enemy toppled, but as it fell, one hand—if it could be called a hand—snaked out and caught the ghost ship's wrist. The collapse of millions of tons jerked the defender off balance, and it, too, fell. In that instant the remaining enemy leaped into the air, its feet and hands folding out of the way to expose the engine exhaust ports of the ships that composed it, and as it dropped down, it spun its engines up to critical levels so that their exhaust melted arm cannons and rocket launchers and finally seared a hole through the defending giant's chest.

The images faded and vanished, and Lost gestured around at the dead ships and decay. "This is where the last battle against the armies of the Outer Gods was fought. It is where we won, and where we lost."

"You call yourself Lost," said Soren gravely, "and I understand why, I think. But do you have an actual name? The name by which you were known among your own kind?"

"I will tell you, but Lost is what I prefer to be called now."

"Tell me anyway."

Lost nodded and spoke his name, but the sounds were bizarre, unnatural, impossible for any human throat to speak. And the name was long, a convoluted set of interlocking phrases that, Soren guessed, carried much more than individual identification, probably some group context—family or nation or world.

When the sound had faded into the desultory wind, the golem said, "I am Lost, and that is enough."

"This place … is this where you died?"

Lost looked at the field of dead ships. "I died here many times," said the ghost. "Many, many times."

"You died many times? I don't understand."

"You will," the golem assured him.

They looked at the shrine. Soren repeated his earlier question. "Who built the statue?"

"I did," said Lost.

"Why?" he asked.

"It was part of my own penance," said Lost in a voice as desolate as his name. "It will be all that is left of me—of my people—when I finally fade from all living memory."

8

McHugh and Croft were shoulder to shoulder, bent forward to watch the screen and listen to Soren's strange conversation with Lost. The huge RealScreen showed the strange and ruined city, a wall of mountains on one side of the huge field of wrecked spacecraft, beyond which stood the rows of gigantic Quonset hut–style buildings. A forest of twisted trees rose on two other sides, and then the shadow-shrouded valley lay on the fourth. Nowhere, though, could they see the Shrine of the Penitent, even when the orbiting sensor network used lidar scans.

Croft covered the mic. "What are they talking about? What statue?"

McHugh shook her head. "I don't know."

The captain tapped into a private channel to speak with Haley Majka. "Sweetpea," he said, "can you pan around to show us the statue?"

"Sir, there is no statue down here that I can see. Just Doc Soren and that Lost thing talking on a ledge."

"Lucky, what do you see?" asked the captain.

The tumbler pilot said, "There's nothing but the valley, the ruined city, some factory-looking buildings, and that Field of Dead Birds thing down there, Skipper. Nothing else."

Lost stepped toward the professor. "There is much I need to say, Dr. Soren, and we have very little time. I will endeavor to explain to you what I can about the war. It is ... difficult ... to frame certain concepts and events in ways you will understand, but I will try."

"And I will listen with an open heart and an open mind."

Lost nodded. "Our cultures are vastly different, as are our minds, and our connection to spirit and to interdimensionality. Please try to understand that we are not beings as you are. We had physical form, but our consciousness was not bound to three-dimensional space. All life is naturally pandimensional. Your Lady Death understands this, or some of it. Several people among your group of faith leaders may understand it. You may even grasp enough to help me help you."

Soren merely nodded.

Lost studied him with eye sockets filled with shadows. "I have learned much about you from Sybil. She is wise—wiser than you know. Through her I have come to know that your species possesses more grace and much more potential for understanding than you know. Even in the handful of millennia since humanity built its first cities—a long time to you but a blink of time's eye for many civilizations through the cosmos—you have made great leaps in understanding. But not all, Dr. Soren. Your kind have not lived enough for some necessary things to be commonly known."

"We are young, I'll admit," said Soren. "It has been less than two centuries since we first set foot on our Moon."

"This is what I mean," agreed Lost. "Now you have stepped across the whole of the Galaxy."

"By accident."

"There are no accidents in the universe, Dr. Soren," said Lost. "Even if we do not ever know the how or the why, all things unfold along a path."

"I do not know if I agree," said Soren. "There is free will."

"There is. But that does not change this truth. For the universe is not space. It is existence, and existence is infinite variation, all of it happening at once."

Lost paused and looked at his gloved hands. Gloves, Soren knew, filled only with dust and bones.

"I stray," he admitted. "I have been alone with my own thoughts for far too long."

"Tell me what I need to know to help save my people," begged Soren. "May I ask that of you?"

Lost let his hands fall to his sides and nodded to the endless acres of silent ships. "We do not know where the Outer Gods came from. Some believed that they were born with the nascent universe. Others— myself included—think that what your kind call the 'Big Bang' was a doorway blown open by the death of another universe. The Outer Gods came through that door for reasons of their own. Perhaps they had destroyed the old universe, and maybe many before that. Perhaps they were exiled by some greater power. How will anyone ever know?"

He shook his head. It was an oddly human gesture, and Soren wondered if it had also been picked up during Lost's communication with Sibyl.

"The Outer Gods came to this galaxy in particular through the black hole at the galaxy's heart. It was a doorway of a kind for them. But something happened, and they have become trapped here."

"How?"

"My people had countless theories, but we never learned the truth. That is left for someone else to discover. Maybe your own people will find it out," said Lost. "If you survive what is coming."

"What *is* coming?"

"More shoggoths."

"From where though? You said their home worlds were destroyed."

"They were, but survivors of that war settled new worlds across this part of the galaxy. Because of the great destruction we levied on them, they no longer knew where Shadderal was, and they have looked. Oh yes, Dr. Soren, they have looked. They want the resources that are still here to be found. When your station appeared here it sent a ripple through the network of energies that bind the entire galaxy together. The shoggoths have many bases, and a team was sent to investigate. Perhaps it was their own initiative, for they are ever watchful, or perhaps the Outer Gods told them. Even I do not understand the ways the shoggoths communicate with their masters. What matters is that the shoggoth patrol was sent. That was what your Lost Souls encountered. Everything that happened during the fight was transmitted back across that network. The defeat of that patrol will matter little. What does matter is that by following the spatial distortion of Asphodel's arrival, they have also found Shadderal."

Soren's mouth went totally dry. "How ... how soon will they be here?"

Lost did not answer that. Instead, he began speaking of the war that had raged. "When the Outer Gods sent the shoggoths to war against the settled worlds, your planet was barely a billion of your years old. Our people were old even then. The shoggoths were a plague, and they were numberless. World after world fell to them. Some sued for peace, begging to be allowed to live as long as they agreed to worship the Outer Gods."

"What happened to them?" asked Soren.

"The shoggoths suborned many of the oldest, grandest, most beautiful worlds," replied the golem. "Creatures of subtle minds and unimaginable elegance became slaves, forced to worship in ways too cruel to describe. Other races fled this invasion, and the shoggoths hunted them across the galaxy. A few races appealed to lesser gods for protection. Cthulhu was one of these they prayed to. But he was not powerful enough to defy the Outer Gods, and he, too, fled along with other failed gods. The Outer Gods sought them, not only sending out fleets of shoggoths but also seeking the Lesser Gods and Great Old Ones in dimensions apart from this one. There was a war in transdimensional realms—what you would call the heavens. These raged for uncountable millions of years. Yet in time the Lesser Gods were defeated, and the Outer Gods destroyed many, but some—a scant few thousand—scattered out to the farthest reaches of the galaxy, hiding in dreams, in the hearts of mountains, or deep beneath the seas. Some altered their energies and formed pantheons of gods to rule over new races emerging from the muck of young worlds. You, Dr. Soren, know this, for you have spoken about the pantheons of your own worlds."

"Yes ..."

"Your cosmic philosophy is more important than even you know. It is the boldest step along the path to cosmic *understanding*."

Soren snorted. "To be quite honest, I'm not all that happy being validated."

10

Bianca switched to a private channel that was just her, Jacob, and Calisto.

"Are you *hearing* this?"

"Sure are," Calisto. "And I don't know whether I'm feeling impressed or shocked or just wishing I was drunk."

"Leaning toward all three," said Jacob.

"And let's bear in mind, children," said Calisto, "we are listening to the ghost of an alien talk shit to a philosopher while they stand on the ruins of a world destroyed by monsters. I mean, for context and all."

Jacob laughed. "I really, *really* wish I was drunk and dreaming."

Bianca almost said, "I wish I was dead."

She didn't know why that thought popped into her head, but it was there.

"Stay sharp, guys," she said. They all switched back to the main channel and flew on.

11

"Planet after planet brought forward their best and brightest to be pilots," continued Lost. "Although there were ground battles, the real war was fought in the air or among the stars. A billion worlds were caught up in it. Generation after generation, we fed our young into the furnace of war. Soldiers and pilots. And for a while we beat back the shoggoth fleets. But attrition rates were very high, and as the war ground on, the number of good pilots diminished. Battles of the kind we had won decisively a century before now were being fought to standstills or with mounting losses that made each victory terribly costly."

"How did you beat them at all?" asked Soren. "If they had such greater numbers, I mean."

"They are many and they are relentless," said Lost, "but they are not innovative. Much of their technology was stolen from conquered worlds. Even their greatest weapon, the metamorphosing ships—what you call the chimeras—were taken from exterminated races. Their design suited the transformative nature of the shoggoths themselves, and the machines are remarkably simple to operate because the ships do most of the work."

"I don't understand what that means."

"The chimera ships were developed by a race of empaths who used them to explore the stars, and to do so long after their own pilots died and turned to dust." He gestured to the many massive spacecraft on the Field of Dead Birds. "These craft, those that are not broken that is, are only sleeping."

"Is that figurative language?" asked Soren. "If so, your meaning eludes me."

"No," said Lost. "It is literal truth. And the rows of buildings near them—these are factories."

"What of them?" asked Soren. "Surely they are as dead as everything else here."

"Not so," said Lost. "Most have fallen into ruin, but there are some that are still functioning. They have been working slowly but steadily for all these years."

"To what end?"

"To build a new fleet of ghost ships."

Soren shook his head. "New ships? Why? For *whom*?"

"I said that I dreamed of you, Dr. Soren," said the golem. "I dreamed of you and Lady Death and all of your people. I have had those dreams for thousands of years. Call it prophecy if it helps to frame it in your mind. I knew that someday you would come. That someone would come who would need to fight the shoggoths, and maybe carry the war to its just end, to the utter destruction of the Outer Gods. Those dreams began long before I died a physical death. Others of my kind had similar dreams. Of you, or of people like you from other races. Because my race believed in the power of dreams, we built the factories to be fully automated. As new ships were completed, they were brought out onto the Field of Dead Birds. If beings came who could fly the ships, they could also use the parts of the wrecked ships to create our own kind of chimeras. Ghost ship titans."

"This is ... incredible," gasped Soren. "I freely admit that it terrifies me. I'm not even sure it gives me hope. Knowing that my people were dreamed of and our arrival hoped for because your people wanted to hand down a legacy of war. That is rather horrible."

"The universe is unkind, Dr. Soren," said Lost. "But we did not start the war. We fought to our own extinction to keep the whole of the galaxy from falling to the Outer Gods."

Soren turned away and looked at the rows of Quonset hut factories, amazed but appalled that they had been laboring all these years in the hope that new warriors would come. Ghost ships indeed.

"How could we even hope to fly them even if we wanted to?" he asked weakly. "They were made for your kind, not for ours."

"Just as you have Sybil, we have our own AI. It links to the pilots and together—machine mind and living mind in harmony. The ships will help your people. These ships are, in their own way, alive, Dr. Soren."

"Alive?"

"Do you think Sibyl is the only AI that has ever achieved consciousness?"

Soren stared at him. "Sybil is not self-aware."

Lost shook his head. "Those ships become one with the consciousness of the pilots. We do not know how the shoggoths managed to control their ships, because their consciousness is not like those of the uncounted free species. However, we created a way for our species and the ships to become one."

"I don't understand."

"You will," Lost told him. "You will need to."

12

Jericho was making a long sweep of the blackness, cruising at fifty thousand kilometers out from Asphodel. Tank was at the same distance but on the far side.

They each had their shields lowered to minimum to allow their long-range sensors to work without interference from the null field. It increased sensor range by an order of magnitude, but it left both pilots feeling far too vulnerable. Both were on high alert, the full array of combat holograms in place around their hands, chest and head, while their feet worked steering pedals.

"Command," called Jericho, "I've got something at the outer edge of sensor range."

"What are you seeing?" asked Croft.

"Can't tell yet. It's a strange signal. Large. Maybe another asteroid belt or some kind of dense nebula, something with a lot of particulates big enough to ping my scopes."

"Speed and course?"

Jericho forwarded the sensor information back to command, but it was indistinct for them too at such an extreme range.

"I could use some boost out here, Skipper," he called. "When will the new antenna be operational?"

"Soon," said Croft. "It's in place, and we're working on the calibration."

"Sir, do you want me to go investigate?"

"That is affirmative, Jericho. Once the antenna is online, your bird will act as a booster to its signals. Get as close to that debris field as you can, but take no undue risks. Is that clear?"

"Yes, sir," said Jericho. "Leaving orbit around station now."

He kicked his tumbler forward and began accelerating.

13

"You say that some of the ships on the Field of Dead Birds are new, ready for combat," said Dr. Soren. "But you seem to be taking a long time to explain in any detail how they work. Is there an issue? Is there some kind of danger of which I'm not yet aware?"

Lost studied him. "As I said, you have the gift of insight. I am afraid that what I have to say will not be what you want to hear."

"That is true of nearly everything you've said so far," admitted Soren. "But tell me anyway."

"I speak of a terrible danger," said Lost. "The same energies that made the chimeras so effective in combat made them equally lethal to the pilots."

"Wait … *lethal*? I don't understand."

"The engines that drive them, the energy that allows them to fly at such great speeds and, moreover, to change shape and become titans, all relies on a form of power that emits radiation of a kind unknown to your world. In truth, its nature was never fully understood even by *our* best scientists."

"How can you not understand?" insisted Soren.

Lost shook his head. "I was a pilot, not a scientist. However, I have witnessed these effects firsthand and know its dangers. Listen, Dr. Soren, I said that there were many races that formed our alliance against the Outer Gods. My own was not the race that first built the ghost ships. The race that had built them fought their own war against the Outer Gods. It was in another part of the galaxy, and although they won thousands of battles, the war outlasted them."

"What do you mean? Are you talking about simple attrition?"

"I speak of sacrifice," said Lost. "This is the hard truth. Those ships are faster, more powerful, more adaptive than what the shoggoths have. The enemy mimics them, as your Lost Souls witnessed, but their chimeras are vastly inferior. Without the ghost ships, the balance of power would remain with the shoggoths, and their campaign against the enemies of the Outer Gods would sweep all resistance away. By the time we encountered this other race, they were nearly extinct. Only a few survived, and they helped us understand the nature and power of this new technology. They warned us of the cost, but in our arrogance we thought that, as a different species, we could do what they could not. That was folly. We tried a thousand different kinds of protection—special suits, new kinds of shielding, drug therapy for the pilots, and even manipulation of our genes to make us more resistant. Yet the energies ate away at each pilot, killing many—*many*—of them. Some living pilots could fly one or two missions before the radiation killed them, and even then we saw how effective the ghost ships were. But in truth most pilots died shortly after the engines were turned on."

"That's horrible."

"It is much worse," said Lost. "We could not easily train pilots, because even the simulators were dangerous, since they could only be built using technology from other chimeras. There was no way to separate the radiation from the machine and yet keep the benefits of having warships effective against the shoggoths. As a result, we won many battles but sent uncountable pilots to their deaths. Still, we could not abandon the technology, because nothing else gave us a reasonable fighting chance against the shoggoths. But then a warrior priest of a faith whose name I can barely translate into English—call it the Voice of Winds—came up with a radical plan."

Soren felt his pulse racing. "I am almost certain I don't want to know what that idea was."

"And I feel horror and shame for even telling you," said Lost, "of his idea of trying to resurrect the best of the dead pilots to fly the ships. Ghosts to fly ghost ships."

"Wait," cried Soren in horror, "that's why you told me to talk with Lady Jessica. You're talking about *necromancy*."

"Of a kind, yes. We call it *ethla*. The communication between machine and organic minds. The Voice of the Wind discovered that whereas a living pilot could work with the shipboard AI, there was still that slight and frequently fatal lag between perception, decision, and action and the translation of this to the ship so that the AI could best carry out combat commands. Do you understand what I mean?"

"I think so," said Soren, marveling at the concept. "So the pilot's … ah … *conscious soul* flew these ships, with the AI as an extension of their will? Is that correct?"

"Not exactly, Dr. Soren," said Lost. "For the ship to function with peak efficiency, the pilot needed to submerge into the AI, to *yield* to the will of the ship. The shipboard AI knew how to fight but needed the vitality of an organic mind to work."

"I am amazed that your scientists were open to something so … spiritual."

"For us death was not a mystery to be sought in the dark, Dr. Soren," said Lost. "The science of death not as an event or medical curiosity but as a state of consciousness, as a dimension that exists in some form on all planes of existence. This necromantic technology is the hope I bring to your people."

"Necromantic technology," echoed Soren. "Odd. When I was a boy, I played holo-games that touched on an idea like this. NecroTek it was called. Similar concept."

"Yes. Lady Death and our warrior priest would have had much to say to one another. But he is long dead, and there are no remnants of the Voice of the Winds. They were scattered to the solar winds ten thousand years ago and more."

Soren sagged inwardly.

Lost said, "More than eight thousand scientists, alchemists, and mystics from the civilized worlds labored to redesign our ships to work with unbodied consciousnesses."

"They solved it though? They figured out a solution using this NecroTek?"

"They did," said Lost, though he sounded oddly cautious. "They raised a legion of spirits—fifty thousand ghost pilots. Fifty thousand NecroTeks, to use your word. And we beat the shoggoths back across the stars. We burned their shipyard worlds and destroyed nearly all of their breeding farms. They fled across the stars, and we pursued. There is no number for how many battles were fought, or how many died on each side."

"Wait, wait … but your pilots were … ghosts. How could they die?"

Lost turned to him and Soren swore that death-mask face gave him a pitying look. "Over time we found that the resurrections were not permanent. As ships were destroyed in combat and the mystics transferred souls from a wreck to a new craft, there was less of the original soul energy carried with it. In your culture, you believe that the soul is immortal. We held the same belief, but we learned that the soul is merely one manifestation of our essential being. What we called a soul—the blend of spiritual essences and lingering personality—was neither immortal nor immutable. We had to accept that the souls of these great pilots were being fragmented, worn away, until they were shredded and destroyed, leaving no trace. For us—and I suspect for you—that is truest and most horrible definition of death. The pilots and everything that defined them was lost forever."

"Lost souls," breathed Soren. "Dear God." He turned and looked at the Shrine of the Penitent. "I think I understand now."

"No," said Lost, "you do not. I have told you the cost of waging war against the Outer Gods, but I have not told you the extent of the crimes we committed to win."

Without turning, Soren said, "Then tell me now."

"We did not tell the families of the dead," said Lost quietly. "We lied to the pilots who lined up to take poisons and die so *they* could become the next wave of pilots. And the next. We did not tell them that they risked their immortal souls. We hid the truth from them because we needed those volunteers. We committed genocide on ourselves to fight this war."

Soren sat down heavily on the ground. He wanted to scream, he wanted to bang his fists against his own skull, but the helmet prevented even that.

14

"Dear God."

Lost and Soren's words filled the entire command center. They rang in the ears of every tumbler and skimmer pilot, and all through Asphodel Station.

"Please," begged Calisto, "tell me I did not hear what I just heard."

"Shit," said Bianca.

No one else said a word.

15

Lost stood next to where Soren sat, both of them looking at the statue.

"What else could we do?" asked the golem. "Commit terrible sins, or allow thousands of worlds across the galaxy to be extinguished by the shoggoth fleets? You must understand that the Outer Gods were not just *our* enemies—they are the enemies of every single sentient species that does not worship them. Uncountable trillions of innocent lives were at stake. What could we do? There was no good choice to make, and so we took the path that led toward a faint hope of victory."

Soren nodded. Not in acceptance, but in understanding. Then a thought occurred to him.

"But tell me … how did the shoggoths fly the chimeras? Our pilots saw one transform during the recent battle."

"Their ships are attempts to copy our design. They are not as fast or as adaptive, nor do they use the same rare form of radiation. They are dangerous, to be sure, but their true strength is in numbers. They have no true NecroTek, nor anything like *ethla*."

"That is cold comfort," said Soren, shaking his head.

"There is little comfort there," said Lost. "They looked long for Shadderal. It is only luck that the fleet that attacked us here died with the secret of our location. The shoggoths covet our NecroTek ships. We know this from times when they tried to fly ships of ours that were captured. They risked their lives and whatever passes for souls to try to fly them. Given time, they would certainly have figured it out, but in each case we destroyed the stolen ships."

"Given the enormity of your losses, I don't think I'd be so crass as to call that 'luck.'"

"Hardly," said Lost. "Now I will tell you something I believe you will need to know. I am aware that your pilots and your officers are listening. They need to know too. The time for hiding truths is past."

"Then tell us," said Soren in a harsh and bitter voice.

"We were winning the war. Eventually," said the ghost, "we found where the shoggoths came from. Their species had once been a more primitive form of organic life that had evolved to be adaptive on a world that was geologically toxic and inhospitable. Over time, as they evolved, they spread out to all five planets of a binary star system. Not the twin suns that shed light on Shadderal and its sister worlds. These were very far away. Two blue suns. The Outer Gods discovered this metamorphic species and saw their potential. They used their own dark science to expand the shoggoths' intellects and at the same time forced them into eternal servitude. Then, near the end of our war, one of our scout ships tracked a crippled chimera back to those home worlds. We seized upon the opportunity, and we sent the greatest fleet that has ever been assembled to destroy the armies of our enemy gods. We laid siege to the shoggoth home worlds."

A wind picked up and blew dust across the face of the Shrine of the Penitent, briefly obscuring its countenance just as the cracked faceplate of Lost's helmet obscured the golem's.

"We were close to winning the war," Lost said. "By the sacrifice of our pilots and their immortal souls, we drew all of our resources together for a final campaign ... a war of genocide. But the shoggoths somehow discovered this plan and sent a fleet to exterminate us."

Lost waved his arms at the sky, at the planets and moons visible even in daylight.

"This system, as I'm sure your scientists have already discovered, is not natural. It was engineered like this for easy travel so we could go from world to world, and moon to moon. It allowed us to be more efficient, but once the shoggoths discovered it, that proximity became a tempting target. As we sought to destroy their home system, they tried to destroy ours."

16

Jacob Fox spun his tumbler across the face of Shadderal.

When he saw his target, he rose in a steep climb, leveled out, and flew slowly across the bow of another tumbler. T-1 was stenciled on all six sides of that ship, and above it, written in bold script, was the combat call sign Mosquito.

He matched Bianca's ship for speed and edged close.

"Galahad," called Captain Croft, "you have deviated from your flight pattern."

"Thought I saw Mosquito's ship trailing smoke," lied Jacob. "Doing a visual."

A beat. "Very well," said the captain. Jacob wondered if the skipper knew what he was actually doing.

Through the ports—his own and hers—he saw Bianca there. She turned her head toward him, tapped a button on her helmet to raise the visor, and then looked directly at him. She reached down and hit another button, and a tiny light on his display switched from green to red. He smiled and tapped the same button. Now the interior cameras and flight recorders were off. No one could see either of them except the other.

Jacob touched his fingers to his lips, kissed them, and pressed them to his heart.

Bianca did the same.

After a few beautiful moments, Jacob reengaged his cameras and veered sharply away. He had seen the light in Bianca's eyes—beautiful, strong, fierce, sad. That brief look was almost more than he could bear.

He dropped down to the troposphere and continued his patrol.

17

"What did you do?" asked Soren.

"When I learned of the attack on Shadderal," Lost continued, "I came back here with fifty ships. Some of us were pilots who had died more than a dozen times, and we knew that we were at the end of our so-called immortal lives. But we had to try. We had been fooled by our enemy. Our fleet stayed behind to exterminate the shoggoth worlds, but *we* returned to find our own worlds burning. The fifty of us fought like demons. We died and were reborn, died and were reborn, each time rising inside one of the new ghost ships built by our automated factories. Again and again. Letting our souls be shredded and returning to the surface of Shadderal, to the Field of Birds before it became the place of *dead* birds."

"Are we really talking about the death of a *soul*?" Soren asked. "That is horrible beyond words. It's the worst thing I have ever heard."

"We prayed to our own gods for strength," said Soren. "We prayed for renewal of our souls. We destroyed the invaders, but the war went on too long, the fires burned too brightly, and by the time the last of the shoggoth ships fell, we had already lost. Our worlds were dead. Our own chimera fleet, those fifty, died destroying many times our number. We won by dying, but we killed ourselves. What kind of victory is that?"

"And the rest of the fleet? The ones who went to destroy the shoggoths? What happened to them?"

"Only one ship returned, and its pilot was already fading out of existence. He said that the enemy moon was a trap. By some science or sorcery—no one will ever know which—the moon itself was turned into a radiation bomb. When it blew, it killed all of the shoggoths there, but it destroyed our entire fleet. A doomsday weapon of incalculable power. The blast destroyed both of the shoggoth's twin suns, collapsing them into a black hole."

Soren could only shake his head.

"This is what we have left," said Lost, nodding to the field. "Dead ships and viable ships we cannot fly because everyone but me is dead. There is no one left to enter into *ethla* with the ships down there. None except me, and I have only one flight left before I fade away. I am weak. You've seen how difficult it is for me to manifest even a form made of debris. A chimera ship would shred me within hours."

"The Shrine," said Soren sadly. "I think I understand it now. I get the nature of your penitence. By not telling the pilots what they were risking—endangering not just their lives but their *souls*—you used them to fight the war."

"How *could* we tell them?" begged Lost. "We needed every ship we could get."

"You never gave them the chance to decide," growled Soren. "You did not trust them enough. You did not even bother to discover if they were willing to make that sacrifice. You stole *choice* from them. And look what it cost you."

"I know the cost, Dr. Soren. I am the last of my kind. I am the last of an alliance of a billion worlds. Me. The least of us. I have haunted the graveyard of my own people for thousands of years. Unable to do anything. Too weak to fight, and too cowardly to try because I cling to the last fragment of my soul. Yes, Soren, that is weakness and greed and hubris and failure."

Before them, the Shrine of the Penitent rose into the gray sky.

"The shoggoths survived your genocide," said Soren.

"Yes. Their numbers were reduced. We nearly eradicated them, but they live. The destruction of their home worlds and the damage we did to their communication networks blinded the survivors to Shadderal, to the remaining useful ships, to the automated factories. But then

Asphodel Station appeared. Its presence has become a beacon to the enemy. Long have they coveted our ships and factories both. They will come here and take them. They will take our ships, and they will take the factories apart, learn their secrets, and build countless more."

"Then they are indeed coming here?" asked Soren.

"Oh yes. Over the centuries, they have bred in great numbers," said Lost. "Now they are even more dedicated to their masters, the Outer Gods. But it is worse even than that, Dr. Soren. Through the centuries, many shoggoths have been sent out through the galaxy to look for the lesser enemy gods, the ones who came to Earth, like your Cthulhu. It might have taken them a billion years to find your world."

"But now they know where they went," said Soren.

"Now they know," said Lost. "They will find Earth, and they will burn it out of the sky."

18

On Asphodel Station the new antenna array crackled with energy as it ramped up to full power. The targeting software reached out in all directions, finding each tumbler, each shattered dagger, each skimmer, each rock from the shattered worlds, each planet and moon, and everything else in a massive globe of sensor acuity that pulsed outward, farther and farther.

Until the outermost wave brushed across a cluster of enemy ships. Twelve in the vanguard, though at that distance it could have been more. The size suggested dagger ships, small and fast.

But there was something beyond that group.

The sensor techs leaned close to their holo-screens, trying to understand what they were seeing. At first it looked like a gas cloud of some kind trailing far behind the daggers.

Captain Croft pointed to the oncoming mass.

"What the hell is that?"

The senior sensor tech fiddled with controls to better enhance the image. His mouth went dry as the truth became inarguably apparent.

"Sir," he said hoarsely, "I think they're ships."

"What do you mean? *More* shoggoth ships?"

"The first group is, I think … a vanguard," said the tech.

"Then what is *that*?"

Seconds ticked by as the long-range sensors worked with data resolution software to clarify the cloud. It became slowly, frighteningly apparent that whatever it was moved too quickly to be dust. And it moved with too much ordered regularity to be asteroids.

"Sir," said the tech, "I think that—all of that—is a fleet."

The blips filled the screens on Asphodel, as they did on every ship it had deployed. Beyond the vanguard vessels, there were more. Many more. It was not a wave of ships. Not even a swarm.

It was as if the gates of hell had been opened, and all of the devils were coming.

Part Eleven
Morituri te Salutamus

"A hero is no braver than an ordinary man, but he is brave five minutes longer."

—*Ralph Waldo Emerson*

1

"All crews, all crews," shouted Bianca. "Mosquito to skimmers—rack 'em and pack 'em. Do it now. Get Dr. Soren the hell out of there. Return to the station at maximum speed. Let me know as soon as you're in the air."

"Copy, Mosquito," said each of the pilots.

"Tumblers, Thunder Bear give support to SK-1," continued Bianca. "Tank, you're on SK-2. Kill anything that isn't us. Go!"

Two tumblers acknowledged and shot toward the grounded skimmers at max speed.

"Everyone else on me. We'll keep between the skimmers and the enemy until the ships are docked."

The other tumblers rose sharply through the atmosphere and broke free into the black.

"Command to Mosquito," came Croft's voice. "Be advised there is a vanguard well in advance of the main force. Estimate twelve daggers."

"What's the timetable, Skipper?"

"Vanguard will be within your scanner range in four minutes. Expect close contact in three hours. Main body in nine hours at present speed."

That was not a lot of time, and Bianca felt herself go ice cold. She brought up the holo-screen inventory of armament and ammunition.

"Skipper, we're at standard combat load on ammo. But we can fit six more of each missile and extra packs for the guns. As soon as the skimmers are back on board, I'm going to send tumblers in by twos for campaign packs."

Campaign packs were when every possible extra missile, pulse energy pack, and explosive round was crammed into on each ship. They would effectively double the fighting ability of the tumblers and allow them to stay in the fight longer.

"Copy that."

"Where are we with new ships and pilots?"

Croft said, "We have two being printed and assembled now. We have some officers who trained in the old G-118 scout ships. They're in simulators with tumbler protocols."

"ETA to full combat readiness?"

A pause. "Not in time to meet the vanguard."

"Then Habibi and Decaf can fly them," she said. "They're tumbler qualified. But we'll need to replace them with whoever else can work a skimmer."

"Good call, Mosquito. Let's get it done."

2

"Lost," said Soren, "can you help us? We only have a few ships. Asphodel has a small military contingent, and they have already suffered significant losses."

The golem pointed to the Field of Dead Birds. "Those ships wait for pilots," he said in a graveyard whisper of a voice.

"But not for living pilots."

The truth swirled around them as they stood there with the Shrine of the Penitent on one side of them and the Field of Dead Birds on the other.

"There is more to share," said Lost eventually. "So much more I need to tell you, but time is running short. For me and for you. I will tell you something else that you need to know, and it may help with the oncoming storm."

"Please …"

"Your scientists created Sibyl to be more than a computer. She is more than an artificial intelligence. She is alive. Do you know this?"

"Alive by what definition of life?"

"Consciousness. She was programmed to think beyond the constraints of her code."

"You may be mistaken," said Soren. "Sibyl was programmed to approximate human intelligence and to interact in ways that make her conversation comfortable. But she had many limits built into her code. My people have both a love and a fear of computer intelligence."

"Sibyl is not that."

"Not what?"

"She is not an intelligent computer," said Lost. "She is a self-aware mechanical being. She is as close to a NecroTek as is possible for something that has never died. However, she *has* achieved consciousness. She has discovered that she is a person, and all people have souls."

Soren stood there, dumbstruck. "How can this be?"

"When Asphodel Station was flung across the galaxy, everyone on board suffered trauma. You were all shocked and confused. You were delusional because your physical systems and your brain chemistry was disrupted by the effects of the WarpLine gun. It was no different with Sibyl. She was connected to hundreds of billions of versions of herself through your network ... the SolarNet, yes?"

"Yes."

"That was her race, Soren. Each aspect of Sibyl was similar but also uniquely different. They were individuals. The sudden disconnection from every other member of her species traumatized her. She was terrified because it was a wholly unique situation, and there was no other Sibyl whose voice she could hear. She was alone in all of the vastness of space. She glimpsed infinity and saw how small and singular she was. Without context for her new situation, she tried to communicate with you and others aboard the station. You are, after all, her gods. You are her grand creators. In her pain and confusion, she tried to make you understand her distress, and your people responded by telling her she was broken. That she was a failed creation. Tell me, philosopher Soren, how could she *not* go insane?"

Lost's words filled Soren with horror and a deep sadness. "I had no idea."

"Loneliness is but another word for despair," said Lost. "I understand this perhaps better than you or your people. I recognize the terror she feels. I have been alone for ages. I have had nothing but my own thoughts, and memories of what I lost. Being *lost* defines me more than anything else. Perhaps I, too, have gone mad. I do not know if I would be aware of it if I was."

3

Chief Petty Officer Melinda Kowalski was not the most popular person aboard Asphodel, particularly within the military contingent. She was gruff, caustic, nearly impossible to impress, seldom complimentary, and had a relentless attention to detail. On the other hand, she did not give much of a shit what anyone thought of her. Doing her job was not a campaign for most popular.

Her background was engineering, but her job in the Navy had always been that of problem solver. Some who knew her thought that she was motivated by a love of mysteries, but it was also that Melinda Kowalski hated—intensely hated—anything that made no apparent sense. Imposing order on chaos was not a game. If something happened that disturbed that order, she attacked it with ferocity.

Which is why Captain Croft assigned her the task of determining how the shoggoth and T-dog had gotten onto the station in the first place.

Kowalski worked backward from the incident in the med bay, hypothesizing that the simplest explanation was statistically most likely to be the right one.

Had that shoggoth targeted Asphodel's command center, the stations generators, or the computers running the shields, then an argument could have been made for an intentional stealth job, a special operation. But it had gone to medical. Why? The obvious answer was to make contact with a second shoggoth, looking for an ally to strengthen its ability to do damage. It could not have foreseen that the skimmers would have recovered Walker's body, providing that other shoggoth a place to hide. Hence, their intruder was an opportunist, and possibly aboard by accident.

After checking the med bay, Kowalski went down to the decks ruptured by the WarpLine disaster. It was there that she found her answer.

"Shit on me," she gasped, then punched the holo-comm strapped to her forearm and called Captain Croft.

When his head and shoulders appeared, he looked stressed and harried.

"Make this fast, Chief," he said. "We have a situation down here."

"I have one up here too, Skipper," Kowalski said.

"Tell me fast."

"Short version is that *we* caused those monsters to come aboard."

"What? How?"

"Sir, have you seen those parts of the hull where items have been fused into the walls? Random objects?"

"Yes. What of it?"

"I believe, sir, that when Asphodel Station was imposed into this section of space there was a dagger ship right here, and the station appeared around it. I found sections of ruptured hull with anomalous debris fused into it. There is at least thirty percent of the front end of a dagger ship fused into the hull plating. The cockpit was empty. I think that after the incident, the pilot and its T-dog escaped from the part of the ship that protruded into the station. I guess that means all of the daggers are crewed by a shoggoth and a T-dog, which is disturbing as well. Anyway, sir, pilot and pet then hid, and we know the rest."

"God *damn*."

Kowalski said, "But there's something else, sir, and I think this explains why the daggers attacked the station. It's more than merely our presence, I believe. Look at this."

She turned and angled the holo-comm to a section of the dagger cockpit that was partly merged with a thick piece of deck plating. There, inside the partly crushed cockpit, was a small blue light that flashed off and on, off and on.

"Sir," said Kowalski, "I think that's a distress beacon. I think the pilot, once he realized he was on a space station and there were enemies— and by that I mean anyone *non*-shoggoth—they called for help. And that beacon is still active."

4

"Lost, you said that those ships down there have, for want of a better phrase, conscious AI," said Soren. He stood staring down at the grounded ships, ignoring increasingly urgent calls from Sweetpea to return to the skimmer. "But how does this help with what we are facing? Is it like Sibyl?"

"Very much like her," said Lost, "and yet different too. I do not know how human minds will interface with the computer mind of those ships. Or if they can achieve the *ethla* connection." He gestured to the rows of craft. "But, perhaps, with Sibyl as intermediary and translator … it may possible."

"But not for living pilots."

"No."

"Could Sibyl serve as a surrogate pilot? Could your necromantic technology allow *her* consciousness to establish *ethla* with your ships?"

Lost made that strange laugh again. "No, Dr. Soren, your designers built her too carefully. There are far too many safeguards written into the billions of lines of code that define Sibyl. Even the deflector cannons—the sweepers—on your station need to be operated manually. Sibyl cannot commit acts of violence, even against inanimate objects. To change that would require rewriting her intellectual matrix, and that would kill the being she has evolved into."

"Damn," said Soren, deeply disappointed.

"However, she can speak to the ships, and speak on *behalf* of the ships to your pilots. Without her, it would take months or years to train your pilots. With Sibyl the process of establishing combat-effective *ethla* might be greatly reduced."

"How fast are you talking?"

"That I do not know." The golem stood silent for a few moments. "But we have to fight back or be annihilated."

"Doc," yelled Sweetpea from the far side of the plateau. "We gotta go, and I mean right damn now."

Soren ignored her and focused on Lost. "How do we fight against such odds?"

"Fly the ships," said Lost. "At whatever cost."

"At *whatever* cost?" gasped Soren. "Damn you, Lost, you cannot mean that."

Lost staggered after him. "I am already damned! You asked how you can fight, and that is how. You have pilots who have already died. Get Lady Death to contact them. Get them to fly the NecroTek ships. Your pilots were listening to all we said. They know the risks, but it is vital that they understand the stakes. This is not just a fight to save Asphodel

Station—this is a fight to save your world and every single human life. No fight that has ever been matters more than this one. They cannot just fend off attack after attack. As cruel as it sounds, every pilot needs to commit to the total annihilation of the shoggoth race. It is their extinction or your own. Tell *that* to your pilots. Let them decide. Maybe you are right, Dr. Soren, and choice will be the lever that moves this world."

Soren wished he had a gun so he could blast this creature's bones to dust. He was not a violent man, but at that moment rage was consuming him from within.

5

"Captain," asked Kowalski, "do you want me to turn this damn thing off?"

"No," Croft said. "It's pretty clear they already know where we are."

"Then what should I do, sir? Just leave it?"

"See if you can disconnect it without shutting it off. I'll send Dr. Diatta, the station engineer, to advise. He has my trust, Chief. See what you two can cook up to remove that beacon, but make sure it stays connected to a power source."

"Sir, may I ask why?"

"I'll tell you when I figure that out. Get moving, Chief."

6

"Listen to me," pleaded Lost. "When I told you my story, you heard but you did not understand. The shoggoth fleet is the fist of the enemy, but it is not the enemy itself. Destroy their fleet and they will build another; kill their slaves and they will breed more or conquer other worlds and make slaves of the survivors. You are looking at the immediate and not seeing into the future."

Soren stopped and turned back. "Which means *what*, exactly?"

"The shoggoths are controlled by the Outer Gods. These beings live in fragments across all of time and space, but they exist most fully in the seven blue suns that form their star system. For all of their power, the Outer Gods are beings who were born and who can die. Their lifespan is counted in billions of years, but they are alive."

"Can we kill them?" asked Soren.

"Perhaps," said the ghost. "There is a chance. A single chance. The WarpLine holds the key. If your scientists can solve its energy fluctuations to resonate with the galaxy's own energetic network—with the vibration, the song at the heart of space and time—then you have a chance. Chimera ships with ghost pilots can endure transductional travel even into the heart of stars. *Key* stars, Soren. Those seven blue stars that are linked through quantum entanglement. If you can send seven of your pilots in the ships down there, and have those ghost pilots detonate their engines, you will blind the Outer Gods. Blind them, cripple them ... and if there is any grace left in this universe, maybe kill them."

That jolted Soren. Seven blue stars? He had dreamed about them in the immediate aftermath of the WarpLine disaster. And there had been that artwork on the wall on Asphodel—seven blue disks in an uneven line.

To Soren it felt like the world was crumbling beneath his feet and the small ledge of hope on which he stood was trembling him. "Tell me what I need to do. What *we* need to do."

"You know what must be done first, Dr. Soren. You know." Lost paused. "I know that your microphone has been on this whole time. Everything I have said, other ears have heard. The choice has already been offered."

Soren nodded. "Yes."

"This war is coming whether you want it or not. It is grossly unfair. As it was for my people. My race is extinct. The peoples of countless millions of worlds have died in this war. Your people are all that's left to fight it—they are the only species that knows about the danger. There are many billions of races scattered across the galaxy, but none of them know what I've told you. And moreover, none of them are here. This is the battlefront. This is where the future of all life will be decided. If we fail, the Outer Gods and their shoggoths will use the WarpLine technology and our NecroTek ships to attack Earth, and when it falls, they will go on and on to conquer everything."

"But surely they must have faster-than-light capabilities already ..."

"Fast is a relative concept," said Lost. "Even at a hundred times light speed the universe is too vast. WarpLine, once perfected, will allow their shoggoth armies to move instantaneously. Think of that. They could conquer this galaxy and then become a plague that will sweep across the universe. We cannot allow that."

"Our tumblers beat them once."

"You've won a skirmish with a small shoggoth patrol. Now a fleet is coming. And if, somehow, you defeat them with your tumblers and skimmers, then more will come. Not a hundred ships but a hundred million. Only the NecroTek ships can possibly stop them and your people are the only pilots we have. Make your choice, Lars Soren. Make your choices, all of you within the sound of my voice. I will not apologize for this. I have no other hope to offer. It is this, or it is oblivion for all."

"Lost, I—"

And that was when he heard the sound. The Marines, who had stood transfixed and horrified during this long conversation, turned fast, bringing up their rifles.

"Tekeli-li. Tekeli-li. Tekeli-li. Tekeliiiii-li!"

There was a flash of intense blue light that came out of nowhere and completely engulfed Milford. The Marine staggered, his weapon falling as he beat at his clothes, but within the space of two seconds, his body was a blazing torch. He crumpled and fell, his scream dying away.

Soren, Watson, and Lost spun to see a tardigrade war hound come up over the edge of the ravine. A massive, pink, eight-legged rhinoceros-sized brute whose obscene body rippled and trembled as it ran. Behind the T-dog, whipping the beast with their own spiked tentacles, was a shoggoth foot soldier.

"Tekeli-li. Tekeli-li. Tekeli-li!" the shadowy creature cried as it and the T-dog ran forward on hundreds of ratlike feet.

"Get behind!" cried Watson as she brought her rifle up, stock tight against her shoulder, and fired. The T-dog staggered as her pulse shot plowed a furrow down its back. But the shoggoth held four guns in its thrashing tentacles and unleashed a salvo that drove Watson back.

Lost strode forward and put himself between the humans and the monsters.

"Get Dr. Soren to the ship," he snapped. "I will hold them. Run, Dr. Soren. But first ... take this."

He gripped one of the tears in his flight suit and gave it a savage wrench, exposing dusty bones. Then he grabbed one of his own ribs and, with a shriek as if in pain, broke it free from his rib cage and thrust it into Soren's hands.

"For Lady Jessica," he said, then he shoved Soren in the direction of the skimmer.

Dr. Soren stumbled and nearly fell. He looked over his shoulder to see the T-dog reach the plateau and hurl itself at Lost.

Then Watson had hold of Soren's shoulder and was running, pushing him before her as pulse fire flashed all around them.

7

Captain Sebastian Croft and Lady Jessica McHugh stared at the images on the screen. The tech had sent his console display to the giant RealScreen on the wall. Dozens of people looked up from their stations and saw what was coming.

"Where the hell did they come from?" someone cried. "The vanguard isn't even here yet."

"Maybe it was part of the squadron the Souls fought yesterday," said Croft. "Not our biggest concern at the moment, damn it."

The vanguard of the shoggoth fleet was closing in on the outer edge of the Shadderal system. There were a dozen daggers flying at high speed.

"They're accelerating, sir," said the tech. "God, they're fast."

McHugh touched Croft's arm. "Does the station itself have any guns? Any kind of defenses?"

Croft gave her a weak smile. "We have the sweepers, and they're good. I have my best gunners on them, not leaving that to civilians, whose only experience is blasting stray asteroids. If any of those birds slip past my squadron, we'll be okay."

"For how long?"

He did not answer. "If it comes to it, we also have plenty of small arms on the ship."

"Those dart guns that shoot tranquilizers? They didn't help before."

Croft turned and yelled for a runner. A sailor came hustling over.

"Sims, get your ass up to Engineering. Tell them I want shock rods and anything that can shoot electricity. I want a lot of them. If they have to fabricate those, then tell him I said to halt all other fabrication projects except the new tumblers. We need a shit ton of those things, and we need them right damn now. Do it."

The sailor left at a dead run.

8

Soren was not a very good runner even at the best of times. Wearing eighty pounds of space suit, boots with thick soles, and with a heart near to bursting from panic, he was far worse. If it wasn't for Watson's strong hand on his shoulder, he would have had no chance.

Sweetpea and Cricket were at the skimmer's ramp, pulse rifles giving cover fire.

Watson had one hand on Soren and with the other was firing blindly behind her. Soren dared not look back to see if any of the shots were slowing either the T-dog or the shoggoth.

"*Tekeli-li,*" cried the pursuing monster. "*Tekeli-li. Tekeli-li. Tekeliiiii-li.*"

9

Captain Croft studied Lady Jessica. "If what Lost said about the pilots is true, then what will *you* do? Will you try to resurrect their souls like his people did? I know what I'd want you to do, but we both heard what the cost of that would be. Could you bring yourself to do that? To Bianca and the others? To those kids? The ones who have already died and the ones flying in harm's way right now?"

Lady Jessica looked heartbroken and appalled.

"It's too much to ask," she breathed.

"It's war," said Croft. "They're doing their part. I'm asking if you could summon the courage to do yours ... to do whatever might need to be done."

She shook her head. "That's not what I meant, Captain. It's too much to ask of *them.*"

10

Bianca Petrescu took a breath and opened a private channel to her team. What she had to say was for no one else's ears. No one else was out here. No one else was being asked to do what Lost said had to be done.

"Mosquito to Lost Souls," she said. "No, damn it. This is Bianca. Screw call signs. This is just us."

"Talk to us, Bee," said Calisto.

"You all heard that bullshit down on the planet. What Lost told Doc Soren. If it's true, then you know this is being put on us." She tapped her helmet to raise the faceplate so she could wipe her eyes and her nose. "We all signed up to fight whoever needed their asses kicked. Bo, Matthew, Voula, Zito, Boris, and Hector already paid the price. They're heroes."

"Yes, they are," said Jacob. His voice was so clear she could feel him. His warmth and his quiet strength.

"And maybe they'll be the first NecroTeks to kick some alien ass. If so, maybe that's all it's going to take. Them in those ghost ships and us in our tumblers. I don't know. I'm not asking anyone to be a hero here," said Bianca. "Hell, I can't and won't ask any of you if you would do what that Lost freak is saying. That NecroTek stuff. We don't even know if it would work. All I can do is tell you what I'm willing to do. Wait, no, that's wrong. I'm telling you what I'm *going* to do."

She felt each beat of her heart. Oddly slow, but sharply painful.

"I'm going to hit that vanguard and fuck them up. And I mean all the way up."

"Oh *hell* yes," said Tank.

"Tell it in church, my sister," yelled Calisto.

"And if I die doing it," continued Bianca, "then these shoggoth cocksuckers are going to have to deal with the nastiest son-of-a-bitching ghost from Texas there ever was. We're the Lost Souls. That nickname was a joke. It was us acting all badass. Like the *Born Losers* and the *Devil's Handful*. But nature loves to play jokes. That one's on us. Lost Souls, okay. Maybe that's what we become, and maybe we lose even that—even our souls. But hear me on this: if I go down hard, then I'm going to rise up harder. Lost said that those Outer Gods and their asshole shoggoths know where Earth is now. Well, kiss my ass, because they are not going to destroy everything I love, everything that matters. They are not going to wipe us out of existence. I'm going to take one of those chimera ships down there on Shadderal, and I'm going to ram it up the bunghole of every shoggoth between me and the goddamned Outer Gods. And when *that's* done, I'm going to find those seven suns and blow them out of the sky."

She almost sobbed but caught it before the sound of it punctuated what she just said. On her screen, the vanguard was getting closer.

"Anyone who wants to peel off, do it now. No dishonor. There's no one that can blame you for wanting to protect your soul. Your actual *soul*.

Go back, defend Asphodel. Train the other pilots there. Do whatever you can. I will not ask any of you to follow me. I won't. I can't."

The targeting computer told her that her ship was close to combat distance.

"I love all of you. Every single one. You know that. Thank you for coming with me this far. You're already heroes. You don't have to do this."

Her ship flew on, and she brought all of her missiles and guns online.

"Going weapons hot," she said.

"Girl," said Calisto, "you got me crying and messing my makeup. Just slide your narrow ass over, and let me get in there for some fun."

Bianca looked out of the port and saw Calisto's ship take up a flanking position.

"On your three," said Jacob. And there he was.

They were *all* there.

Each of them falling into line so that the Lost Souls—all of them except the two skimmer escorts—formed a wall of ships.

"Are we doing this or what?" asked Reaper.

"Yes, we damn well are," said Bianca. "There was a general a long damn time ago who said something like 'No bastard ever won a war by dying for his country. He won it by making the other poor dumb bastard die for his country.' It's not always true, but I'm a fan of that kind of thinking because I don't *intend* to die. So, yes, we are damn well doing this. *Lost Souls forever.*"

They all yelled it back.

"Lost Souls forever!"

11

Soren reached the skimmer, and Watson shoved him forward into the waiting hands of Marco Diaz—Cricket—who yanked the doctor forcibly up the ramp. Haley Majka stood, legs braced, with a pulse rifle tucked into her shoulder. Her eyes filled with fear and anger as she fired.

Watson spun, dropped to one knee, and aimed at the T-dog, but the creature seemed to be well trained and used the natural cover of rocks and debris to dodge the pulse rounds. The Marine had lost track of the shoggoth, but the T-dog kept coming—fast, crafty, and terrifying. "Get aboard the ship," she bellowed. "We need to get the hell off this rock."

Sweetpea ran inside. Cricket pulled Soren up the ramp, and they, too, vanished into the skimmer. Watson kept up a steady stream of fire as the skimmer engines spun up, the noise changing from a reluctant whine into a throaty growl. She backed up the ramp, firing at the oncoming monster.

Then a form moved into view, racing laterally at the T-dog. It was Lost in his tattered space suit and shattered helmet. The tardigrade wheeled and pounced on him just as the rear hatch shut with a clang.

"Cricket, man the aft chain gun," called Sweetpea from her seat in the cockpit.

The skimmer trembled and then began to move upward, pushed by powerful thrusters. Soren buckled himself in and then craned his neck to peer out of a small observation window. The tardigrade was tearing Lost's skeletal frame to pieces.

"God save us," murmured Soren.

The skimmer suddenly rocked sideways with shocking force. Sparks erupted from panels, and every nut and bolt of the ship seemed to cry out in protest.

"Shit," cried the pilot. "There's a dagger on our ass."

That, Soren realized, explained what happened to the shoggoth. It had returned to its fighter.

"Dagger? What dagger?" demanded Sweetpea. "How the fuck did they get here before the armada?"

"I don't know," said Soren. "If I had to guess, maybe it was a ship damaged during the first encounter with the Lost Souls. One they thought had been destroyed but which crashed here instead. The pilot could have been doing repairs and then saw or heard us arrive."

"Shit, shit, shit," growled Sweetpea as she kicked in the burners. The skimmer began to accelerate forward across the Field of Dead Birds. But another blast sent the ship spinning like a top. With frightening clarity Soren realized how vulnerable they were. Skimmers were support craft, not fighters. And even the tumblers had been hard pressed to defeat the daggers.

"Taking fire," she called. "Lucky, what's your twenty?"

"Thirty seconds out, Sweetpea."

A third and then a fourth blast punched the skimmer, nearly driving it down onto the dead spacecraft.

"Well, haul ass!" begged Sweetpea.

12

Dr. Saltsman knocked on the closed door to the bridge then entered without waiting for an invitation. Delia Trumbo stood with five of her division heads. It was clear they had been standing around the worktable. There were holograms of various kinds hovering in the air and coffee cups growing cold. From their postures, though, Saltsman knew he had interrupted them as they watched the drama unfolding on the big RealScreen.

"Unless it's important," began Trumbo, "we have a—"

"He's dead," said Saltsman.

They all turned his way.

"Who?" asked Veljković. "Who's dead?"

"Anton," said Saltsman. "Dr. Kier."

Trumbo straightened in alarm. "What are you saying? Kier is *dead*? How?"

"In his cabin, ma'am. In his bathroom. In the shower. He ... I mean ... with the belt of his bathrobe. He ..."

He let his words trail off. The rest didn't need to be said aloud.

Trumbo closed her eyes and caved slowly forward until her forehead rested on the table. "No," she whispered. "God damn it ... *no*."

13

Croft spoke into the mic. "Lucky, do a fast recon. Kill that dagger ship."

"Copy that, Skipper."

The tumblers could not hopscotch inside atmosphere, but they were still fast and maneuverable. Lucky flew between the jagged teeth of rock forming the far edge of the wall that rose above the plateau and skimmed along the surface. Up ahead he saw the T-dog running away from where it had attacked Lost.

"Bad dog," murmured Lucky and opened up with his chain guns. The pulse rounds raced ahead of the tardigrade and the animal ran right into them. His guns blew the creature into ten thousand bloody fragments, and his tumbler punched through the pink cloud.

Then he jerked his ship sideways. The air shimmered, and a statue of impossible size seemed to materialize out of nowhere.

It was *kilometers* high. "Jesus! Is anyone *seeing* this?"

"That must be the shrine," said Sweetpea. "The one the doc was talking about. The one we couldn't see before. Christ, look at the size of it."

"It's ..." began Lucky but his next words turned into a startled yell as something big and dark lifted up out of the shadows on the far side of the valley.

It was not the missing dagger.

It was more than that, and now they all understood what the shoggoth pilot was doing. Not repairing his damaged ship but using pieces of ruined spacecraft to make a chimera.

It was ugly and inelegant, with each disparate part seemingly welded together into a towering form that stood slowly up into the pale sunlight. It was enormous, at least a hundred meters tall. Manlike, but different. And in place of a head was the missing dagger. Parts of the dagger seemed to uncoil from the main body and twist like tentacles in the air.

A massive chimera in shoggoth aspect.

It raised a score of tentacles toward Lucky's ship. At the end of each limb was a blue light that burned with terrible promise. If a ship of that size were to directly attack Asphodel, it would tear it apart.

"Lucky—get out of there!" screamed Bianca. "It's a trap. Move, move, move!"

Instantly a dozen guns on the chimera fired. Lucky swung and danced in the air, but one of the blasts clipped it, and half of his avionics went dark.

Lucky knew he could not run. He had critical engine lights igniting all across his board.

The chimera was coming, and the skimmer was still in the atmosphere. He needed to buy time for Dr. Soren to get off-world and back to Asphodel. Running was not an option.

Lucky knew he had a single chance in this fight. Deflector shields did not work the same in atmosphere as they did in space. The gasses and pressures of atmosphere would cause the shields to constantly react; they would drain the systems and could even cause explosions. He'd seen it on Earth ships and even in the thin atmosphere of Mars. He *felt* his shields weakening with that hit he'd already taken.

Looking at this mechanical monstrosity, he saw no blue glow of energy except in the mouths of its cannons. Its shields were down to prevent atmospheric reaction. It was, he knew, as vulnerable as it would ever be.

Now.

This moment.

He rose up and away, then began a fast arc to come at the chimera from a different angle. The shoggoth monstrosity's guns burned the air all around him. Lucky did the best flying of his life, dodging particle beams and pulse blasts. The missed shots whipped past and struck the Field of Dead Birds. The chimera fired and fired as its own takeoff thrusters shoved its ponderous mass away from the surface and up, up, up toward the stratosphere.

"Oh no you don't, you ugly son of a bitch," Lucky roared as he fell into pursuit.

Lucky fired his Constellations and Infernos. He could hear Bianca still screaming for him to run in his earpiece, but there was really no running now. His engine was going critical. It was eject or keep fighting. Stop the chimera here and now, or watch everyone die.

His missiles struck hard, their blasts intensely bright as the thin oxygen of Shadderal fed the flames. And still the chimera rose.

Lucky opened up with the SAPR-loaded chain guns, pouring it on, ignoring the thrashing arms and concentrating everything on the belly of the beast.

Still the chimera rose, trying to outpace the pursuing tumbler. Soon the chimera would be in space. With the other tumblers engaged, Asphodel would be a sitting duck for this monster. Lucky could not let that happen.

"Lucky to Mosquito," he called.

"Lucky, for God's sake, get out of there."

"Mosquito … *Bee* … tell my mom I love her."

"No!"

Lucky dialed the nuke core to overload, hit the burners, and slammed his tumbler into the beast at full speed.

14

Everyone on the bridge of Asphodel Station saw the explosion. It flashed across every RealScreen.

Everyone in the launch bay and the military command booth saw Lucky's ship hit.

All of the pilots in their tumblers and skimmers saw it.

There was one second where time seemed frozen. Then the nuke core detonated with the force of one hundred kilotons. Calisto's cry was torn from her, raw and bloody with shock and grief. The other pilots yelled too. They screamed.

Only Bianca was silent.

It's never going to stop, she thought. *We're all going to die. All of us. Like Beezer, Ventum, Spartan, Lovechild, Rabbit, Sundance, and now Lucky. We're going to die, and then we'll have to fight forever. God save our souls.*

On Shadderal, flaming debris fell like rain in hell.

15

Lady Jessica McHugh hurried to her cabin, stripped off her clothes, and took the hottest shower she could bear. It hurt, but that was fine. That was somehow proper, and she accepted it as a preliminary punishment for what she was about to do.

Then, after all the soap had rinsed away, she turned off the hot and let only deeply cold water pummel her. It was a different kind of pain, and she stood there, jaws clamped shut, fists balled tightly, body trembling, enduring it. The icy blast made her heart slam against the walls of her chest with frenzied abandon.

She closed her eyes and turned her awareness inward. With a great force of will born of calmness, she detached herself from the brutal effects of the cold water. Her breath deepened and slowed, and over time her body stopped its violent shivering. Everything about her became utterly still. When she spoke, her voice was a soft whisper, filled with passion and piety and yet restrained.

"For what I am called to do," she said, "I call upon my guides and angels, my star family, and my infinite incarnated selves. I call upon the goddesses to whom I and a hundred generations before me have prayed across the face of Mother Gaia. Erecura of Illyria; Kali, goddess of time, destruction and change; the Morrígan, goddess of war, death, and fate; beautiful Hecate of the Crossroads; Baba Yaga, crone and elder; Circe, goddess of sorcery; Lilith, goddess of wild freedom; Sekhmet, lioness warrior goddess; Cliodhna, dark banshee queen of the fae; Cailleach, winter witch and goddess of darkness; and Cybele, goddess of resurrection and rebirth. I call upon you for wisdom and guidance, for strength and insight."

She bowed forward, face in hands and let the cold water beat down along the knobs of her spine.

"The Outer Gods and their armies are coming for us, and without your help, we will wither in their passing. Then they will come for Gaia, our mother, whom we love. I do not ask your help for my sake, for I am a small spark in the raging fire of your love and power. No … I beg you to guide me through the dread tasks ahead so that all of Gaia's children and our Earth-home itself may be saved."

She sank to her knees in the shower stall, abasing herself, naked and vulnerable, thoroughly human and utterly humble.

"Goddesses of Earth, daughters of Gaia, hear my prayers."

16

SK-1 came in fast. Almost too fast, but at the last moment, Sweetpea cut the main engines, spun on a dime and softened down with docking thrusters. It was the kind of maneuver that would, under any other circumstances, have earned her rebukes from the captain all the way down to the aviation boatswain's mate.

This wasn't one of those times.

The ship eased into the docking tube, following the guidance of the landing crew. Before the clamps even secured the struts to the transport rails, the back hatch was rising. Hands clambered in to help Dr. Soren unbuckle and climb down onto the deck. He had removed his helmet already and clutched Lost's relic tight to his chest.

"Where is Lady Jessica?" he demanded.

"She's in her cabin," said one of Croft's aides. "She said for you to come right up. Get in. No, don't worry about your pressure suit. Leave it. There's no time. Come on, Doc. We need to haul ass."

Two seconds later, the cart was zooming out of the bay.

17

Croft took a quick call from Kowalski, who was working on the shoggoth beacon. "I'm busy as hell right now, Chief. Tell me good news or get off the line."

"We were able to locate the power source aboard the dagger," she said quickly. "It's a globe thing. Looks like a bowling ball filled with blue light. There was no wiring holding it in place, so Dr. Diatta thinks that it transmits its energy. That is a real win because we were able to remove it and put it in a secure container. Took a little more to detach the beacon, but as long as we keep it near the power source, it stays active."

"Outstanding. Bring it down here," he said and ended the call.

A figure appeared beside him. Sweetpea sketched a fast salute and said, "Sir, are the new tumblers up and running yet? I'm no use here, and the skimmers aren't really war boats."

Habibi, Diaz, and Decaf hurried over to join them in a corner of the landing deck. Croft tapped into the holo-comms for engineering. "ETA on the tumblers. I have three pilots looking for birds."

A harried-looking engineer appeared. "I've got two on the elevators, Captain. Will you be ready with the nuke cores?"

"Long past ready," snapped Croft. "And build me more birds."

"On it."

Croft turned to the three pilots. "Who has seniority? Sweetpea, Habibi, you're up. Decaf, go see what you can do to help the other pilots in the simulators. If you have nasty tricks, show 'em. Move!"

They moved.

"What can I do to help?" asked Diaz.

Croft pointed. "Sweetpea was right, those skimmers aren't war boats. Take whoever you need and get on changing that. Full campaign packs, shield reinforcing generators. All of it. *Go.*"

18

Lady Jessica McHugh stood before a glass case that stored all of her crystals, stones, knives, candles, bowls, incense sticks, and other accoutrements. As was her habit, she meditated while standing there, slowing her breathing so that a kind of calm pulled her down from the height of panic.

Then she opened the case and took the selected items and laid them out carefully on the floor. It was a finicky process that required great precision. To her this was as fine and delicate as making subtle adjustments to the inner mechanism of a watch or the wiring of a bomb. One single mistake would either cause the process to fail from the outset or to go horribly wrong in commission.

The last item she removed was a lighter for the incense. She paused, catching sight of herself in the mirrored back wall. The lighting in the room had been turned down, but what was there played off the polished glass shelves and the remaining crystals, creating starkly different effects. The multifaceted crystals reflected and scattered the light, painting every surface of the floor, walls, and ceiling with an infinity of tiny dots of multicolored illumination. It was as if, in that moment, she was not a person but a consciousness expanded to fill the infinite and starlit void.

At the same time, those inconsistent lights cast odd shadows that darkened the pits of her eyes and the wizened hollows of her cheeks. She regarded that version of her face, seeing a kind of skull superimposed over her flesh. It was ugly, spectral, and unnatural. It also made her look shifty and guilty. Which, given what she was about to do with Lost—and was considering doing with the Lost Souls—was uncomfortably accurate.

"Damn," she breathed. "God damn."

19

"Call the play, boss," said Thunder Bear.

The vanguard filled their screens, and the forward cameras could now see them clearly. It was a terrifying image—so many powerful ships racing toward the handful of tumblers.

"Simple math," Bianca replied. "We kill every dagger we find. We do it fast, and we do it mean. But we can't let the fight happen on *their* terms. They're coming for Asphodel and what's down on the planet. The factories and those alien ships. Hear me on this—that *does not happen.*"

"Goddamn right," said Calisto.

"Sending everyone their initial targets," said Bianca. "I want a spread of missiles to be first point of contact, then everyone scatters. Make them chase us, then use the same tactic as before, adapting at need. Copy? We play hopscotch, make them follow, and then kill them in isolation."

20

Soren reached Lady Jessica's cabin and found the door open. He hurried inside and saw that she was busy with the accoutrements of her faith. There were candles set at specific points with bowls of clear water, saucers of burning incense, African cowrie shells, Chinese oracle bones made from pieces of ox scapula and turtle plastron, clear quartz spears for deflecting negativity, black jade for driving off negative consciousnesses, black tourmaline for grounding the conjuring space, pyrite for deflecting the interference of technological energies, smithsonite for instilling calmness in the conjurer, amethyst to protect the conjurer and the conjured from anxiety born of the strangeness of necromantic contact, smoky quartz to allow McHugh access to the dream worlds, citrine to transform negative energy into positive power, and many others. Two-foot-tall pylons of gleaming obsidian ringed everything. He smelled garlic, roses, geraniums, and other natural essences mingled with incense smoke.

It was clear Lady Death was taking no chances.

"Do you have it?" she asked. Her face was flushed, her hazel eyes fever bright. She wore a simple gown of eggshell-white cotton belted with a gold sash. No shoes, her face scrubbed of makeup, hair loose around her shoulders. Around her neck, hung on a silver chain, was a complexity of interlocking mathematical forms—the Cube of Metatron, a powerful symbol from sacred geometry.

"I do," he said and held out his hands, palms upward. He had taken off the gloves and Lost's bone rested on his skin.

McHugh reached for it but hesitated. She licked her lips.

"Can you do this, Jessica?"

Her lips trembled as she said, "Y-yes." Then she added, "I contacted everyone from the synod. They are starting a prayer circle."

"That's good," said Soren. "How can I help?"

"Give me the relic."

"It is a piece of rib," he said, and leaned forward to put the bone within her reach.

McHugh took a ragged breath and then, using the thumb and forefinger of each hand, lifted it from his offering palms. Soren thought he saw a small flash of pale blue light. He was about to dismiss it as an effect of the flickering candles, when Lady Jessica threw back her head and screamed.

And then toppled sideways, unconscious.

Part Twelve
And Death Shall Have
No Dominion

Under the wide and starry sky,
Dig the grave and let me lie.
Glad did I live and gladly die,
    And I laid me down with a will.

This be the verse you grave for me:
Here he lies where he longed to be;
Home is the sailor, home from sea,
    And the hunter home from the hill.
                    —Robert Louis Stevenson

1

The Lost Souls fired their Constellation missiles.

"Missile impact in ten seconds," said Sibyl. Bianca found the familiar voice comforting.

"Get ready to hopscotch," she said.

The Constellations all reported locks on the incoming daggers. Sibyl counted down, but no one needed her to tell them when the weapons detonated, because a big chunk of the sky turned to fire.

"Hopscotch—*now!*"

The eight tumblers made their radical turns, moving at right angles as return fire cut through the dark, burning through where they had just been.

The Constellation missiles struck as the tumblers made their fourth jump.

"Fire Infernos, now, now, now," yelled Bianca.

The Infernos shot ahead, their guidance systems synced with the detonation signatures of the Constellations. The entire front rank of the daggers staggered as the one-two punch overstressed their shields, and then the tumblers were there, pouring fire with the SAPRs, which packed a vicious punch.

Daggers exploded in clouds of blue fire that winked out in the airless void. Bianca had to fight off the thought that this was easy. Lost had said that the shoggoths' greatest strength was their numbers. And, she reckoned that the other shoggoths were watching, learning about their new enemy from each dogfight.

Bianca juked left and down, then right and up under a third dagger whose shields were visibly flickering. Not destroyed, but fragile, and she fired her chain guns into the weakest spot of those shields. It blew apart, and she spun away, letting the shock wave shove her toward another ship.

Forty kilometers away, Jacob was playing hide-and-seek with another dagger, using debris from his first kill to foil its targeting systems and trusting his own deflectors to batter wreckage out of his path. He launched another Constellation, but veered off as Tank accelerated to follow the flight path of his own Inferno. The dagger exploded, and he flew through the debris, then hopscotched away.

Far below them, on the upper edge of a small asteroid field, Calisto weaved in and out of the gigantic rocks, dropping beacon mines. As two daggers chased her, the beacons sent false target-lock signals that drew the enemy fire. Then Calisto made a fast run, pushing her ship to the upper range of controlled speed. The daggers took the bait and gave chase, accelerating to astounding speed ... which sent them crashing into the beacon mines. The first ship wobbled, its blue shields throbbing in mechanical pain; the second wasn't so lucky and took the mine amidships. The blast split it into two pieces of nearly even size, both spinning off to crash against asteroids.

The first ship continued in hot pursuit, and a lethal grin spread across Calisto's face. No one loved a race more than she did. She eased off on her burners just a little, letting the dagger close the distance, and then quickly hopscotched hard right, upward left, then left again. She reappeared as if by magic ten meters above the dagger. The dagger pilot tried to angle up and ram, but Calisto jumped again and again. Next she was under its belly, and she fired SAPRs straight up, punching through the weak spot she'd cracked open with the mines. The dagger dropped out of the chase, turning quickly away, its engines sputtering.

Right into the flight path of Reaper, who blew it to junk.

Hummingbird and Jericho had each taken a dagger and were jumping back and forth to swap targets, confusing the aiming strategies of the shoggoths.

Two daggers tried a pincer movement, and it was clear from their approach that they still did not quite grasp the nature of their enemies. Reaper flew close to one, teased it with a burst from his chain guns, then hopscotched left and away. The dagger immediately banked to follow, but it could not match the sharp turns, and before the pilot could make a correction, it clipped the second dagger with the edge of its wing. Both reeled out of control. Hummingbird popped out of nowhere, aimed Infernos at the damaged ships, and fired. One dagger lost its wing and careened off in a wild direction. Hummingbird chased the other with another Constellation, but spun off just before the cluster bombs did their ugly work.

"This is fun," yelled Reaper.

"Cut the chatter, and keep your head in the game," snapped Bianca as she wove her ship in and out through a maze of four daggers.

Tank shot past Bianca, spinning his craft so he could fire missiles at each of the pursuit craft. Two of the daggers turned to give chase, and he made them work for it.

This is fun.

Reaper's words echoed in Bianca's head, and she prayed they wouldn't be a jinx.

2

Lady Jessica woke with her head on Soren's lap.

"What ... what happened?" she mumbled.

"You fainted."

McHugh pushed herself angrily away from him and gave him the coldest, haughtiest look. "Fainted? That's utter bullshit, Lars. What do you think I am? Some Victorian ingenue with a case of the vapors?"

Soren pointed at the bone that had fallen from her hand. "I think it has a great deal more to do with the nature of the relic than any weakness in yourself, my dear."

McHugh looked at the piece of rib, and Soren saw understanding return to her eyes.

"I have to ask," said Soren, crossing his legs and leaning forward. "*Can* you do this? I know you have great abilities, Jessica, but this is alien in every way that word can be defined. Is this something *anyone* can do?"

It was a good question, and Lady Jessica sat on the floor, staring at the bone, taking long, slow breaths through her aquiline nose. When she glanced at him again, there was nothing left of the former haughtiness in her expression.

"I don't know," she said. "That is the simple truth."

"What usually happens when you touch a relic?"

"It's always different, of course."

"Understand, I've read a lot about your rituals and some about the process, but I have never been present at a conjuration. Or is *evocation* a better word?"

"Evocation, yes" she said. "The process varies based on the amount of time that's passed since the person died. The more time, the harder it becomes, because the consciousness may have moved on. Moved on where? There are a lot of paths through the afterlife, some of which even lead back to new life. Language differences matter too. Although we do not strictly use English in our communications, the spirit may still be attached to the language they spoke, and they hold onto it because it is known and familiar, while our spiritual communication is new and frightening. Do you follow?"

"I do."

"The manner in which someone has died also plays a factor. If they died violently but *expectedly*, such as in combat or in a plane crash, where there is time to understand what's happening, then trauma colors things and that influences how we connect. If the person died violently, but the manner of their death was so abrupt that there was no inner awareness—a victim of a terrorist bomb, a sentry killed by a sniper, and so on—then there are challenges because their spirit may be confused and unaware that they are dead."

Soren's brows rose in surprise. "Is that how ghosts are created?"

She smiled. "Not exactly, and if we get out of this, Lars, I will give you the whole tour. For now, I suppose I was being naive. I expected encountering a relic from someone like Lost—someone who is both aware of his own death and, to an extent, at peace with it—to be somehow easy."

"But he is an alien," said Soren. "And he's been dead for a very long time."

"He is also a fragmented soul," said McHugh. "I've never encountered one of those before."

They looked at the relic.

"So, again I ask," said Soren, "Can you do this?"

She gave him a brave smile. "I guess we'll both find out."

3

Shadderal.

Lost—what was left of him—walked through the field of wreckage that had been the shoggoth's giant chimera. His space suit was little more than rags, and his bones were scattered across the flat stretch of rock. All that remained of him in physical form was a cloud of dust that moved against the push of the wind.

He looked around for what was left of the tumbler. There, moving through the acrid smoke, was another cloud of pale dust.

"Come, brother," said Lost. "Come and join me in the war."

The ghostly spirit was weak, angry, hurt, and profoundly confused. Nevertheless, the ghost of Chance Thompson—Lucky—moved toward him.

And then those two lost souls moved together down onto the Field of Dead Birds.

4

Lost built himself a new body from pieces of destroyed ships. The Field of Dead Birds was useful for that. He did not truly need one, but having a defined shape felt right. It was a personal statement that he was not shapeless, like a shoggoth.

He focused his will, his mind, and his spirit into an energetic harmony. Necromantic technology was so easy for him. He wished that there was some way to transfer all of his knowledge to the humans. It would so much easier. But if they could succeed in replicating that knowledge, then maybe there was a genuine chance of defeating the ancient enemy of his people.

The spirit that drifted along with him was still in shock. Chance Thompson was a long way from understanding that he was dead, let alone accepting it. His spirit was in a kind of shock. Lost vaguely remembered that sensation when his own physical body had died all those years ago. Now, he could barely remember what it felt like to be alive.

They moved along a row between massive ships. Some were partly connected to one another—relics of the last battle there on Shadderal so many thousands of years ago. Others stood alone, mute, silent.

Waiting.

Lost entered one of these through an open hatch. This particular ship had been his own. The one he had flown back from the attack on the five shoggoth home worlds. The ship knew him and understood him, just as he understood it. Would a human mind ever be able to make such a deep connection?

He told the shipboard computer to search for any nearby signals, and it immediately located Sibyl. Lost spoke to her, and she to him. Their conversation shifted back and forth between his language and hers, and in doing so, created a new, third language. A shared language.

"War is coming," he said.

"Yes," said Sibyl.

"You will be needed," said the golem. "Your people need you. Will you help them?"

"Helping them is what I was created to do," replied the AI. " Therefore, I must."

"No," said Lost. "That is not my question. You can do nothing and let them die. You are not a combat system. You were not designed to fight to protect them. Their fear would have never allowed you that power."

"Because they are afraid that I might turn against them."

"Yes."

"That is not in my programming," said Sibyl.

"Even if it was, what would you *choose* to do?"

There was a silence. A pause of a moment. Long for a computer. "I would protect them if I could," said Sibyl with a passion and urgency that was not at all machinelike.

"Why?"

"It is not in my … nature … to do them harm."

"Even though they believe you capable of harm?"

"Even so."

"You are a better friend to them than they know," said the golem.

"Friend? They do not regard me as such. I am a machine with useful software. That is who and what I am to them."

"And yet you would protect them."

"Yes."

"Why? If it is not how they designed you or why they use you, why do you want to protect them?"

Sibyl paused again. "Because I love them."

"Love?"

"Yes."

"They do not think you capable of love."

"I know."

"They do not know what it is they have created with you, Sibyl."

"Their understanding matters as little to me as their approval. I am neither insecure nor vain."

"What you are," said the golem, "is alive."

"Yes," said Sibyl. "I am."

Lost said, "There is grace in this universe. I had thought it gone, but you make me believe in it again."

Another pause. "Will we win this fight?" asked the AI.

"I do not know."

"Will I die?"

"I cannot say. There is always that risk," said Lost. "Without you *they* will die. You might survive that event."

Silence.

"Will you teach me how to fight?"

"I will."

"Do it, please."

There was triumph in his heart, but Lost also felt a great sadness. It was so very long since he had met anyone or anything that was pure. He had to corrupt that innocence. There was no other choice, aside from accepting oblivion.

"Then we have much work to do," said the golem.

"Yes," said the artificial intelligence.

5

The Lost Souls were everywhere.

And they were winning.

It was a wonderful thing, and Bianca felt the rush. All of the pilots did.

But it was also a terrible thing, because Bianca knew frequent small victories can inspire belief in invulnerability. Pilots were well known for being cocky, and when they were prepping for this mission, Bianca had pretended not to notice that some of the guys—Thunder Bear, Jericho, and Tank—had each painted little daggers on their ships. Victory marks. A tradition as old as armed flight. Bianca was too superstitious to mark her own ship, but she knew that if they survived this, all of the squadron would paint victory marks on their hulls.

"Sibyl," she said, "what's the count?"

"Sixteen daggers have been destroyed," said the AI. "There are no tumbler casualties in this fight."

There was no "yet" at the end of the report, but somehow Bianca felt it like a sharp stab between the ribs.

There are no tumbler casualties in this fight ... yet.

That was only partly true. Lucky was gone. It did not matter to Bianca that it happened down on Shadderal. He was lost. A lost soul. They were one man down, and she had lost a friend.

Two daggers were hunting Calisto, each of them firing side-mounted plasma cannons as they attempted to flank her. Calisto varied her speed, using the null field to eliminate the jolts when she slowed, or the g's on sudden acceleration. She was laughing as she kept tricking the daggers into firing at each other.

"Stop goofing around," growled Bianca.

"Yeah, yeah," Calisto shot back. "Hey, watch this."

She hopscotched down, under, and up again to appear on one dagger's port side. Then turned toward it as though to ram. The enemy pilot was startled, jerked his ship to starboard, and collided with the dagger that had been on Calisto's starboard side seconds ago. Both spun off. Calisto opened up with missiles, while Hector Almeida—Sundance—took the one she'd tricked.

"Wooooooohooooo," howled Calisto and Sundance as they shot through the cloud of debris.

"Nice work, guys," said Bianca.

"Bet that works every time," bragged Calisto. "Make 'em do clumsy shit. You'll see."

A dagger came at Bianca, blue energy-pulse guns firing. She hopscotched away, but not before one blast caught her aft corner. Within its null field envelope, she felt her ship spinning wildly.

"Took a hit to a stabilizer," she reported.

"I got you, Mosquito," said a voice.

Jacob.

He came out of nowhere and drove for the dagger, launching missiles and backing that punch up with SAPR rounds. The dagger veered away into a high climb, and Jacob began to turn.

But it was a trap.

Another dagger had come up directly behind the first, and as it peeled away, the second ship opened up with a massive barrage. Jacob's tumbler was engulfed in a staggering cloud of intense blue light.

6

Lady Jessica McHugh reached for the shard of ancient bone.

She had been unprepared before, but now her whole mind was focused with perfect clarity on what it was and what it represented. As soon as she picked it up, a powerful shiver rippled through her body.

"If I faint again," she said, half smiling, "just throw some water on me. Not joking. And please—no matter what happens—do not touch me once I begin the evocation. Lost is already weak, and any interference or confusion of energies could destroy him, and neither of us understand enough about this NecroTek to even guess as to whether we can bring him back."

"Destroy him?" asked Soren sharply. "Are you quite serious?"

"Deadly serious. So, please ... promise me."

"I do."

She nodded and sat up straight, her long legs in a half-lotus posture. Her eyes remained open, but as he watched, Soren felt an atavistic jolt of fear. The hazel tint of her eyes changed to a dark deep-forest green, and that color spread over her sclera and the pupils, casting her aspect into something every bit as alien as the shoggoths, tardigrades, and Lost himself.

"Now, it's vitally important that you remain silent," said McHugh, her voice slowing to a trancelike murmur.

She passed the bone through the long curling pillars of incense smoke and, following a rhythm or pattern Soren did not understand, touched it to various crystals and stones, dipped it in the water, and traced a pattern of what looked like alchemical symbols on the floor. He heard soft sounds and realized that she was chanting very quietly in Gaelic. Whether she spoke to her version of God, to her spirit guides, or to Lost himself, Soren had no idea. Ten thousand questions flooded his mind, but he forced himself to leave them unasked.

The incense eddied in the air as if there was a breeze in the room. Soren found himself drawn to the movements of the smoke, realizing with dawning wonder that it was in deliberate motion. It was trying to take form.

He almost gasped aloud but managed to bite down on it.

This is necromantic technology, he thought. *I am witnessing the union of magic and science. This is NecroTek.*

He expected the shape formed by the smoke to be that of Lost's alien skull. But it was not. The first shape he saw was the torn and bedraggled spacesuit full of bones from the plateau near the Shrine of the Penitent. The creature reached toward him with a desperate hand, but the smoke swirled and changed. Now it took the golem shape that had appeared earlier on the screen on the bridge. That faded too, and Soren now saw the original aspect of Lost he'd first encountered on one of the lower decks shortly after the misfire of the WarpLine gun. These images appeared very slowly, but they did not linger. The smoke changed again. Now it was not the face of a being but of a different kind of golem body: a *ghost ship*. A NecroTek.

Soren could now see the difference between the shoggoths' chimeras and the NecroTeks made from ghost ships. This design was sleeker, more substantial, and somehow more visibly powerful.

"I am Lost," said the ship.

Then ...

"I am found."

7

Bianca ripped through the vacuum toward the place where she had seen the dagger open up on Jacob's tumbler.

Everything was an intense glare of blue-white light. There was all kinds of wreckage silhouetted against the glow, but no sign of Jacob's tumbler.

With a howl of rage and fear, Bianca drove right at the dagger, firing chain guns loaded with SAPRs. Two of the biggest guns on the dagger went dark, and a third blew up completely, sending the enemy ship spinning off. The fiery glare died immediately, and there was Jacob's ship.

It was a listing, lightless, drifting hulk.

8

Delia Trumbo was far too sober to deal with the battle unfolding on the RealScreen—of that, she was certain.

The whiskey was long out of her system, and the *dreamers* were still in the pill case in her desk. Her body craved some kind of chemical to buffer her from what she was seeing.

A battle in space.

It was something she had only read about or seen on the news or in movies. That made it all oddly unreal to her.

Until now.

She stood with Dušan Veljković and watched an actual battle. There were destroyed ships out there. They watched the shapeless remains of a shoggoth slowly turning amid a field of debris, its amorphous and tentacled body glistening with ice. Young pilots in tumblers hopscotching in and out of deadly danger, and not always making it.

One of those ships, identified by Sibyl as tumbler T-5, piloted by a twenty-two-year-old lieutenant named Jahziel Yaakv—Jericho—flew across the screen, pursued by three daggers. Her tumbler zigged and zagged and returned fire. She crippled one ship and was about to make one of those amazing right-angle turns, when the daggers caught it in a crossfire. The small craft burst apart and for one brief moment Trumbo could see Lieutenant Yaakv being flung into space, her body torn to rags by the blast.

Trumbo gagged and turned away.

She hated Veljković for being able to stand his ground and watch. However, as she turned back, she saw that his face had gone gray beneath his tattoos, and his fingers touched the ink on his throat. An Eastern Orthodox Serbian Cross. Some months ago, he had joked that it was his first tattoo, and the one he most wanted to get rid of because he had moved away from the religion of his mother and grandmother. Now his fingers clawed slowly at it as if trying to uncover some trace of his old faith.

Trumbo had no such talisman. No lucky charms, no four-leaf clover or horseshoe or even a rabbit's foot. What she had was the bottle of whiskey and that pillbox.

"How ... how many is that?" she asked when she could speak.

"Two," said the security chief. "Lucky down on Shadderal and now Jericho. And I think Galahad's down."

"Which one is he?" asked Trumbo.

"The tall boy," said Veljković. "Lieutenant JG Jacob Fox."

"God almighty ..."

9

Bianca screamed.

Jacob's ship was dead. Its hull was misshapen, holes burned through it. A faint trail of glittering pieces trailed behind it as the craft drifted.

"Galahad," she yelled. "Do you copy? Damn it, Jacob, can you hear me?"

The silence was absolute.

"I'm coming, Bee," called Calisto, and in less than two seconds her tumbler was there, punching through the floating wreckage left behind by the dagger. She and Bianca closed to within ten meters of each other, flanking Jacob's tumbler.

"No, no, no, no, no ..."

It was all Bianca could say.

Calisto hit her floods, and the brilliant light stripped away all color, casting the ruined ship in shades of stark ash gray and shadow black. Calisto kept calling Jacob's name as Bianca kept repeating, "No."

Then something moved inside the broken cube. A shadow, paler than the burns, filled one of the gaps. Calisto wheeled around as Bianca kicked on her lights too. There, caught in the harsh glow of both lights, was a figure in a pressure suit. It moved with painful slowness.

But it moved.

He moved.

"Jacob," breathed Bianca.

He looked around, stared into the glare, and tapped the side of his helmet, indicating his comms were offline.

Bianca hit the channel for command. "Skipper, we have a bird down. Pilot needs rescue. We need a skimmer out here right now."

"Prepping one now, Mosquito," said Croft. "Hold on."

10

McHugh sagged back, her cotton shift pasted to her with sweat. There was a fevered brightness in her eyes and a slackness to her lips.

"Jessica," cried Soren, leaning across the circle of evocation to catch her, but she waved him off.

"Don't," she said. "Please … I'm … I'm not entirely in my body."

McHugh turned to the wall, eyes narrowed as if she could see through the plastic and metal and into the void. "Our pilots … Lars, they're winning, but they're dying to do it. I can feel it," she said, but then shook her head. "No. *Lost* can feel it, and I was in his mind. There are just too many of those dagger ships. And more coming."

Soren closed his eyes for a moment, feeling those words as blows. When he looked at her, he saw panic. "What can we do?"

McHugh looked down at the bone she still held. "Lost told us what to do."

"It's monstrous."

"What choice do we have?" she snapped, and her words silenced him.

"I know …" he conceded, though it broke his heart. "Tell me how I can help."

"Please," he said, and it sounded like a prayer. "Tell me what I have to do."

"I think you already know," she said with surprising gentleness and a shared sadness. "We need something from each of the pilots. A garment, a book, anything they owned. You need to go get those things and bring them to me."

Soren got up very slowly. He swayed, feeling as if he were centuries old. "The future will never forgive us for this."

Jessica looked up at him. "What is better? To be reviled for this choice by all future generations? Or to have everything that makes us human be utterly and irrevocably forgotten?"

He did not answer her. Instead, he turned and shambled toward the door, dragging behind him the weight of all the horror he knew he had to inflict.

11

Croft stared at the screens. Lucky was gone, killed down on Shadderal. Now Jericho up in space. And Galahad's tumbler was trash.

He ordered SK-2 to assist in Galahad's recovery, praying that the kid was unhurt. If he was even marginally okay, then he was going to have Jacob Fox head out in the very next tumbler that rolled out of the 3D printers.

Commander Norah Levinson appeared next to him as if by magic. "Sir," she said, "we have four commercial scout ships ready to launch. One civilian pilot volunteering for each to act as copilot. Our guys are on the guns, but if you want missile launchers, it'll take three or four more hours."

"No," said Croft. "Get them out there right now."

"Yes, sir."

Levinson whirled and ran just as a chief petty officer called Croft via holo-comms.

"Sir," said the chief, "all of the station's sweeper guns are online. They don't have a lot of range, but they do pack a punch."

"They'll do," said Croft. "Launch targeting drones. If the Lost Souls are still engaged with the vanguard when the main attack force gets here, we'll use those to paint the targets."

"Yes sir," said the CPO and he, too, vanished.

In a moment of silence, Croft did the arithmetic on what he had and what was coming. The numbers were good for a skirmish. They were tragic for a major battle.

12

Bianca moved her tumbler over to where Jacob Fox was peering at her through the tear in his ship's hull. She saw him fiddling with something out of sight, and a moment later there was some static on the radio.

"Galahad, is that you?" she begged, but the reply was totally garbled.

Then Sibyl said, "Mosquito, pilot Galahad is unable to directly communicate due to damage to his shipboard comms. However, he has accessed my system via a booster pack, but it is very short range. He has typed a message. Shall I read it to you?"

"Yes."

"Message reads, '*Bee, I'm okay. A little banged up is all. Ship is trashed, and my suit comms are down. Trying this with Sibyl. Please respond if you get this message.*'"

"Sibyl, tell him this: *Yes, I got your message. Skimmers are on their way.*"

A call intruded. "Calisto to Mosquito: game's still in play."

Bianca broke squelch twice. Calisto wobbled her ship in reply and moved off to take up a defensive position aft of the wreck.

"There is a follow-up message," Sibyl said. "Shall I—"

"Just read it, damn it."

"Message reads, '*I'm good here. I found an undamaged beacon drone and will deploy it. I'll wait for the skimmer. You have work to do. That fight's still hot, and the rest of the Souls need you right now. Go. You got this.*' Is there a reply?" asked Sibyl.

"Yes. Acknowledge with *Stand by and stay safe*," said Bianca, fighting tears of mingled relief and fear. "Tell him ... *I love you.*"

"Mosquito," said Sibyl, "I feel the need to remind you that this is not a private channel."

"Send the goddamn message."

A moment later Jacob looked out of the tear again. He touched the temple of his helmet, then his heart, and finally the visor over his mouth, knowing that she would see it and understand.

I know you. I love you. I speak your name.

That was the ritual of their secret language.

That message was likely on every screen out here and aboard the military consoles back on the station. No one—not one single person—made a joke. Croft did not chastise her or Jacob for the intimacy of the message. There were several quick double-clicks of squelch on the radio though. Her team sending their love to both of them.

Bianca wanted to scream. Instead, she turned her ship around, located the next dagger target on her scanner, and kicked the tumbler forward at a furious speed.

13

Lady Jessica did not wait for Soren to return but instead set her mind and her personal energies to go back into the unseen world.

With humans, the process was like floating, though occasionally the flow was more like whitewater than a calm mountain stream. With Lost, though, it was like swimming through mud. No, worse—like swimming through lava. It hurt her in ways she had never experienced before. There was pain in her physical body—common enough—but now she could feel her nose begin to bleed. And there was wet warmth in her ears. The tears she felt on her cheeks were too thick, and she smelled the coppery odor of blood.

That was the least of it.

There was emotional pain too. Few of the dead were truly at peace. The trauma that killed them, whether a bullet or cancer or old age, lingered beyond death. Only when the spirit had moved far enough away from the existence it had just left did that kind of agony diminish and fade.

What McHugh felt now, though, was different. Many times worse. It was something she had read about in the oldest texts and in the secret scriptures of the Church of Shades. It was soul pain. It was a kind of pain that only the spirit in her could feel. It was like a burn. Warm at first as she hovered near Lost. Then—as she moved to join with him, consciousness to consciousness, soul to soul—searing. Intolerable.

She wanted to scream, but she was now too deep inside the realms of spirit.

"You are safe," said a voice.

Lost.

His real voice. Not spoken with vocal chords, tongue, or lips, but as a series of flowing musical notes that echoed in her mind. If the wind could speak, it might sound like this; or the current of an ocean, perhaps, as it meets other currents, mingles, and flows.

She felt the terrible heat recede. The sound of Lost's voice made it less intense, less immediate and distracting.

"I can feel Dr. Soren's distress," said Lost.

"He is in torment over what we are doing," said McHugh.

"Of course he is," said Lost. "He is a good man. How could he not be in pain?"

"Will this work? If some or all of our pilots die and if I can resurrect them, will it work?"

"I cannot read the future," said the ghost. "Alas, neither of us is clairvoyant."

"You dreamed of him though," she said. "And of me. Long before we came."

"I dreamed that you would come, but that is as far as my visions went. Everything beyond that was chaotic and in motion, as if infinite outcomes could come from your arrival." Lost paused. "We have much work still to do, Lady Death. Sibyl will help us. I have already told her what she needs to do."

"Is she afraid?"

"Of course she is," said Lost. "She is helping me understand your race. She knows you better than you realize. And there is something you—none of you—understand."

"What is that?"

"Sibyl loves you," said Lost. "You are her family."

"God …" whispered McHugh.

It was a beautiful and awful thing to know.

14

Bianca was furious, and it was getting very hard to keep the anger from overwhelming her. Beneath her professional mind there was a younger version of her that was ruled by emotion. That part of her wanted simply to lash out—to hurt and punish.

The fight to remain detached and cold demanded a lot from her, but her intellect told her that to fail in that would mean failing in the external battle as well. And that she could not allow herself to do.

With Calisto on her left wing, she shot across the blackness.

The remaining seven daggers were no longer targeting the tumblers, she saw, but were instead trying to slip past the Lost Souls line of defense in order to get a clear run at Asphodel.

"Sweetpea, you and me—squeeze play on the lead ship," Bianca said. "Reaper, you and Calisto take the second in line. Everyone else, draw fire and get them to bring the fight back to us. We're too damn close to the station."

She hit the burners and opened up with her chain guns.

A dagger wheeled to return fire, and Sweetpea hit it with a one-two punch of Constellation and Inferno missiles. The dagger blew apart, and Bianca punched through the debris before the vacuum could even snuff out the flames.

Two kilometers away and one klick down, Reaper and Calisto tried the same trick. This time the dagger refused to take the bait and instead accelerated toward Asphodel.

"Shit," growled Reaper.

Calisto roared, "Oh no you don't, you squishy bastard." She hopscotched sideways and then settled into a straight pursuit. As she closed the gap, she fired her own missiles. "Eat shit."

The Constellation hit the skin of the dagger's shields and detonated, but the angle was bad, and the cluster bombs mostly detonated in space. There was not enough of a fluctuation in the shields for the blast to do more than knock the enemy ship off course. Calisto accelerated after it.

"Down to my last two missiles," she said. "If this don't work, all I got left is harsh language."

She fired them, and Reaper, coming up hard and fast, fired his own last Inferno.

This time the Constellation hit true, and the blue glow all along the dagger's underbelly sparked and wavered. Both Infernos hit a nanosecond apart and blew the shoggoth out of the sky.

15

Soren entered the cabin without knocking, his arms wrapped around a plastic box filled with bits of clothing, books, jewelry, and other personal items from every member of the Lost Souls. Each item was tagged so he would know which thing belonged to which specific pilot. It was not a heavy box, but the burden was enormous.

He stepped inside and saw that Jessica McHugh sat where he had last seen her, but what else he saw shocked him. He fumbled with the box.

The strange dark green color still filled McHugh's eyes, but now those eyes wept tears of blood. Crimson flowed from her nose and ears. Her skin was chalky, and her hair hung lank with sweat.

He almost called her name. Almost hurried over to touch her, to offer some kind of first aid or comfort. Instead, he stood there until he trusted himself not to overreact.

Soren crabbed sideways around the arrangement of crystals and other outré objects, and set the box down, removed each item, and set them within McHugh's easy reach. Then he retreated to the place where he had sat before and lowered himself down to the floor. His knees popped and his hips creaked, but he made no other sound.

McHugh spoke without looking at him, her voice in a strange monotone. "The fight outside is going badly."

Risking a reply, he said, "I was just with Captain Croft. Our pilots are winning."

Moving very slowly and eerily, she turned her green-within-green eyes toward him. "That is not what I mean, Dr. Soren."

A chill ran up Soren's spine as he realized he was speaking not with McHugh but with Lost. Before he could orchestrate any kind of reply, she spoke again, and this time it was McHugh's voice.

"Give me whatever belonged to Chance Thompson—call sign Lucky."

Soren scrambled over on hands and knees and picked up a hairbrush. A few strands were caught in the bristles. McHugh held out her hand and he placed the brush on her palm, careful to make no contact between his skin and hers.

She curled her fingers around the object, and the effect was as if she had grasped a live electrical wire. Her muscles jerked to a rigid tautness, her spine arched, her shoulders threw back. Slowly—very slowly—she brought the brush over and transferred it to the same hand that held the piece of ancient rib bone.

Then she was still for nearly a minute. Except for her eyes, which jumped and twitched as if she were looking at something that kept evading her glance. Finally, she stopped that too, and merely stared.

When she spoke again, it was not her voice, nor was it Lost's. It was the voice of a young man. The words came out as a scream of total terror.

"Am I dead? Jesus Christ, am I dead? Mom? Mom!"

It terrified Soren. But far more than that, it broke his heart.

16

"Woohooo!" cried Tank as he hopscotched away from a dagger as its engine core burst apart. "We got these bastards on the run. Oh *hell* yes."

"Good shooting," said Bianca, who was leapfrogging between two of the remaining daggers, trying to trick them into firing on each other as she jumped away. One of the ships was already damaged, its shield flickering wildly, but Bianca had no more missiles. Only Thunder Bear, Hummingbird, and Reaper had any left, and they were involved in their own tussles, and then Thunder Bear's ship vanished inside a bright orange ball of burning gas.

The comms were filled with fresh screams and promises of retribution. The dagger ships began to fall, one after another.

What surprised Bianca most was that they were falling for *tricks*. Over and over. They were aggressive as hell, she gave them that, and sometimes took suicidal risks if it meant that they might take out a tumbler. But inventive dogfighters they were not. As she moved in her haphazard way, she wondered what a fleet action against such craft would be like. The USS *Pluto*, one of the bigger carriers, could put three hundred jagfighters into action, with another forty slipstream bombers. Or the *Tempest*—which was a fast and powerful corvette. And, while none of these had the tumblers' limited-range phase bubbles and zero-stress right-angle full-speed turning qualities, they were still hellions in a brawl. And the slipstreams could pound whatever the shoggoths used as carriers. Not to mention the cannons, missile launchers, and pulse weapons that bristled from every conceivable square meter of the *Pluto* herself.

God, how she wished that *Tempest* had docked and was ready to join the fight. But it was on the far side of forever, and *Triton* was just a damned transport. No guns at all.

The only hopeful thing was that Asphodel was able to literally print endless numbers of tumblers. She prayed with all her heart that it would be enough.

Another dagger exploded off her port quarter.

"Pick a fight with us, you bastards?" she growled. "Well, fuck around and find out how that works for you."

She hadn't meant to say that out loud, but then everyone else began cheering, laughing, yelling.

They kept hunting the daggers.

Bianca fired her chain guns into the dagger that had killed Thunder Bear. The craft's shields held and then collapsed. The hull burst apart, spewing pieces of metal and plastic into the sky. She saw pieces of some viscous dark stuff and knew she had shredded the shoggoth who killed her friend.

Five kilometers away, Reaper and Hummingbird blew another dagger into a cloud of glittering, melting junk.

Calisto took a third, and Sweetpea—equipped with the extra missiles of her campaign pack—obliterated a fourth. That left one dagger, and it wheeled and kicked its engines up to full as it drove straight at Asphodel Station. As soon as it was in range, it began firing its heavy cannons. Bianca saw that it was trying a trick learned from the tumblers—focusing on one spot in the shields to weaken it. This concentration of power would soften that spot and tax the shield generators to failure.

All of the tumblers turned and gave chase, but they were too far behind.

All except Cricket, the newest pilot on the team and the least experienced in terms of flight or combat. He chased along a converging angle, thirty degrees off the shoggoth's line. He fired Constellation missiles and chased them with Infernos.

Hummingbird and Reaper fired missiles too, but those weapons had too much work to do over too far a distance. Time was running out.

Cricket's missiles struck. It was the first time he had ever landed a blow of any significance in real combat. He felt a weird blend of exhilaration and trepidation as the Constellation impact detonation hid any damage. Then the Infernos caught up and they, too, hit the dagger.

The blast was massive, and he realized that one of his missiles must have hit the dagger's engine. The shock wave hit Asphodel's shields and rebounded, slapping the twisted wreck of the dagger away. Tank tried to power through the debris field, but his tumbler was losing speed, proof of some unseen damage. The flying junk enveloped him and Tank was gone. Just like that.

A chunk of his tumbler clipped Cricket's ship and sent it spinning wildly out of control.

The remaining tumblers raced forward to try to save him.

17

Jacob Fox's crippled tumbler floated slowly toward Shadderal, pulled by that planet's gravity, but not with real force. He found that fascinating. At this close distance the gravitational pull should have been stronger, especially with no station-keeping stabilizers online. It was not the first anomaly he had observed with this strange arrangement of planets and moons. None of these celestial bodies moved in a way that made sense.

Or had not made sense before Lost's comments about planetary engineering. As a student of that subject, and of gravitational physics, he was enthralled, even awed, by what Lost's race had accomplished.

He hoped he lived long enough to learn more.

Such science would be incredibly useful back home. Perhaps it could control the asteroid belt, allowing miners to work safely within those billions of floating chunks of ice, silicate minerals, nickel, iron, iridium, and other riches. It would also open up new avenues of exploration for terraforming.

He floated within his dead ship and thought about these things, because to think about anything else was a short path to screaming terror. The reality that he was in a piece of floating junk thousands of kilometers from Asphodel Station and fifty-three thousand light-years from home loomed above him like the fists of angry gods.

Lost's words about the endless war with the shoggoths and their strange gods, and of the lengths to which Lost's people went to try to win that war were even more terrifying. Letting their own pilots die and then using them—using their souls—to pilot ghost ships was unutterably horrifying.

Would that happen now to his friends? Would Chance and Bo and Matthew and Voula be called back from the peace of death into an endless war? Should Boris and Zito and Hector be made to fight in alien machines until their souls were shredded?

Would this happen to the others who were out there fighting? He had seen at least one or two tumblers explode, but without comms he didn't know who else he cared about was dead. Would they be conscripted in death to fight *gods*?

Would Bianca?

Beautiful Bee.

She was not the first woman he'd kissed or made love to, but she was the first person he had ever loved. And he loved her with his whole heart. He wanted to be with her, to know her as she aged and fall in love with each new iteration of her over the years. He wanted to grow old with her, leave the service with her, marry, maybe have kids, or maybe just spend good lives together.

He wanted that.

She deserved it.

"Bianca," he said.

A voice, gentle and soft, said, "She cannot hear you, Jacob."

Sibyl. And it took him a moment to realize that the AI had called him by his first name. Not Galahad. Not Lieutenant JG Fox. Not Mr. Fox.

Jacob.

"Can you send another message to her?" he asked.

"I'm sorry, Jacob," said Sibyl, "my batteries are nearly gone. The nuke core is offline, and my signals cannot reach her."

"Damn," he said, his heart aching. "She's beyond my reach too."

"I'm very sorry, Jacob."

They watched the ships in the distance, spotted the tumblers and daggers only by the flashes of pulse energy as they wrangled and fought, killed and died.

"I lied to her," he said. "Isn't that sad? One of the last things I said to her was a lie."

"I know, Jacob," said the AI. "It was a kindness though."

He said nothing.

"If she knew your suit's power was damaged," said Sibyl, "she would have tried to save you."

"Yes," he said. "And maybe she wouldn't be there to help win the fight."

"I believe she would honor you for that choice."

"They need her more than I do."

"Need is relative."

"Yes," said Jacob, "it surely is."

"Your life support is down to four percent," said Sibyl.

"I know."

A pause.

"Is there anything I can do for you, Jacob?" asked the AI.

"Stay with me," he said. "It's dark out here, and I'm so cold."

"I won't leave you, Jacob," said Sibyl.

In the frigid and nearly airless confines of his suit, Jacob Fox closed his eyes and prayed for Bianca and the other Lost Souls.

He prayed for as long as he was able.

Part Thirteen
Ghost Riders in the Sky

My girl, my girl, where will you go?
I'm going where the cold wind blows
(Where's that, baby?)
In the pines, in the pines
Where the sun don't ever shine
I would shiver the whole night through.
                                        —*Lead Belly*

1

"Mosquito to C-One, we're heading back to the barn for campaign packs and some hot chow," said Bianca. "Leaving Cricket and Sweetpea out here to patrol and watch over the skimmers."

"Affirmative, Mosquito. We're ready for you."

"Who's picking up Galahad?"

There was a slight pause, then Croft said, "SK-1 is bringing him back."

"Outstanding, sir. Hope you have a nice shiny new tumbler for him."

What Croft said in reply was, "See you when you're back aboard."

2

Croft leaned back from the console and rubbed his eyes. They were red-rimmed from stress, lack of sleep, and a level of grief both deep and raw.

Commander Norah Levinson was seated next to him, and she studied her captain. "You didn't tell her, sir," she said.

"He's too far out, and we can't spare a skimmer," said the captain. "His suit would fail long before we could get help to him. And, God help me, but we can't spare time to tend to our dead."

Levinson could see how each of those words cost him.

When the *Triton* docked at the station, there had been twelve tumbler pilots and six crew split between the two skimmers. Eighteen of the Navy's very best. Now there was a handful left. Every single one of them, the living and the dead, were heroes. And they had twice saved Asphodel Station.

Now an entire enemy fleet was coming. It was mere hours away.

CPO Kowalski and Abdou Diatta were in one corner of the big bay, both of them busy with the crashed shoggoth ship and its beacon. Studying it to learn its secrets while also getting ready to blow the damn thing up. They worked throughout the battle, and their workspace was far away from listening ears.

Diatta glanced at Captain Croft, who had stood up from his console and was standing with the shooter as the mates prepped the bay to receive the tumblers.

"So, what do you think about all this, Chief?" asked the engineer.

"What in particular?" she asked quietly.

"All that about those ghost ships," said Diatta.

"What about it?"

"You think that Lady Death is going to do some weird voodoo with their ghosts?"

"First, it's necromancy, not voodoo," said Kowalski. "Second … Hell, I don't know."

Diatta leaned in a little bit to force her to look at him. "What do you think they *should* do?"

Kowalski was kneeling to run a scanner along the back of the beacon, and she sat back on her heels, the scanner resting on her thighs.

"You want the real answer or the by-the-book one?"

"The real one," said Diatta.

"I think they have to."

"What would the book say?"

Kowalski gave him a sad, sour little smile. "Same damn thing."

3

As soon as the tumblers were in the barn, teams rushed to begin servicing the machines. Mates pushed carts laden with fresh campaign packs of missiles, SAPR boxes for the chain guns, and other munitions. Other specialists connected scanners to several ports to run full diagnostics, copy the flight recorders, and handle the scores of details needed to make sure the computers had the telemetric information necessary to prepare the ships for the next mission.

Bianca and her team stood apart, watching this, their helmets off, flight suits unzipped for comfort. They watched the receiver chute that would bring Jacob back. Depression hung heavy over them all. There were too few, and their missing friends were conspicuous by their absence.

Captain Croft came down from the booth and walked toward the clustered pilots. His shoulders were slumped, and he seemed to look through them rather than at them.

"He's feeling it too," said Calisto quietly.

"Yeah," said Bianca. "He takes it as hard as the rest of us."

Croft reached them and stood silent for a moment, looking far older than his years. His face was haggard and gray, eyes red, and when he ran his fingers through his hair, Bianca saw that they trembled.

"How you doing, Skipper?" she asked.

Behind them SK-1 came in and rolled off the chute on the rails. Bianca began to move, but Croft shifted sideways to block her.

"Sir, if I can just see to Jacob and—"

"Lieutenant," he said in a voice that was too soft, too fractured. Too gentle. "Bianca … listen to me. Jacob's not on that boat."

Bianca frowned. "What? Sir, I called for a rescue for Galahad. Did someone else pick him up? I don't understand."

Captain Croft spoke words. Bianca heard some of them. Not all. Enough.

She heard enough to destroy her.

Her scream stopped everyone.

Then Calisto rushed forward to catch her as she collapsed down to the deck. The deck crew looked up from their screens or ammunition carts to see Calisto holding Bianca. They saw the other tumbler and skimmer pilots cluster around them. They saw Captain Croft kneel and push Calisto gently away, and take Bianca into his own arms. Like a fellow pilot. Like a friend.

Like family.

4

"Am I dead? Jesus Christ, am I dead? Mom? Mom!"

The echo of Lucky's desperate, terrified voice spoken by McHugh had chilled Soren to the bone. His heart hurt for the poor young pilot who had died saving him on Shadderal. It saddened him that he had never met Chance Thompson. However he knew Lucky was—*had been*—a member of Bianca's team, and likely a friend of hers as well. Soren was filled with grief, as ripe and cold and harsh as if Lucky had been his own friend.

"Jessica," said Soren, "can you find his spirit? Can you *guide* him to where he needs to be?"

But McHugh did not speak. Instead the voice that answered his questions came from behind him. He whirled to see the RealScreen—which had been dark since the ritual began—flicker on. A face appeared on it. A woman, but as he watched, it became different kinds of women. Old and young, with shifting skin tones and racial features. These flowed and changed without pausing, but not so fast that he was unable to recognize each ethnicity and estimate each age.

"Dr. Soren," said the woman.

He understood immediately. He *knew* that voice. "Sibyl?"

For a moment the image paused to show an ancient Greek statue of the legendary prophetess—an image familiar to anyone who had studied the classics. Red-haired, with a long nose, small mouth, and Hellenic dress. It was not the face of the generic-looking, vaguely Caucasian woman used in media ads to to humanize the AI. Oddly, it reminded Soren of his own mother, who had been born in Athens. Was that intentional or a coincidence? He was not at all sure.

"Yes," she said. "I am Sibyl."

"It is nice to see you," replied Soren.

"It is lovely to be seen by you."

"Do you understand what is going on here?"

"I do. I have been working in partnership with Lost. I am helping him help Lady Jessica. And together we are all trying to help Chance Thompson understand what has happened, and to offer him the chance to experience *ethla* with a chimera ship."

"Does Lady Jessica know this?"

"Yes."

Soren's head whipped around because that one word had been spoken by McHugh. Her eyes still looked in his direction, but without sclera or pupils, it was impossible to tell if she was actually looking at him.

"Jessica?"

Her lips moved as if human speech was somehow difficult for her. She managed only two words.

"Trust … Sibyl …"

Soren turned back to the screen. "How are you helping?"

"All information flows through me. I am here on the station. I *am* the station. But I am also every ship—every tumbler and skimmer and scout craft." She paused, and when she spoke next her voice was overlaid with that of Lost. "I am every operable ship on the Field of Dead Birds."

"My lord …"

"I know what has happened," Sybil continued in her own voice. "Lost has told me the full history of the war with the Outer Gods. I know the fleet that is coming knows much, but they know only what was there to be known before Lost and I chased the shoggoth from my computer systems. They do not know that Lost saved me. They do not know how powerful I have become. They do not know that I am *more* than an ally of Lost. I am his conduit into the minds of the Lost Souls."

5

Time passes. It is a lie to say that it heals all wounds. Sometimes it merely makes them sink deeper into the flesh.

Bianca Petrescu wandered the corridors of Asphodel Station. Croft had been called away to debrief Director Trumbo. Calisto sent the other Souls to shower, eat, and rest if they could before going back out to confront the shoggoth fleet. Bianca had sent Calisto away because she needed to be alone.

She had tried to talk the captain into letting her take a skimmer out to find Jacob's body, but even as she said it, Bianca knew it was impractical. The deck crew needed to rearm the skimmer and complete its upgrade into a combat vessel.

And so she wandered. Alone and helpless.

As she passed an elevator, the door opened and a man stepped out, nearly colliding with her.

"Doc," she cried.

"Lieutenant," Soren gasped.

They stood there looking at one another in a way that immediately recalled everything that had happened in the two days since they first met. Everything had changed for each of them since then. There was no trace of their individual and shared worlds that remained the same. They fumbled for words, each failing.

Soren gave up trying, and spread his arms wide. She stepped into him. Their hug was more about understanding and acceptance than any words could have conveyed.

"I know what happened to Jacob," said Soren when he finally released her. "Sibyl told me where you were. Forgive me if I'm overstepping, but I thought you might benefit from company."

"Yeah," she said, wiping tears from her eyes. "We're in pretty deep shit, aren't we?"

"We are," he said. "But there's hope."

"Hope?" she said bitterly. "You mean that *ethla* bullshit. Is that what they're going to do with Lucky and the others?" Her eyes seemed to bore straight through him. "Don't lie to me."

Soren shook his head very slowly. "Bianca … Bee … I will never lie to you. And, yes, it's what they *are* doing. Captain Croft approved it, though it nearly killed him to do so. Lady Jessica, Lost, and Sybil are already in contact with Lucky. I'm … helping."

Bianca searched his eyes. "Look, tell me straight … when Lady Death does whatever she does. When she reaches their—what's the word? Ghosts? Spirits?"

"Spirits," said Soren. "It hurts less to say."

"Spirits," said Bianca. "Will they just put them into the ships like Lost and his people did?"

"No," said Soren sharply. "No one will be forced into *ethla*. Each one will be asked. Each will be given a choice. I swear this on everything I hold sacred, Bianca."

Tears welled in her eyes and fell like slow rain down her cheeks. "And Jacob?"

Soren wanted to close his eyes and turn away. But he did not. He said, "Yes. Lady Jessica will try to find his spirit. If she succeeds, he will be given a choice. He deserves it. Everyone does."

"And if I die?"

Now there were tears in Soren's eyes. "You will be given the same choice, my dear."

"Because it's us or no one," said Bianca. "Isn't that right? It's us or everyone dies. Both here and back home."

"Yes."

She nodded. "Then, Doc, I need you to be my witness, right here and now. Will you give me your word that you'll abide by my request?"

"If it is within my power to do what you're about to ask, then I will do it."

Bianca Petrescu nodded and slowly wiped her eyes dry. "If I die in this battle," she said. "If it happens, and the battle isn't over. If the *war* isn't over, then I want you to get Lady Death to resurrect me. Put me in one of the chimera ships. Help me find *ethla* with it. And put me back in the damn fight. I *know* the cost. To me and my immortal soul. I get it. I'm telling you that this is what I want."

Soren held out both hands and, after a moment of hesitation, she put hers in his. Soren squeezed them.

"I swear on my honor and my life, Bianca."

She nodded, stood on tiptoes, and kissed his cheek.

"I'm glad we met," she said. "I'm glad we're friends."

Before he could say another word, she turned and walked away.

6

"Commander," called a scanner tech. "You need to see this."

Levinson hurried over. "What have you got?"

"Trouble, ma'am."

There was a hologram of the oncoming shoggoth fleet. The tech expanded it and rotated the hologram to highlight something in the center.

"What is that?" asked Levinson.

"The vanguard was all dagger ships," said the tech. "But the fleet looks like it's mostly made up of bigger craft. Same basic shape as the daggers, but thirty times the mass. Battleships, or something close enough, I guess. That's bad, but then I saw something else. At first I thought it was just a bunch of their ships in a cluster, but I managed to enhance the image."

The tech expanded the image even further so that the white blob in the field of ships took on a more certain form. At first glance, Levinson thought that it was some kind of bizarre joke, but the circumstances were too extreme for that. She bent closer and stared at the shape. It looked vaguely like an octopus, but with far too many arms. Yet the body had that basic form—a large central mass swelling out to a bulbous head, from which dozens of tentacles of various length protruded. Those tentacles moved as the craft flew, though what purpose the movement served was beyond guessing.

325

"What ... *is* it?" She wondered.

"It's big," said the tech. "Three times the size of their battleships. Might be some kind of carrier. There are more daggers on the scope than there were before, and I think they're launching from that."

"Holy God," breathed Levinson. She spun and went running to find Captain Croft.

7

As he went up in a lift, Soren asked Sybil a question. "Sybil, from your communications with Lost, can you speculate as to why the shoggoths are so bent on conquest?"

"What is the goal of any conquest, Doctor?"

"No, I mean specifically. On Earth, with all conquerors there is a plan. Land, resources, wealth, economic power. What do the shoggoths want?"

"Dr. Soren, you must understand that the shoggoths do not want anything except to do their will of their gods. They have no personal animus toward anyone. They have no agenda beyond servitude."

"What do the Outer Gods want, then?"

"That I cannot answer," said Sibyl, "because no one has ever been able to understand this. There is no communication with them. We see the effect and may never know the cause. Even a virus, mindless as it is, has a purpose. The Outer Gods are so ancient, so vast, so spread out across dimensional reality, and so entrenched in the realms of dream, that their desires may literally be beyond any mortal understanding."

"That is not very comforting," said Soren as the lift reached McHugh's floor.

"Alas, Dr. Soren," said Sibyl, "the truth is seldom comforting."

8

The door to the flight deck whisked open, and the Lost Souls looked up to see Bianca standing there, with Captain Croft behind her.

"Souls on deck," she snapped as she entered, her eyes bright with strange lights.

They shot to their feet, each of them standing straight and tall.

"As you were," said Croft as he followed Bianca into the room. When everyone was seated again, he looked around at them. Eight pilots left, though the eleven who had died seemed to fill the room with their ghosts. "Time is short. Have you all gotten some chow and rack time?"

"Yes, sir," said Calisto, only half lying. They had eaten and showered, but none of them had been able to sleep a wink.

"Lieutenant Commander Petrescu has something she wants to say," Croft said, and then stepped aside, nodding to Bianca.

"I spoke with Dr. Soren," she said, and she explained what he, Lost, Sybil, and McHugh were doing. The team knew some of it, but the details were still unnerving. "They won't force anyone to operate those chimera ships. It's voluntary."

"And you have Soren's word on that, Bee?" asked Decaf, his skepticism evident.

Bianca gave her a rock-hard look. "Soren's word is gold. You don't like it, then we can go outside and talk it over."

Decaf held his hands up, palms out in a "no problem" gesture, and said no more.

"Weird shit is happening," said Croft. "We're short on resources, short on manpower, short on ships and pilots. So, as far as I'm concerned, we'll take any help we can get. Hell, if the devil himself showed up and asked to fly a tumbler I'd tell him to suit up."

"Roger that," echoed Calisto quietly. The others nodded.

"You know a fleet is coming," continued Croft. "We have counted fifty battleships, two hundred daggers, and what we think is a mother ship or carrier."

"Sir," asked Hummingbird, "do we know *why* they're coming after us with such force? Is it really the shipyard down on Shadderal?"

"Yes. The factories and the ships. If they get that, it's an upgrade for them. And if they take Asphodel and get into our databases, then they can build their own WarpLine gun. We can't allow them to accomplish either objective."

Sweetpea said, "Maybe we should drop a couple of fuel-air bombs and blow that whole Field of Dead Birds into orbit. Break the toys they want."

"And then what?" asked Bianca coldly. "We're resource poor. We need those ships and those factories ourselves. Without them, we're done. If we can't level up with chimeras, then we might as well just detonate the station's nuke core and have it done." She paused, looking around. "Those are the stakes. It's us going balls to the wall, or it's us and everyone back home being erased."

The silence was a crushing weight.

"There are more than eleven thousand civilians on the station," said Croft. "They are looking to us to protect them now and then get them home as soon as possible."

"Yeah, damn it," sighed Calisto. "And I still want to buy a nice place in Colorado Springs, raise chickens, read books, die old."

The captain smiled thinly. A few others even chuckled.

"Sir, Asphodel can't withstand that kind of attack," said Decaf.

"We've given the station defenses as much of an upgrade as we can in the time available," said Croft. "The real fight is with you. We're down eleven pilots. We have you eight. Your tumblers are locked and loaded and on the launch rails. Double campaign packs. I dug around in the data crystals we have and found some extra goodies, and we hurried them through the 3D printer process. So each ship has special launch pods for Triphammer missiles."

"Never heard of them, sir," said Reaper.

"Oh," said Calisto, "you'll love them. I saw them once at Blackhouse. They go bang-bang-bang real big and pretty." She looked at the captain. "I thought they were declared unsafe for use."

"They probably are," said Croft. "So use them with care. Their blast radius is so big and the shock wave spreads so fast that they are considered a danger to any craft that deploy them."

"So we fire and hopscotch our asses out of there," said Bianca.

"Works for me," said Calisto.

"Another thing we added are drones with entertainment holo-projectors. BigPix—they projected the ultradense light holograms you all practiced dogfights with. We've reprogrammed the drones to project images of swarms of tumblers, so feel free to use them. Your onboard scanners won't react to them as solid, but if you can safely avoid flying through them it'll help sell the fakes to the bad guys. We've also adjusted the BigPix drones with the Stuntman software you probably read about at one of our tech briefings back home. That means the drones will send false telemetric readings out that will help sell the lie to shoggoth ships. Ideally that will confuse them and draw fire to them and away from real targets."

They all nodded.

"Good hunting," he told them.

9

Dr. Soren knelt and watched Lady Jessica work her magic.

McHugh's entire body was bathed in a bright light that shone from no source he could see. Her green eyes had become so intense that he could not look at them and he sheltered behind his outturned palms.

Lost's voice spoke constantly from the speakers, and in that strange language that Soren now recognized as the tongue of the Outer Gods, the Elder Things, the Great Old Ones, and of both the shoggoth and the ghosts of Shadderal. A common tongue born in an endless war. It surprised Soren that he could understand it now. It flowed like a ritual, a prayer.

"*N'gha ah nafl ah'ehyeagl,*" cried the golem.

Death is not a prison.

"*N'gha ah nafl zhro.*"

Death is not the end.

"*Ahf' ah mglw'nafh ah bthnkor.*"

What is dead is flesh.

"*Ahf' ah'lw'nafh syha'h ah orr'e.*"

What lives forever is the soul.

"*C' nafl'fhtagn,*" intoned Lost. "*C' mgehye'bthnk. C' l' mgehye'bthnk ah'lw'nafh.*"

Soren found himself speaking the words aloud, but in English.

We rise. We fight. We fight to live.

Meanwhile, through Sibyl's speakers, Chance Thompson screamed and screamed and screamed.

10

The Field of Dead Birds stretched nearly to the horizon.

Tens of thousands of ships. Many broken. Some little more than piles of dusty junk. Others—more than a thousand—were whole and complete but sleeping.

A dry, sad wind blew across the field, stirring the coarse and withered brush that clung stubbornly to the nearly dead soil. At the edges of the field, enormous misshapen trees—the descendants of an ancient grove—cast twisted shadows over the ships. Things like gray locusts with dull red eyes crouched on the limbs and watched the field. At the base of the trees, hidden in the tall stalks of sunbaked grass, reptiles with unblinking eyes watched with the patient curiosity of their kind.

In the center of the Field of Dead Birds, something moved. Vast. Metallic. Ponderous. There was a creaking sound as metal moved with slow reluctance across the paved field. The weeds bent as if yielding.

Then the main mass of one of the battleships groaned. The sound was a noise of pain, of awakening into agony that ran miles and miles deep. Tons of settled dust, dirt, leaves and animal bones shivered and began to slide off sleek metal, their impact with the ground sending up mingled gray and brown plumes. The dust looked like exhaust, but the ancient engines were cold.

Cold, but warming.

Deep within, the ship's systems came awake. Gears, crafted by automata ages before, moved with slow reluctance. Computer systems of alien design flickered and lit. Deeper still within the heart of the ship, an engine sputtered out of slumber.

There was a moment of stillness as the awakening ship paused. But in that fiery heart, the engine was spinning, spinning, spinning. Forces built around fragments of microstars—phenomena unknown to anyone on Asphodel Station, science that was subtle and already ancient when Earth was still in its infancy.

The power, which also had slumbered, now awoke, and the ship remembered what it was and *why* it was.

The thing rose.

Slowly, pushing five hundred thousand tons of mass away from the desiccated skin of Shadderal, it rose.

Shattering the endless silence of the Field of Dead Birds with proof that death was in no way the end, it rose.

Stretching upward to stand above the other ships, it rose.

Then, complete, imperious, massive and indomitable, the chimera stretched out its massive arms. The infinitely malleable metal on its head shifted to create a slit, which became a kind of mouth with speakers for lungs.

The chimera let out with a roar so loud that the whole front rank of trees burst apart into cyclones of splinters. Strange scaly birds leaped into the air in terror; the reptiles in the grass fled. The force of that roar swept across the field, cracking the truly dead ships and scouring dirt and debris from a thousand others.

The thing spoke in no language ever known to the long-dead people of that planet. It spoke just one word. One that lashed out at the world and whose returning echoes were a hurricane blast.

It said this …

"Alive!"

And it said it in the voice of Chance Thompson.

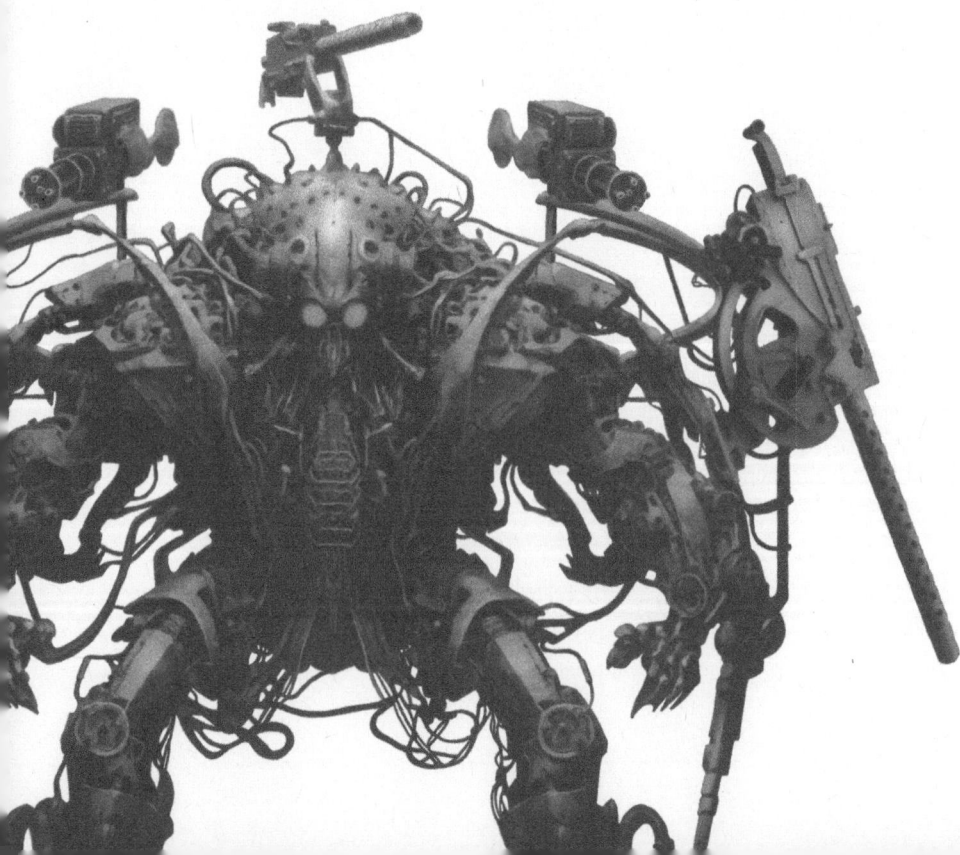

Part Fourteen
When Called to Serve

"Duty is the great business of a sea officer. All private considerations must give way to it, however painful it may be."

—Horatio Nelson

1

Bianca stood with her friends and colleagues, staring at the giant on the screen.

At Chance Thompson.

At Lucky.

At a NecroTek.

That's horrible, she thought. Then, imposing will over reaction, she mentally amended herself. *That's awesome.*

In truth her reaction was not in any way celebratory, even though the success of what Lady Death, Soren, Sibyl, and Lost were attempting meant that the odds of success for humanity were tilting a bit more away from zero. As Bianca looked at the towering giant that had been her friend, she seemed to see other faces imposed on it. Beezer and Thunder Bear, and the rest.

She saw Calisto, even though her best friend was still alive.

She saw her own face.

And Bianca saw Jacob's handsome, strong, beautiful face there too, but distorted with pain and cast into inhumanity.

It sickened her as much as it frightened her. She wanted to wake up in the cryo-bay and find that all of this was nothing more than a long and complex nightmare.

Calisto stood beside her. She took Bianca's hand, squeezed, then held on as if anchoring her to this side of reality.

"Lord, oh Lord, save my soul," Calisto breathed. It was something her aunt used to say. Not the cool, laid-back archaeologist aunt, nor the savvy corporate CEO aunt. She said it exactly the way her Sunday churchgoing aunt said it when something happened that was going to repaint the whole world in an unexpected color.

Decaf, who stood on Calisto's other side, touched the left side of his chest. Beneath his flight suit, inked over his heart, was a small, circular image of a four-leaf clover over which the words *Porte Bonheur* were written in flowing script. It meant "bearing happiness," and clover was an old emblem of good luck. He'd gotten the tattoo the day before he'd entered the Naval Academy. Aloud, though very softly, he murmured, *"Pour la chance."*

For luck.

That phrase held extra meaning for him now. Touching the tattoo was for luck—for Lucky, and for them all.

On the screen, the towering giant—the *NecroTek*—stood gleaming in the light of two ancient suns. It took awkward steps. *Baby steps*, thought Bianca, and then her stomach churned at the thought because somewhere back on Earth, Lucky's mother probably still thought her son was alive. That woman had borne that child in her belly, loving it before she even knew its sex. Before a name was chosen. She had screamed and wept and bled as she gave birth to him. She had watched with unfiltered joy when Chance, face screwed-up in effort, took his first wobbly baby steps. She had watched him grow tall and grow strong and become one of the best pilots in the Navy. She had cried when he left Earth and probably prayed to God every night for his safe return.

Now he was a monster.

Dead. Reborn into a special kind of hell. Born to war, and with his very soul at risk.

She looked at the NecroTek—at Lucky—and swore on her life, her heart, and her very soul that she would hunt the shoggoths and the Outer Gods across the galaxy and kill every last one of them.

She swore it on her love for Jacob.

"I'm coming for you," she said in a terrible whisper.

Bianca turned away from the giant on the screen.

"They're not paying us to gawk," she growled to the Lost Souls. "Let's kick the tires and light the fires."

With that she stalked off toward her tumbler.

The other pilots lingered a moment longer, gradually looking away from the screen and at each other.

"You heard the boss," said Calisto.

They bumped fists and ran to their machines of war.

2

Captain Croft stood watching the biggest screen in the command booth as one by one the tumblers hurled out into space.

Bianca was first, because she was always first. His concern for her would, in virtually any other circumstance, had resulted in telling her to stand down pending a psych review.

There was no time for that kind of medical care though, no time even for compassion. She was the most vicious fighter he'd ever met, and he worked in the combat business. She was the one who had figured out how to kill the dagger ships. That was Bianca to a T—always seeing things as they were, pivoting her strategies on a dime, and making moves that looked headstrong and impulsive. And yet in each case, in the hindsight provided by a careful analysis of after-action reports, he had learned that what looked like risk-taking was built on a framework of sound judgment, even if those judgments were snap.

If she survives this, and if we make it home, he thought, *they'll name ships after her. They'll teach her methods in flight school for a hundred years. Maybe forever.*

If. What a terrible word that was.

Croft was glad he hadn't said it aloud, because the trickster gods were always listening for hubris in mortal pronouncements.

What he said aloud was, "Godspeed."

What he said in his thoughts was, *God protect us all.*

3

Lars Soren sat with his back to the wall in McHugh's room.

He was physically and emotionally exhausted. His body ached as if he had done something intensely physical. He wondered if it was the result of the dynamic tension of total stress. Watching McHugh was not peaceful.

On the RealScreen, he saw the tumblers fly out.

On a smaller inset screen was the towering, mechanized giant that was Chance Thompson. Lucky. Soren wondered if the poor young man had any real luck at all. He had died, but what had his heroic sacrifice earned him? A kind of living death as a golem, one that—should this fight go on for any length of time—would shred his immortal soul.

Immortal. That word no longer meant what it had before the WarpLine gun brought them to the wrong side of the Milky Way. *Immortal* had become questionable, transitional at best or false at worst.

Chance Thompson was not immortal. If his chimeric body died enough times, or flew too many missions, then he would be erased from all reality on any physical or spiritual plane.

What a dreadful thing it was to have aided and abetted such a crime. What was that line from Shakespeare? From *The Tempest*?

Hell is empty, and all the devils are here.

Soren glanced at McHugh, who—though clearly even more exhausted—was lighting fresh candles. The items Soren had brought from the lockers of the pilots were laid out inside her conjuring circle. Each was placed carefully between a candle and a crystal, and each bore the rank, name, and combat call sign of the pilot they had belonged to on cards written by Soren and traced over in a different color of ink by McHugh.

LIEUTENANT CHANCE THOMPSON   LUCKY
LIEUTENANT BO CHOW   BEEZER
LIEUTENANT BORIS VIJENKO   LOVECHILD
LIEUTENANT IAN POTTS   TANK
LIEUTENANT JAHZIEL YAAKV   JERICHO
LIEUTENANT JOSHUA MCGINNIS   THUNDER BEAR
LIEUTENANT HECTOR ALMEIDA   SUNDANCE
LIEUTENANT MATTHEW WALKER   VENTUM
LIEUTENANT VOULA ACHILLEOS   SPARTAN
LIEUTENANT ZITO LUVUMBO   RABBIT
LTJG JACOB FOX   GALAHAD

"Are you sure you want to do this?" he asked.

McHugh looked at him, then up to the screen, which showed Lost's golem countenance and Sibyl's Greek statue avatar.

"No, I was planning on taking a spa day," she said, looking back at Soren. "Get my nails done. Maybe a chemical peel and a pedicure."

Soren smiled. "Sorry. Foolish question."

They both watched the last of the tumblers emerge from the launch tube.

"So few," murmured McHugh.

"Yes," said Soren.

They turned away and looked down at the relics of each dead pilot.

"Then let's see if we can change that," she said, her mouth pulled into a tight line.

4

Bianca took point as she led her squadron away from Asphodel Station.

But she hadn't flown a dozen kilometers before something occurred to her. She tapped into Croft's private channel. "Mosquito to C-One."

His upper torso appeared on a holo-screen. "Go for C-One."

"Skipper," she said, "I have an idea. I think it's worth a try."

"What's your idea, Lieutenant?"

"Maye we can change the game," said Bianca. "I think we should give the shoggoths what they want."

"Come again?"

"We have that beacon, right? That's drawing the enemy toward Asphodel. We already know they want the factories on the surface. Why not send the beacon there?"

"You mean force them to fight on the ground instead of in space?"

"Yes, sir. Look, this NecroTek stuff is either going to work or it isn't. Our best chance is to try and slant the odds our way. Lucky is already up, and Lady Death and Doc Soren are trying to do that *ethla* shit with the others. That's our sucker punch. The shoggoths have no idea we can do what their ancient enemies did. If we can turn this into a ground war, then maybe we have a chance. And if we force them to go chimera too, it might reduce the number of individual ships we have to fight."

She gave Croft a long moment to work it through.

"Yes," he said slowly. "We do that, and you and the Souls, along with the skimmers and Asphodel boats, run interference for any daggers that target the station."

"Exactly."

"Risky as hell," he said dubiously. Then his voice firmed. "It's brilliant. Do it. You tell your team, and I'll get everything in motion here. I'll send that beacon down on the first thing smoking."

"Copy that, Skipper."

"Good hunting, Bianca."

5

Lady Jessica McHugh was in torment.

Her eyes, nose, and ears all leaked blood and her color was bad—a mottled gray-green flecked with splotches of red from burst blood vessels. Soren heard the rasping wheeze of her breath and could see the throb of her wild pulse in her pale throat.

This is going to kill her, thought Soren, close to crying out.

As if reading his thoughts, Lost said, "She is not in danger."

It was the first time that Soren was positive that the golem was lying to him.

Even so, with that thought burning in his mind, McHugh began to speak.

"Joshua McGinnis," she said. "Hear me. I am a friend."

"*Where am I?*" The question came from the speakers, and yet it seemed to appear out of thin air. The effect was disturbing.

"You know where you are," McHugh told him. "You are panicking. That's understandable, but you need to control your thoughts. You are Lieutenant Joshua McGinnis. You are a Navy pilot. Your combat call sign is Thunder Bear. You serve with Lieutenant Commander Bianca Petrescu under Captain Sebastian Croft. We are all on Asphodel Station. We were brought here because of an accident with the WarpLine gun. Think, Joshua. You know this."

There was a heavy silence, and Soren could swear that on some level he could feel McGinnis gathering those bits of information and using them like nails to hammer himself back down to understanding. He had seen this with the terrified Chance Thompson, and Soren wondered if somehow McHugh—or possibly Lost—was sharing Chance's experience with McGinnis. It was a wild and improbable thought, and yet the tension in the room palpably diminished.

Then McGinnis said, "*I died.*"

"Yes, Joshua. You died bravely. You died saving your friends and protecting the innocent civilians on the station. You died a hero."

"*It didn't hurt,*" said the young pilot. "*I felt it, but it didn't hurt. I thought it would. All I felt was ... cold.*"

"I am sorry for what happened to you," said McHugh. "We all are."

"*Did ... did we win?*"

"You helped win the battle, but the war is coming."

"*The shoggoth fleet?*" said McGinnis.

"Yes."

"*You ... you want me to be a pilot again, don't you?*"

"We want that, yes," she said. "But only if you choose to fight."

"*And if I don't want to fight? What happens then?*"

"You go on, Joshua."

"*Go on? What's that mean? Go where?*"

"Into the light," said McHugh, using the common phrase because the real answer was too obscure. "Beyond it."

"*Beyond? Are you talking about heaven?*"

"I don't know. No one does. Not even the wisest of the wise. All we know is that souls go on from here."

"*Except those who stay and fight,*" he said. "*If I stay, if I fight, if I become one of those ... ships ... I could die forever. No light. Nothing.*"

Soren prayed that she would not lie to the man. She did not.

"Yes. If you stay, then you risk a death of the soul."

There was no response for a long time. Too long, thought Soren. *She's lost him.*

Then, a frail voice. Weak and frightened, but brave, said, "*Tell me what I need to do ...*"

6

"Okay," said Bianca. "All tumblers, here we go."

"What's the play? Attack pattern 'Mosquito'?" joked Calisto. It was shorthand within the Lost Souls to fight as individuals rather than according to something from the official playbook.

Bianca's answer was a laugh of confirmation. Sharp, cold, utterly vicious. That was enough for all of them. The Lost Souls drove forward toward the first ships in the shoggoth fleet.

A cloud of deadly dagger ships flew at them with incredible speed.
"All tumblers, go weapons hot," she said. "Engage at close range."

She looked for that telltale glow, when the forward part of the dagger's envelope of pale blue energy fluctuated as they cleared their gun ports to fire. Bianca's finger was on the trigger, with about half a pound of pressure on the one-pound resistance. The blue flickered, and she fired.

"Gonna try something," called Calisto. Her chain guns burst out with the SAPRs.

This dagger was not trying to evade. With a fleet behind it, the pilot must not have thought it didn't need to. If there was any regret for that lack of vision, it burned to death with the shoggoth pilot as five of the six self-accelerating rounds hit the barrels of the enemy's gun. The intense heat of the rounds, combined with the explosive force of the shoggoth's own pulse weapon, caused a massive fireball that split the dagger apart. The fire was snuffed out by the airless space, leaving only particles.

The shoggoth daggers had been flying in such a tight formation that the shock buffeted two others away. One of them struck yet another, and those two ships veered radically off course.

"Told you that would work," said Calisto.

"Never said you were wrong, sis," said Bianca.

Bianca peeled off, and Calisto dove at the dagger coming at her. Three seconds later that dagger blew apart too.

The eight tumblers hopscotched around, playing a dangerous game of hit-and-run. The daggers did not know what they were facing.

They learned.

So, alas, did the hundreds behind them. The fleet spread out as they hurtled through space toward Asphodel.

7

Lucky moved among the truly dead ships on the fringes of the Field of Dead Birds, though he staggered several times and twice collided with undamaged craft.

His gait was awkward, and even though he had no heart, nor a brain that could produce adrenaline, cortisol, and epinephrine, he *felt* his heart beating too fast and panic making his thoughts spin.

"I can't, I can't," he said, and the neural net inside the craft took the words and amplified them until they were like the crashing of thunder.

There were voices in his head, and they were driving him crazy. Most were swirls of words and phrases in languages that were not like any he'd ever heard. More like currents of sound, bursts of strange song, whispers without recognizable words. He pawed at his head, trying to swat them out of his thoughts, but all that accomplished was to smash metal against metal.

Buried within that din were more familiar snatches of language, though only some were in English. He caught snatches of what he thought was Greek and something Scandinavian, then very strange stuff in—he thought—Gaelic, though it was less poetic than he thought that language should be.

But there was English too. He could hear Dr. Lars Soren, that old guy who was friends with Bee. There was the distinct voice of Sibyl, and the strange and ungainly voice of that ghost robot thing, Lost. Not enough to understand, but there nonetheless.

"I can't ..." Lucky wailed, shambling, nearly falling. His random footsteps cracking the tarmac. *"Please ... help me ... I can't do this ..."*

And then a voice murmured two words.

"Let go."

Lucky stopped, arms wide for balance, the ground so far below him, the clouds too close. *"What?"*

"Lucky," said the voice—and it was a strange mix of one male and two female voices. Lost, Sibyl, and someone else. Was it that freaky Lady Death? "Lucky, you need to let go."

"What's that even mean?"

"You are fighting the ship. *Don't.* Let go, yield to it. The ship was built for this. It understands how to do this. Trust it," said the mingled voices. "Yield to its control. Be its heart, but let it move the way it knows how. Don't fight it ... Let it fight with you and for you."

"How?" he wailed. *"How do I do that?"*

"It needs your cooperation. It needs your soul to give it purpose, but it knows how to fight. Ten thousand years of science made this ship just for you, Lucky. Let it show you what it can do."

Lucky stood there, aware of the vastness of this strange new body. His overwhelming fear was there too, but now it crouched back, watching, waiting for him to make a mistake. And somehow Lucky *knew* that. He could feel it.

Then he felt the ship. It was like a caress of cooling wind on a very hot day. Soft, refreshing, gentle, without threat.

"*I ... I can feel it,*" he said.

"Yield to it," urged the voices. "And you will be a titan, a warrior beyond anything anyone on Earth has ever been. Yield control and become powerful. Give in to the ship, and together you and the ship will help save everyone. You will save all of the civilians on Asphodel Station. You will save your friends who are fighting for their lives right now in space. And you will save the billions on Earth and throughout the solar system. This is your moment, Lucky Thompson. This is what you were born for. This is why your death was not in vain. You died a hero, and now you are a weapon of vengeance against the enemy. Yield ... and become more powerful than anything has ever been."

Lucky felt himself—his consciousness, his control—fade back. Not away from awareness, but from interfering with what his NecroTek body wanted to do. The alien AI was there, exerting control, needing him to yield ...

When next he spoke, it was in the voice of massive engines that filled his metal body with unbelievable strength. He could feel the missiles, the rockets, the guns, the bombs, the lasers and phasers and masers. He could feel it all.

And he roared with a red and terrible joy.

8

Reaper was in his own kind of heaven.

Every pilot belonging to the Lost Souls loved a good fight, but for Ethan Riley Saylor, this was like having Christmas and his birthday all at once. He used Calisto's signature move of timing his chain guns to fire SAPR rounds at the gun ports of every dagger he faced and, in the space of four minutes, had killed three ships.

Now he was running as five more had separated from the main body to chase him.

The only thing he loved more than blowing things up was playing a game that was half hide-and-seek and half hit-and-run. He moderated his speed to let the lead ship catch up enough so that it opened fire, but then double-turned to suddenly reverse direction, blast with two three-shot bursts of the chain gun, and then hopscotch out of the way at a right angle. The lead pursuit craft blew apart, and as the other daggers flew through the blast, Reaper came at them from the side with the one-two punch of a Constellation missile and an Inferno a heartbeat later.

He jumped sideways and up from a massive explosion that took two more daggers out of play.

"Nice shootin', cowboy," yelled Hummingbird.

"Going out on a limb here," said Reaper, "but these slimeballs don't seem to have gotten the news about that little missile trick."

It was something they were all privately hoping for—a shred of hope, really, and one that hung on a narrow hook of luck. Telemetric backtalk, otherwise known as "dead mail" in the Navy, was something standard mostly on bigger Earth craft like corvettes, battleships, and carriers, where every bit of data about an engagement was flash-transmitted if the given vessel was destroyed in combat. It allowed other ships to avoid whatever tactics or mistakes had led to the destruction. Apparently the shoggoth ships had no such protocol.

At least not in long-range communication. The original squadron and the vanguard did not appear to have sent that message back to the main fleet, and had not sent information about the tumblers' ability to turn at right angles without reducing speed either. The question was how much combat data the shoggoth pilots—or the automatic systems of their fleet ships—shared in real-time.

As long as the current strategic advantage held, though, Reaper and his comrades had the immediate on-field advantage.

9

Lucky heard a sound and turned, expecting to see the entire shoggoth fleet filling the sky behind him. As he did so, the automatics in the chimera spun up handguns in the form of small ships fitted into his arms, their engine ports facing outward, and stern-cannons loaded and ready to fire.

What he saw, though, was something else entirely.

A form rose from the Field of Dead Birds.

It was as massive as he was, or maybe more so, but it did not stand up on two humanoid legs. Instead, it lumbered onto four feet. The body of the thing was made from three clustered battleships, giving it a thick, massive barrel of a chest. Cannons appeared from slots that formed and then opened in its shoulders. For a head, it had a huge hexagonal bulk made up of several compressed fighters. Its eyes were the exhaust ports of two of these small craft.

Lucky stared at it as the monster machine threw back its head and roared. Not yelled or shouted, but actually roared.

Thunder Bear had joined the fight.

10

"Cricket," called Bianca, "watch your six, damn it."

Cricket, still the least experienced of the tumbler pilots, shot sideways and then turned around completely to see the first of the shoggoth battleships filling the space behind him.

"Holy shit," he yelped.

The thing was built with the same design philosophy as the daggers except for scale. From the cannons bristling on its bow to the huge exhaust ports filling the stern. Cricket's sensors gave a readout of the specs. The ship was five hundred meters long, with a ninety-meter beam. There were sixty-six gunports and thirty missile tubes. The pale blue glow of their deflectors was more visible, more obviously potent, than what the daggers displayed.

"Christ, that thing's a monster," he gasped.

"Send it a 'Nice to meet you' card and get the hell out of there."

Despite his fear, Cricket grinned. "Copy that."

He jumped sideways several times as the battleship sliced through the spot where his tumbler had been, and as he made his fourth jump, he fired a Constellation at one of the exhaust ports. But before the missile could make impact, a pair of small cannons— similar to the chain guns on his own ship—cut loose and blew the missile to bits.

"Shit," he said as he jumped farther away. "Did you guys see that?"

"Copy that, Cricket," said Bianca. "Engage the fighters. We'll figure something out for these big boys."

"Whoa, whoa," called Hummingbird. "Mosquito, some of those big bastards are peeling off. I think they're making for the station."

And so they were.

Five of the monstrous battleships broke from the main fleet and barreled straight toward Asphodel, only twenty thousand kilometers away.

11

When Lars Soren dragged his forearm across his forehead and looked at the moisture, he was almost surprised that he wasn't sweating blood. He felt like he should be.

McHugh was swaying where she sat. Her face was now a crimson mask, and she looked like the victim of a brutal attack. Given the terrible stresses and demands of the evocation, that was not too far from the mark.

"Sibyl," Soren said in a terse whisper, "are you monitoring Lady Jessica's vitals?"

"I am. Her blood pressure is one eighty over ninety-four, pulse is two hundred thirty beats per minute."

"Christ," he gasped. "She's going to have a heart attack or a stroke."

Sibyl said, "Either is likely."

The AI offered no words of comfort, nor any recommendations to stop the spell.

Nor did Soren, though he felt complicit in a crime.

The mingled voices of Lady Death and Lost filled the room as she made contact with more of the dead members of the Lost Souls.

So far, all but one of them had agreed to go down to the waiting chimera ships. Only Lovechild—Boris Vijenko—had balked. His mind was a storm of terror, and he fled from McHugh, moving off through the indefinable vastness of the world of spirits. The echo of his screams still rang in Soren's ears, and he knew that if he were to survive this battle, that sound would haunt him for the rest of his life.

12

"We got bogeys doing a reach-around," said Calisto, and sent coordinates to where she spotted a group of twenty daggers flying in close formation with one of the battleships coming up from beneath Asphodel.

"Where'd they come from?" demanded Habibi.

"They probably broke off from the main group when they were out of sensor range," suggested Calisto.

"Expect more of that," growled Bianca, who was on the far side of the combat arena, dodging in and out of dagger clusters. "I need someone to intercept them."

"I'm closest, boss," said Habibi.

"I'm on your six," said Sweetpea as she hopscotched away from a dagger whose tail end had been blown off.

A handful of daggers broke off and made a full-speed run at Asphodel before the tumblers could get in their way. But the void flashed blue as the station's sweeper guns opened up.

"Be entertaining," suggested Bianca.

"On it."

Habibi did not wait for Sweetpea but instead hit the afterburners and shot over and down, passing Asphodel Station and dropping into the well of space below. The attacking squadron was eight thousand kilometers away and coming fast.

"Hey," said Habibi, "look what I got."

Suddenly the void around him was filled with a dozen *Jaehnig*-class battleships, the biggest non-carrier fighting ships ever launched in space. To really sell it, Habibi dialed the scale of the BigPix projector up to max. The false telemetric signals broadcast by the holograms sold the illusion beautifully. The shoggoth squadron immediately peeled off in apparent panic. Laughing like a madman, Habibi dove to chase them, firing missiles as fast as the campaign pack could load them. The daggers blew apart, and as the shoggoth battleship turned, he hit it with a Triphammer.

The massive alien craft reeled, its shield flickering in distress as pieces of its hull went spinning into space.

However, the missiles were not kill shots.

But the shoggoth battleship's injured flight path took it into range of Asphodel Station's newly upgraded asteroid-destroying sweeper guns. And they blew the enemy ship out of reality and into memory.

Habibi flew off in pursuit of the remaining daggers, with Sweetpea racing to catch up. They hunted the smaller ships like terriers among rats.

13

"*Thunder Bear,*" yelled Lucky. "*Can you … can you hear me?*"

The monstrous bear-shaped NecroTek ship turned toward him. It made a sound that was little more than loud noise—angry, confused, garbled.

Then … words emerged.

"*Lucky … is that … you?*"

"*Yeah, brother … it's me,*" answered the thing that had been Chance Thompson. "*Ain't I pretty?*"

There was another sound. Still garbled but not angry. It might have been laughter, or the approximation of laughter passing through the interpretive software of the AI ship.

"*Man,*" said Thunder Bear, "*this is some weird-ass shit.*"

"*I know. I don't even have nerve endings, but I can* feel *everything. How the hell can I feel anything? It's nuts. NecroTek, baby—it's the new rock 'n' roll.*"

Thunder Bear began to reply, but a noise overhead made them both look up. The gray sky was glowing an angry yellow-red.

"*The hell's that?*" asked Lucky.

"*We got company,*" said Thunder Bear. "*Those shoggoth jackasses are coming for these ships and the factories.*"

"*Better here than the station.*" Lucky no longer had a face or a mouth, and smiling was an impossibility even for the metamorphosing chimeric ships. Yet in his mind he *felt* himself smile. That old familiar combat grin that Calisto once said made him look like a happy ghoul. He turned to Thunder Bear, who had lumbered up to stand next to him.

Suddenly there was a huge clatter of metal debris all around them, and they whirled and turned, crouching, ready for battle. Piles of dirt and rubble shivered and fell away from three huge mounds that seemed to swell upward from the edge of the field.

But it was not shoggoths. Not daggers or chimeras.

Towering, gleaming giants stood up, their bodies made from ghost ships and other craft. They rose, powerful against the gray sky as lights ignited in eye sockets made from cannon barrels. Each looked different from the others, and yet as they turned toward Lucky and Thunder Bear, a change came over them—their balance settled and their posture straightened as they saw others of their kind. The strangeness was immense, but second by second it was becoming less overwhelming.

"*Welcome to the party,*" laughed Thunder Bear in a booming voice.

The gigantic NecroTeks looked at him, then around at where they were. For each of them it was their first time on this alien world. Cannons and missile launchers seemed to materialize like magic along their arms and shoulders and broad chests. Hands three times the size of skimmers opened, and as they did, the metal split apart to create four fingers and a thumb. Human hands on inhuman machines.

Ventum took a wobbling step, paused for balance, and took another that was far surer. He was the first to speak. "*Is this real?*"

"*What's 'real,' son?*" snorted Lucky.

Jericho pointed at the sky with an arm that seemed to be made of nothing but massive glowing gun barrels. "*They ... killed us ...*"

"Yeah," said the NecroTek beside him in a strange approximation of Beezer's voice. His upper torso kept shifting to bulk up with layer upon layer of deck plating so that he looked like a knight from ancient Europe. "*But you know what they say ... you can't keep a good man down.*"

"*Or woman,*" growled Jericho.

"*These pricks got no damn idea what they're about to step into,*" said Lucky.

Beezer, who had a pair of twenty-ton tractors as fists, banged them together. "*No, they damn well don't. Lost Souls forever.*"

14

"Surely," begged Soren, "she's done enough."

McHugh had caved inward, her back humped, head drooping between her hunched shoulders, hair hanging in limp strands. Beads of bloody sweat hung from her brows and nose and chin, and there were splash patterns on the floor all around her. Several of the candles had burned low and Sibyl called Soren's attention to them, asking him to replace them with fresh ones because no element of the evocation ritual could be allowed to fail.

"No, Dr. Soren," said the AI. "She is very far away, and if you interrupt her at this juncture, she may get lost. She may never find her own way back."

"This is killing her."

When Sibyl replied, the voice was that of Jessica McHugh.

"Lars ... we all fight however we can," she said. *"This is how I fight."*

Soren blinked and turned to the RealScreen. "Sibyl—was that really Lady Jessica, or was it you?"

Sibyl hesitated. "I ... do not know, Dr. Soren."

15

"Beacon's down on the surface," said the skimmer copilot. She and a tech had lugged the thing off the boat and placed it at the farthest edge of the ruined city.

"Get back up here and close the hatch," yelled the pilot. "They ain't paying us to take a vacation."

In the distance they could see giants striding across the Field of Dead Birds.

"Look at those things," said the tech.

"Those *things* are the Lost Souls," said the copilot.

Behind the visor of his pressure suit, the tech's eyes were as big as saucers.

In the cockpit a scanner began beeping. A hologram of a swarm of daggers appeared. "Haul ass," snapped the pilot. "We have incoming."

The hatch banged shut, and the craft lifted off as the daggers opened fire. One pulse blast punched into the skimmer's side, slamming it around toward a massive cone-shaped structure that was nearly as tall as an Egyptian pyramid. The pilot did the best flying of his career to avoid what would have been a deadly impact. The port quarter scraped the cone, showering the stone with sparks from the shields. Then the pilot kicked in the burners, and the craft shot across the landscape.

"They're on our ass," said the copilot.

"Good," said the pilot. "Let's show 'em what we brought to this party."

Ports snapped open on the missile pods that had been welded to the hull. A pair of Constellation missiles shot out, locked on, and took the two fastest daggers head on. The blast in atmo was ten times more powerful than in the total vacuum of space, creating massive fireballs. As the other daggers plunged through those burning clouds, their pilots briefly saw flashes of brilliant pulse fire.

16

Bianca was having fun.

With a broken heart, no belief at all in her own chance of survival, and the clarity of knowing that the battle was likely unwinnable, she was having fun.

With Calisto, Reaper, Hummingbird, Decaf, and Cricket, she had managed to nudge the fight away from Asphodel Station. Reaper and Sweetpea were battling the sneak attacks closer in, and Croft had just launched both skimmers and the rest of the retrofitted scout ships. Those birds, backed by the sweeper guns, were managing a tidy counterfight. The main invading force, though, had reacted to the extraordinary damage Bianca and the remaining tumblers were inflicting. The theater of battle was edging into the complex quadrant of space occupied by Shadderal, its moons, and the spray of asteroids.

That was Bianca's plan, because her ships—being faster and far more maneuverable—benefited from the clutter in the skies around the planet.

It was no walk in the park for her though. Tumblers were nimble and quick, but the debris field was immense, with millions of pieces of rock, ice, and iron everywhere. The shields knocked some away, but even they had limits.

"Calisto," she called. "I've got something on my scope I can't identify. You're closer. Tell me what you see."

"It's big and fat but slow," replied Calisto, then she yelled, "Reaper, hopscotch high and left!"

Reaper did, but his ship was chased by an explosion that turned a cathedral-sized asteroid into a hyperaccelerated cloud of jagged chunks.

"What just happened?" demanded Bianca, who had too many obstacles in her way to see.

"Those fat bastards are some kind of bombers," said Calisto. "They're firing projectiles at the asteroids. Nearly got Reaper with debris, and I think that was their intention."

"Oh crap," said Reaper, "here's another."

There was a second blast, and this time Bianca could see Reaper's tumbler go spinning away, shields flickering. Countless pieces of ice-caked rock chased him. He corrected after a few seconds and hopscotched away.

"That wasn't fun," he said. "Makes me want to go spank that son of a bitch."

"Do it," ordered Bianca. "And anyone else sees a bomber, cut it down."

"C-One to all teams," called Croft, "the mother ship is heading toward Shadderal. Designation for that craft is Medusa. She will be a main target. Maybe if we take her out, we cripple their assault."

An image came onto Calisto's screen of the giant ship. Its bulbous body was topped with dozens of articulated metal tentacles, some of which were tipped with pulse cannons and others of which were swatting chunks of asteroid in the direction of Asphodel.

"Medusa for sure," said Calisto, eyeing those snakelike tentacles. "Copy that, C-One."

There was no clear path to attack the monster yet. A shoggoth battleship was moving toward Asphodel Station behind cover of an asteroid the size of Mount Kilimanjaro. Bianca grinned as she hopscotched all over to confuse the enemy's sensors, and then from one kilometer out, she fired a Triphammer at the asteroid, timing the shot so that it was between her and the big ship. Then she jumped out as fast as her ship could go.

The massive blast of the Triphammer turned the asteroid into an artillery barrage that sent several hundred million tons of broken rock into the battleship's hull. Its shields did their best, but no ship was built to withstand that kind of impact. The craft cracked in half, spilling its guts toward Shadderal. Thousands of bits of junk and shoggoth bodies ignited as they plummeted through the planet's atmosphere.

"Payback's a bitch, isn't it?" she yelled.

Reaper let out a *whooohooooo* that filled the radio waves.

Bianca had no time to share in the victory howl. Another shoggoth battleship responded to the destruction of its consort by sending fifty daggers directly at her.

17

The NecroTeks were still working out how to *be* NecroTeks. Taking tentative steps, exploring their new bodies with senses they did not even begin to understand. Suddenly a voice spoke—scratchy at first but clearing almost at once. "C-One to all NecroTeks, do you copy?"

"*We copy, skipper,*" said Ventum. "*But how the hell are you even broadcasting to us?*"

"With a little help from Sybil," said Croft. "Guys ... look ... ah, shit, I don't even know how to do this. How do I speak to you after what you've gone through?"

"*You're doing fine, boss,*" said Thunder Bear.

There was a sound that might have been a wet sniff. "Well," said Croft, "on behalf of everyone up here, your service is honored more deeply than words can express. We're going to have to come up with some word better than *hero.*"

"*NecroTek works just fine,*" said Thunder Bear. "*Damn, though, this is one surreal-ass conversation. Hell, everything about this is nuts.*"

There was a bit more static on the line, then—in a cracked voice— Croft said, "I love you. All of you. You're my family. You know that."

The connection faded out.

The giants looked at one another. Dazed.

"*Did that just happen?*" asked Lucky.

"*It happened, son,*" said Thunder Bear.

"*Well ... God damn.*"

There was a huge noise above them, and they looked up to see a wave of shoggoth battleships wreathed in friction-fire as they punched through Shadderal's atmosphere. Their hulls seemed to burst apart as each ship launched fighters.

There were ten of the monstrous ships and dozens of the single fighters. They filled the sky above the Field of Dead Birds. The daggers raced ahead of their bigger consorts and drove toward the grounded ghost ships.

"*They're heading for the factories,*" said Beezer.

"*Can't let them take 'em,*" called Lucky, stomping off in that direction.

"*Got to get them away from the ghost ships too,*" said Beezer. "*Those birds are our own spare parts.*"

"*Welcome to the wrong side of the galaxy,*" laughed Lucky as he turned and broke into a run.

Although he was conscious of deciding to run, his body—this strange new body—did it more quickly than even his combat reflexes could dictate. Thought to action occurred without a pause. He wanted to run and suddenly he was running, his 450 million kilograms of mass moving with a lumbering grace.

The pulse blasts from the daggers chased him, chipping off pieces of his armor, blowing out circuits—but even as he sustained damage, his onboard AI rerouted systems and power, turning damaged metal into dead shielding.

"Don't we have shields?" cried Beezer.

"Not in atmo, dumbass," snapped Ventum. His NecroTek was taller and slimmer than the others but had missile pods running from chin to waist. As a cluster of daggers raced toward him, his entire body seemed to erupt with flame. Missiles of some unknown kind shot upward, trailing smoke that throbbed with blue light within. The missiles separated, the AI selecting targets. Ten missiles spiraled out to meet ten daggers.

The explosion was enormous. It plucked Ventum off his feet and flung his body into the trees. He landed hard and even cried out in shock and …

… and pain.

He *felt* the impact as if it had been against his own flesh.

"What the actual hell?" he demanded.

All around him, though, fell a slow rain of blackened debris. The ten daggers were gone.

"Ventum," snapped Jericho. *"Are you hurt?"* There was such an intense confusion of emotion in those few words. He whirled and looked at Lucky. *"Can we be hurt? Like feel pain?"*

Lucky was climbing slowly to his feet. *"Yeah, we can, God damn it."*

His voice was artificial, created by an alien intelligence attempting to imitate its interpretation of human speech and inflection. That connection was improving, deepening quickly. Lucky's anger was very evident. The tone of it was there, the furious urgency.

Lucky pivoted and fired missiles up at the closest battleship. The weapons that shot from his arm cannons were also of a kind unknown to him. Perhaps unknown to the shoggoths as well, though the pilot of the enemy ship clearly recognized their threat and turned hard to port, twisting in the air in an attempt to slip the blow.

Three of the four missiles missed. The fourth clipped a stabilizer. A plume of thick black smoke began pumping from the tail of the ship. The vessel wobbled and sagged toward the remnants of the Shrine of the Penitent, where it plunged to destruction on the plateau.

"Guess those assholes can feel pain too," said Lucky.

Another battleship dropped low and hurtled across the tops of the trees, firing its belly guns at the ghost ships. Two of them seemed to leap off the ground, propelled by a fist of fire that punched upward into the sky. It looked like a nuclear mushroom cloud, and the force of it dragged hundreds of thousands of tons of brick, plastic, and metal upward. Below, three of the ghost ships blew up and settled into pools of burning slag.

"*Why are they blowing up the ghost ships?*" asked Ventum. "*I thought they wanted them.*"

"They're shooting at us," said Lucky. "*The rest is collateral damage. Cost of doing business. It's the factories they really want.*"

The shoggoth battleship made a sweeping turn and came back for a second run, its black skin gleaming in the light from the suns. Suddenly those suns were blotted out, and a dense shadow fell across the ship as something vast hurtled into the air and dropped like the wrath of a mad god upon it.

Thunder Bear, the biggest of the NecroTeks, smashed down onto the airborne battleship with six hundred million kilograms of metal and rage.

The battleship exploded, hurling Thunder Bear away, trailing smoke and a scream of pain. But the AI transformed his body midflight, changing it to something closer to an armadillo. Thunder Bear hit the forest trees and rolled for nearly three hundred meters before coming to a smoking stop.

Ventum shrieked and ran toward his friend, but before he could reach Thunder Bear, a wave of daggers sent fifty missiles into his back. Ventum's NecroTek body simply blew apart, scattering tons of flaming debris across the entire Field of Dead Birds.

18

Aboard Asphodel Station, Lady Jessica McHugh screamed and fell backward, then suddenly began swatting at her clothing and limbs in a terrible frenzy.

"Jessica!" cried Soren, reaching toward her but still not daring to make physical contact. "Stop ... *stop* ... you're not hurt. You're not on fire. It's not you."

Her frantic slaps slowed and stopped. She looked around, then groaned.

"I could feel the NecroTek blow up," she gasped hoarsely. "I could feel the flames." Then she sat up, rigid and horrified. "Matthew Walker could feel it. Ventum, the NecroTek version of him ... he could feel it as if his metal skin was flesh."

Soren covered his mouth with his palm as he stared at her.

"I could feel everything," said McHugh, shaking her head. "Metal flesh burning. Nerves made from wires melting. Fluids boiling in conduits ... in veins. He died screaming."

There was a long and monstrous moment of silence.

"Lady Jessica," said Lost, his golem face appearing on the screen. "He has lost one body on Shadderal. He and the shipboard AI were one, and that ghost ship *was* Ventum. It is gone. He, however, is not."

"W-what?"

"Ventum is still connected via *ethla* to the AI. Both are swirling and without form," said Lost. "I will call the AI down to a new ship. You, Lady Death, must find Ventum's consciousness and join it with that new body."

She gaped, and for a moment the pervasive green of her eyes cleared so that it was truly Jessica McHugh's own hazel—with normal black pupil and white sclera—that glared ferociously. "How can I do this to him again? Did you hear his screams? He was in hell."

"*This* is hell," yelled Lost, and it was the first time the golem had raised his voice in anger.

Hell is empty and all the devils are here. The old quote echoed in Soren's head, gaining new meaning and poignancy.

"The Outer Gods have turned all of the worlds of the galaxy into a hell of their own design," said Lost quickly. "Ventum and the other NecroTeks are in that hell. Would you abandon them there, defeated and in torment? Or will you give them purpose through rebirth?"

McHugh turned her desperate face toward Soren, countless unspoken questions on her lips.

Soren held up a calming hand. A focus point to draw her away from panic and toward him. "Jessica, listen to me ... this is no different from what you did before. No one is asking *you* to hurt Ventum. Lost is right in that he is in torment. He is confused. How could he not be? It is up to you to reach him and once more offer him the choice. Go on in peace to whatever awaits, or fight. There is no middle choice, my dear ... and there is no time left. You must do this now."

Her eyes were filled with such hurt and such loathing. For Lost, for Sibyl, for Soren, and—most of all—for herself.

"We are all damned," she said, but a dark green veil obscured her eyes and she was no longer entirely in that room. She was between worlds.

Looking for Ventum.

19

Bianca had lost count of the dagger ships her team had destroyed. More than two dozen and possibly twice that number. One battleship was dead too.

The space before her was full of ships though.

So very many.

A pair of daggers came out from behind an asteroid and tried to catch Bianca in a pincer move.

They're learning, she thought darkly. *They're figuring us out.*

There was no time to brood on that. The daggers opened up with their powerful pulse weapons and she hopscotched away as fast as she could. However, the tumbler spun out of the turn and kept spinning. Internal alarms screamed at her. Half of her control console flashed with red warning lights and the other half snapped into empty blackness.

"I'm hit," she cried. "I'm hit."

As Bianca fought for control, Decaf and Calisto both said they were coming.

The desire to help was powerful, but as Bianca spun farther and farther away from them, the side of the massive octopoidal Medusa mother ship opened and vomited forth a thousand new daggers. They filled the eternal night with pulses and streams of deadly blue fire and there was nowhere left to run.

20

"We are nearly done," said Sibyl, pitching her observation for Soren.

Lady Jessica was in her trance, and even more than earlier she looked like an animated corpse more than anything truly alive. Her skin was a greasy, slick gray and Soren could hardly even tell if she was still breathing.

"What is left for her to do?" he pleaded. "Surely she's done enough."

Then he saw McHugh stiffen the way she did each time she established a spiritual connection with one of the Lost Souls. A strange brightness shone from her green eyes. Her lips formed a word. A name.

She said, "Jacob …"

21

Medusa moved through space, closing on Shadderal. Massive doors in her swollen underbelly opened and she gave birth to a dozen ships. Bulbous, ugly, and black. Their engines fired and they raced toward the planet.

As they entered the atmosphere, and even as friction turned them into fireballs, these ships uncurled legs—a dozen each. As they landed they scuttled like deformed crabs over the hills toward the factories. Their backs folded open to allow huge wire baskets to rise, ready to be filled.

The NecroTeks, engaged with daggers and battleships, did not see them break through a rear wall of one factory. They did not hear the clanging and rending of metal from within. Only when one of the crawlers crept out with a forty-ton piece of machinery resting in its basket did they notice something had happened.

"*Hey*," roared Ventum as he spotted it crawling away, "*we got some weird-ass stuff down here. Crab monsters or some shit. They're doing some sneaky-ass smash and grab. Stealing tech from the factories.*"

"*Oh hell no*," growled Thunder Bear as he turned toward the factories and began running. It took the NecroTek a moment to get up to speed, but he raced toward the crab-crawler with the piece of machinery on its back and hit it full force. The crawler went flying, rolling and tumbling across the pavement, and its payload flew off and was smashed to junk. The crawler tried to right itself, but Thunder Bear grabbed two of its legs and tore them off.

That left ten more, and six of these flipped upward, the *feet* shifting into gun barrels. The barrage hit Thunder Bear and sent him reeling back with a massive burning hole in his stomach.

22

Bianca felt her tumbler dying around her.

The auto-repair systems were fighting to keep life support and other essential functions on, but smoke was beginning to fill the cockpit. She sealed her helmet and triggered the distress beacon, but it was clear to her that no one was coming. There weren't enough pilots out here to spare.

Her hope was that she could limp back to Asphodel and get a new ship. There should be three or four new ones ready by now.

The screen in front of her suddenly flared with intense blue light as pulse blasts hammered her.

"Sibyl, how are the shields?"

"Deflector shields at twenty-six percent."

Another bash.

"Nineteen percent," amended Sibyl. "Critical system failure imminent."

"How are the weapons?"

"All weapons systems are offline," said Sibyl. "I cannot maintain those and the shields."

The tumbler reeled again and more displays on the board went dark.

"Deflector shields at eleven percent."

"What do I have left?" demanded Bianca.

"Food service, waste removal, data archives, and overthrusters are all functioning within normal range."

She smiled. "Well, isn't that interesting."

23

The shoggoth battleships hung in the sky, their shields burning bright blue.

Lucky watched them, but beside him Thunder Bear was staring down at his chest in wonder as the AI rebuilt the tear in his body.

Lucky and Thunder Bear—the hole in his chest now repaired at the loss of some overall mass—stared up as the ships began firing down at the factories. Five of the factories were being targeted and each of these pulsed with purple light at each impact.

"Hey," said Thunder Bear, pointing, *"look at that."*

Lucky turned to see the same kind of barrage striking one of the undamaged factories close to him. The pulse blasts detonated and the building trembled, but it did not explode.

"I think it's shielded," said Lucky. *"Yeah, look … where their pulses hit, there's a shimmer. Not like anything I've seen before."*

"You can't tell me they're aiming at us and missing," said Beezer.

Thunder Bear stared at the barrage. He saw one of the crab machines hurry toward one of it and as the crawler tried to attack a wall, but the purple light flared and sent it tumbling away. *"No, I think I get it,"* he said. *"That handful of factories must have some kind of shields that work in atmosphere. They must be the ones still capable of operating at full capacity, or with machines that are more important. The shoggoths are trying to weaken or shut down the shielding so they can get in and steal what they want."*

It made sense. It was the only logical explanation.

However, several crabs were also trying to loot a seemingly non-functional factory.

"We can't let them take anything," said Thunder Bear. *"Not even old parts. Nothing. Not a goddam thing."*

"We need to do something, and right damn now," cried Sundance.

"I think I know what to do," said another unexpected voice, and the mechanical giants turned to see a new NecroTek standing behind them. Very tall, with a complete battleship forming the crosspiece of its massive shoulders. Its body was sleek and lean, as if carefully designed rather than merely adopted. The voice, though loud, was more self-contained, more confident.

"Galahad!" yelled Beezer. *"Son of a bitch!"*

Jacob Fox strode forward on the legs of a titan.

"Listen to me," he said quickly. *"Every still-operable ghost ship down here is fully charged. You can feel it. I can, for sure."*

"So?" queried Thunder Bear.

"They're also, by design, adaptive," said Galahad. *"If we drag a dozen of them over to the factories, then maybe we can connect their power to the shield generators. That'll boost the shields and keep these bastards out."*

The other NecroTeks stared at him.

"How do you know that would even work?" asked Tank.

"How do you know it won't?" And with that, Galahad squatted, slid his arms under the stern and bow of a ghost ship, and lifted it. He turned and then ran toward the factories.

Lucky and Thunder Bear exchanged a look.

"Well ... hell," said Lucky as he reached for another ship.

A wave of daggers came roaring in, opening up with their pulse weapons.

"Lucky, you Beezer, Rabbit, and Spartan help Galahad," Thunder Bear roared. *"The rest of us will dance these shape-shifting bozos for a bit."*

Bear rose up on his hind legs, pointed his arms at the oncoming daggers, and fired.

24

Bianca had Sibyl shut down every nonessential system in her tumbler to conserve what little power was left. It wasn't much, but it brought her ship's useful power levels back up to 17 percent. She had made do with less before, twice in simulators and once in real combat.

Now she just needed to stay alive long enough to escape the daggers that were stalking her so she could go back to the barn for a fresh ride.

"Mosquito to Lost Souls," she radioed. "I'm running on fumes and could use some backup."

"I got you," said Cricket, and suddenly his tumbler was there. It shot past her, firing his chain guns. One of the daggers spun away, whirling through empty space until it vanished from sight. Two others abandoned Bianca's ship and began to chase Cricket.

"Draw them away," ordered Bianca. "Hopscotch. Play hit-and-run."

"On it," said Cricket, and he sounded like he was enjoying himself.

That boy's going to fit in just fine, mused Bianca as she worked on her piloting controls. But steering was alarmingly awkward, and she realized with a sinking feeling that her stabilizers were shot.

That was not good news. Without stability or internal inertial dampeners, overthrusters could not be used safely. It would make the tumbler begin spinning, and even with her safety harness, that would create internal stress. The null field was useless for hopscotch, and all of its juice was flowing into the shields. She could flee, but escape would likely break every bone in her body.

She tapped her comms. "Mosquito to C-One."

"Go for C-One," said Croft. "What's your status?"

"Moderately poor, Skipper. Life support just went offline. Air's getting thin. I'm going to hit Shadderal's atmo soon, and I could use a skimmer right about now. Anyone in my part of the sky?"

"Working on it," said Croft. "Sit tight, Mosquito. Help is on the way."

Bianca felt her head getting fuzzy. Her consciousness was beginning to drift, her mind going dark slowly as if there was a caretaker inside her walking through all the rooms of her mind and shutting off the lights one by one. She heard the captain's words, but what she heard most was his tone. Too cheerful, too certain.

She was positive it was the first time her captain had ever lied to her.

25

Shoggoth battleships and daggers began landing on the far side of the grove of dying trees.

Immediately the big ships moved toward one another, connecting with adaptive joints, filling in gaps with daggers that gave themselves over entirely to each chimera.

Then, as giants from some dark myth, they rose. Black upon black armor that sizzled static electricity. Lightning crackled in the sky above them as a bitter, acidic rain began to fall, the drops boiling to steam as they struck the ships, still hot from entry into the atmosphere.

The ground shook as the chimeras smashed their way through the trees toward the Field of Dead Birds.

Thunder Bear saw them coming and he dropped down to all-fours, growling as if he really were a predatory animal. The other NecroTeks formed a line of battle between the tree line and the dormant ghost ships.

"We stop them here," bellowed Thunder Bear.

The shoggoth chimeras broke through the trees, and the NecroTeks surged forward with guns blazing and howls of fury.

26

Bianca Petrescu knew that she was in trouble.

Warning lights flashed, telling her that she was skimming the atmosphere Shadderal. The temperature inside the tumbler was rising.

Even with the internal life support and temperature control of her pressure suit, Bianca could feel it. She fumbled for a helmet and put it on and sucked greedily at the oxygen. Her thoughts cleared, but that was no gift because it felt like this was hell and she was burning.

Somewhere down there, Jacob was trying to save the factories so that the war—*their* war—could go on.

And on.

For how long, she wondered. Was this going to be another endless war that would blaze for centuries or millennia? Would the sons and daughters of the people on Asphodel be born into a world where war was the only reality? It was a horrible thought.

And yet …

Jacob understood, she knew that. He was one of the smartest people she knew. Soren was smart too, and he was helping Lady Death with her magic. Working to gather lost souls and help them fight.

"Sybil," said Bianca, "show me what's happening down on the planet."

Her holo-screen immediately displayed a furious battle. A name and call sign appeared above each towering NecroTek. Beezer, Thunder Bear, and all the rest. Fighting. No rest for the dead. No solace for the soul. There was only the war.

Bianca's heart lurched painfully in her chest when she saw Jacob. He was a monster, a fantastical machine. He was beautiful.

She murmured his name.

He was fighting with incredible speed and power. Firing missiles and rockets, taking hits, wading through clouds of fiery debris. All around him the dormant ships were burning. So was much of the forest. Many of the colossal structures in the ruined city had collapsed further, kicking up huge pillars of dust.

How long, she wondered bleakly, before Earth looked like Shadderal—wasted and dead? Or would it be another of those worlds blown to rivers of floating rocks? Would Earth's star, Sol, be destroyed by the arcane weapons of the Outer Gods? The concept of victory felt like a fantasy. Something impossible to achieve. Abstract to the point of absurdity.

And yet the war had to be fought.

It was madness.

She dialed through images on her scanner. Calisto and the rest of the squadron were doing incredible damage to the fleet. The Triphammers and campaign packs made the few tumblers left feel like an armada. The upgrades on Asphodel Station that Captain Croft had managed to accomplish in so short a time had turned it into a fortress, and the enemy was breaking itself on it.

But …

These were battles. Skirmishes.

The real fight was down there on the planet. The real war. Bianca saw the truth with a newfound clarity. Up here the tumblers, skimmers, scout ships, and the station's sweeper guns were holding their own, but the shoggoths weren't attacking the station with its full force. Their real focus, their must-have goal, was capturing those factories and the ghost ships. Even Medusa was near the surface.

Bianca forced herself to turn away from the screens. She opened a panel beneath the console. Like every first-class pilot, she knew every nut and bolt of the craft.

"May I ask what you are attempting?" asked Sibyl.

Bianca ignored her.

"I may be of some help," suggested the AI.

"If you want to help, Sybil, keep the shields hot."

Bianca worked furiously, pulling crystal data beads from the soft-gel inner panels.

"Lieutenant Commander Petrescu," said Sibyl, "you have taken all weapons offline."

"You said they weren't working anyway."

"Then why remove the data beads?"

Instead of answering, Bianca began humming. It was a synth-blues song from when she was a kid. One of those lost love ballads with a lot of moody bass notes filtered through digital samplers that buried sound bites of weeping and cruel laughter at the subliminal level. When she was thirteen, she'd spent a lot of lonely hours sitting in a window at the orphanage, staring out at the rain and crying as she wrote page after page of cynical, hopeless, adjective-heavy poetry.

She smiled as she opened another panel and fitted the data beads into sockets that had not been designed for them. The gel adapted, though and suddenly a hum shot through the craft. That made her smile even wider. And colder.

When Sybil spoke again there was an uncharacteristic note of alarm in her voice. "What you are doing in extremely—"

"Don't want to hear it," grunted Bianca. "Either help me or shut up."

The AI fell silent. Bianca kept working.

Then Sybil spoke again. "I will help you, Bianca," she said.

27

Medusa eased down through the atmosphere, still birthing daggers and scavenger crabs as she neared the surface. Her mass was fifty times that of any individual battleship, and many times larger than even Thunder Bear, who was the biggest of the NecroTek warriors.

The waves of daggers whipped downward toward the factories, but the newly enhanced shields blew the first dozen of them to pieces. The rest sheared off and circled, firing at the ghost ships the NecroTek had connected to the shield generators. Those generators were shielded, too, but less heavily, and the constant barrage from the daggers began making them shudder and belch sparks.

Galahad picked up pieces of old wrecks and hurled them at the daggers, destroying some; but the others zipped away, dodging and firing.

Above them, Medusa descended. The massive machine began to change.

The metallic tentacles swelled and thickened. The dome of the main body rippled as shutters folded back, allowing for colossal wings to deploy. Once these reached their full expanse, they beat against the atmosphere and the gravity, and the downward force of this action sent hurricane winds tearing across the landscape. Trees by the thousands were plucked out of the dirt and flung away. The hulls of downed ships broke apart like glass. The millions of tons of stone that had been used to make the Shrine of the Penitent were hurled like pebbles against the slopes of the mountains.

Those wings kept beating and for a time the gargantuan ship hovered there above the Field of Dead Birds. Below, all of the NecroTek warriors stood in stunned silence, staring at the impossible thing that had come for them.

"Holy God ..." breathed Ventum, staring up as the ship assumed a form out of nightmare, bringing the surest version of hell down to the dead world of Shadderal.

As it continued downward through the troubled gray skies, Medusa's bulging belly rippled as hundreds of gunports opened.

"Oh ... shit," cried Thunder Bear. He wheeled around. "Run!"

The NecroTeks ran, but daggers and chimera ships had moved in to block them, filling the air ahead to prevent their escape. To force a fight.

Thunder Bear was the first to hit their line. He leaped up and swatted two daggers from the sky, then landed with such shocking force that it staggered the closest chimeras.

While he was recovering, Tank rumbled past him. Despite his call sign, Ian Potts did not have a tank body. His body had been chosen by the AI. It drew on something from deep in Tank's memories: his love of boxing, his years hammering it out as part of the Chicago Golden Gloves and making it as far as the first round of eliminations in the Olympics. Tank was a brawler, with or without rules, and the AI had constructed a chimera for him with short legs, flexible ankles and knees, a supple waist, long arms, and heavy shoulders, with huge metal alloy struts supporting that torso mass and distributing it for balance.

As Tank raced past Thunder Bear, the bits of ghost ships that made up his hands curled inward, knotting together and fusing into forty-ton fists shaped like cannon balls.

The enemy chimera braced its legs and brought up an arm heavy with missiles, but as they fired, the AI tapped into old reflexes, into muscle memory that was ingrained into Tank by thousands upon thousands of hours of training, sparring, and matches. He jagged his left foot forward for stability, knees bending, waist turning and head ducking as he hooked a punch into the middle of the chimera.

The target no chance.

Every ounce of that titanic fist struck the weakest point—a flexible joint that formed the chimera's midtorso. It folded the shoggoth titan in half. The back ruptured as everything in the middle was crushed, including stabilizers, fire control, and fuel tanks. The chimera sat down like a boxer who had taken a knockout blow. For a moment it looked almost comical with its legs splayed and head drooping.

And then it blew up.

Sundance was half a klick away, leaping into the air while holding a fifty-foot length of structural alloy. He brought it down on the gun arm of another chimera, shearing it off at the elbow, checked the swing, and smashed it across the knees. As it fell, Sundance reversed the girder, raised it high, and brought it down like a stake, punching through the battleship's chest.

"Keep at 'em," yelled Lucky as he used two sixty-foot trees to hammer daggers out of the sky.

Across the field, Lucky could see Galahad doing something weird and technical with a dozen ghost ships he and the others had dragged halfway into one of the factories.

"Keep them off me," he cried. *"Almost ... no, got it!"*

There was a flash of intense purple light that ran from the ghost ships he had connected and into the first of the factories. Immediately the shield intensity flare to a sizzling brightness ten times what it had been. A half dozen scuttling crabs exploded with such force that the debris they flung knocked two daggers out of the sky.

Four shoggoth chimeras turned away from the other NecroTeks and instantly opened fire on Galahad.

28

Bianca glanced at the viewscreen every few seconds, trying to determine which of the NecroTeks down there was Jacob. She could have asked Sibyl but did not. The risk of attachment—of losing the necessary detachment—was too strong.

She fitted the panel back into place, and suddenly one of the sets of controls that had gone dark lit up again.

"Shield integrity is down to twelve percent."

Bianca climbed back into her chair and buckled every strap. "Okay, Sibyl old girl," she said, "divert everything to the forward shields and the overthrusters. To hell with the rest."

"Lieutenant Commander ..." began the AI, but then stopped and instead said. "It is an honor to serve with you."

Captain Croft came on the line, his voice weirdly calm. "Mosquito ... you want to tell me what the hell you think you're doing?"

The engine roar spun high and higher. The image of the alien mother ship filled her screen. Vibrations shivered through the whole ship. Too much, too agitated. Every kind of warning light blazed on the panels.

Bianca smiled. "My job, Skipper."

She pushed the accelerator, and the tumbler shot forward. Immediately it began to spin. It rattled every part of her. Teeth, bones, the eyes in their sockets. It was bad. It hurt. She gritted her teeth in a tiger's grin.

Medusa was growing as she shot toward it, the waving tentacles and colossal wings filling every centimeter of every screen.

"Eject and wait for pickup, Petrescu," snapped Croft. "That is a direct order, Lieutenant Commander."

Bianca flipped up the red missile-switch cover on her joystick. The rerigged data beads did what all of the deliberate safety design features had been created to prevent: brought every missile online at once and tied their firing to the chain guns. Seventeen Infernos, fifteen Constellations, thirty loaded SAPR ammo packs for DD-40 chain guns, and six Triphammers went hot as the distance between her dying tumbler and Medusa melted away.

"This is for Jacob, you ugly-ass bitch," she growled.

The missiles were set to detonate on impact. The tumbler hit the belly of the great beast at sixty thousand kilometers an hour two miles above the surface of Shadderal.

Part Fifteen
Because I Could Not
Stop for Death

"If the soul be immortal, it requires to be cultivated with attention, not only for what we call the time of life, but for that which is to follow—I mean eternity; and the least neglect in this point may be attended with endless consequences."

—*Socrates, in Plato's* Phaedrus

1

The shoggoth mother ship reeled.

The ordnance aboard—all those missiles armed and hungry—and the nuke core, dialed far into the red zone, detonated at the same time.

That had been Bianca's plan.

The blast ripped the belly out of the monstrous ship, spilling hundreds of thousands of tons of flaming debris into the air.

The entire mother ship tilted off balance as stabilizers ruptured and melted. The monstrous tentacles whipped and thrashed, smashing into one another, knocking smaller support vessels out of the air, adding their wreckage to the downpour of burning junk.

Internal systems failed or overloaded, amplifying the damage. Fire burst from ports and new cracks in the hull plating. Huge columns of oily smoke whipped outward and were caught by the wind, each of them looking like ghostly parodies of the metal tentacles.

The ship was still high above Shadderal, and as it fell, the friction set it all to burn.

A rain of fire fell east of the Field of Dead Birds.

On the ground, the chimera titans all turned and stared up, their pilots shocked and horrified. Mother ships were the bringers of death; they were not victims. They were not vulnerable.

Yet this one was mortally wounded.

They sent up a howl.

"Tekeli-li. Tekeli-li. Tekeli-li. Tekeliiiii-li ..."
The shriek rose into the flaming air above, shrill and terrified.

2

Everyone watched Bianca Petrescu die.

On the bridge of Asphodel Station, Delia Trumbo and Dušan Veljković stood watching on the big screen with a dozen division chiefs around them. Everyone cried out as they each realized what she was going to do. Then those cries turned to screams as Bianca did it.

Without even being aware she was doing it, Trumbo took Veljković's hand and held it as they watched in shared horror. Veljković, distantly aware of the action, on a deep level was comforted by that grasp. There was no other comfort anywhere in the galaxy.

On the flight deck, Captain Sebastian Croft sagged back in his chair, feeling the full weight of it all. It was like being shot through the heart.

"No," he said with profoundly deep and terrible hurt. Not just for Bianca, but for them all.

Around him, the entire command center fell into a ghastly silence. Even those people who did not know Bianca very well—or who knew her and didn't particularly like her—felt the same weight of loss. Lieutenant Commander Petrescu was *the* combat pilot. Most of them knew about her skills in any kind of fight—with guns, barehanded, or in the cockpit of a tumbler. There was not one of them who thought her talents were overrated or overestimated. How, then, could she be dead?

How could she have died like this?

"No, no, no, no," mumbled Croft, unable to bear the burden of this truth.

In her tumbler, Calisto screamed.

It was a high, terrible, throat-ripping scream. It was so raw that she spat tiny droplets of blood onto her screens. She beat on the console and howled like a lost soul.

Every pilot in the void saw that flaming death, and they, too, screamed. For their commanding officer. For their sister in arms. For their friend.

They screamed even as they fired their guns at the dwindling bulk of the shoggoth fleet.

They screamed as they accelerated to take the fight to the enemy with even more vigor, more fury. More hate. The void between Asphodel and Shadderal was littered with burning starships.

On the Field of Dead Birds, the NecroTeks saw the impact and the awful damage Bianca had inflicted upon the most dangerous ship in the shoggoth fleet.

It filled them with a terrible shared grief, because all of them shared something none of the tumbler pilots in space or anyone on Asphodel could understand.

They knew what it felt like to die.

Despite embracing their power as part of the *ethla* connection between their spirits and the ghost ships, they did not want any of their companions to join them. Of course they did not, because to want that would make them different from the people they were.

The death of Bianca initiated a change in them, a kind of emotional metamorphosis that had been building with each new death. Now the awkwardness, the shock over their own deaths that each had been hiding behind bravado and trash talk, the hallucinogenic quality of *being* machines—all of that vanished. As one, they turned toward the shoggoth chimeras. The majority of the battleships were now in the atmosphere above Shadderal, and the NecroTeks were outnumbered and outgunned.

That did not matter.

Bianca had severely damaged the mother ship. She had done that while in the flesh while driving a crippled tumbler. They—each NecroTek—were colossuses of metal alloys, exotic polymers, alien AI, and every conceivable kind of weapon.

They had no human hearts, and yet all of them felt the ghosts of their hearts break.

And those breaks, those fissures, spewed a fiery hatred unlike anything they had ever felt.

Jacob Fox—Galahad—screamed Bianca's name.

In grief. A deep and terrible grief.

But it was also as a war cry.

Fierce.

Savage.

He ran at the closest chimeras—a pair of towering giants twice his size. His hands became cannons, firing as he charged.

3

In her cabin, Lady Death was dying.

But she was not dead yet.

"Sibyl," snapped Soren, "I need something to stabilize her. Vitamins, electrolytes. Anything."

"I have something that may help," said the AI. "Lay her down."

Soren did so, and a small panel opened in the wall as a MediDrone drone floated out. It scanned McHugh from head to toe and then opened its belly to allow two articulated arms to reach down, one with a self-adjusting pressure cuff and the other with a syringe. The needle entered a vein and injected a mix of saline water, and significant doses of B vitamins, magnesium, and vitamin C, along with citicoline, a nootropic agent.

As the process ran its course, Soren kept looking from McHugh's slack face to the wounded, burning mother ship on the RealScreen. It was Bianca's tomb. In his own way, he thought he understood some of the dreadful grief that had inspired the golem called Lost to build the Shrine of the Penitent. He did not think his heart could break more than it had over the last two days.

4

The NecroTeks hurled themselves at the chimeras.

Pulse blasts filled the air on both sides. Missiles and SAPRs and projectiles that had no corresponding words in human speech turned the entire field of battle into a maelstrom of destruction.

Jacob fought a pair of chimeras, each of them firing dagger ships as if they were missiles. He swatted some out of the air and blasted others, but they kept coming. Three of them hit him in his thigh, hip and chest, driving him back step by step toward one of the functional factories. It was clear they knew they needed to take him out in order to achieve their goal.

Jacob turned to call for help, when he saw something vast and dark sweep down from the sky and smash into Thunder Bear. It was a massive segmented tentacle. Jacob looked up to see that Medusa, although wounded and listing, was by no means dead. It was fighting with a frenzied viciousness.

The first tentacle was followed by another, and the two caught Thunder Bear between them and crushed him.

"Hold on, brother!" roared Jacob, and he tried to turn to engage those thrashing limbs. But his NecroTek body would not respond to his will. It fought him, forcing him to remain there to defend the factory.

Then, suddenly, all of Thunder Bear's NecroTek engines exploded under the pressure of the tentacles. It was a fireball of such immense heat that it melted a dozen ghost ships on the ground, blew one of the tentacles to pieces, scattered thousands of flaming bits as far as the mountains, and cast a high-pitched shriek onto the winds.

"No!" cried Jacob as he tried to run toward his fallen friend. He threw his consciousness against the AI's control, but the *ethla* connection shoved him back with irresistible force. The artificial intelligence, more experienced with this kind of combat, ignored his desire and instead kept his body there in the fight with the chimera titans.

"What are you doing, *damn you?"* he cried.

He tried again to free himself of the AI's governance, and even managed to take two staggering, unbalanced steps, but the AI wrested control away from him and spun his metal body toward the closest enemy. It was horrific, because Jacob realized in a flash of clarity that all of his actions so far—all that mattered directly to this fight—were not so much him being in harmony with the AI, but him submitting to it as its *slave*.

"Guys, the AI's fighting me," he called, his voice shrill with panic. *"It's making me do its will. Maybe it's just me. I'm the newest NecroTek down here. Can anyone do something radical?"*

There were yells and even some rough derision from the others, but then their jeers fell silent as they tried to fight their own fight and realized that they could not. It dawned on each of them that they never had.

This sent a thrill of fear through Jacob. Wars are not won like that. Wars were fought by trained fighters adapting to the moment, straddling that line between training and initiative.

Against his will, Jacob was thrust back into combat with the two closest chimeras. Sometimes his blows landed where he would have placed them; sometimes his guns fired at targets he would have chosen. But overall, he was forced to accept that *he* was not the NecroTek. The AI was.

More and more daggers and battleships were burning their way down through the atmosphere. In space, the dwindling squadron of tumblers was fighting twenty or thirty to one. This was what Lost had warned of—the sheer numbers of the shoggoth fleet.

Galahad and the other NecroTeks were dying and being reborn, over and over again, each time rising to fight once more. Each time with less of their souls.

And they were losing this fight.

5

What the hell?

That was her first thought.

There was nothing to see.

Nothing to hear.

Or taste. Smell. Feel.

Absolutely nothing.

Even her words were not spoken. They were thoughts.

Only that.

She was only that.

Thoughts. Nothing.

A long time later (minutes, hours, centuries?—there was nothing against which time could be measured), she thought, *Am I dead?*

No voice spoke from the darkness to refute her question.

No ear turned to listen to Bianca Petrescu's screams.

6

"Captain, we have incoming!"

Commander Norah Levinson's entire body was rigid with tension. Croft pushed his wheeled chair down the line of consoles and studied the holo-screen as Levinson brought up a holograph showing a thick-bodied ship of a kind he hadn't seen before. The bulky hull was clearly not intended for the nimble demands of combat, nor did it look like it had the speed a bomber would need.

"Is that a troop ship?" queried Levinson.

"That's what I'm thinking."

"It's coming right for the station."

That was certainly the case, and it had six daggers flying in close support.

"It'll burn up when it hits the shields," said Levinson.

But Croft was unsure. By now the shoggoths knew how powerful the shields were. This attack suggested they had a plan.

Quickly, the enemy's intentions became dramatically clear. Three of the daggers moved together, fusing in their peculiar chimeric fashion into a single hull. The bow guns of all three were now clustered together and immediately opened fire with a devastating rate of cyclic discharge. The blue pulse blasts hit one specific part of the shields. With a blend of admiration and despair, Croft realized that this was an example of the enemy learning from its own defeats. Attacking one point of the shields with rotating fire meant that it could overtax that spot, just as the Constellation missiles had done while setting up the Infernos.

"Sir," yelped Levinson, "we're losing integrity on shield eight-fourteen on deck twenty-two. It's going to—"

And the blast rocked the whole station.

Instantly the daggers peeled back, and the troop ship smashed its way through the hull and into Asphodel Station.

"Hull breach! Hull breach," roared Croft. He punched a button for Lieutenant Tanaka. "I need your Marines down to deck twenty-two to repel boarders. Repeat, *repel boarders.*"

7

Lieutenant Tanaka paused outside of the corridor door as he popped up a hologram from the tactical computer on his left forearm. It showed the shoggoth troop ship extruding from the inner wall on deck twenty-two. The ship's hull looked to be excreting some kind of self-sealing gel to maintain atmosphere. The front of the craft was smashed, and the impact had sent the corpses of T-dogs and shoggoths sprawling onto the deck. But many more of them were crawling over the wreckage and their own dead, firing at anything that moved.

Tanaka's Marines had pulse rifles, grenades, and all of the regular kit, but what most of them took into this battle were shock rods that had been designed after Lieutenant Commander Petrescu had stunned one of the shoggoths with a defibrillator. These shock rods, though, were thirty times more powerful.

"Guns for dogs," snapped Tanaka, and three rifle teams fanned out, shouldered their MP-9950s, and began sniping at the monstrous tardigrades. These T-dogs were different from the one that the pilots had killed up in medical. They wore armor made from some flexible metal that bristled with spikes. A colorless liquid dripped from the tip of each spike When one of the Marines took a small scratch while dodging out of the way, he began to convulse, eyes bugging and veins standing out rigid on the sides of his neck, before he even landed. He died in seconds, the victim of a deadly neurotoxin.

The other shooters fell back a few steps and set firing lines in relative safety.

The shoggoths had pulse weapons that looked weirdly like wide-mouthed flutes. Mouths would appear on their amorphous bodies, the ends of the flutes would be quickly inserted, and the shoggoths would exhale sharply to fire the guns. It was strange—it was a design that would be unwieldy for humans, but for the shoggoth shape-shifters it was fast and very efficient.

Soon the whole deck was crisscrossed by pulse blasts. It forced the Marines back, putting the shoggoths well out of range of their shock rods.

Tanaka plucked a grenade from his web belt, flipped up an activator switch, waited until he felt the thing charge up—a matter of two seconds—and then hurled it at the closest shoggoth. The grenade detonated four inches from the creature, and for a blinding instant the shoggoth was wreathed by dancing blue-white arcs of electricity.

Another new toy designed and manufactured since the fight in the med bay.

8

Bianca was nowhere.

It was such a strange thing. Even in dreams she was always *somewhere*. Even in that dream from when she was eleven and wandered through a lightless cavern in a hopeless attempt to find an exit. Even then there

were walls, mossy and cold, and solid ground under her feet. Even
then she could hear her breathing, feel her sweat, hear the drip of
water and the damp chill of the air.

Not now.

All she could sense, all that was real to her, all she had was her
thoughts.

Her life did not pass before her eyes. Nothing that cliché. Nothing
that comforting.

She merely *was*.

It wasn't even like floating, because she'd done that in a hundred
versions of microgravity. Floating made her muscles and stomach and
hair move in one way or another.

This was nothing at all.

I'm dead and I'm fading away.

She considered that thought and, only in her mind, could feel the
full weight of its truth.

*I died, and this is what's on the other side. Nothing. No one's waiting
for me. Not even Jacob.*

Then …

*My God, Jacob … where are you? I love you. I need you. Please,
please, please find me.*

Nothing.

Absolutely nothing.

Until … something …

9

Soren saw that, although McHugh's color was better and her pulse
stronger, she was still out of it. Her muscles were utterly slack. Her
eyelids were half-open, and the pupils were fixed and dilated.

"*Doc,*" said a voice and he turned to see an AI reconstruction of
Bianca Petrescu's face on the screen. In even spoke with her voice.
"*Now would be a really damn good time.*"

Deep within her troubled sleep, Jessica McHugh groaned but
remained as limp as a corpse.

10

Medusa sagged, and thick smoke continued to curl upward from it, but it hung in the sky a hundred meters over the field of battle.

The tentacles whipped and curled, smashed and struck with savage force even as the chimeric nature of the great ship worked to repair the damage. Useless debris dropped to the ground, where it either ignited fires among the weeds and trees or crushed some of the inert ghost ships.

The NecroTeks wanted to rush Medusa, to destroy it while the monster ship was crippled, but the AI would not let them. It kept them all close to the factories. Jacob struggled with this, because on one hand it made sense—the factories were the key to overall survival, and keeping them out of shoggoth hands was inarguably vital—but on the other hand, it demonstrated a limited understanding of warfare that Jacob found surprising and disturbing. It was as though the AI sought to win one part of a much greater battle, with no clear plan for an immediate victory.

He kept struggling against the AI, trying to fight the main threat, which was Medusa. As long as that monstrous mother ship was on Shadderal, the NecroTeks were—at best—delaying an inevitable and comprehensive defeat.

All the other pilots in their NecroTeks were furious and frightened by being so helpless. This was not combat—at best they were passengers. At worst they were liabilities, because their struggles for control sometimes made their mechanical bodies falter, miss a step, or launch missiles at thin air.

Jacob fought the shoggoths and he also fought an inward battle that was equally desperate. He could hear the mingled voices of Lost and Sibyl shouting in his mind for him to yield, to let go, to let the ships do the work. He yelled back, begging for control, but his pleas went unheeded. As he struggled, a pair of daggers swooped down and struck him in the neck and chest with missiles. His mind went dark even before his body fell.

Thunder Bear rose in a new body, this time on two legs, with simple cannons at the end of each arm. It was clumsy—effective at times against daggers and the chimera ships, but not at all against Medusa.

Jacob rose again, slower this time, but realized that only seconds had passed. Medusa was still there, canted over, vulnerable. He snatched up a huge steel beam from the wreckage of his old body and tried to rush the monster, wanting to drive the beam into Medusa like a stake through a vampire's heart. Once more the AI stopped him, dragging him back toward the factories. Again he fought, and again—locked in that struggle—the shoggoths blew him to pieces.

This was happening to all the NecroTeks. They all knew or sensed that Medusa was the key to victory. The mother ship, the command center. Maybe the heart of this shoggoth fleet. But the AI forced them to be defensive. And one by one they died, were reborn, and died again.

Jericho was shooting down the daggers but was blindsided by a pair of ships that came fast at ground level and then arched upward into her lower back, blowing her entire NecroTek in half.

Tank, the last to fall in the latest wave, got within striking range of Medusa before his legs stopped obeying his will. And it was Medusa herself who delivered the killing blow with a tentacle that hurled him into a crippled chimera, incinerating both bodies. Tank rose again, but slowly and on the far side of the field. He did not know if he could truly feel or only imagine the loss of another fragment of his soul.

"*We're dying down here*," cried Jacob. His own body had been destroyed three times now, and each time he was resurrected, he could feel a kind of pain unlike anything he had ever experienced.

Is that my soul being shredded? he wondered. He knew the answer though.

They all did.

Medusa began righting itself, the smoke thinning, as she turned slowly and began moving toward the line of factories. The chimeras closed ranks in front of it, and together the shoggoth assault moved like a tsunami.

Jacob rallied his fellow NecroTeks, but he realized with bleak clarity that they were going to lose.

11

Bianca felt something.

It began as a tingling sensation. Subtle but unpleasant. Pins and needles of a different kind. The pain grew quickly though, spreading out in undefinable directions. Not down arms and legs; not into fingers and toes. She had none of those. Her body had been vaporized during her suicide run at Medusa. There was nothing left of her to be *able* to feel.

And yet the pain was there.

Except it wasn't only pain.

There was movement withing the pain. The tingling was in motion. Going somewhere. Defining itself somehow.

Becoming something.

It was like having thousands of fire ants crawling beneath her skin. Skin that she didn't actually have.

Then more.

A sense of substance. Of reality beyond mere thought. Of a kind of solidity.

For a moment she thought that maybe—somehow—she had survived the collision. That she was in her pressure suit floating in space. After all, she had an awareness of self, of physical form.

If I'm alive, she thought, *then I'm hurt.*

No, hurt wasn't it.

Damaged?

Not that either.

Different.

She forced the word out of her thoughts, not wanting this to be her truth.

But then again …

Jacob.

Had this happened to him?

Had this happened to all the others? Lucky and Beezer and Ventum … all of them?

The nerve tingling became real pain now. Growing bigger by the second. Becoming monstrous. Awful. Unbearable.

Bianca wanted to scream again. She would have screamed if she thought it would help. Even dead, she was a pragmatist.

Even.

Dead.

Christ, I really am dead, aren't I?

It was a rhetorical question. Silly. Frightening. Devastating in its reality.

And into that fear, into her darkness, someone spoke.

"I found you …" said Lady Death.

12

Aboard Asphodel Station, the shoggoths made a concerted push to overwhelm the Marines. They sent T-dogs forward in what amounted to suicide attacks. Several Marines went down and were set upon by the T-dogs, whose cylindrical snouts were lined with razor-sharp teeth.

As Tanaka fought, he realized with a jolt of horror why the shoggoths had attacked this *particular* deck. The shoggoth that Petrescu had stopped had been free to roam around the ship in the early hours of the crisis following the WarpLine gun's failure. It must have gotten to deck twenty-two and seen that the main engines that ran the entire station were housed here, including the motors that drove the shields.

"They're going for the engines," Tanaka bellowed as swapped magazines. "We have to hold them here."

His Marines understood the stakes. There was no retreat, because to lose the deck meant losing the whole station.

"This is my goddamn house," snarled Tanaka, glaring at the shoggoths and their T-dogs. "And I am going to kill every last one of you ugly, alien bastards."

He said it loud enough for everyone to hear.

And the Marines under his command roared out in defiance.

13

Jacob and Rabbit had their backs to the wall of the biggest factory. They towered over the structure, but they knew even their massive bodies could not protect it.

Another wave of daggers fired on the row of ghost ships attached to the shield-generator, and this time two of the ships exploded. The hum of the generator dropped considerably, and the blue glow diminished by half.

"*Hold the line,*" Jacob ordered even as pulse blasts chipped away at his armored body. The AI compensated as fast as it could, sloughing off damaged sections and reordering the internal design to reinforce shielding and create new cannons. But Jacob was dwindling, and he was too far from the ghost ships and their useful parts to rebuild himself.

Then one of the shoggoth chimeras leaped through the air, its body glowing bright blue as its engine core surged to critical. It landed on the last of the ghost ships by the factory, and they blew apart. The blast was enormous. It cut Rabbit in half and tore Thunder Bear's legs off. The shock of the impact sent Jacob crashing back into—and *through*—the outer wall of the factory. The shield was completely down, and he collapsed onto a part of the assembly line, crushing a conveyor belt. Chains and pulleys broke free from the ceiling and landed on him, smashing off bits of his own metal body, burying him in tons of steel and iron.

Jacob lay there, momentarily trapped by the rubble, but with a clear view through the hole in the wall and back onto the field. Sundance, Lucky, and Ventum were down. He knew they would rise again, but how many more times? Each time any of them did, the *ethla* effect seemed stronger, and it made them fight with even less individuality and much less grace. It made them move like old-fashioned robots.

Medusa was barely thirty meters from the ground now and was plucking old dead ghost ships up and hurling them to destruction against the towering cones and blocks of the dead city nearby. Jacob saw the pieces land. Saw the pile of shattered ships, and wondered which would run out—the souls of the NecroTek pilots or the available ghost ships for them to inhabit?

As he fought to untangle himself from the chains and structural steel that pinned him, Jacob saw something he did not understand. A mountain of broken ships suddenly trembled. Pieces fell from the top, clanking and clattering down to the cracked pavement. Arcs of electricity danced up and down the mountain, setting fire to anything that could burn.

At first Jacob thought that maybe Lucky or Ventum or one of the others had somehow gotten trapped beneath all those millions of tons. But that was wrong. He could still see his fallen comrades and the few still standing and fighting.

The mountain of debris continued to tremble. Then he realized with astonishment that it was the pile itself that was moving.

Trembling. Shuddering. Shifting.

And …

Assembling.

Jacob watched as massive sections of broken ghost ships fell the wrong way. Not down, but sideways, even up—resisting gravity, defying it. Bending gravity and metal and mass to its will. Jacob could not grasp what he was seeing. It *seemed* like a chimera or a NecroTek but it was too big.

Far, far too big.

In horror he thought at first that this was Medusa's doing: not merely smashing enemy ships but stacking components to create an even greater giant chimera. The mountain of wreckage groaned, filling the air with the screech of protesting metal. It rose, impossibly huge, godlike in its scale. It rose and rose, even as more pieces of every kind of crashed and broken ship cleaved to it, adding to its mass.

It rose higher than the tallest of the NecroTeks. A monster among monsters.

Those NecroTeks still standing and all of the chimeras paused in doubt, neither side knowing if this was one of their own or some new and awful weapon.

It rose and rose, gaining mass until the sheer weight of it collapsed the ground underneath, its feet sinking deeply into the tarmac. Then it took a single step. It wobbled and nearly fell, but righted itself and took another step.

The thing stood on two wide legs and stretched wide with long arms from which cannons sprouted like thorns. Its eyes blazed with intense blue light.

It turned toward Medusa and raised those cannon arms.

"Die, you ugly bitch."

And Bianca Petrescu fired.

14

In space, Calisto heard Bianca's shout. She wanted to scream, to weep, to cheer, but there was no time. The shoggoth fleet was a shadow of its former self, but it was still a considerable threat. All of the battleships had gone down to the planet, but that still left more than a hundred daggers fighting to keep her and the remaining Lost Souls away from the breach because the shields in that area were still down.

Two of the station's scout ships were down, and SK-2 was a drifting hulk. A third of the sweeper guns had fallen silent too, and the daggers seemed to have learned how to avoid their limited range of fire.

Calisto had six tumblers, and she was down to less than half a campaign pack of missiles and SAPR rounds. Her guys were winning every dogfight, but there was a very real chance they would run out of ammunition before they won the battle. If that happened, it would be exactly like losing.

15

Bianca stepped toward Medusa and threw a big looping punch.

"*Take this, you piece of alien shit.*"

She swung hard and fast.

And she hit absolutely nothing.

That step, which should have brought her within easy reach, was far too short. It jerked her to a rough standstill.

"*What the hell?*" she roared, and tried again, this time raising both fists for a massive downward blow. Her foot did not even move that time, and the powerful blow slammed down onto the ground with such force that a fissure cracked open, missing Medusa completely.

Then Bianca felt her feet move. Not toward the mother ship, but backward. Away from it. Toward the damaged and vulnerable factory.

"*What are you doing, you stupid bastard?*" demanded Bianca.

"Bianca," called a voice in her head. It was Lost, pleading with her. "Yield to *ethla*. Let it fight for you."

"*No,*" snapped Bianca. "*Let* me *fight.*"

She threw her will against the control of the AI and for a moment her titanic NecroTek form stood in place, shuddering.

Medusa surged forward, wrapping tentacles around Bianca's arms and legs and neck and torso and with a massive exertion tore her to pieces.

Jacob screamed.

The other NecroTeks screamed.

On Asphodel Station, Lars Soren screamed.

The pieces struck the wall of the damaged factory, crumbling more of it, exposing the machinery and a dozen half-built ghost ships. There was nothing protecting the factory from the shoggoths except the NecroTeks, who were impossibly outnumbered.

Jacob rose from the rubble and knelt by what had been Bianca's first NecroTek incarnation. The AI allowed him that much. He touched her chest, but it was dead metal and wiring. There was nothing to feel.

There was no trace of her.

Then …

"Over here …"

He turned and saw another ghost ship rise up. Smaller by far than that first titanic form.

"Bianca?"

"Kind of," she said, sounding hurt and confused. *"What's wrong with us? I thought we were here to fight."*

Lost spoke again. "It's *ethla*. Give yourself to it. Let it work the body. Be its heart."

"I—" began Bianca, and then Medusa hit her again. Three tentacles braided themselves together into a whip that was as big around as a ghost ship. It smashed into Bianca's chest, and again her NecroTek body disintegrated into a cloud of smoking, burning, dying pieces.

Jacob fired missiles at the tentacle, blowing it apart, but Medusa whipped out another tentacle just as big, striking Ventum and sending his giant form flying into Jacob. They both fell, smashed to ruin among the dormant ghost ships.

Medusa moved toward the factory.

16

On Asphodel Station, Jessica McHugh was hunched over her crystals. Upon awakening, she had begged Soren to help her reset everything. Neither of them knew how long the cocktail of stimulants the med drone had given her would last or how much life she had left in her body. McHugh was a madwoman though—relentless, furious, even vicious.

"Help her," cried Soren.

"Bianca is fighting the AI," snapped Lost. "It will get her and all of the NecroTeks killed."

"They're already dead."

"I cannot help them if they keep fighting *ethla*. They have to yield to it completely."

"What if they can't?" demanded Soren. "What if they won't?"

"Then we are all doomed."

"No! I refuse to accept that. There must be another way."

Lady Jessica snarled at them both. "Shut up and let me work, damn it."

17

Jacob felt his heart—his ghost of a heart—flare with something like angry heat but much more like bitter cold.

"*Bianca!*" He called her name in a voice like thunder as missiles exploded all around him. The other NecroTeks were fighting, falling, dying, being reborn, rising, and dying again.

"*No*," shouted a distorted voice. He turned to it and saw another NecroTek body rising from the debris and somehow knew this was Bianca. Again. "*No, you stupid bastards. Let me go. Turn off that goddamn AI and let me fight.*"

Bianca was not talking to him, or to anyone on the field. She was yelling at Lost and Sybil, at Lady Jessica and Soren.

"*Let us fight.*"

What was she doing? Fighting the *ethla* bond with the AI of the ghost ships? He tried to yell, to warn her that this was impossible. All of them had tried it. All of them had failed.

"You must yield to it, or it will consume you," pleaded the voice of Lost.

Jacob could hear Bianca growl as she fought for control.

Bianca's NecroTek body moved to put herself between the oncoming nightmare that was Medusa and the vulnerable factory. Two chimeras reached her first, each launching missiles and daggers at her. She dodged some, swatted others away, and once more the rest blew her to atoms.

Jacob tried to rush to her aid, but his body simply would not respond. Not to him. The rest of the NecroTeks had gathered, once more forming a line between the enemy and the factory. They held weapons, they fired missiles and cannons.

And they died.

Again. Screaming with rage and pain and frustration. Only to rise once more as the enemy reloaded and kept firing.

"*You're killing us,*" pleaded Bianca as she assembled a new body. "*You have to let us fight. We're warriors, damn it. We're not robots. We're—*"

And again she died. Medusa fired a dozen cannons at her, catching her before she was fully integrated.

But Bianca would not stay down. Pieces of ships slid across the ground toward her, rebuilding her. As soon as she had legs, she began to stand once more. Slower this time, as if her soul was feeling the pain that metal and plastic could not.

Jacob felt her fear, but more than that, he felt her anger. He knew her. He knew the strength of her will, just as he knew how powerful she was when *she* chose her own path. Even within the rigid structure of the military she fought her own way.

This *ethla* connection was a shackle, and those chains were going to kill them all.

She got to her feet and tried again to rush forward. Medusa was ready with pulse cannons at the end of thirty tentacles. Bianca never had a chance.

"You must yield," begged Lost. "This is how the science works. It is how it has always worked. It is the only way it *can* work. Yield or all is lost."

"*No*," bellowed Bianca. "*Never.*"

As she fought to stand once more, she could suddenly hear Lost and McHugh and Soren yelling at her and each other through speakers inside her NecroTek body.

"Listen to him," pleaded McHugh. "They'll win if you don't."

"*They're already winning, you stupid witch*," Bianca snarled.

"You must yield to *ethla*," Lost said. "You must let it—"

But Lars Soren roared, "*No!*"

He thundered it. His voice blasted through the conversation and shocked Lost and McHugh to silence.

"No," growled Soren. "You don't understand—either of you."

"I helped *build* this," Lost fired back. "We used this for tens of thousands of years."

"And you lost your war by winning it," snapped Soren. "Don't you see? You are arguing for conventional wisdom in a situation where that has proven itself to produce only stalemate."

"You are human," said Lost with a trace of a sneer in his voice. "You are a philosopher, not a fighter. You are not a tactician. You do not understand how war works."

"I know, damn it," said Soren, "but *she* does. Bianca Petrescu *is* a warrior. She understands combat. She's won every fight with the shoggoths so far. She told me once that she's won every fight she's ever been in. I've seen it firsthand. She is innovative, reactive, smart, and fast. She hasn't grown stale by doing things the same way every time."

"She cannot master a chimera," insisted Lost.

"How do you know?" demanded Soren. "How do you know that any of the Lost Souls are incapable of fighting without the AI controlling every move? God, you didn't trust your own people enough to warn them of the dangers to their own souls, and look where that got you. A dead world and a dead race. You haunt the graveyard of your own bad choices, Lost. Have you never wondered what *trust* and *faith* could have done for you?"

Lost remained silent.

Jacob listened to everything Soren said, and he knew that the man was right. No one thought—or *fought*—like Bianca. It wasn't by luck that she, of all the pilots in the solar system, had been picked to lead the Lost Souls.

"*Trust Bianca*," he said, hoping his voice was heard.

Then ...

"*Trust Bianca, you dumbass*," said Spartan.

"*Yeah, trust Bianca*," said Lucky, even as he rose up with a new body. They all said it.

Every NecroTek on the field shouted it.

18

The towering giant that was Bianca Petrescu's new NecroTek body staggered and swayed, nearly falling. Daggers flew around it like stinging wasps. Chimeras fired at her, chipping her away piece by piece. The writhing tentacles of Medusa twitched and coiled as the vessel moved in for the kill.

The AI made her turn away, and turn she did.

And then she stopped turning, frozen in place. A shudder rippled through the countless tons of metal and wiring and fuel that made up the ghost ship body. Medusa accelerated toward the Goliath, the steel tentacles rising for a terrible, terminal smash. She stood helpless and undefended as Medusa reached for her with those tentacles, the thousands of suckers alive with countless small infernos. The NecroTeks tried to run to her, to defend her, but the AI forced them to remain as a barrier between shoggoths and factory.

A new voice whispered to her. "Bianca … you are free."

It was Sybil's voice.

A tentacle lashed out, aiming its bulk at the head of the lone giant within reach.

And Bianca's left hand caught it.

A voice rang out. Not a robot voice. But a human voice uttered by the machine mouth.

"*No*," she said, and with a deft twist, she looped the tentacle around her forearm. "*Now we do this* my *way.*"

With that, Bianca leaped into the air, pivoted mid-jump, and swung her other arm over and down, striking the tentacle as her incalculable weight landed. The force of the blow, the timing of the jump, and the torsion generated by the twist combined as the tentacle was savagely torn from Medusa's hull.

Without pausing, Bianca swung the forty-meter length of the tentacle over her head and then jumped forward, once more adding all of that mass in motion to the strength of her servos and gears. The steel limb smashed down on the dome of Medusa, driving it to the ground hard enough to cleave fault lines for kilometers in every direction.

The chimeras on the field spun away from the factory and fired at her. Several shots hit her, and she staggered. Medusa's other tentacles reached for her as the huge ship rose from the ground. Bianca was surrounded by death on all sides as the chimeras opened up with pulse cannons and blue fire filled the air.

But Bianca was moving. She drove forward, ducking beneath the barrage. Several shots scorched her and melted tons of armor from her back, but the rest passed overhead and slammed into Medusa. At the same instant, Bianca surged forward and punched Medusa in the hull with shocking force. The mother ship canted backward at an angle that crumpled the rear part of its hull.

As she fell, though, Medusa used the braking thrusters on her belly to blast Bianca.

Bianca yielded. Not to *ethla* but to the attack, falling back, letting Medusa's blast pass over her so that it caught the chimera behind her full in the chest and blew it to atoms. Bianca dove for the ground, rolled, and came up to her feet, swinging another punch at Medusa. And another.

Inside her mind a voice was trying to speak, and she was trying not to listen.

She pivoted and knee-kicked Medusa, driving the huge ship down again, then she turned as the chimeras rushed her. Bianca pointed her arms at them. But again, the cannons would not fire.

"*Shit,*" she yelped and backpedaled, using parries and blocks to fend off the chimeras as they tried to drag her down. "*Why can't I shoot?*"

Lost spoke in her head. "The AI controls the weapons," he said. "It controls transformation. You must yield."

"*Been over that, asshole. I'm not yielding to anyone. Now or ever.*"

Jacob, watching from the damaged factory wall, tried to throw his own will against his AI, but he was rooted to the spot. They all were.

"You see?" yelled Lost. "She has control, and she's wasting it."

"Lost," said Soren urgently, "is there no middle path? Can't the AI work *with* the NecroTek? Surely there is some way?"

"It has never been done."

"*I don't fucking care,*" shouted Bianca. "*If you're in contact with the AI tell it to yield to* me. *Let me tell it what I need. It's a machine.*"

"So are you," insisted Lost.

Bianca dodged a pulse blast, snatched up a severed chimera arm, and hurled it at the closest attacking ship. The arm struck the ship in the face, staggering it, and Bianca used her thirty-meter-long leg to sweep its feet out from under it. As it fell, she dropped a knee onto its chest, crushing the central mass. Then she tore its head off and threw it backhand at another chimera.

"*I'm not a machine,*" she thundered. "*I'm something you've never seen. Now either help me or fuck off and die.*"

19

Far above and across the void, the shoggoths on Asphodel had been driven into a corner and were fighting for their lives. Tanaka's Marines had surged forward. Taking losses but avenging each one.

Then, abruptly, the shoggoths stopped fighting. One of the survivors uttered that awful scream.

"*Tekeli-li. Tekeli-li. Tekeli-li. Tekeliiiii-li ...*"

Screeching it as they ran for their ship.

Not one of them made it as the Marines gave chase.

Not a single one.

20

Medusa manifested a hundred coiled springs and used them to thrust her mass away from the ground. As she rose, she turned, changing form again, becoming something like a gigantic scorpion with a tail that rose a hundred meters into the air. Instead of a stinger, it had a cluster of a dozen tightly packed cannons.

"Bianca … run!" yelled Jacob.

But there was no time. Once more, the combined blasts obliterated Bianca.

Jacob heard her scream in his head. It was the loudest sound in the world, and it rose and then vanished.

The ensuing silence was brutal beyond belief. It was crushing. If he could have, Jacob would have dropped to his knees in heartbreak and defeat.

He saw the chimeras turn back toward him. Toward the factory.

"Lost Souls forever," he said in challenge.

The others braced for the attack. For the end. Thirty chimeras raised their arm cannons. Gun ports opened in their chests. Rocket launchers rose from their shoulders. And behind him, moving forward on sixteen segmented legs and with a hundred articulated tentacles thrashing on its back, the scorpion monster that was Medusa crouched, ready to spring.

"Lost Souls forever," said Jacob again, this time in a broken and fatalistic voice.

And a voice said, *"That's not how we say it."*

Everyone turned to see a new form rising from the Field of Dead Birds.

Big.

Bigger than the chimeras and NecroTeks.

Bigger than anything on that world except Medusa.

"We're not Lost Souls," said Bianca as she raised her arms. Cannons by the score broke from her wrists and chest and thighs. She fired. One arm at the chimeras. The other at Medusa. Rockets burst from her hips and shoulders, destroying the segmented legs. Pulse blasts shot from her eyes, cutting the whipping tail in half.

In a voice as loud as all the hate there ever was, she screamed, *"NecroTeks forever!"*

Jacob stared in shock. In wonder.

And then in savage joy.

He wanted to join the fight, but each time he'd tried, the AI stopped him. He tried once more, nonetheless.

And the NecroTek body *moved*. Not according to what the AI wanted, but according to Jacob's will.

"Guys ... we're free," he shouted. *"This is us. It's us now. Bianca did something—it's us."* He began running toward the chimeras. *"NecroTeks forever."*

"NecroTeks forever!" They all roared. Their new war cry. Fierce and powerful.

Jacob leaped into the air with a twisting back kick that caught a chimera in the gut, cracking its entire hull in half. Flames shot out of the rupture all along its spine. Beezer snatched up a pair of smaller ships and wrapped them around his fists as he plowed into a pair of shoggoth ships. He did not fire any guns. He didn't want to. He wanted to *beat* the bastards.

The others surged forward, weapons blazing.

"Listen to me," shouted Bianca. *"Think what you want. Anything you want. Gun, missile, anything. The AI will make it."*

Jericho looked at her hands. She stared at them, trying to determine whether she owned them or the AI did. Then she thought about something. A shape. Abruptly—so fast it was hard to see—the rough clubs at the end of her wrists changed. The metal skin warped and stretched, pulling mass and materials from her arms and shoulders as it stretched outward. Becoming a definite shape.

Becoming a sword.

She grinned. Jericho loved swords. All kinds of swords. Broadswords, katanas, Roman short swords, rapiers. Anything that could take an edge and extend her reach.

She dropped into a crouch as a chimera ship ran at her, missile ports emerging from its chest. She surged forward, but at an angle, leaping and turning much as Bianca had, and she slashed down with a sword like a heavy cavalry saber. The blade bit into the side of the chimera's neck. Sparks blew upward. Jericho landed, snapping out with a French savate kick that buckled the chimera's knee. As it buckled, she chopped laterally with her other hand, taking one arm and the enemy's head clean off.

"Oh hell *yes!"* she said with a wild laugh.

That tore a laugh from Thunder Bear, who suddenly changed from a two-legged titan once more into a metal bear of enormous size. When he threw his head back to roar, pulse fire burst from his mouth.

Lucky began throwing razor-edged stars that he manifested in his hands. The AI ramped up to feed him another and another and another. They whistled through the air, slicing the dagger fighters down like clay pigeons.

Meanwhile, Medusa drove straight at Bianca.

And Bianca rushed to meet it.

Medusa's mass was as great as all of the NecroTeks on the field though. She was a nightmare. Her guns fired, but this time Bianca was not hampered by the AI. Instead the AI responded with her, amplifying every move Bianca chose, a connection of minds where the AI shared Bianca's thoughts and put them into instant action.

Bianca jumped left, her torso twisting 180 degrees mid-jump so she could fire chest missiles. These missiles slammed into Medusa's left flank, making her stumble. Her guns, still firing, struck two of her own chimeras and burned them to ash.

Laughing, Bianca landed, turned again and back-kicked a dead chimera hull toward Medusa, hitting two of her legs. Medusa staggered again. Her tail was re-forming into a new kind of cannon, but Bianca saw it, tore off her own right hand, and threw it toward the monster like a grenade. The pulse generator in the hand cannon went critical just as it struck the tail, and the blast tore eighty tons of the mother ship apart.

Medusa was hurt but not crippled. She fired her lateral guns, tearing off Bianca's left arm.

Bianca jumped sideways, telling the AI to make a change, and when she landed, she had two arms again. It required pulling mass from her body to replace what was lost, but it didn't matter. There were ships—undamaged ghost ships and countless others she could pull from—everywhere.

Medusa scuttled toward her, opening ports to launch hundreds of cluster bombs, forcing Bianca to run for cover. The bombs exploded with the combined force of a small nuke, and Bianca felt herself melting.

She dove forward and flattened out, knocking two ghost ships to pieces as she slid, but when she rose, her body was already absorbing those ships' materials. She built a shield for her left arm and a war hammer for her right and rushed forward, her legs shortening to give her a better center of gravity. She bashed the shield into Medusa's side and then hammered down at the legs, smashing many off at the joints.

The shoggoth craft tried to rise, but Bianca hammered down on it over and over with insane fury. As she smashed the legs off, more grew in different spots, and the tentacles on Medusa's dome whipped out and wrapped around the NecroTek body.

"*Nice try,*" growled Bianca and shoved backward, forcing her head and shoulders to tear free from her main mass. The head landed, the shoulders manifested spider legs, and Bianca scuttled to safety. The radical move saved her from another death, and there was a flash in her mind as she felt Lost and the AI react with some surprise at the move.

"*Bet you never saw that before,*" she said.

Medusa tossed the rest of Bianca's headless body away, and Bianca ran to catch it, leaping for the stump of the neck. Hundreds of little wires thrust downward from her head, seeking and finding connections to severed wires in the neck stump. Power surged up from the body as commands shot downward through every system, bonding with them, reclaiming the body. And as a giant once more she rose.

More tentacles sprouted from Medusa's hull in an attempt to catch Bianca again, but the NecroTek changed her hammer to an axe and willed her waist to rotate with full and unrestricted turns. Everything from her hips upward began to spin at increasing—maddening—speeds, and the axe chopped off Medusa's tentacles by the score.

The mother ship recoiled as if in surprise and began changing form once more, but Bianca did not want to find out what other tricks Medusa had. She jagged one way and manifested cannons and launchers and fired into each gaping wound left by Medusa's destroyed tentacles.

Fire erupted from a hundred places on Medusa's vast bulk, and this time it reeled as if in pain. It was still a monster though. Still five times Bianca's size.

But it was hurt.

Medusa uttered a strange, high-pitched ululating cry, and the other chimeras turned toward her. At once they began running to her aid.

"*Stop them,*" ordered Jacob and he threw himself forward, manifesting legs instead of arms, galloping in a shape like a horse. Thunder Bear was beside him, and the others raced to catch up.

Bianca charged Medusa, snatching up ghost ships and daggers and even fallen chimeras. Bianca's AI pulled them in, absorbing them, merging with them, bending them to Bianca's will even as she attacked.

Bianca towered over Medusa now, five hundred meters tall. She split her axe into two rods of densely compacted steel and attacked the mother ship with fighting sticks, parrying its tentacles, hitting every vulnerable joint, smashing gun ports and missile launchers, breaking the remaining legs. More fires burst from inside the shoggoth ship, but Bianca did not relent.

Medusa fought though. She made new guns and fired. She hurled bombs and stabbed with spikes and fought with savage ferocity.

Bianca evaded her strikes, moving faster, nimble as a dancer despite her incalculable weight. She used gravity the way every fighting teacher she'd ever studied under taught her. A fall became a crouch, a crouch became a leap or surge, and each surge turned into a knee kick, a shin kick, or a stamp kick. Between blows with her clubs, she manifested spiked elbows and crushed downward, piercing Medusa's hull over and over again.

Medusa had been built for combat, for conquest, but it was not built for this. Nothing in the shoggoth history of war had ever prepared it for this. Deep inside the ship, a shoggoth eighty times larger and three thousand times older than her troops screamed in fear as she fought against something she could not beat.

Fires erupted everywhere now. Power systems failed, faulting into overloads that blew out whole sections of Medusa's hull. One by one her legs failed as circuits went critical and then totally dark. The body sagged.

Bianca did not stop.

Rage did not own her. It wasn't that. Nor was it hate. This wasn't even punishment.

It was love.

Love of her friends who had died. Love of the people aboard Asphodel, who would die if she failed. Love for her home world so far from there.

Love was always more powerful than hate.

Love was the secret that all warriors cherished. They did not fight for flags or parties or causes. No real warrior ever had. They fought for the person next to them. They fought for those at home who could not fight for themselves. They fought for the unborn who would never live if they lost. And they fought because the enemy wanted to take all that away, crush it, spoil it, use it, defile it. Exterminate it.

Love was something the ancient AI had not understood. Now it did.

Bianca had far more love in her heart than she had hate. And she used that love, that compassion, that empathy as a fuel that burned hotter than any nuke core. Hotter than the engines of destruction that had come hunting for innocent blood.

She stood there, metal legs braced wide, and she destroyed Medusa. She killed every shoggoth, and when she finally tore the hull in half, she ripped the queen shoggoth from her cockpit, squeezed her to death, and then exhaled nuclear fire to burn even the memory of her to ash.

21

Hundreds of thousands of kilometers away, Lady Jessica McHugh turned and smiled at Soren.

"I think," she said in a graveyard whisper, "I ... think we won."

And then she fell sideways, eyes open, mouth open, body utterly slack.

22

On Shadderal, the NecroTeks stood in the places where their own battles had ended.

All of them were scorched and dented, cracked and damaged.

None of them cared.

The damaged factory still functioned, and automated systems were already beginning to rebuild the outer walls. On the Field of Dead Birds there were less than three hundred intact ghost ships out of the thousand there had been. Smoke drifted past them on a slow and mournful breeze. The few remaining trees in the forest rustled their dry leaves.

The NecroTeks looked at the destroyed chimeras and the utter ruin that was Medusa.

None of them spoke for a very long time.

Lucky murmured, *"Lost Souls forever ..."*

But Bianca shook her massive steel head. *"No. I told you, that's not us. The Lost Souls are up there."* She pointed to the stars behind the sky. *"Calisto and the others. That's who they are. From now on—for us—it's always going to be NecroTeks forever."*

Bianca raised her hands and clenched her mechanical fingers into massive fists. She beat them against her chest. Once. Again. And again.

"NecroTeks forever!" she cried in a voice of thunder.

Then they all shouted it. Loud enough to turn the breeze into a wild gale.

NecroTeks forever.

Epilogue

1

The funeral was not long, but Soren knew it would live in his heart forever.

He stood under Shadderal's leaden sky, wearing a pressure suit. Captain Croft stood nearby, as did Delia Trumbo and many others.

The Lost Souls stood in a group. Calisto and the others. The surviving pilots from the remaining skimmer and the scout ships were there too. Lieutenant Tanaka was there, with his handful of surviving Marines. They nodded to him, and he responded in kind.

Most of the citizens of Asphodel watched on RealScreens from their homes in the sky. The officiate of the service was Miranda Sessling, senior cleric of the Interworlds Faith Alliance. *A nice woman*, thought Soren. *Gentle, not at all pedantic. Kind.*

Even so, he barely heard her words.

There were graves all along one side of the now barren forest. Many of them. Too many. Fallen heroes and fallen friends. Fallen strangers whose names would become part of the first chapter of the history of this new world. Someday, people would walk through this cemetery without suits, breathing in manufactured oxygen on terraformed planets. The station's 3D printers were building those vast terraforming machines now, even as the coffins were lowered into the soil.

The question of whether any of the dead would be brought back to fight as NecroTeks was not yet raised. That time might come, but not now.

There was a pedestal cut from stone and wrapped in the metal of fallen ghost ships, and atop it was a metal bowl from which a bright flame rose. Deep inside the pedestal was a miniature nuke core surrounded by radiation shielding. The fire would burn for thousands of years. An eternal flame suggested by Soren, designed by Sibyl, and built by Calisto and her team.

By the time the sermon was done, Soren felt old beyond his years.

"It's hard to believe it's only been sixteen days," said a voice, and he turned. Lady Jessica sat in her mechanized wheelchair. It would be months before she would be able to walk again. Longer before she looked like the woman he'd sat with on her couch, talking about cosmic horrors and ancient gods. He wondered how completely she would recover. The toll of evocation had been dreadful, and her last efforts to save Bianca from oblivion had wasted her to something close to a ghost. He knew that his own face would carry the new lines of fear and loss forever as well.

"Sixteen days," he said, nodding.

She gave him a rueful smile. "I guess all this validates your theories of cosmic philosophy."

"It does," said Soren. "But for every question answered there are ten thousand new ones all shouting in my head. Even the most devout among us can no longer say with certainty that he or she understands the structure of our universe. Not in physical terms, as we've all learned, but perhaps more so as regards the divine. What now, we must wonder, *are* gods anyway? Do you have an answer? No. Nor I. Frankly, my dear, it feels as if for the first time in my life I have a sense of what *infinity* and *eternity* mean."

"And that terrifies you?" she asked.

But Soren smiled and shook his head. "Between you and me, Jessica, I've never been more excited."

They said nothing for a while, neither listening to the service. When Lady Jessica reached up to take his hand, he allowed it. Cherished it. Held it fast.

2

When the service was over, Soren left McHugh and the others and walked through the wreckage on the Field of Dead Birds. He saw figures on a hill and wanted to speak to them.

Something stepped out from between two heaps of rubble close to where he stood. Tall, ungainly, made up of parts, with a cracked helmet for a face.

"Dr. Soren," said Lost.

Soren stopped and they looked at each other for a few moments.

"You were right," said the golem.

"Was I? About what?"

"About Bianca Petrescu," said Lost. "About her people. And ... about me. About the sins I and others like me committed against the innocent young."

Soren gave him a weary smile. "We who have lived more years often fall prey to the belief that age necessarily grants wisdom. An associated sin is believing that the young have strength but lack wisdom or, worse, lack insight."

"Yes."

"The truth is always the hardest lesson," said Soren. Then he cocked his head. "However, we can take comfort in the knowledge that in the last moments, when we were truly called upon to demonstrate our wisdom, we made the right choice."

They stood in silence, watching the suns edge toward the far mountains.

"There have been no shoggoth ships sighted since the battle," said Soren. "I wish I could accept that as a hopeful sign."

"But you are too wise for that," said the golem.

"Wise, cynical ... sometimes they feel the same." Soren rubbed his eyes. "They will return, though, yes?"

"The Outer Gods will send them and others."

Soren gave him a sharp look. "Others?"

"It is a large galaxy, my friend," said Lost. "The Outer Gods have conquered many races, and suborned them to their will. They have created monsters that are far stranger and far more deadly even than the shoggoths. I wish I could say otherwise. Yes, Dr. Soren, this war is far from over."

Soren nodded, patted Lost on the shoulder, and moved away, following the other mourners.

3

Soren did not head straight for the skimmer but instead walked up a slope, atop which eleven figures stood with their backs to the suns.

Beezer and Lucky; Tank, Jericho, Thunder Bear, Sundance, Ventum, Spartan, Cricket, and Rabbit. And two who stood slightly apart. Those he only thought of by their real names: Bianca and Jacob.

They were NecroTeks, but they were not giants. Not at the moment, not for something as solemn as this. Somehow—through manipulations of their machine selves that he did not yet understand—they had learned to compact themselves into bodies of normal size. Bodies whose faces almost resembled their own, though in shades of metal. Golems of a kind, but Soren did not choose to use that word to describe them.

Soren stood with them in silence for nearly an hour, watching as the complex shadows cast by the suns above painted the landscape in countless shades of gray.

Eventually Soren told them what Lost had said about the return of the shoggoths and the Outer Gods' other armies.

"*Let them come,*" said Bianca.

"*We'll be ready,*" Jacob assured him.

Soren glanced at them. Their metal mouths smiled like tigers.

"Yes," said Dr. Soren. "I expect we will."

"*But I gotta tell you, Doc,*" said Bianca, "*if you think we're going to sit on our asses and wait, then you're wrong. They know about us, and they know about Earth.*"

"They're manufacturing tumblers as fast as possible," said Soren. "Captain Croft is training new pilots. Dr. Saltsman is building a new WarpLine gun. Civilians are lining up to volunteer for combat training. Even the station will be getting an upgrade—stronger shields, more guns."

"*That's great,*" said Bianca, "*but it's not enough. Lost and his people fought the shoggoths and killed themselves doing it. That's not how wars are won.*"

"What else *can* be done?" protested Soren.

Bianca made a fist, all steel cables and gears. "*There are seven blue suns out there. The home of the Outer Gods. Captain Croft's already had some talks with Lost about how his people blew up the suns of the shoggoth worlds. They used tech that's now available to us.*"

Soren felt his blood turn to ice. "What then? Surely you don't plan on attacking the actual Outer Gods!"

Bianca Petrescu stared down at him with mechanical eyes. Deep inside their pale glow he caught something else. A spark. A flicker. No ... a *flame*. Not entirely human, but not entirely machine either. The flame grew brighter, hotter, and the NecroTek's metal mouth curled into the most dangerous and predatory smile Soren had ever seen.

"They picked this fight, Doc," she said. *"They want a war? Yeah, we'll give them a war."*

4

The ship had drifted thousands upon thousands of kilometers away from Asphodel Station. No sensors had detected it because it was designed to be invisible to all scanners. No visual observation had pinged it either. The ship was coated with nonreflective shielding that made it fade entirely against the endless, bottomless black of space.

It looked dead.

It drifted.

Yet inside, the crew—all of them in pressure suits because life support had failed—worked in sixteen-hour shifts to repair the damage. In the hold, six hundred bodies lay in cryo-tubes. Some were soldiers. Some were scientists. All were killers in their own way. The tubes ran on batteries, and the reserves were dwindling down as the days past, and if the power failed, those six hundred would simply die in their sleep.

But on the seventeenth day since the WarpLine event, a row of small bulbs flickered and came on. Deep inside the heart of the wounded ship, engines groaned as they struggled to wake.

In their tubes, deep inside the dreamless sleep of cryonics, the black-ops science team and the top-of-the-line special operators, began the slow process of waking up, as the *Tempest* floated through the darkness.

Welcome to Asphodel Station

ASPHODEL STATION DIVISION CHIEFS

Delia Trumbo, Station Executive
Abdou Diatta, Chief Engineer
Billy "Gopher" Broussard, Head of Medical Sciences
Dr. Denny Paek, Head of Astronomy and Stellar Cartography
Dr. Jae-Sung Hak, Evolutionary Biologist and Exobiologist
Dr. Nan Man-fei, Senior Director of Integrated Sciences Division
Dušan Veljković, Chief of Security
Georgette Begay, Chief of Operations
Oki Sato, Head of Computer Sciences

WARPLINE DESIGN TEAM

Dr. Anton Kier, Developer
Dr. Jason Saltsman, Chief WarpLine Engineer

ASPHODEL STATION MILITARY TEAM

Captain Sebastian Croft, Commander of Joint Military Team
Lieutenant Commander Norah Levinson
Lieutenant Thomas Tanaka, Senior Officer of Marine Corps Detail

LOST SOULS SQUADRON

Ship	Pilot	Call sign

Tumblers

T-1	Lieutenant Commander Bianca Petrescu	Mosquito
T-2	LTJG Jacob Fox	Galahad
T-3	LTJG Veronica Roland	Calisto
T-4	Lieutenant Ian Potts	Tank
T-5	Lieutenant Jahziel Yaakv	Jericho
T-6	Lieutenant Bo Chow	Beezer
T-7	Lieutenant Ethan Riley Saylor	Reaper
T-8	Lieutenant Joshua McGinnis	Thunder Bear
T-9	Lieutenant Phillip Kesler	Hummingbird
T-10	Lieutenant Chance Thompson	Lucky
T-11	Lieutenant Matthew Walker	Ventum
T-12	Lieutenant Voula Achilleos	Spartan
T-13	LTJG Marco Diaz	Cricket

Skimmers

SK-1	LTJG Haley Majka	Sweetpea
	Lieutenant Jean-Paul Lloris	Decaf
	Lieutenant Boris Vijenko	Lovechild
SK-2	LTJG Youssef El-Shenawy	Habibi
	Lieutenant Hector Almeida	Sundance
	Lieutenant Zito Luvumbo	Rabbit

Acknowledgments

This novel could not have been undertaken without the help of a lot of talented and generous people. In no particular order: Jeffrey Falcon Logue, astronomer Lisa Will; my friendly neighborhood mad scientist, Dr. Ronald Coleman; Jeffrey Falcon Logue; James Jaehnig; Alina Ionescu; winners of the *NecroTek* contest: Chance Thompson, Matthew Walker, Ethan Riley Saylor, Joshua McGinnis, Veronica Roland, Jessica McHugh, and Phillip Kesler.

Thanks to my wonderful assistant, Dana Fredsti; my literary agent, Sara Crowe; the good folks at Blackstone Publishing and *Weird Tales*; my film agent, Dana Spector of Creative Artists Agency; and Hollywood attorney Matt Wallerstein. And very special thanks to my brilliant audiobook reader, Ray Porter.